The Seq

HEATHCLIFF

The Sequel to Wuthering Heights

Lin Haire-Sargeant

G
Gainsborough Press

This edition published in 1996 by Gainsborough Press

First published in the United Kingdom in 1992 by
Century

Random House, 20 Vauxhall Bridge Road, London SW1V 2SA

Random House Australia (Pty) Limited
20 Alfred Street, Milsons Point, Sydney,
New South Wales 2061, Australia

Random House New Zealand Limited
18 Poland Road, Glenfield
Auckland 10, New Zealand

Random House South Africa (Pty) Limited
PO Box 337, Bergvlei, South Africa

Random House UK Limited Reg. No. 954009

A CIP catalogue record for this book
is available from the British Library

Printed and bound in Great Britain by
Cox & Wyman Ltd, Reading, Berkshire

ISBN 0 752 90350 0

To my parents,
Elizabeth S. Haire
and
Alvah Chambers Haire,
and my daughter,
Sage Anetta Green,
with love.

Acknowledgements

I am lucky to have friends who are as talented as they are generous; their help was essential in creating what is good in this book.

Every month for almost five years MaryKay Mahoney, Candice Rowe, Peggy Walsh, and I have gathered around MaryKay's kitchen table over pizza and champagne to read our stories to each other. So when I began work on this novel, they heard each chapter as quickly as it rolled off the laser printer. Not only their critical perspicacity, but the range of their backgrounds – MaryKay's in Victorian Studies, Peggy's in drama, and Candy's in the teaching of creative writing – made them the ideal critics of *Heathcliff*. I am grateful for their substantial help, with this project and many other things.

A second writing group helped too. This one grew out of my friendship with Rebecca Saunders, on whose perceptive critical assistance I have depended since we started graduate school. Soon after I began *Heathcliff*, she and Ellen Troutman invited me to attend an exciting workshop they were forming: they were to write poetry with Helene Davis, author of *Chemopoet and Other Poems*, guest poets (including David Zaig and Ivan Rodriguez) were to present their work for criticism, and at the end of each poetry session I was to read a chapter of my novel. Though this was rather like following an elegant plate of sushi with a huge slab of chocolate cake, the odd combination worked: the poets and their art prospered, and I got the benefit of their keen ears and insights. Thanks, gang!

Yvette Grimes deserves quadruple thanks: first, for providing the word processor upon which this novel was written; second, for teaching me how to use it; third, for her editorial suggestions, often enthusiastically sanguinary, invariably witty; and fourth, for always having urged me to write fiction.

Julia Dubnoff was rich in encouragement during the writing of the book, and, once she read it, prolific in interpretation. I greatly appreciate her contributions in both respects.

Thanks to my daughter Sage for liking what I wrote, and for performing many acts of thoughtfulness that allowed me to work undisturbed.

Martin Green gave *Heathcliff* his sharpest critical focus, though never his easy approval. Ever champion of the comic muse and nemesis of the gothic, he kept me in balance between them – or tried to. My thanks also for his guidance in the matter of getting the book published.

Other friends who helped are Larry Berman with his music; Jeff Butts, Janet Campbell, Bob Gale, Ugo Giambarella, Julian Jordan, and Sam Riley with their appreciative reading; Karen Henry, Devra Kunin, Olga Pelensky, and Jeff Snyder with their publishing advice; and Liz Ammons, Linda Bamber, and Robert Stange for their classes on the novel.

Thanks go as well to Liz and Jim Trupin, literary agents, and Claire Zion, Associate Executive Editor at Pocket Books. Their good will and kind assistance far exceeded professional duty.

Finally I would like to thank Janet Gezari, who taught an extraordinary graduate seminar on Charlotte, Emily, and Anne Brontë at Tufts Summer School, 1990. As she lectured through the cool June evenings, three slight female forms, almost obscured by the glare on the glass, seemed to hover just outside the classroom windows, and someone dark and brooding to lurk in the shadowed angle behind the door. And when Professor Gezari asked what Heathcliff had done in those years he was gone from Wuthering Heights, I thought I knew.

Heathcliff

The Return to Wuthering Heights

1

Third January 1844. A letter written sixty years ago, by a man dead for forty! Little had I imagined when I left Brussels on New Year's Day, that this, and not wistful memories of Monsieur Heger, would be the chief preoccupation of my homeward journey.

For I had thought with pleasure of Monsieur, and of Monsieur alone, for so long – almost for the whole tenure of my stint as a teacher at the Pensionnat Heger. From him alone did I receive a smile, a friendly greeting; the others shunned me until, in time, I was quite frozen into my little end of the dormitory: teachers and students alike, following Madame Heger's slyly insinuated lead, encased me in an icy silence – broken only when my one friend in this chill continent innocently warmed me with his kind words for half an hour. How short a thaw, and of late how infrequent! Madame was jealous; Madame wanted to be rid of the English mistress; Madame always got what she wanted.

I had loved; the object of my love was married. No matter now. I was separated from him, probably forever. And not one tender word had been spoken on either side; of emotion, except for that which rightly flowed between master and pupil (for he had taught me much), there had been no passage between us. Mine alone had been any deep feeling, and remaining singular, it had at length shrivelled to this with me: a placid countenance, a lip that never quavered, a dry, clear eye. Though the calendar might still count me a young woman, I had left my youth, and any hope depended tremulous upon it, in Brussels.

To my homecoming I bore only my misery. I felt it as a great stone in my throat, that must never be choked out, but suffered to lodge, though it stifle and starve me.

For if I gave true voice to my trouble I would stun those I loved. Their tender image of me would be crushed.

I had two sisters, gifted in sympathy. Broad-minded and devoted though they were, they could not, should not accept the unlawful form my idol had taken. No, I must make this grief my familiar; it must be my uncomfortable companion on a path otherwise solitary – a pilgrim's path, that abandons homely hearth and cot to wander cliff and crag and crevasse in the severe mountains beyond.

On New Year's Day, then, I left him I love to take the packet from Antwerp. Docking on English soil, I was driven directly to the Leeds train through the swarming thoroughfares of London. On my first visit to the great city two years before I had felt it surge around me like a harsh, tumultuous river, animated and animating; then, in it, I had known myself for the first time as *alive*; all my previous life had seemed but a gentle dream. Now I moved through London's streets like a somnambulist; like a somnambulist I passed through the great hollow station and was led to my seat in the carriage. I meant to take notice of as little as possible; the image of my lost master was still lucid in my mind's eye, and I wished to protect it from the blurring influence of more immediate scenes.

My master! What worlds of reverence and love this phrase conjured to me! I, who had at first in my proud English way resented giving mortal man the title European usage required, had in time willingly conceded it to *M* Heger. Ever mercurial, stern or playful by turns, he was accomplished above the average, even above the exceptional, in his ability to impart knowledge. This earned my reverence. But what drew from me my love was nothing visible in him – oh no, it was something of another order from the external powers many admired – something privately and uniquely precious – the power he possessed of drawing me out. With others I might be dumb, awkward, and dull – indeed I believe I was widely thought to be nothing else – but with him I *felt*, at least, articulate, easy, and keen. How could I name him other than master, who ruled my best self? Little wonder, then, if I clung to his remembered image; it was all I would have of him from now on.

But eventually the curtain of memory dissolved; my perceptions entered the train compartment. I was forced to alertness by an abrupt sensation of motion. The train had started; the world, in the form of metal rails, signal signs, and an occasional snowflake, fell backwards past the darkening window. The chuff of the engine quickened its tempo.

I was not alone. Across from me but nearer the corridor entrance sat an elderly white-haired woman whose chin jerked up and down as she knitted. (It was probably this rhythm, in chance conjunction with the rhythms of the train, that brought me at first out of my reverie.) Having noted her, I gradually focused my attention on another person in the compartment with us, whom I discovered to be a moustachioed gentleman with fine, silver-grey hair. He was richly but sombrely dressed, in one of the latter stages of mourning. He sat very quietly by the window, his grey-gloved hands folded over the top of a propped-up walking stick, his eyes never wavering from the speck on which they were fixed, a speck somewhere beyond, certainly, the vanishing point of any perspective that could meet an outside observer's eye.

His apparent case so resembled my own that perhaps I smiled slightly in fellow feeling: at any rate he shifted his attention from the speck to me. We exchanged pleasant nods.

'If there is any adjustment I could make to the window or shade,' he said, including our web-weaving companion in his address, 'you have only to indicate your wish.' I smiled and shook my head. The old lady frowned and exasperatedly snapped her knitting needles, but otherwise took no notice of the gentleman's utterance. He bowed and returned to his contemplation of the speck in the glass, and I, despite my misery, to my covert observation of him.

He was perhaps sixty years old, of middling height, and in body spare rather than portly. His skin was fine of texture and delicately blooming; almost the glow of youth illumined its fine wrinkles. His countenance had a kindly, reflective, benevolent cast, but certain lines of the chin and mouth revealed a turning inward, a somewhat finicky care of self, a lack of outward force. I thought he was one of those men who, seemingly, only obey the dictates of a higher law when they treat themselves to the best of everything. How different this mild, benign countenance from the excited, humorous visage I had left on the other side of the Channel!

My musings were interrupted by the advent of a train employee asking for our booking receipts. The gentleman's and my own were checked against the record and returned without comment, but the old lady's was subjected to a long, silent scrutiny, of which she deigned not to take notice. My male companion and I, however, watched the process alertly, with that fatalistic pessimism common to travellers sensing a snag in the vast machinery in which they have enmeshed themselves. Our suspense was ended, finally, by the man's utterance: 'You have an Ipswich booking.'

'Certainly, young man, for it is to Ipswich I am going!' This the woman delivered in a tone of utmost disgust, with not a beat of knitting or chin-jerking skipped.

'Not on this train, you're not. We're for Rugby, Derby, and Leeds.'

She looked up. 'You are impertinent, and should be reported. This is the Ipswich train.'

The train man shrugged. 'As you like, ma'am. But we'll be pulling into Luton in five minutes. If you get off there and cross the platform you'll be able to get back to London in time to catch the Ipswich train.' He continued on his rounds.

Unshaken from Ipswich orthodoxy, the old lady returned to her knitting. The gentleman and I exchanged a rather worried glance; we saw that if we did not do something quickly, we would become trapped witnesses to a prolonged and tedious storm of outrage. 'Pardon me, madam,' said he, leaning towards her, 'concern for your welfare prompts me to speak. This train *is* bound for Leeds; I am going there myself.'

(Then he and I, at least, were fated to spend some hours in each other's company.)

The woman now put down her knitting and glared at the man over her spectacles. 'But I am going to Ipswich.'

'Nonetheless, this is the night train to Leeds.'

I nodded in confirmation. Continuing to glare, the lady in a tone of great scepticism said, 'Let me see what you showed him.'

Obediently we reached for the receipts, hurrying because the train had already begun to slow for its stop in Luton. Mine the conductor had secured in a clip above my head, and in rising to get it, I displaced from my lap the book I had been holding. It tumbled to the floor. It was precious – a parting gift from him I had left in Brussels – so I dove for it. Unfortunately, at the same moment the gentleman also bent to retrieve it.

We cracked our heads together very smartly. Simultaneously his cane and my eyeglasses scattered wide; simultaneously our hands flew to our stricken pates.

The pain was nothing; the mere physical shock would never under normal conditions have drawn from me the least expression of emotion (unless it had been laughter), but somehow this blow was psychic in its force: it breached my stone reservoir of grief.

I sobbed – and the torrent once released could not be moderated; try as I would I could not stop crying. The gentleman squelched any pain *he* felt the better to assuage mine. But his murmured apologies and expressions of sympathy for a while made me sob the harder; I had for so long been without the honey of common kindness that its gift from a stranger stung rather than soothed.

'I am really alarmed – ' he said at last, fanning me with his handkerchief. 'I fear you are injured. I will leave you only a moment while I summon help – a female attendant perhaps – '

'No – No!' The idea of public exposure penetrating my brain, it was somehow enabled to control my sobs; as they diminished I more clearly conceived of how completely I had played the fool, and my distress, though quenched outwardly, was inwardly directed towards the sad spectacle I had made of myself. This sobered me in earnest. I wiped my eyes. 'Really, the bump was nothing. I cannot explain the cause of my outburst. I am sorry; it was absurd.'

'Absurd or no, it has accomplished one thing.'

'What?' I asked, reassuming my spectacles and smoothing the hair from my eyes.

He nodded mutely towards the other end of the compartment. It was vacant. The lady, whether from disgust at my outbreak or motivation more obscure, had shaken the dust of our tent from her feet and removed herself and all that bore her stamp.

This made me smile. Encouraged, my companion continued, 'Your argument has been of service to her in spite of herself.' He pointed out the now-stationary window to the train platform, where the old woman, skirts and knitting whipped by a snowy wind, was being supported by a porter to her proper place on the London side. 'She will arrive in Ipswich as planned, and all because of you.'

'Sir, you are very kind.'

'Not at all. I perceive that you have perhaps been under some nervous strain, have suffered some loss. No – do not trouble yourself to explain.' He shook his head reassuringly. 'I venture to think that I understand.' With a gesture he indicated his state of mourning. 'I am too well acquainted with the blows of a depriving fate to fail to recognize their consequences in another. But allow me to introduce myself. Our shared ordeal has made us old friends by now. I am Charles Lockwood, of London and Kent.'

'I am Charlotte Brontë, from Yorkshire, daughter of the Reverend Patrick Brontë.'

Once our acquaintance was established, talk came easily. We made such an exchange of observations as seems almost inevitable for fellow-travellers these days: the ease and speed of railway as opposed to coach travel; the relative dangers of each; the alteration the English countryside has undergone beneath the hand of the railway engineer; the spread of scientific thought and practices and how they bid fair to extinguish local folk ways, even in pockets of deep country.

The porter entered to light the oil lamp. 'We're in for a stormy night,' he commented as he left. Indeed the weather had thickened considerably in only the last few minutes. The flakes visible outside had gathered mass enough to make a curved yellow swirl as they entered and passed through the speeding shaft of light from our window. The motion mesmerized me for a while. Something it told of separation, something of futility, something of vacuity: I turned my back to it.

'With your permission.' Mr Lockwood pulled the shades, and the walls seemed to huddle together with us, instantly making the little room brighter and snugger. 'Such cold and dark does not match – or perhaps matches too well – my mood this evening. It recalls forcibly something I have made a concentrated effort to forget these many years past.' I must have looked surprised, for he continued, 'Pardon me, that perhaps sounds overdramatic in your ear, Miss Brontë, but there really is an order of events whose power for evil does not diminish with the passing of years, but rather intensifies. However, you are too young to know that yet; pray God you never will.'

Maybe the sharing of this tiny safehold of light and warmth, put together with a consciousness of speed, cold, and dark without, gave us the odd illusion that we had known each other for a long time. Or maybe our intimacy had been unnaturally advanced by that violent contact of heads that had begun it. That, at least, is how I explain what followed: my boldness in query, his readiness in answer. At any rate, instead of receiving his intriguing statement with the silent nod politeness demanded, I gave voice to the curiosity I felt:

'What was it happened so long ago, Mr Lockwood, that has such power to affect you still?'

He lifted the blind and peered behind it a moment before answering. 'I am puzzled as to how to answer your question simply, yet truthfully, Miss Brontë. The simple answer would be this: that all my distress arose from my chance contact with a man named Heathcliff.'

I started in surprise.

'You know the name?' Mr Lockwood asked, also surprised. 'I have heard it; does the Heathcliff you speak of come from a town called Gimmerton?'

'Yes, from a farm named Wuthering Heights, near Gimmerton. It is there, in fact, I am going. But Heathcliff has been dead these many years.'

'Pardon me, but it cannot be the same Heathcliff then,' I said. 'The man I have heard spoken of is living, or was a year ago.'

'But how singular! The name and the man were alike unique, and he had no surviving issue. How could there be two Heathcliffs, and both in Gimmerton? In what connection had you heard of him?'

I parried the question, wishing not to pursue this line of inquiry till I had ordered my ideas, which were now in considerable disarray. 'Some Gimmerton folk attend services in Haworth, where my father is Perpetual Curate. Perhaps the name appears in the church records.'

Here he exclaimed over the coincidence of our common destination, and we counted over our little stock of mutual acquaintances and neighbourhood associations. He remembered our churchyard, and it developed that many of the walks and byways frequented by my sisters and myself had once been trod by Mr Lockwood. My mind calmed by these commonplaces, I reverted to our former subject:

'How did you know this obscure Heathcliff, then?' I asked.

'I rented a manor house from him for a year,' said Mr Lockwood. 'But he was well-known, a rich gentleman, the biggest landowner in the vicinity.

'Then it is indeed unlikely that we are speaking of the same person, for the Heathcliff of whom I have heard is a vagabond of the moors, a true child of nature.'

'Stranger and stranger, for those phrases would have described my Heathcliff perfectly at the opening stages of his career!' Mr Lockwood exclaimed. 'He started out as a farmhand, and ran wild through the neighbourhood with his playmate and foster-sister, one of the Earnshaws. What, have you heard of her as well?'

If I had, I chose to keep the knowledge to myself. 'The Earnshaws are an old family in the district. But you say Heathcliff was a farm labourer? – How did he transform himself to a rich gentleman?'

Mr Lockwood smiled. 'It is curious you should ask. I have in my possession a document written by Heathcliff himself, expressly to explain just that mystery.' He reached inside his coat and pulled out a thick packet wrapped in a Mulready; addressed, I could see, to himself. This was odd. Mulready wrappers were an innovation of last season, yet here was this gentleman maintaining the sender had been dead for decades!

'I suppose he wrote it to you some years ago,' I ventured.

'Certainly he wrote it many years ago – about sixty it would be now, when he was a young man just come into his fortune – but he did not write it to me!'

'How did you get it, then?'

'It was recently sent to me by a third party.' Deflated, I listened without further interruption as he continued: 'No, the document was addressed to that same Miss Earnshaw, Catherine, or Cathy as he called her, with whom he had grown up. He had run away from her home to escape the wretched circumstances of his life there. Cathy's older brother had made him almost a slave, you see. He wrote the letter after he had been gone several years, to explain to his old playmate how he had raised himself during his absence, and to ask her to marry him.'

'Did she do so?' I inquired.

'No, she never received the missive, and so remained ignorant of her foster-brother's whereabouts. She married another man, though she loved Heathcliff best.'

'That was a sad fate for them both.'

'For all concerned; the tragedy touched many lives. Yet it is hard to say positively that things would have been better had the star-crossed lovers married.'

This I could not let pass unchallenged. 'When people love, and love supremely, should they not be together?'

'As a general rule, but this is an exceptional case – yet I cannot say.' He shook his head, fingering the bulging brown packet.

'But why didn't the letter reach Catherine Earnshaw? And how did it come to you?'

'You will get the best answer to both questions from this.' He now opened the packet and drew from it documents of two distinct types: one set, by far the larger, a thick bunch of brittle and yellowing papers inscribed with heavy, dark, spiked characters; the other a handful of fresh white sheets covered with a light, fluent, old-fashioned hand. He thumbed out the latter. 'Here, you shall read this covering letter, just as I found it two days ago when I opened the package. It is from a Mrs Dean, the housekeeper of the property I rented from Heathcliff. She it was, incidentally, who told me most of what I know about that man. But her letter will explain.' He handed it to me.

Gimmerton
26 December 1843
Dear Mr Lockwood,

You will remember me, I hope, as Mrs Dean, the housekeeper of Thrushcross Grange at the time of your tenancy.

You were good enough then, some forty years past, to let me gossip with you about our family's history, especially where it touched Mr Heathcliff, your old landlord and my old employer, and I venture on the memory of your good nature to think an addition to that history will interest you still.

Heathcliff's tale, as I told it you, had a gap in the middle of it; I said no one knew what had become of him during those three years that he had been gone, or how he had got his fortune. That was a lie. I knew, though no one else did: I had found out by reading the manuscript I now send to you.

It is a long letter from Mr Heathcliff to my then mistress Catherine Earnshaw, mother of my present dear mistress. I have had it hidden in the bottom of my work-box for almost sixty years, a fair lifetime for some, and not a day of those sixty years has gone by but I wondered if I had done the right thing in so secreting it.

Mr Lockwood, I stole this letter. It was brought in by a little post-boy on a bright morning, the day before Miss Catherine's wedding to Mr Linton. I remember she had gone to the Grange for a few hours to be with her pretty Edgar, as she called him, and I was in the house smoothing her wedding gown over a dress form and thinking of past days, when a voice behind me said, 'Please, missus, Mr Heathcliff's waiting,' and a little hand reached me an envelope. If the boy had said the devil was waiting he could not have given me a sharper taking!

Now Heathcliff had then been missing three years, and I was pretty sure he was finally gone out of my mistress's head, and better so, so I gave the boy an orange and a play-pretty from my apron pocket and bid him wait. I took the letter into the next room, prised up the seal undisturbed, and skimmed the sense from what you hold in your hands, before giving the boy an answer. You may be certain I read it through and through many times later, and cried over it too, though Heathcliff would not have thanked me for my tears!

Now that I am old and, Dr Kenneth says, in my last illness, my thoughts turn and turn again on my actions during my life. Taken in the balance, I think I have nearly always acted for the best, or at least in the best way I knew, but this one instance sticks in my mind and will not be thrust out. I thought of telling my mistress, but hesitated to add to her troubles, since she has recently been made a widow – as I think you know, she married her cousin Hareton Earnshaw, so taking back her mother's maiden name as well as her property, and a happy marriage it was, too, these many years; the more to grieve her when he went.

Mulling matters over I hit upon you, sir, as one outside the troubles I stirred with my deception, yet in a position to understand them. I need your help to make my peace with the past and rightly prepare to meet my maker. I ask you to read what Heathcliff wrote and tell me honestly what you would have done in my place.

Ellen Dean

I looked up from the page. 'It is to her you are going.'

'Yes, I am going to her bedside, her deathbed perhaps, to comfort her.'

'It is a most kind, a most generous action, and I honour you for it, sir. To travel such a distance through this weather to aid a friend you have not seen in decades – it is admirable.'

'It is necessary. Do not give me more credit than I deserve. I am compelled to action by complicated motives, only one of which is friendly feeling for a woman who served me well and kindly during an unhappy period of my life.'

Here I was silent, though many questions crowded to my lips. Mr Lockwood regarded me for a minute.

'Miss Brontë, something in your countenance speaks of true judgement, true benevolence.'

I liked not this flattery, but could do no less than bow my head in its acknowledgement.

He continued: 'These qualities in your physiognomy give me the boldness to ask of you a favour, for you have it in your power to help me.'

'That seems unlikely, but if it is so, then I will gladly comply. What is it you would have me do?'

'If you will be so kind, Miss Brontë, read this.' He

indicated the other document, the letter from Heathcliff. 'I know the manuscript is long, you are weary from travel, and perhaps disinclined to tangle yourself in the troubles of a dead man. Yet I ask you.'

'Though reading the letter would clearly benefit me, by gratifying my curiosity, I fail to see how that gratification could be of use to you!'

'It is simple: I hope that you may be able to solve the conundrum that confounds me – how to comfort the living, yet do justice to the dead. In fact I ask of you the same favour Nelly asks of me: to read, and to judge.'

Just then the train made a sudden lurch sideways: the jolt caused one of the blinds to snap up. We jumped, then laughed at our jitters, but I think we were both glad to again draw the shade over the wind and white that flashed outside. The porter entered with foot warmers and blankets. We received them gratefully, for the cold was deepening. When we had finally settled ourselves again, Mr Lockwood, indicating the manuscript, said:

'You hesitate – '

'Indeed, I do not; I will read it gladly!' I reached out, but he held it tantalizingly beyond my fingertips as he framed his next speech:

'I must confess I had forgot something just now; the account contains some language and incident that must be shocking to a lady – '

'Mr Lockwood, though I am the daughter of a clergyman, I have read freely all my life and have, moreover, lived in Brussels these past two years. I am not likely to be shocked.'

'Still, I could easily summarize the main points of the story, especially since to read every word of it would take you all night – the span of time, by the way, it took Heathcliff to write it. You need actually read only those parts where Heathcliff – '

I held up my hand. 'No, please, do not tell me. I *wish* to read every word. Of course I am tired, as you must be, but as I am absolutely unable to sleep while travelling, I will find more relief in losing myself in this manuscript than in vainly seeking rest.' (Or in longing for *Monsieur* in Brussels, I mentally added.) 'Before I begin, however, I have a particular reason for repeating my previous question, though it may seem impertinent to do so. What is it about the memory of Heathcliff that has the power to disturb you now?'

'I will tell you, though my answer will strike you as strange. One snowy night, a night much like this, I stayed at Wuthering Heights as Heathcliff's grudged guest. There, between fitful dreams, I saw, or thought I saw, a ghost. It made a kind of assault on me, and I was ill for weeks afterwards. Still, the full effect of the visitation, or hallucination (I do not insist on others' credulity), did not make itself known to me till years later.'

I nodded. 'Did the ghost have an identity?'

'It was the shade of Catherine Earnshaw.'

'Thank you. I am satisfied.' He handed me the manuscript, and as I touched it, I fancied a little thrill ran up my arm from my fingers. I settled myself near the lamp to read. Mr Lockwood leaned back as though to rest, but through half-closed eyes for a while kept up a covert surveillance of my progress. I took good care that my face should not betray the intensity of the interest with which I began, for the pages that hid Heathcliff's secrets might also conceal some of my own.

2

Gimmerton, 10 April 1784

Cathy

It is I, Heathcliff – I am come back to you. I write this in my sitting room at the Boar's Head not two miles from where you lie asleep, and tomorrow I will wait in a carriage – my own carriage, Cathy – on the road behind Pennistone Crags, for the one word that gives me the right to claim you. Send that word and claim you I will, though to do it I must shed heart's blood in every room at the Heights, and wade through the results to carry you out. One word, and I am at your side; one word, and in an hour we fly beyond the petty torments of that bottle-tyrant Hindley, and all others who would keep us apart.

But first you must read this account of my actions since I have been gone, so you will understand why I left, what strange imperative kept me away for three long years, and how it is that I am now in a position to rescue us both. I have had my fill of secrets; I would have none between you and me. I would have no misunderstandings sunder us, as they did often during those last months at the Heights, when unthinking you hurt me and, hurt, I rebuffed you, so I will tell you all – even though some parts will make as painful reading for you as they do writing for me.

So avert your eyes from nothing, omit nothing. I ask it, though I feel every minute that delays our reunion as a knife-twist in my breast. Still I write, still I ask you to read.

I have good reason for my request. You will see it soon enough.

Cathy, I am a gentleman. Strange shifts of fate and my own bitter perseverance have made me so. I have been educated, both in mind and manners. I have a fortune, sufficient to sustain us together for the rest of our days. I will never shame you again. I even have a name. But stay; I must reveal all gradually so that you may feel as I felt and comprehend as I comprehended. From this moment I would have us parted in nothing. Read, then, and know that I wait, my body torn between agony and bliss as I imagine what the next hours may bring.

You will remember the night I left. Goaded almost beyond endurance by Hindley's unspeakable persecutions, made wretched by the many days you chose Edgar Linton's company over my own, but enduring still for your sake, I was finally broken by one sentence I heard you utter: 'It would degrade me to marry Heathcliff.' (Even now my cheeks burn as I write it.)

Not marry me! Despite the distance separating our stations, we were and are unalterably, fundamentally joined, we could not be parted, it were blasphemy to deny it. But you *had* denied it! I heard you! Before I knew why or how, I had run out the door, past the gate, between moor and sky, halfway to Pennistone Crags.

There was to be a storm that night. The clouds were thick roiling masses of murky matter only rendered darker by the beats of sullen light that limned their coils. Through some elemental trick, the moors emitted a sulphurous glow, eclipsing the welkin, overturning the wheel of earth and sky. It was right; this was the very wheel to break me.

For what was I? I thought I saw it then. Ploughboy, scullion, wretch – though I knew my degradation, I could not find words to frame it. You had said it often enough – I did not trouble myself to speak, I had no conversation.

That the power to make it had been beaten out of me by Hindley did not signify when I was put into the balance with Edgar Linton. Often and often had his visits in the past months barred me from the house and from your presence. But why should you not prefer his company? He, with his fair unclouded face, his happy words, his harmonious movements, must please and charm any discriminating taste. I saw, as in a flash from the lurid heavens, my own hulking form, blackened countenance, sputtering speeches, set beside Edgar's impeccable demeanour. Then indeed I knew the meaning of pain.

As I stood in the quickening wind, I imagined thrusting that blond face into the depths of Blackhorse Marsh (into the same ancient muck you and I used to overleap, daring it to pull us down), crushing those pink ears in my hands till they wrung blood. My fingers ached with the pleasure of it! But it was I who was mired, in poverty and ignorance. I opened my mouth to the wind and howled. How could I shake off the filth that encumbered me? How could I free myself? Where was my hope?

No answer came. There was no hope, only the instinct to struggle. Struggle I must, if only for sufficient advantage to kill Edgar Linton, if I could not rise above him.

I tried to consider my situation in a cold light. It was clear that I must escape Hindley's rule before anything else was possible. A mist rose between me and the thought of where I would go, but at least I had the means of going *somewhere* at my disposal. In the barn I had secreted a small hoard of gold – gold dropped from Hindley's pockets in drunken fits or stupors, that I had claimed as slave-price for my labour. I must retrieve it, and take myself to a place where I could batten on hatred to conquer – or avenge.

I came back to the Heights just as the first hot drops spat from the clouds, and from behind the barn I watched you as you stood motionless by the wall, looking towards Gimmerton. (Were you watching for me, or Edgar?) The storm's explosions seared your sky-turned face: my eyes kissed it and cursed it. My heart was a stone. I sought my hoard in the secret cavity behind Joseph's rabbit traps; I tore a lock of hair slippery with my scalp's blood to leave in its place; it is there still, I suppose. The storm reached a mighty climax as I slid open the threshing door; the barn shook, a bolt descended and outlined the

Heights with thin coruscating fire. I left. You were a stubborn dark shape by the wall. That was the last time my bodily eyes saw you.

Where would I go? What did I know of the world beyond Gimmerton?

An answer began to grow in my mind. Though I had been created to consciousness sleeping in the coach bed next to you, my birth song the wind soaring through the fir trees outside the window, there was a dim-remembered dream before that creation. If I worked my mind back through the dark journey that had first brought me, wrapped in your father's coat, to the Heights, I found a city – a river, ships, sailors' flashing teeth, bread snatched from a tavern floor, a gold coin somersaulting forever on its way from a pirate's toss to my waiting hand. A city of giants, for I was a child scurrying among knees. I remembered, too, even more dimly, a low, whitewashed room with a cross on the wall, blows and prayers, an earthen tunnel under a wall with the stink of the river on the other side.

These bare scraps of odd associations, meagre though they were, formed the only map I had to the country of my origin, and the only clues to my parentage. For I did not spring from the festering river mud like a toad; I had had a human father and mother, however low, and it was growing in my mind that I would claim my birthright. I knew from Nelly's tales that the city where your father had found me was Liverpool, and to Liverpool I would go.

I pass quickly over the rest of the night. In Blackhorse Marsh the storm confused me. Three times I stumbled off our secret path to wallow in the slough; three times I struggled to release myself from its pull. The third time, utterly exhausted, I must have lost consciousness for a space – I woke to the delectable taste of bog mud in my mouth and to the agreeable vision of a hole-eyed, slash-mouthed ghoul face three inches from my own. It must have been the ancient corpse of a Saxon sacrifice, such as are preserved by the peat to be offered up to the world of the living in times of turbulence – Nelly had told of these things. But in my panic, I thought it was a demon sent from hell to fetch me – which misapprehension probably saved my life, for revulsion and terror alone lent me the strength to free myself from the mud. I choked out the filth I had swallowed, then through the clearing dawn made my way to Gimmerton, thence to Manchester market day hidden in the straw of a cheese wagon.

Tired and low in spirits though I was, still the excitement of the market crowd, with its buyers and sellers from all stations, ignited in me an emotion that was at once pride and resentment. Though I was now lower than the dung-smeared cretin emptying the outhouses, I felt rising in myself the power to scorn even the lordly merchant who flipped the cretin a coin and slapped his gold chain against his belly. I would be a gentleman who could buy and sell gentlemen like these!

The best way to Liverpool was, I found, by canal. I asked a man loading great bolts of cloth into a barge the price of passage. He answered me with a kick, saying he'd have no gypsy thieves aboard. As soon as his back was turned, though, I pulled myself up out of sight on the top of the pile, and rested in cotton and wool through the deepening afternoon, till we glided into Liverpool.

It was quite dark when I slipped from among the stacks of cloth (not neglecting to foul as many of them as I could with the swamp mud that still clung to my garments and boots, as payment to the barge-master), and made my way unremarked past the dock men.

I paused. I could see little. The air around me was thick and murky, made nauseous by effluvia from the decaying mud flats that stretched everywhere, and perhaps also from the breath of the ramshackle dwellings among which I now stood.

This was familiar. Memory teased me with tiny cuts, knowledge oozed as from knife wounds in the river. Secret blood, that as soon as let, dispersed unrecognizable downstream. A reflection of a barge floated by and lost itself in the mist.

I walked then, without pattern or plan, turning as the heart within my breast turned amongst the uneven winding lanes. Though I constantly heard faint voices and laughter, I saw no human form. At many a corner I felt a dull quickening of memory, but I gained no clear access.

For a while off to my right there had been no flicker from windowed lantern or candle, only a great black mass. I stopped and looked at the dark form. Gradually its outlines impressed my straining eye. I was standing next to a high wall, behind which slowly undulating shapes – trees, I thought, moved by the sluggard motion of the thick air – could be discerned. Beyond this, I knew, or thought I knew, was a large building.

I followed the wall as it curved unevenly to my right. At one point, where its meanders brought the river nearer, moved by a sudden impulse I fell to my knees and plunged both hands into some weeds growing at the base of the masonry. Nothing, but something should have been there.

Eventually I saw glimmerings of light ahead. At the same moment I noticed, and was aware that I had been hearing for some time, faint cries and growls, like those of wild beasts. What was it I was circling, then? Was it a pleasure-park, filled with animals? The notion is not so far-fetched, for as you know from the stories your father used to tell us, Liverpool slave ships from the West Indies and Africa bring back sundry curiosities, including fantastic beasts. Perhaps this wall enclosed a rich man's menagerie. Why, then, did my memory seek it out?

At length I came to a thoroughfare, lit only by torches of passing coaches but bright to my dark-adapted eye. I saw, between the bars of a gate I now approached and behind the wall I had circuited, the building of my memory. It was an imposing, symmetrical Palladian edifice (as I now know), with very high narrow windows. My frame shook, with fear or elation, I knew not. Fancy conquered reason: if this had been my residence I had been a lord's son and could easily triumph over a simple country demi-squire like Edgar Linton.

I observed two men by the gate. One, liveried and pike-armed, held a lantern that illumined the other, a gentleman, who was apparently questioning him. Determined to do likewise, I approached the pair and waited for a pause in the conversation. I must know what this house was.

As I came near him, the liveried man made a move with his pike as if to strike me. The gentleman, however, restrained him.

'Hold, friend,' said he. 'I have a fancy to hear what this goblin or ghoul might have to request of humankind, for ghoul he is, and has recently risen from his tomb. See! The very grave-clouts cling to him.'

I looked down at my clothes, suddenly aware of the dirty sight I must be on a city street.

'Nay, look at me, let me see your face when I speak to you, lad,' the gentleman said. I almost ran away then, but, anticipating my action, he snapped his walking stick out to bar my path. 'State your business.'

I had half a mind to make him eat his words in the form of his own stick crammed down his throat (though he was strongly built, I was taller than he and could have done it), but the weight of my mission made me stay my hand.

'My business is none of yours.

'Yet I make it mine. Speak.'

I determined to ignore the gentleman's rudeness, so I fixed my attention on the watchman's face. 'Whose house is this?'

A flick of the gentleman's cane brought speech from the servant. 'It belongs to the Church.'

'Yet it is not a church.'

My informant laughed. 'You have the right of it there.'

'Who dwells within, then?'

At that moment an uncanny shriek from the building made both me and the gentleman start. The watchman laughed again. 'Your brothers, by the look of you.'

Lightheaded from emotion and fasting (I had had no food except for a penny bun at the market), I was momentarily dazzled by the image of brothers of my blood and countenance within, perhaps ready to welcome the lost one of their number to the familial hearth. Then the gentleman, seized by one of those sudden convulsive impulses I afterwards found to be characteristic of him, snatched the lantern from the other's hand and thrust it full in my face.

The watchman sneered, 'Here's a pretty one, sir! Well fit to join them inside, with his nasty brow and wild eyes. See him snarl! This one should be tied down, sir, I'll warrant he bites!'

I could see the gentleman's eyes searching out mine over the lantern's glare. They held a strange expression. His voice came slow. 'Boy, are you of this house?'

Something in his tone made me silent. He thrust the lantern so near my head I could feel its heat singe my hair. 'Speak.'

'What is this place?' I asked.

The watchman answered. 'It's the madhouse, boy. St Nicholas madhouse. The bloodiest lunatics in England live here.'

I fell back as though I had been struck full in the chest with a rod. Lantern and cane smashed to the ground as the gentleman sprang to detain me, but I twisted away and ran, I cared not where.

Mad! This was my history, this the hungry hand of fate that had reached from the past to put a throttle-hold on my throat. Now I remembered, or thought I did – for madness may conjure fantasies that seem facts – I remembered the little whitewashed room: a cell. The tunnel under the wall: an escape route, dug with the preternatural energy of the frenzied. Harsh words, kicks, blows – demon child. A child locked up, perceived as inhuman and dangerous even then. How much more to be feared and loathed now, grown to a man's height? No wonder I had ever been shunned. No wonder that even you, Cathy, had turned from your dark star to the happier light in Linton's brow.

I became aware that I ran through deserted streets, wider than those I had quitted, lined with quiet houses, each of which had a large garden. Not a soul moved or spoke. The only sounds were the clatter of my boots and the pulling gasps of my breath. I had the night to myself.

I slowed to a walk. Even madmen must rest. I entered the darkest garden and flung myself on the grass under a tree. Here, mad or sane, I would sleep, and hope to wake to a clearer vision of myself and my future.

But then, deep within my sleep (and sometimes since in dreams) to my mingled sorrow and delight I saw you – but as never – in life, Cathy. Wild, wild, *this* Cathy's mien – her lips where she had bitten them black with blood, her eyes, fierce, fixing me with an agony of fury and bereavement. The bloody lips did not move, but I heard your voice, dear beyond remembrance, from afar, as though you had slipped from this world lightly as down from a thistle, and were tormenting me from the other with these words, harsh and strange:

When you left I stood by the wall. The slippery rain ran down my throat and choked me. You had gone and I knew you would not be back.

Through the rain, mist rising from the bog formed your wershape, and mine too, as we used to be when we were all in all to each other. I saw you lurch from the cloud with the meagre grace that satisfies as no feast.

Believe me, I want you, believe me it is you I must have, forgive me Heathcliff it is for you.

The mist rose from the ground and penetrated my stomach and made me weak. It wound up from Gimmerton kirkyard in long wet clots. I willed it catch you home but you were stubborn.

Nelly had said it would come to this; my castle crumble in a heap at last, for all my devices.

The mist covered my eyes and I fell against the base

of the wall, into the running mud. It slid between my fingers and all around, cold, cold. This is how the grave will feel when I lie in the kirkyard, I thought. This is my future.

It's then you will return, isn't it? I'll hear your boots above me tamping the harebells while I writhe in the muck beneath. Up there you'll pause to read my gravestone. Up there the sun will warm your coat, you'll inhale the fresh breeze and let it out with some fine tune you'll find to whistle in the minutes before you stroll away . . .

No, my lad, not so easy.

I'll cast off the stupor of death. I'll twist my hands up through the mud, no matter how chill. I'll make the roots' white tangle crackle as I claw a way through, no matter how my dead flesh rips. Nothing will hinder me then, whose joints are driven by more than muscle.

The greensward bulges, my fingers pierce it and rise in the air. Strange graveflowers on starved stalks, weaving. Yes, you see, but you don't move. You can't move. The bones clamp your ankles. I'll have you. Here. With me.

The voice diminished, the fiery eyes receded, and I knew no more. But oh, Cathy, if those broken cries were your own – if the dream I had that night was no dream but a true vision, such as sometimes visits sainted men or damned, carried by agents of the netherworld to further the designs of fate – then, oh my darling, drop this page and speed to me now, that your voice so terrible still in echo may plunge, may drown, may quench itself in the flood of our embrace.

3

A brightness in the air pressed upon my eyelids and I came to consciousness, but did not open my eyes. I was smitten with a mighty longing for you, Cathy, and the Heights, and it seemed that my throat must burst if the growing light did not disclose you near me. All that had passed in the last hours was paraded through my mind. My heart felt as though it had committed a great crime that parted it from yours – the greatest crime that ever was, for no ordinary crime could come between us – mayhem, treason, murder – any and all would be blinked away like motes of dust, provided our essential souls remained. But what was my soul? All I knew of it might be a mad dream. Indeed you yourself, Cathy, might be a lunatic phantasm spun out of a moonbeam on a white-washed wall. I might never have left the madhouse – at this moment, instead of lying in fresh grass, I might be worrying my filthy straw, celled, chained, drooling, my mind caught in a web that is not there.

'He weeps.'

That voice had its origins beyond the world bounded by my eyelids. I lifted them. A dark shape interposed itself between me and the dawn. As I stared it resolved itself into the semblance of the man, the gentleman who had questioned me last night. He sat not three feet away from my head with his knees drawn up to his chin. I could have felled him with one blow had he been flesh and blood, but the unlikelihood of his being present in anything but my diseased fancy kept me still.

'Who are you?' I asked without moving.

'He speaks,' said the man, 'and in a human voice, a voice different from his dream-ravings.'

'What have you to do with my dreams?' I sat up to gain

more of an equity with my dream-phantom, if dream-phantom he was.

'He moves,' said the man. 'He has a strong frame, but it shivers from the cold – that at least is a human trait. Here, boy, warm yourself,' and he unwrapped the long cloak he wore and draped it over my back.

I shrugged it off. 'Who are you?' I asked with more force. 'I *will* have an answer.'

The man laughed. 'Softly, my brave Bottom! An answer you shall have. I am Mr Are.'

'How did you find me?'

'I followed you. You were not hard to track. You snorted and bellowed through the streets like one possessed.'

'And you stayed here all night?'

'Yes.'

'Why?'

'I had two reasons. The first was that I feared to leave a being as fierce as yourself loose in a respectable neighbourhood.'

'And the second?'

'I have need of a servant. I wish to hire you.'

The paradox in the dyad did not strike me then; I was far too dazed for logic; but the strangeness of the man's behaviour did. Now, as the dawn spread around us, I saw that he too was shivering; he was as beaded with dew as I was; the knees of his light-coloured britches were soaked through from kneeling long at my side in the wet grass, as certain indentations there also indicated. Perhaps it was not I, but Mr Are, who was mad.

He attempted to dispel my doubts. 'Ah, Master H, you bridle, your brow clouds, you think I act strangely. Well, I am a strange man with strange fancies sometimes, and it is my fancy now to attach you to myself. What say you?'

'Why do you call me "H"?'

He pointed mutely to my chest. I put my hand there. Next to my heart was the medallion you gave me on your fourteenth birthday graved, 'H from C, 1779', with its intaglio of two larks flying. It was safe, but he must have opened my shirt to read the legend; I clapped my hand to where my money was kept.

'What next, the imp suspects me of thievery! Don't worry, your hoard is undisturbed. You must not blame me for seeking to discover what kind of being I would take into my household. Did you come by the gold honestly?'

'It is mine.'

'An equivocal answer, but let it pass. What can you do, Master H? Come, lad, don't glower, I mean what can you do in the way of work? How have you earned your bread hitherto?'

'I have been made to labour in the field from dawn to dark, to work in the stable, to be the lowest country menial, a churl, a bumpkin.'

'Yet it is not a bumpkin's voice. There is some mystery there. Can you read?'

'Yes.'

He pulled a book out of his pocket and handed it to me. Very well; I opened it and read at random:

Struck by that light, the human heart,
A barren soil no more,
Sends the sweet smell of grace abroad,
Where serpents lurked before.

'The soul, a dreary province once
Of Satan's dark domain,
Feels –

Mr Are raised his hand. 'It will do. Your measures are halting, but correct. Who taught you?'

'A curate engaged by the house.'

'Engaged to school the stableboy? My credulity falters.'

I was silent. I did not choose to parade my history before this stranger.

'And "C"? Who was she, Scholar H? Some serving wench sneaking a kailyard romance? A blooming poppet ripe for ploughboy kisses? Nay, a scullery maid would scarce have money to purchase that chain – it is gold. Perhaps C is some lusty widow, buying young flesh with trinkets.'

I leapt up and knocked Mr Are back on to the grass. 'She is as far above you in spirit as I surpass you in strength. If you speak of her again, I will rip the lips from your face.'

Mr Are lay stunned for a minute, then he roared, whether with laughter or ire I could not tell. 'Ha! You would, wouldn't you, H? There is something I recognize in your wild eye that convinces me you utter the truth. It will bear watching; it will bear watching.'

I felt half-inclined to put an end to the man's unaccountable paroxysms by kicking his breath away, but upon observing his countenance definitely mould itself to a mask of tragedy, and the roars change to almost-sobs, I turned on my heel.

'Hold!' The chameleon sobs again seemed laughter. 'Can you not take a jest, man? What I said was in play – light-hearted banter.'

'*I* am not one you can play with.' I began to walk away.

'Yes – you are right. *H* is not one to be played with. *H* is not to be trifled with. With him you cannot share a jest, enjoy a joke, pass a light-hearted half-hour in repartee. No; no; with H all must be blood and tears. Ah – you turn, your lip curls, your fist clenches, you would smite me again! Well, no reasonable man could question your power to do so. I certainly do not. Here I sit on the wet ground, winded by your previous blow, half-palsied from chill and inanition – you could mince me to dog-meat in thirty seconds. But would it not be a better idea to help me to my feet? Then we could go to my inn (where I have no doubt my drowsy manservant still wakes for me), dry ourselves before a good blazing fire, drink coffee, eat rolls and bacon, and talk business.' He reached up his hand.

I wanted to knock it away and have done with this unpleasant gentleman and his stupid conceits, but my stomach argued otherwise. What harm could there be in accepting his breakfast? 'You can help yourself,' I said, crossing my arms. 'But I will come with you.'

Mr Are heaved a mock-pathetic sigh and with exaggerated difficulty struggled upright. 'Such, I perceive, must be my meed. So be it. I will grasp my thorn fast and lick the wound for comfort.'

The servant girl who unlocked the inn door gasped and jumped back when she saw me, but on recognizing Mr Are let us in, then covered her mouth with her hands and ran away.

'Ah, Master H, you have made a conquest. We must soon do something about that unfailing charm of yours. You are like the king who turned all he touched to gold in the amazing invariability of your effect on others. But first, to business.' And snapping his fingers by the ear of a man, evidently his servant, who napped in a tipped-back chair in the hall, he ordered the mazed and jolted waker to freshen the fire in the sitting room, and bring coffee and breakfast for two.

Mr Are seemed in high spirits as we settled at the hearth. 'It is well; it is well.' He rubbed his hands together. 'That will steam the damp out of our bones, will it not, H?'

'Stop calling me that.'

'Gladly, if you will provide me with an alternative.'

'My name is Heathcliff.'

The gentleman seemed singularly struck by this piece of information; at least it stopped his flow of talk for ten seconds, quite an age for him.

'Heathcliff – *Heathcliff*! It is an outlandish, an unlikely name.'

'Like it or not, it is mine.'

'Surname or Christian?'

'It serves well enough for both.'

'Then it must serve me, I suppose.'

The servant brought coffee, rolls, and meat. Famished, I fell upon them.

'Gently, Master—Heathcliff; we must not whine and

slaver over our crusts; it scares the lower orders. Have you had aught to eat today, or rather yesterday, lad?'

I did not pause to notice these natterings, but turned my shoulder to shield His Highness from the sight of my feeding, since it offended his high-flown notions. I heard him snap his fingers again.

'John, do you see this boy?'

'Yes, sir.'

'What is your opinion of him?—Don't shuffle, man.'

'Begging your pardon, sir, he's dirty!'

'Dirty? Dirty? You amaze me! Dirty? When I never saw such a clean lad in my life?—the original lily-white boy. But if you say he is dirty, John, then we must wash him. I know you set a high standard for your employer. Take a good look at him, John.'

'Why, sir?'

'Because I want your eyes to make his measure. As soon as the shops open you must buy him a suit of clothing, all complete, as decent as you can on short notice. It will be better than he has at any rate, and Mrs Fairfax and her minions will fit him up properly later. Then when you come back you must throw him in a large vat filled with boiling water and a strong corrosive, stir the whole for ten minutes, and strain the results. We may sieve out a recognizable human being for our labours.'

John looked doubtful; I rose, stuffing some bread into my shirt. 'That is the end of your insults, Mr Are,' I said, 'for I'll not stop to permit a repetition. Good day to you.'

As I bowed satirically Mr Are cast so savage a glance towards John that the latter fairly reeled out the door backwards. Mr Are thrust his hand into his pocket and pulled out a heavy purse.

'Sit down, Heathcliff. Let us stop this taradiddle and talk sense. You want occupation; I want a servant. Let us agree that the gold I pay you will be sufficient to gild an occasional insult, as you call it, or jest, as I do. Come, what do you want per annum?'

The purse bulged full. I had noted in the courtyard the

excellence of a carriage with 'Are' blazoned on its crest, and now took in the sound richness of all this man's appointments. It suggested a wealth far beyond what I had seen; my brightest measure of elegance at that time being the Lintons' residence, the idea of attaching myself to a standard that eclipsed it was attractive, if I could do so without damage to myself. And I had proved that I could easily master this strange gentleman. Why should I not take advantage of his fancy? He would doubtless try to exact from me a subservience I would not yield, but why should that concern me now? At any rate it was the best, the only prospect I had before me. The man might be eccentric to the point of madness, but was I in fitter state? All things considered, I thought I could do no better than close with him. Accordingly, I named as wages fifty pounds, twice what Hindley pays Joseph. My interlocutor laughed.

'Greedy, Heathcliff, greedy! 'Ware of killing the goose that laid the golden egg! You frown—I see you are a hard bargainer. But I am harder; you shall not do me down. I will meet you halfway. We will—*double* that figure. One hundred pounds, take it or leave it!'

I suppose my jaw dropped in amazement.

'Ha! You open your voracious maw to gobble me and all my substance—but I am too canny for you. I find my Scots blood rising: you must resign yourself to diminished returns. What say you to two hundred pounds?—Nay, not a penny more!'

I could do nothing, finally, but laugh aloud. Mr Are pulled a long face.

'Ah—I see you at last comprehend the seriousness of this undertaking. But it is too late; you are no match for me when it comes to driving a bargain. Two-hundred fifty—guineas per annum it is, and board and clothing. Now, Heathcliff, own you were worsted. Let us shake hands on it, and no hard feelings.'

I proffered my hand to Mr Are. For such a wage I could afford him his jest, but mentally I noted well; for insults he would pay in even higher coin.

4

We removed, then, by the carriage I had seen outside the inn, to Mr Are's house in the country, some seventy miles nearer London than Gimmerton. Cathy, imagine my emotions as I travelled thither – every mile, on the one hand, taking me further from you than ever I had been; but every hour, as it might happen, advancing me on the road to our reunion.

Not yet having been assigned a servant's duty and concomitant station, I was put snug inside the coach with Mr Are. This state of affairs much perplexed and troubled John, whose job it was to ride up top and tend the luggage. Every five minutes he popped his red face upside-down to peer through the window, no doubt fearing to catch me gorging on his master's blood. I had the double satisfaction of disappointing his expectations, and returning his hot stare with my cool one. Nothing had I to do with the great gentleman John served except observe him at my leisure, since he, exhausted after the silly vigil he had set over me the night before, dozed and softly snored in the corner of his seat.

Mr Are was a man of middling height and athletic build, broad of chest and narrow of hip, dark of hair and skin. His face, stern or satirical by turns when animated, was in unguarded repose almost a perfect pattern of sorrow. He was uneasy in his slumbers. The joltings of the carriage would sometimes half wake him, sometimes toss him into deeper coils of dream – he called out once, a woman's name I thought, but did not trouble myself overmuch to understand. Time enough later to ferret out all I needed to know, if I needed to know anything.

In dress I thought him an affected dandy. He had taken a cool perfumed bath while I had my scalding one, had changed all his linen down to his skin, and donned strange and exotic combinations of clothing, such as I had never seen – lemon-coloured gloves and topcoat, a paisley vest, a striped satin scarf, a gold-ornamented ebony cane. And of these costly accoutrements he was careless; when John spilt a goblet of red wine on his sleeve as we sat to lunch at a wayside he brushed an embroidered handkerchief at it without inspecting the stain or slowing his flow of words.

I had marked his manner – his quips and jokes, his imperiousness – without knowing whether to ape it or despise it. It was necessary that I become a gentleman. Good. To become one I must have before me a proper model. Better and better, since a reputed gentleman sprawled and snored in front of my eyes. But could I stomach the necessity to re-form myself in this image? No, my instincts shouted; still, I resolved to force an open mind for the near future, and be content presently with only keeping my balance.

For, though calm on the outside, inside I was all turmoil. While part of my mind was weighing and measuring what profit I could make of Mr Are and his strange preference, the other part was yet reeling from the shock of new knowledge of my origins, and new understanding of old memories. And what I had learned was but the shadow of what more there was to learn, which might be ten times more horrible. What could I have done, as a child, an infant almost, to have justified incarceration in a madhouse? The deed must have been nothing short of demonic. And what of the night before? If I had entered the institution and stated my story and made such inquiries as I had planned, would not the keepers have swiftly laid hands on me and returned me to my cell? Was I even now subject to instant loss of liberty and livelihood if anyone plumbed the secrets of my identity? The idea was fantastic in the extreme, since even I had scarce plumbed those depths, and was doubtless safe enough unless I gave myself away. Yet I sat well back from the window when we passed through a town.

It was dark when we arrived at Mr Are's estate, so all the knowledge of the manor house I received when I followed its owner through the front door was an impression of brilliant colours, fine wood panelling, and warm lights glinting off many polished surfaces. A genteel-looking elderly woman, the housekeeper probably, issued from one of the doors to the hall nodding a greeting; in her soft wake came other servants. Mr Are bid John take me to a bedroom on the second floor, so I was hustled up a large staircase and through an even larger gallery. I heard Mr Are's loud voice booming orders to those below as I flung myself on the dark shape John indicated as the bed. Framing neither prayer nor curse on this the portal of my new life, I lost myself in sleep. Time enough to weep when I was dead, now I must prepare myself to live and strive.

I woke abruptly, aware that the latch on the door had just clicked. For a second I thought Joseph had come to rouse me with a blow and a sermon, then in a flash I knew myself transported to a new scene, far beyond Joseph's sinewy grip; alas, as far as from your warm touch. No one was in the room, but there was a tray of food placed on a table by my bed; the unseen bearer's parting had wakened me.

I ate, dressed, and left the room. Not a soul was stirring that I could see or hear. The gallery, lit by a very large window at the end near the stairs to the entry hall, was evenly flanked by a series of closed doors like the one from which I had just emerged; presumably there were bedrooms behind them. I went downstairs.

As I descended a motion caught my eye. It was the opening swing of the front door, a massive oak panel carved with thorn trees. I ran to look outside, but no one was in sight. Perhaps the door had been left ajar to air the house, and now swung in the warm wind. But I could see no other sign of housewifery in progress. Where were the servants of the night before?

I passed from room to room. All was sumptuous; all was still. The tall dining room windows (they reached almost from floor to ceiling) were hung with brilliant purple curtains trimmed with peacock-feather fringes, now dancing gaily in the fresh breeze. The fourteen chairs round the very long table were upholstered in the same purple. There were many articles of what I now know to be chinoiserie: massive china and brass vases on the tall mantel, painted fans on the wall, a pale green pottery bowl piled high with dusky plums. I picked up one of these and bowled it down the centre of the shiny table; it splatted on the floor off the far end. I pitched it out the nearest window, then filled my pockets with the rest.

The parlour, connected to the dining room by a curtained archway, was more of the same, only done up in white and cherry red. The windows there were open too. I could hear insects humming in the flowers outside and could see two fat tabbies sunning themselves on the garden wall; still I heard or saw no sign of human life.

Tales came to mind, first the one Nelly used to tell us about the time of the Black Death, when people, one of every two in England, had dropped unwarned, in the middle of their occupations – baking, brewing, ploughing – and putrefied where they lay for want of survivors to bury them. Perhaps in each bed upstairs lay a corpse, perhaps all in the house were dead, and there was no one left to hinder me picking over their leavings as I liked. Or mayhap I had been transported into one of those fairy tales where the hero walks alone through a beautiful frozen landscape, the people in it still quick but stiff, like green pith under winter bark, motionless and unspoilt forever – seeing with their rigid eyes everything that takes place, but unable to prevent the hero wreaking his will upon them.

These were pleasant fancies – I thought of more not so pleasant. Perhaps it was the last trump, come just as Joseph had said it would. The crack of doom had transported all the just to heaven in the twinkling of an eye (perhaps the very second I lifted my lids in my bedroom this morning), leaving me alone on earth, to be captured by Satan and his legions when they thundered up from the fire below. Or (most likely of all) I *was* mad – the deserted house a hallucination I suffered as I walked through its peopled rooms. Even now Mr Are might well be standing by the mantel taunting me, John might be restraining me, while I, lost in folly, neither saw, heard, nor felt them.

I had a sudden impulse to test my theory. Half fancifully, half superstitiously, I made a pact with myself that if the next room I entered was also devoid of humankind, then I was proved lunatic and might as well slit my throat straightaway. I walked quickly to the door on the far side of the parlour and flung it open.

There was a flutter and a clang. I had surprised a housemaid polishing the brass grate in a fireplace. Her blank face stared interrogatively, she mouthed a perfect O. I shaped my mouth the same, only bigger, and snarled in the bargain. The silly thing chirped 'La!' and clattered away to the nether part of the house.

Cheated of my fancies, I pushed aside the curtains of the nearest window and stepped out into the garden. The corner of my eye caught a white flash – a man's stockinged leg had been swiftly withdrawn behind a hedge. Looking sharply, I was able to discern the shape of someone – John, perhaps? – standing motionless in the shrubbery. He could only be watching me.

I was fast losing patience with this game, whatever it was. Thinking I might as well give the spy something to report, I threw my plums at the kitchen cats, and when they had scurried for cover, took up white stones from the path and aimed them at a row of empty flowerpots set up on the wall – but the sequence of crashes grew monotonous; I berated myself for putting on a dull play, even for so unbidden an audience. Then I thought of the fine horses that had pulled the coach. They might give me more scope for show.

By following occasional echoes of neighs and whinnies I found the stable at last; it was on the far side of a thorn thicket so dense I had no thought of passing through, but skirted the edge till I had reached my goal.

It was as grand in its way as the house. Enormous double doors stood open to a lofty and darkly atmospheric gallery, criss-crossed by scores of dusty light shafts from a double row of small high windows. Below, parallel ranks of long horse heads swivelled to my progress as I strolled the path between them to the other end. These animals had been tended well, and tended this morning, but as in the house, not a soul was in sight. Stay! The horses near the double doors quitted their contemplation of me to inspect a new object, obscured to my eyes by the glare from outside; apparently I had been followed.

'Well, if they choose to continue that game, they must bear with the consequences,' I thought angrily. I went into a storeroom containing large cabinets filled with all the tools of a farrier, and hung floor to ceiling with the finest Spanish tackle. Taking the best saddle and bridle, I fit them on a bay mare, the most spirited horse of the bunch (except for a fine twitchy fellow in the corner whose recently patched cell and rolling eye bespoke his treacherous nature). Conspicuously taking no notice of any spectator, I led the bay from the barn, mounted her, and we were off; if the spy cared to join me, I would give him a run for his money.

I galloped the bay through a rolling field behind the stable, took the stone fence at the end on the fly, and raced up a fair-sized gorse-thatched hill crowned with oaks. At the crest I pulled up. What met the eye in every direction was fresh, green, pleasant country, except for one smoke-thickened blot on the horizon, the manufacturing town I had heard mentioned as the chief market centre of the vicinity. Nearer at hand was a little village (called Hay, as I later learned) nestled between two gentle hills. Otherwise there were neat farms and houses, one or two besides Mr Are's of some apparent stature, pleasantly arranged among checker-boarded hedgerows, groves, and meadows. It was a prospect to delight a doll; how different from our troll's scape of crag, moor, and bog!

I took my bearings by the sun and found north-

northwest, which by my reckoning was the direction in which lay Gimmerton and Wuthering Heights. Suddenly my anger melted, and my spirit flew out to you, Cathy, over rolling hills, over smoking chimneys of midland factories, over Manchester market, over marsh and rill and beck, to your side, to brush soft across your glowing cheek.

How was it possible we were parted? How often and often had we sworn by what we cherished most, our common soul, that no force on earth or in heaven would sever us? How often had we pressed heart-to-heart, the great throb of nature beating in our breasts as one, and whispered in each other's ear that we would always be thus together?

How often indeed! Yet here I was, as far out of your knowledge as you were beyond the reach of my five senses. The argument to leave you had seemed irrefutable, irresistible, a few days before, with your hard words ringing in my ear. Now, sitting astride a strange horse atop a strange hill looking towards a horizon that obscured you, I was not so sure I had argued aright. Was I not as much to blame, leaving you without a chance of explanation on either side, as you to betray me? My offence might even be the greater, since I had acted, where you had only talked.

Suddenly I had a wild urge to gather up the reins, kick the horse's flank, and ride, ride, ride hard and steady towards that point in the clouds beyond which was the physical fact of *you*, until I rode into sight of Wuthering Heights – up the hill, through the gate, into your embrace.

I almost did it; the willing bay anticipated my signal and gave a start forward, but I pulled her back. I had seen my hands on the reins – horny, calloused, grey with work – and they reminded me of the life that surely lay in wait for me if I returned now: ceaseless, degrading toil, broken only occasionally, after a while it could be not at all, by hurried moments with you. And perhaps even now you were holding Linton's sweetened and pumiced palm, pressing it and kissing it as you used to mine –

The thought was too much to bear. I released my restraint on the bay and we tore down the slope, but turned on a large arc between the two hills, down the main street of the little town (how the people scurried from our path!), and finally back to the stable. Coming down the drive to the house we skirted too close to a thorn tree, and a protruding branch grazed my horse's hip. By the time we halted it was streaming blood. I staunched its flow easily enough (you remember our trick of cramming cobwebs into a wound), rubbed down the sweating beast, and put her back in her stall.

I returned to the house; if I were to be dismissed for my escapade I had better find out sooner than later. But the lower rooms were as vacant to all but sun and wind as I had left them; only at the end of the great table in the dining room there was a place set with sundry dishes, familiar and unfamiliar. There being no one to stop me, I made out my dinner.

My exploration of the house ended with the discovery of a large library at the other side of the main entrance hall from the dining room, for there I found one of the glass bookcases unlocked, and spent the length of the summer day perusing its contents. As you know, it had been long since I had done anything like study a book, and at first the myriad black letters on the pages might have been swarms of biting ants for all the benefit they conferred on me, but by and by bits of Curate Shielder's old teachings returned, and I began to put together in my mind a system by which I might employ these books, and some of those whose titles I could see through the glass in the locked cases, to climb out of the ignorance in which I knew myself to be enmired. If I had passed whatever strange test my spies had in mind, and if the domestic routine here was really lax as it had seemed this empty day, then I might find many opportunities of stealing an hour in the library, or of thrusting a volume or two into my shirt for midnight perusal. Now I stopped reading only when reminded of hunger by the fading light.

The whole afternoon had passed without my having seen a living body in the house, only I had at times been aware of a burst of far-off murmuring, as though a door had been opened, then hastily closed upon a conversation. So it was with some curiosity that I entered the dining room again. Here I found the table illuminated by freshly lit candles and my old emptied dishes replaced by brimming new ones. Inwardly shrugging at the elaborateness of the trick someone persisted in playing on me, I consumed the repast in lonely splendour, took up a candlestick, and went to bed, thinking that if this day had been a fair sample, I was indeed embarked on a singular career.

In retrospect the whole episode seems fantastic in the extreme, almost to the phantasmagoric, and certainly should have struck a clear warning even to my befuddled brain that all was not as it should be, but I was so confused with many extremes of emotion and sensation, so troubled with thoughts of you, that the day's silence and surveillance made a fit part of my experience, almost to be expected.

The next day, however, began much differently. An ungentle hand on my shoulder woke me. 'Get up,' said John, 'and quickly. Master Edward has somewhat to say to you. He stood by impatiently while I dressed, and finally with a snort took over the tying of my unfamiliar cravat. 'You came out of a thieves' den, or worse, I'll warrant,' he said, jerking my collar around my ears. I longed to take over the management of *his* cravat, forcefully and decisively, but grit my teeth and forbore. There would be plenty of time to crop this cur's tail.

John led me to the sunny room where I had surprised the maidservant yesterday. Mr Are sat at a small table with breakfast laid before him and that same servant brewing coffee in the rear.

'Heathcliff, I have decided on your duties. Do you wish to hear them?'

I shrugged. It made no difference what I answered; he would say and do what he liked. Now, playing to his salaried audience, he continued brightly:

'For twenty-three hours out of the twenty-four you must skulk around the house and stable like a mad monk, scowling at all inanimate objects and kicking the animate. You must gallop my fiercest horses till they think the devil mounts them, you must paw through my best books till their very bindings crack with the intensity of your attention, you must scare the cats, curse the dogs, curdle the cream, and generally make yourself as disagreeable as possible to beast and man. Is that understood?'

I nodded. Of course I saw he was satirizing me, but I waited to see what else he would say. This was but prologue.

'Good. To receive your daily agenda of disagreeables, each morning you must stalk into this room: you will find me standing inside a golden pentangle that simultaneously shields me from your evil energies and binds them for my own use.'

'As long as it is made of gold, it will serve,' I answered.

'Excellent! The prudence of my course is confirmed! Having summoned you, then, I will say the spell that speeds you to your morning's task. Ah – !' (appealing to John, who kept a noncommittal expression on his face) 'Is it not sweet to own a spirit, and such a spirit? Do you not think our household *ton* heightened by such an airy addition, John?'

'I'm sure I have no opinion on the subject, sir.'

'And I am sure you have, but we will let it pass. The important thing is to set tasks for our genie. Are you listening, Heathcliff? Very well; in the afternoons you will help Daniel in the stables; he must see to his own incantations, however; I have enough on hand with devising mine.

In the evenings – I know not; you may commune with your deity; they say the thorn thicket was once the site of a witches' coven. But the twenty-fourth hour, I say again, is my own.'

'All the hours are yours, since you buy the right to direct them.'

'I direct to this purpose: during the twenty-fourth hour you must act like a civilized human being. The instant the clock strikes on that hour you must play the puppet; your head jerk upright from its customary lowered position, your body straighten itself, its habitual ogre's hunch become the poise of a marble Antinous. You must meet your companion's eye when he speaks to you; you must answer him intelligently, comprehensibly, and civilly. You must smooth your brow and erase the cloud that ever darkens it. For that hour, Heathcliff, you will laugh. I order it so.'

I turned away. I could not countenance this foolery. As though reading my mind, he continued:

'Understand, I perceive that you are damaged goods, and proud in the bargain, but I have taken it into my mind to mend you, in the outer appearance anyhow. I have a position to maintain. My servants must be presentable. I can't have one who looks like he'd much rather slit a guest's throat than serve him dinner. You must take on the semblance at least of a Christian body. How now, goblin, what say you to a change of skin?'

I looked about to see if John and the serving maid (whose name I found later was Leah) smiled, or blushed, at this evidence of their master's lunacy. But both stood stock-still and impassive, as though nothing could be more normal.

I responded to that part of his ravings which seemed most concrete: 'This twenty-fourth hour, then, when I shall *laugh*, is it to be literally the twenty-fourth? From eleven to midnight?'

'You are jealous of your witching hour? Yea, I would wean you from your cloven-hooved master. Come to me at eleven, Heathcliff. We shall sup together each night, you and I.'

'Sup together?'

'Yes. You shall be my guest, Heathcliff.'

I surveyed the delicate crystal and silver set before this

silk-clad gentleman, who was just now lifting to his lips a bowl of china so tender that the morning sun behind it made it glow like a lamp, and imbued the hand that held it with a roseate flush. This made me think of my own hands as I had seen them the day before holding the horse's reins. Today they were washed, it is true, but no amount of washing could erase that horny musculature, just as no amount of play-acting could make me a fit occupant of this room. Then indeed I laughed, and laughed long.

Mr Are put his finger to his chin. 'Something – could it be the dulcet quality of the tones that escape your throat? – tells me, you laugh not with pleasure, but in mockery of my invitation. I wonder why?'

For answer I thrust the palm of my right hand into the sunbeam in front of his nose. The crusted callouses and dirt-ground lines made such an ugly sight I almost flinched. He, however, stared calmly at what I showed him for a minute or two, then looked me up and down.

'I suppose it is a ludicrous notion,' he mused at last. 'A muzzled bear set to sip tea at a doll's table. Very well; you shall have it your way.

'What is my way?'

'We shall sup, and sup each night, but I will come to *you*!'

Here John, by his face as puzzled as I, did show a slight reaction – so I showed nothing, but folded my arms and awaited elucidation. As none was offered, I resigned myself to abide in a state of mystification till the stroke of eleven that night.

I paused briefly in my reading to shift position and pull another shawl over my shoulders; the train compartment grew frigid. Mr Lockwood had fallen quite asleep; his face in repose looked at once older and less formed than it had waking, as though conscious attention alone had held it to its previous lines. His hand had slipped from its covering and now lay palm upwards on the chilly seat; I gently drew a fold of blanket over it.

I turned my eyes back in the direction of the manuscript, seeing, however, not the words on the page, but something else floating above them. It was a face. I gazed at it long, for there my mind found much to interest, much to vex.

Reader, what visage do you imagine me to have conjured up into the dim air of the train compartment? Perhaps you think it most likely that I had attempted to visualize the countenance of him whose letter I read – that I had, out of pique or boredom, sketched in my mind's eye a glowering, sneering gypsy face, splattered with mud. Or maybe you would take a different line, and venture that not fancy but memory ruled me, and had imprinted on my retina its constant motto – the laughing, wry lineaments of Monsieur Heger, so recently and reluctantly abandoned, so jealously cherished. Or perhaps you would say, with regretful certainty, 'No – the face that haunts her is the product of neither fancy nor memory, but simple flesh and blood, and sleeps now in shadow, half-swaddled, before her – after all, she is bereft, sore, rejected – too ready to transfer her pitiable affections to this unsuspecting stranger.'

You would be wrong on all counts. It was my sister's face that hung in the dark before me, my sister Emily's face.

No common face, Emily's. Perhaps a first glance reveals nothing extraordinary – but a first glance provokes a second; a second, a third: Emily, full of lip, high of brow, smooth of skin, her lustrous eyes having something in them of deep thought, something of laughter, something of scorn. They are eyes that entice, yet permit no familiarity except to the favoured few, and then on her terms, and her terms only.

I counted myself among that few, but never by familial right. Emily and I had always been at once more to each other than common sisters, and less. We might pass weeks constantly together, night and day, speaking only to each other, having the same object in view, and sharing that common, and commonly unique, object, in intense and secret discussion. Some weeks it would be no error to say we shared one mind. Then, suddenly, something would change – a window would shut, a door would slam, Emily would blink, and I would be shut out – for how long? Weeks or months sometimes I would wait in uneasy suspense, perhaps forming a substitute alliance with my brother, Branwell, in pursuit of that object, in childhood the meat and drink of life to me.

I hardly know how to term our secret pastime, invisible to grown persons; my father and our housekeeper, Tabby, if they saw anything, saw the insignificant games of children. Emily and I, and Branwell, and my sister Anne too, had, since we were little, engaged in imaginary plays – plays whose characters, setting, and stories became so sweet to us that we preferred them to the tangible world of parsonage, church, and moor. As we grew older the plays grew in complexity – we began writing down what we played, as other people might keep a record of the day's events. Gradually we began to apply more and more of conscious art to our records, seeking to replicate in black and white the thrill we experienced in action. This grew; as the years passed, we created entire nations and their customs and histories.

Though I was eldest, Emily was leader. Prolific of invention were we all, but Emily's powers were of another order. Where we would sweat out the details of an incident – an elopement, a shipwreck, the clash of two great armies – and wrangle amongst ourselves to get it right, she had but to speak: a thing was so, and so, and so – and thus it spread itself before our eyes, detail multiplying upon detail, till we had to shake our heads at the wonder of it. None of us could contradict her; not because if we did she would leave and refuse to play more (though this was true), but because her vision was more beguiling, more seductive, more clear than any we could compel.

Emily's ability to sway reality with her words became

stronger with time. She had but to say, 'Imagine this . . .' and I would see it, would see and hear and feel what Emily put before me. The longer I listened to Emily, the stronger my conviction would grow that what she described was *real*; more real than the four walls around us, the chairs we sat in, the features of our own faces.

Sometimes I would see the direction one of Emily's stories was taking and want to prevent it. I might become so hysterical at the approach of some tragic denouement – the assassination of the hero, the early decline of the heroine – that I would be unable to sleep or eat. But wheedle, threaten, or cry myself into a fever, it was all the same – Emily would never relent. 'The story has its own laws,' she would say. 'I cannot change them; I can only impose them. That is the limit of my power. I make the characters do what they must do. They have no choice, and I have no choice.' There was no help for it. The loved personage would live out its doom, and I would cry myself to sleep at last.

Reader, again I hear you speak. 'Most touching,' you say, 'but why trouble yourself, and, more to the point, why trouble *me*, about it now?' Very well, I will tell you.

Heathcliff, *this* Heathcliff, whose yellowing pages I now read, was, according to Emily, a living human being of about our age. The tale of his childhood at Wuthering Heights was not a new tale to me. I had heard it before, not as the story of one long dead, but as a present outrage.

Up to this hour I had known of Heathcliff as Emily's friend; her *exclusive* friend, for she never allowed us to meet him. Now, I had in my hands words written by the same young man, but written sixty years ago. The coexistence of the letter and the friend was an impossibility. If the letter was authentic, the friend was a fraud – or vice versa. And I could not doubt the authenticity of the letter.

For years I had secretly wondered, what was Emily's sense of her own creations? If she could so easily lead me over the line of belief, what about herself? Did she distinguish her private fiction from public fact? And if she did not, what did that make of her mind? What did that make of her sanity?

I had wondered, I say, before; now, on the train, I positively feared.

I remembered the times when Branwell and Anne and I, bored because shut in by rain, perhaps, or giddy from staying up past our bedtime, would beg Emily to frighten us. 'Oh, please, Emily! Please, Amalia, scare us! Scare us!'

If, after teasing, she assented, she would turn her back for a minute. The rest of us would draw closer together, seeking to steal courage from contact, but instead transmitting from hand to sweaty hand a delicious acid current of fear.

Then Emily would turn, would simply look at us. She would not distort her face in the slightest: it was the same everyday, rather handsome, rather severe, face – till we saw her eyes. Her eyes! They dared us to look closely, yet we resisted. Something in them compelled, something in them repelled! Not death – that was comprehensible, that we knew – but a thing incomprehensible, yet inevitable. Inevitable, yet blank. That waited for us behind Emily's eyes.

Mr Lockwood stirred; I lowered my gaze to the manuscript. If he woke, let him not wake to the misapprehension that I watched him sleep. Gradually the letters insisted on their meaning and I began to read again.

5

Later that day I and my few effects were removed from the bedroom in the house to quarters attached to the stable, built adjoining it on the second level, up the rise of a hill. The head groom, Daniel Beck, had had them till he moved to a nearby cottage with his bride. At first, reminded of my banishment from the house after your father's death, I regarded these new arrangements as insulting, but once I was installed in the tidy apartment, awash with clean breezes from the apple orchard on the hill, I felt differently. Here, in the room's broad hearth, its row of copper pans, the solid oaken furniture, was a stout reality to place against the fairy-tale dreams which seemed Mr Are's preferred habitation, and in and out of which he had pulled me like a stunned heifer on a rope ever since our meeting. The gold and silver world of the great house had spun my brain up in a glittering whirlwind, but now I was set down in a room I could understand, with an hour or – so to get my bearings before Daniel came back. The ground gradually steadied under my feet.

As my mind quietened, I set myself the task of considering my situation seriously. What manner of place was this strange household? and why had its master brought me to it? Though I had even then (at almost the lowest point in my life) a considerable sense of my buried power and worth, I was too much of a realist to think that any stranger would be able to divine it; he would have to be seer indeed who could overlook the forbidding aspect of the present Heathcliff to those days past when he had been favoured son of a prosperous household, or to project a future where the banked embers of his genius might spring to flame. Was Edward Are such a prophet? I thought not. Though he was magician enough when it came to shifting and shaking his little world around him, it was my opinion, in those early days anyway, that he had more of *wit* – agility and (because of his wealth) power to surprise with eccentric combination – than he had of *understanding*, real penetration of surface appearance to truth beneath.

Self-love did not blind me; I knew my surface had few qualities to appeal. And in all my converse with Mr Are I had been either reticent or rough. Why hire me, an unknown and perhaps dangerous quantity, when he could have had his pick of twenty stableboys from the neighbourhood, all vouched for since their first squalling at the baptismal font? But that was the lesser part of the mystery: why pay this stranger five times what by the most generous calculations his services could have been worth? And, above all, why insist on supping with this surly, overpaid underling?

Moreover, Mr Are's manner to me was strange out of all reckoning. Though I knew about as much concerning the habits of the upper classes as I knew about the habits of a pack of wild orangutans, yet I knew this – moneyed gentlemen did not every day spend such a store of attention and vivacity as I had had from Mr Are on the likes of me; not without a definite object in view.

As I sat on my stout feather bed covered with its good linen counterpane, gazed out upon the orchard and rolling pasture beyond, with the soft whinnying of the horses below-stairs in my ears, I began to get a glimmering of what that object might be. I remembered Lord Vathem – as you will, Cathy, if you think back to our fourteenth summer, when we would cross Pennistone Crags to his house of an evening to spy on him; he was tall and long-nosed and wore a crimson-powdered wig – Lord Vathem and his footman. The latter, you will recall, was a young man of fresh countenance and arched eyebrow, slight like a girl, only with a boy's smooth-muscled body. The lord had built a fantastical little house, a *cottage orné* as I now know, with a ginger-breaded tower and gargoyles spitting water from the four corners of the roof into a moat below. You and I would wade through this toy moat (goldfish, not dragons, swam sentry in it) to peer through the griffin-leaded windows. You recall what we saw the last time we went there: spindly Vathem, bowing and strutting like the Lord of the Cranes, in private congress with his footman, who acted not like a footman when they were alone, but a flirting, coy lady, flaring and snapping a fan. Once we saw them begin to fondle and kiss each other we turned and ran away, having no wish to witness a he-mating. Nelly said later that the dalliance between these two was the talk of the common folk for miles around, that the masked lady Lord Vathem had danced with till cockcrow at the Whitsuntide masquerade ball was no lady but the footman, and the high quality he had up from London for the occasion took it in stride, being well up to tricks of this sort, every man jack of them.

Could Mr Are be of Lord Vathem's mould, then, that found its pleasure in the embraces of its own sex? And had his desires fastened upon me as their object? The idea alarmed me in the extreme. I suddenly saw, point by point, how such an unlikely conjecture yet explained every oddity I had encountered – the marked pains Mr Are had taken in following me and securing my services, the large salary, his manner towards me, his refusal to be repelled by my harsh ways. So weighty, in fact, seemed the evidence as I piled it up piece by piece, that I almost sprang from my bed and left the place forever at that moment.

Yet I did not do so. Again I came back to the incontrovertible fact of my own marred appearance. Troll, gypsy, ghoul, warlock – all these Mr Are had called me, all these fitted me well enough. But light-of-love footman? Little as I understood of such matters, still I could not conceive that my rough flesh could promise delight to anything masculine. And despite his foppish clothing, Mr Are was nothing if not masculine.

No, the more I thought of my dirty and forbidding aspect, the more preposterous did my suspicions about

Mr Are's motives seem. I became a little disgusted with myself for having harboured them, even so fleetingly. I had admitted that Mr Are belonged to a class of person whose manners I did not understand; he himself was evidently an idiosyncratic member of this (to me) exotic caste; was I likely to mine with ease the motives beneath the manners? No. All the more reason, then, to press towards acquiring those manners myself – and to do that I must stay here.

This was the core of my reason for putting aside suspicion of Mr Are. I own it; ambition grew like a hot flame within me. At home I had seen the elegance of the Lintons' clothing, the grace of their deportment, the ease of their conversation, and hated these things even in their beauty because they were closed to me, and as you admired them shut me off from you. I exulted in ugliness, since it was at least indisputably mine. But now elegance, grace, and ease suddenly were placed – deceivingly it might be, but might *not* be – within my reach. And I wanted them. Previously I had desired such changes in my being only insofar as they made me a fitting mate for you. Now I began to see they could be good in themselves. I began to feel pride in them, even in advance of their acquisition, and impatient of what would keep them from me. The seed of desire for what Mr Are could give me if he continued in his present path was already rooted, and perhaps with it grew an inclination to trust him.

But if trust tempered suspicion, suspicion tempered trust. I resolved to be well on guard: if ever I caught a hint of Mr Are behaving to me as Lord Vathem did to his footman, my fine master would abruptly find he had lost his senses – if not all, forever, at least the temporary use of two or three of them.

These thoughts rolled around my brain more than once as I did my work in the stable that day, but each time I came back to the same conclusion: that no conclusion was yet possible. I tried to question Daniel Beck about Mr Are, but all I could get out of him was that 'Mr Edward was a good master, though strange in his ways.'

More he would not say, except that Mr Edward had had even more quirks and pranks about him before he inherited the estate upon the death of his elder brother a few years back; the servants thought the loss had sobered him. I could but marvel at the notion that a higher level of eccentricity had been possible, but I kept that to myself.

Eleven o'clock found me reading by candlelight in my room. The night breezes were moist and fresh, the firmament brilliant with stars, and the air full of the chirp of tree frogs from the orchard. I was so engrossed in the new ideas introduced to me by my book (it was a treatise on perception by a Scottish philosopher), that I had almost forgot what had been appointed to happen at that hour. Then I heard muffled footsteps, a clattering, the creak and thud of the stable door being flung back. I unlatched the door that communicated between my room and the stable (it opened on a stair down to the stalls) and gazed in amazement at the scene below.

Mr Are stood in the middle of the floor, the gesticulating centre of a swirl of activity. 'Lanterns! Lanterns!' he cried. 'Quick, hang them high! We must see what we are about! Here, Frederick, help John with the table!' All the manservants in the house, it seemed, were in motion before me. One with a long pole was hanging lanterns on to the rafters, two were positioning a good-sized table in the middle of the aisle between the rows of stalls, a fourth bore chairs, one under each arm. Another stood by holding white linen, which he spread on the table as soon as the others had set it down. The horses blinked drowsily at this turn of events and one or two of them whuffled softly, but for the most part they took it unmoved; I supposed they had seen their master do stranger things. I, however, had not, so I stood agape.

The table was laid with linen and plate; the chairs were pulled to; lanterns and candles were lit. Mr Are clapped his hands. 'To the house, quick, and bring the food before it cools.' His minions scattered to do his bidding. He looked up at me. 'Heathcliff, come down. You see I have tunnelled a mole under your battlements, and have now set up an outpost in your very camp. Are you for a fight, sir? Or will you parlay?'

I walked down silently. He seemed to wait for an answer, so I said, 'You are pleased to make sport of me, and pretend that I could turn you out of what is yours. Apparently you expect me to join in your game, perhaps to assert that I would fain keep you from entering this place. You want us to engage in a mock-duel of wits, to cross artificial insults like cork-tipped foils – all the show of antagonism, with none of its point.'

'Bravo, Heathcliff; the first victory must go to you.' He bowed over the candle-flame.

'But I am telling you that experience has not prepared me to play this game, and even if it had, my nature does not bend to it.'

'Faugh, lad, that is exactly what we must remedy. Here – come here.' He gestured impatiently. 'We are to sup; you must wear the proper dress.' I saw he carried clothing draped over his arm, an embroidered waistcoat and a velvet frock-coat. 'Come, come. Take off at once that lugubrious smock, along with that shocking frown. We must always meet any occasion in proper costume, if only to gain licence to consign it to Tophet and enjoy ourselves.'

I took off the linen work smock with which Daniel had supplied me, and put on what Mr Are held out. The frockcoat was somewhat short in the arms, but otherwise the garments fit tolerably well.

'They will do,' said Mr Are. He buttoned the bottom three buttons of the waistcoat, and adjusted the frock-coat so it fell in easy folds. 'Now – before the servants return you must stand properly.'

I shrugged. 'Why should I play to them? They will only think me a fool.'

'It does not matter what they think. It is your own thoughts about yourself that matter, and your present posture tells but an ill story of those.'

Remembering that he had previously unbraided me for stooping, I stood upright.

'Yes, that is a start,' he said, 'but do not swing your paws at your side like an ape.'

'Where else can they go?'

'Here – and here.' He rested his right hand negligently in the breast of his waistcoat, and placed his left fist on his hip.

'Why there?'

'No man knows, yet there is where every man of breeding puts them. To depart from the pattern is to expel yourself from the pack, without profit and to your own detriment. Save your original ideas for matters of moment.'

I self-consciously assumed the pose he modelled.

'Right! Yet not so stiff! Not so stiff! It is good to discipline yourself to stillness – already, in our brief acquaintance, I have been pleased to see you do so, composure being a primary tenet of gentility – but you should not be so locked into place that you look *unable* to move. It makes those who see you uneasy. No, not only should a gentleman be himself at ease, he should by his looks, his manner, his words, his *everything* put others at ease as well.'

I might have asked him how many *others* he thought he put at ease with *his* manner, but I heard the servants approaching, the grumble of their voices preceding them down the path. They stilled their tongues however as they entered the doorway. Mr Are, beaming his pleasure the while, directed the placement of the covered dishes upon the table. 'Roasted chicken – there – stewed plums – there – boiled greens – wine just there – salad – excellent! Now leave us. Two gentlemen dining alone may serve themselves. No, let the doors remain open. The stars are brilliant, and the breeze fresh. John, return in an hour. Mr Heathcliff, will you sit?'

I sat down and waited to see what Mr Are would do next. He poured wine in our two glasses. I began to raise mine to my lips. He stayed my hand.

'Ah – ah – you cannot drink in company without first proposing a toast, lest your friends think you drink only as a means to stupefaction, and not to enjoy their good fellowship. To whom or what, then, will you drink tonight?'

I thought for a moment. 'I will drink to plain dealing.'

He laughed and lifted his glass. 'To plain dealing, with all my heart. It is precisely what I hope for.'

I drank with him, then said, 'You think you have not received it from me?'

'I would like to know more about your history, and about your hopes for the future.'

'You have hired me to work in your stables. So long as I do my work, why need you concern yourself with more?'

'I *need* not concern myself, yet I do.' He had lifted the dome from the chicken; it sent a savoury smell into the sweet night air. 'Watch how I carve this, Heathcliff – no skill serves a gentleman so well as niceness in carving. Never set your companion's teeth on edge by sawing through a bone like a tipsy surgeon. Separate delicately at the joint – so. And serve deftly and neatly – so – without dribbling gravy on your friend's breeches or squirting grease in his eye. You shall serve me tomorrow night. Now you must say "thank you, sir"; an item, by the way, that seems to have been stolen from your stock of phrases.'

The words he requested stuck in my craw, but I managed to mutter, 'I am glad enough for the meat, and for the lesson too.'

Satisfied for the moment, Mr Are carved himself a piece of the fowl and began to eat. The wide stable doors were open at both ends, so we could see the starry sky on two sides. It was high summer; the air that blew in was heavy-laden with spicy smells from ripened fruit and flower and herb; it overlay the barn smell of hay and healthy animals most pleasantly. The leaping light from our candles glinted off the horses' milky eyes and was lost in their dusky coats. We ate in silence for a while.

Then Mr Are put down his fork with the air of someone about to make a pronouncement.

'Heathcliff, I propose to teach you how to act like a gentleman. What say you?'

I cleared my throat, but the words I prepared choked me. He offered so precisely what I wanted that I feared to speak.

'You are silent, insulted, perhaps. The young are ever in love with themselves. Control your pride, Heathcliff; it is only the outer man, the crust of the spirit, that I would change. What is inward, no man beside yourself can truly know, and no other can touch.'

I blurted out: 'I am not proud or in love with what I am. I desire to change, I *must* change, I must become a gentleman – it is necessary to all my hopes.'

'What are your hopes then, lad? He will not trust me, he is silent, he lowers his eyes – but not in puzzlement as to how to answer, I'll warrant, for to be so positive about the remedy he must have studied well the nature of his disease. Hmmm . . . I'll wager there's a lady at the bottom of the matter, a certain C – but I'll not venture a name, the sudden leaping of your eye to mine and the blackening of your expression recalls to me your warning that you would tear the lips off my face if I ever made another attempt at guessing it. Well, though my lips may not be well-shaped, they are useful, so I think I will endeavour to retain them.'

He held my gaze for a while, then continued, 'Yet your reaction tells me I am correct. She-Who-Must-Not-Be-Named, then, is at the base of your ambition. Stay, do not scowl, I mean no disrespect. A woman is as often the source of a man's elevation as she is of his folly. You must raise yourself to a gentleman to gain favour in her eyes.

Still I said nothing. Interpreting my silence as consent, he nodded for me. 'In future we will take that as given. Heathcliff, cheer yourself. There is no intrinsic barrier to your success. Your natural parts are good – you are quick of perception, there is nothing wrong with your wits. As to your heart – well, your disposition, though on the face very bad, may yet prove sound; I hope it may not be worse. Your frame is well-shaped, exceptionally so when not deformed by slouching. Your face, too, is very well, even handsome if you do not scowl – as you do now: your brows have drawn together like thunderheads breeding lightning. Why must you fashion yourself such a hobgoblin?'

In fact, his favourable mention of my person, accompanied as it had been by an assessing and adjusting touch to my shoulder, called up the whole line of conjecture I had spun out earlier, and I suddenly saw things differently: elegance became grotesquery; kindness turned to cruelty; encouragement, mockery. Seduced by the golden swirl of Mr Are's fancies, I had almost made a fool of myself. I was about as much in place eating off this dainty table with its gleaming white damask as was the ugly brown spider, suddenly dropped from the rafters, now scuttling over it.

I brushed the foul thing to the floor and crushed it beneath my boot. 'You are right. I am nothing but a hobgoblin – a creature of mud and dung you picked up while slumming in Liverpool. Why do you bother with such filth? Tell me!'

Here he made a motion with the wineglass he held as though to wave away my question, but I would not let it go. I could stand no more of his evasions – I reached out to grab the dismissing wrist, and in doing so knocked the wineglass out of his hand. The skittish horse in the corner stall reared and neighed; the glass shattered on the floor.

Before I knew what had happened, my chair was overturned and I was pinned to the stall behind me, a horse's breath hot against my back, and Mr Are's hands, almost choking me, at my throat. His wild glare scorched my face.

'By God, boy, take care when you go up against me. If I had been wearing a sword, as I used commonly to do, you would at this moment be run through and skewered.'

I returned his scowl. 'I want to know your reasons. I *will* know them.'

He glared at me a minute longer, then grudgingly released me. 'You see, Heathcliff, though you are several inches taller than I am, and twenty years younger, I can best you, because I am master of the arts of fencing and boxing. We must add them to your syllabus.'

'Your reasons.'

'Ah, yes, my reasons. But why do you wish to know them?'

'I want to make sure I am not running up a debt I might be unable to repay.'

'Humph! The creature actually shows signs of honour! I should be loath to discourage that. Very well, you shall have an explanation. It seems you deserve one.' Here he went to the door, ostensibly to get a breath of air as he settled the lace at his throat, perhaps actually to frame his reply.

Mr Are's form against the night sky seemed to alter its contour from second to second, changed by the leaping shadows that played on it. Searching out the source of this illusion, I saw that a spider had ventured near one of the lanterns to harvest a snared moth; it was the death-struggles of the prey and the greedy springings of the carnivore, silhouetted and magnified, that so fantastically metamorphosed my companion's broad back.

'Heathcliff, I *will* give you the explanation you demand – but just now, seeing this brilliant display of innumerable lights stretched across the heaven, each one a huge fiery ball like to our sun, perhaps with other earths and other lives circling it, I am reminded of how fleet are our little seconds on earth, how puny our struggles, how minuscule our force, for good or ill.'

At that instant something quick and fluttering flashed through the dark, in one door and out the other – perhaps a bat or a night swallow. During the second it passed, its wings and shrill cry seemed to fill the stable. Then it was gone.

Mr Are turned to face me, decision written in the gesture. 'As to my reasons, what would you say if I told you it has for some time been in my mind to create someone in my own image, to make my stab at immortality by reproducing myself, as it were? What would you say?'

'That you should marry and have children.'

He shook his head. 'No, it cannot be. Never. I cannot explain; let it suffice that there are strong, there are insurmountable reasons that I cannot marry.'

'Even so, your remedy is clear. You should take to ward a young orphan, unformed and willing, and take it from your own class.'

'So it would seem, so it would seem. Yet I have chosen you.'

'You still give no reason.'

Mr Are turned again to the night. 'The truth is, Heathcliff – and I find this a subject difficult to broach, so bear with me – the truth is, your person resembles, at all points, that of someone I once held dear and then – lost, lost forever.'

I thought of what Daniel had told me. 'Your brother?'

He seemed to stiffen. After a minute he said, 'Let us not utter the person's name – I am superstitious in this one area, the more because the resemblance is amazing, stupendous – I knew when I saw you in Liverpool – well, never mind what I knew, only mind what action the knowledge led to: fate had put you in my way; I knew it was a sign I should take you for my ward. Yet fate arranged the meeting outside a madhouse; perhaps that was a sign too.'

'What do you mean? Do you think me mad?'

'Do you think yourself mad, Heathcliff?'

'You were outside the same madhouse. Should I think you mad because of it?'

'Perhaps – perhaps.' We had both been standing; now Mr Are returned to his seat at the table. He tossed the contents of his water-glass into the straw of the stall nearest him, and filled it with wine. 'Pray sit down and finish your meal, Heathcliff; these are weighty matters we discuss, but that is no reason to starve ourselves.'

'You would do well to be cautious,' I said as I resumed my seat.

'This warning sounds in my ear curiously like a threat. You arouse my interest. Go on, pray.'

'I am not tractable.'

'No argument is needed to convince me of that assertion; experience vouches for its truth. Yet I believe you will prove tractable enough when it suits your own self-interest. Next!'

'I have nothing of the softness of which gentility is moulded. I warn you, my nature is rough and hard. It would be poor stuff to shape, in anyone's likeness, let alone a gentleman's.'

'What mealy-mouthed cant!' he snorted. 'You mistake the case entirely. Gentility born of softness is inferior stuff, like to crumble, and coarse in detail. Go on, let us see if you can do better!'

I did go on. 'I have trusted a human being once and once only, there unconditionally and completely. With me this instance is unique. My capacity for human connection is already spent. To speak plain, I do not trust you now and probably never will.'

'Ah – I sense the shade of She-Who-Must-Not-Be-Named again. Well, you have warned me, and that is honourable. If I wanted encouragement, I might find it in the circumstance that you have given your trust once, and are therefore proved capable of the act.'

I shrugged. 'It may be. But I have been so ill-used, even by her' (the truth slipped out here, Cathy) 'that I feel little inclined to place into another's hands the power of affecting me. I will keep my independence, and my counsel.'

'That is understood. You and I are alike, Heathcliff; each of us by nature stands alone, his breast the tomb of memories, of hurts, of vows, long dead, and secret from the world, yet shaping every one of his sentiments towards it, feeding every one of his actions in it. Is it not so with you?'

'Yes.'

'As it is with me. Like recognizes like; my intuition told me you were a fellow slave to an inner tyrant.' He reached across the table and grasped both my hands, holding my eyes with his. 'Since we share, then, the base from which our beings spring, we may understand each other better than two others outwardly more alike, yet lacking our hidden connection. Is it not so, Heathcliff?'

'It may be; the theory has yet to be proved.'

'Good,' he replied. 'It is a small communality, but it runs deep and true.' He released my hands abruptly and picked up a dish. 'Will you have a syllabub?' He held out the sweet-smelling mess; I rejected it; he served himself a goodly portion.

'I think, then, your objections are disposed of,' he continued after having swallowed, with gusto, a few spoonsful. 'Now we can make our plans. You are – what? Seventeen or eighteen?'

I nodded, in truth not knowing if he were right or wrong, since my years before I came to the Heights were unnumbered.

'And you had – how many years of tuition from the good country curate?'

'Four or five.'

'What did he teach you beyond reading?'

'To write and figure, some Latin, some history, a little natural philosophy.'

'A very little, I'll warrant. But you have a start. We will build on it. After breakfast tomorrow morning, and every morning, you will go to the library. You will not leave the room till you have mastered the lesson I will have laid out for you. Every evening at supper I will affirm that mastery, or expose its lack. Is that understood?'

I nodded. 'Will supper be here, then, or in some other place?' I could not suppress a smile as I imagined a succession of ever odder venues for our meals – the graveyard, perhaps, or the market square at Hay, or the roof's battlements.

'It will be here, for the time being. I have taken a fancy to this dining hall; the air, as it rushes down from the hills, is sweeter than in the house (for which I have an aversion anyway), and these faithful servants who attend us' (he looked up and down the uniform rows of horses' heads) 'are more noble and stately than any we could command elsewhere.'

'What do you demand in return?' I asked. 'You are not fool enough to give this much for nothing.'

'You are right, though your construction is far from flattering. I want a great deal. I want cooperation, cheerful cooperation if possible, from the sullen, half-wild stableboy I propose to raise to a gentleman of distinction. I admit I have all the vanity of a latter-day Pygmalion to satisfy. For my labours I demand your success.'

'Is that all?'

' "Is that all?" ' he mocked. 'You flatter yourself if you think that all is little. Part of the delicious appeal of this whole enterprise is its difficulty. My ambition is large, and must be satisfied with a large challenge.

Just then Leah, the servant girl from the house, entered and drew up behind Mr Are. 'Please, sir, John said – ' she began, but got no further, for at that moment came what seemed like an explosion. We jumped to our feet. It was the black horse. It reared high and struck its hooves again and again against the slats of the corner stall.

I immediately sprang towards the beast with the intention of stopping it from doing itself an injury or from shattering its prison. I heard Mr Are behind me curse Leah (which action seemed unreasonable even for him) and tell her to run outside. Meanwhile I had snatched a rope from the wall and looped it; I flung it up to gain the horse's neck, but he reared out of my reach. I saw Mr Are come forward with an iron bar raised, perhaps to stun the animal.

I shoved him aside. 'Let me try this.' I took a ladder from its hook and leaned it against the far wall. Mr Are still tried to hinder me, shouting something or other of caution, but I shook him off and climbed to a rafter that ran above the frantic animal. I crawled out; from that vantage I was able to drop the noose over its neck. I tightened my hold gradually, just till I got its attention; it momentarily stopped its rearing and flicked its eyes behind, trying to spot what restrained it.

I saw my chance; I swiftly and lightly dropped down on the horse's back. Before it could well react I lay along its neck and began stroking its sweaty coat and whispering charms into its flattened ear, just as I did to tame the wild ponies on the moors when we wanted to steal a ride. The horse bucked in earnest a few times, but I managed to stick. Its protest became half-hearted; it was distracted from whatever had caused its frenzy by the mesmerizing rise and fall of the old chant I crooned to it. In two minutes it had subsided altogether; when it was perfectly quiet I dismounted, stroking and whispering the while, gave it some oats, and climbed out of the stall to the tune of its steady crunchings.

It was Mr Are's turn to be amazed at the proceedings. 'Now I am sure you have something of the devil about you, to calm Beelzebub as I have just seen you calm him. He almost killed one of my servants last year; it is still not known whether the man will regain the full use of his legs. The horse is mad; I must have him put down.'

'But he is a splendid animal.'

'I agree; that is why I have postponed the onerous duty, but in his present state he is useless: either he stays sequestered here or becomes a positive danger to the neighbourhood.'

'What is wrong with him? There was no cause for his fit.'

'Ah, but he had cause, as he saw it. Leah came in.'

'*She* has ill-treated him?'

'Indeed, no, except it be in inciting the poor brute to do itself an injury, when she had been warned never to enter the stable. No, for some unfathomed reason Beelzebub, who was shaping very well indeed under Daniel's training last year, suddenly began going mad, just as you saw him, at the sight of anything in petticoats. Last Christmas during a riding party he threw my guest, Miss Ingram, when she attempted to mount him, and trampled the groom who was holding the reins. No, there is really no point in keeping him; Daniel says there is no cure. He must be destroyed.'

I stroked the horse's muzzle, lifted his head from his feed, looked into his now-mild eyes. 'Destroy him if you like; it's your loss, but I can put him right,' I said.

Mr Are peered at me with interest. 'How, where others have failed?'

I shrugged. 'It is enough for you to know that it will be done. I am not without influence with this fine fellow.'

'Influence indeed – yes, he will listen to his litter-mate, for I am now convinced; you are twin foals of the devil. Go ahead, then, I will put off his execution. But you place yourself in danger.'

'It's my own risk.'

'Very well. Only have a care – I find I could *almost* as ill stomach burying you as I could Beelzebub.'

I bowed satirically. This was one compliment I was able to believe.

We heard hurried footsteps; Leah had called up help from the house. Finding nothing else to do, the men removed the plates and food; the furniture Mr Are caused to be stored in a room under the stairs.

'Till tomorrow, Heathcliff,' called Mr Are from the barn door, 'or rather till tonight, for we have slipped by the witching hour. Mind you learn your lesson well.'

After they had left I busied myself with quietening the horses and making all secure. Once I was satisfied, I lowered the lanterns and blew them out. I mounted the steps to my bedroom door.

I opened it. At once a tremendous blow sent me flying forward. My nose slammed against the floorboards. I felt my back pinned by the full weight of a man's knee in the small of it, and my arm painfully twisted behind me. A voice whispered grittily in my ear:

'I know who you are, you dirty gypsy beggar, though Master Edward don't.' It was John's voice; him I could throw off at any time, but I decided to defer that pleasure till I had heard what he had to say.

'Hold still and listen,' he grunted. 'You think you'll wheedle your way round Master Edward. Well, maybe you will, for a while. But don't think you fool me. He's too good to live, sometimes, Master Edward is, and someone's got to look after his interests if he won't. So remember; I've got my eye on you. Move one inch out of line and I'll slit your throat, and do my master and the world a favour.'

Here he released his hold on my arm to grab my hair, certainly with some improved torment in mind, but before he could complete his plan I had unbalanced him and rolled on top. I beat a short tattoo on the floor with his head, then yanked him upright by the hair. I thrust him up against the wall, as I thought, but the back of his pate hit the window and shattered a pane of glass in it. One of the flying shards struck above my eye; I pulled the great sliver out but was momentarily blinded by the ensuing gush of blood; in the meantime my attacker staggered out the door and was gone.

Handkerchief to my face, I ran after him, but all I saw outside was the half-moon rising above the apple trees, bleaching out the stars with its chalky light.

I was born to smile just as you turn your face to the door, and to wear a mask when you look back.

After the storm I was ill. I heard them say I would die, was dead already, so I let myself dream.

Our mother came to the edge of our bed, but she was in grave-clothes so I ran from her.

You ran from me, Heathcliff. You wanted to be done with me

You changed yourself into a hawk and flew far, far

into the blue above the moor where I stood, until you were only a black speck against the sun –

But I became the spreading oak you homed to when your wings sagged. I closed my branches around you against the changeful moon.

But you saw it through my leaves. Coiling out of yourself you became a loathsome curling serpent, hissing venom –

Yet I was not afraid. I became the little bird that sang so sweet you rose your neck in the air and danced.

But you danced out of your skin and left it shimmering. I looked up. Now, on the very tip of a high mountain, you were a stout castle, a castle with a hundred windows, at every window a huntsman's hand, in every hand a bow, in every bow an arrow cocked, to pierce me if I found you out –

But I became the bright lantern set in the highmost tower of the castle, beaming you the safe path home over the cruel mountains.

And I saw you coming, against the light, your outline as it was when you stood in the kitchen doorway from outside, and I in shadow
dazzled.
Then I woke and Nelly said hush
it was only a cloud across the sun, a
branch in the wind, a
bird on the sill
hush my darling

6

So I entered Mr Are's household and contracted, in the same midnight hour, to tame Beelzebub and to tame myself. In truth, I felt more in common with the dark fiery beast than with any human creature at Thornfield.

I understood him. The same ungoverned pulse measured our beings, our spirits moved in the same blood-red aether. When he tossed his mane, rolled his eye, stamped in exasperation with his bonds, shivered with impatience to be flying across the field – I felt the same. But it was my part to thwart him, though I felt most acutely *with* him.

He must be my opponent, whom I loved because he was my twin. I must use against him all my intimate knowledge of the hot blood we shared. But that blood I must freeze in myself – I must be all icy reason and control. If he knew me as his like and equal, he would carry me with him into rebellion.

I fixed my intent and laid plans. My duties in the stables were not of the low order they had been at the Heights – that drudgery was accomplished by a crew of small boys under Daniel's orders – here I was required only to help Daniel with skilled operations: dosing, foaling, gelding, training. But now I added to my labour the entire care of Beelzebub. (He is a fine horse, Cathy! Sixteen hands at the shoulder, coal-black, strong-boned, muscles rippling like spring water!) I gave him his feed, I groomed him, I mucked out his stall. And in all my dealings with him I moved neither nervously nor stealthily. I aimed to be so steady that he would soon be able to predict my actions, and finding his predictions accurate, come to trust me.

Every day while I curried his coat I sang the same old

ballad, one of those you used to sing, for its melancholy melody seemed to arrest his attention:

An earthly maiden sits and sings,
'Hush, ba, loo lillie,' this maid began;
'It's little I ken my bairn's father,
Nor less the land where he dwells in.' & etc.

You remember, the mysterious lover comes to her bedside in the dead of night to claim his child and make himself known: ' "I am a man upon the land, I am a selchie in the sea," ' 'and prophesy the time when the maid would kill both him and their son. A sad and unlikely tale, but Beelzebub made no critique, unless the invariably sedative effect the song had on him expressed one.

So the horse was managed. I had a harder task in managing myself. How often, with what sharp desire, I burned to brush away with a curse and a blow the petty fettering rules imposed by the tutors Mr Are soon provided me, or by that man himself, and thereby confound my worldly ambitions! Somehow I refrained, and I thank the angel, or devil, who miraculously froze my hand, for, wherever else my course in these three years has taken me, it has at least brought me to you in marriageable state.

After several months of steady schooling Beelzebub was completely broken to the long rein, but I had never ridden him. For this I needed space and privacy. I asked if I might have exclusive use of a small enclosed pasture, nestled between hills, for the horse's exercise. I wanted to be safe from any chance passage of womankind; a few fits Beelzebub had taken when serving women skirted the stableyard had proved to me that he still bore his unreasonable prejudice. Mr Are assented, and gave orders that the field in question should be out-of-bounds to the household during the afternoon hours.

It was early October: Beelzebub had not willingly borne anyone on his back since he had thrown the lady and made his murderous attack on the groom. How should I mount him? At last I decided to let him run free in the pasture till he was tired, then jump on suddenly.

After he had frolicked an hour, I ran along next to him with my hand on his shoulder (on this signal I had taught him to match his gait to mine). How wild and free was the motion! How I wished to run thus with him chest-to-chest forever, leaping the horizon at last and climbing the clouds! But instead, in an instant, I caught the pommel and vaulted up to his back very smoothly.

My thighs had tensed themselves to ride the whirlwind, but there was no need. I found myself guiding Beelzebub around the corners of the field as easily as if he were a cow led to be milked. Well and good, I thought to myself, but let a servant girl from the next farm happen to take the shortcut to Hay that traversed yon end of the pasture, and I would find my milch cow had grown horns.

I took Beelzebub to a rise at the middle of the enclosure and dismounted. I stood next to him and gazed into the eye, the dark pupil with its milky surround, that regarded me so calmly. 'You look a veritable Houyhnhnm for phlegm and respectability, but I know that there is a mob of Yahoos within ready to riot at the first sight of the enemy. This must not be; I say so. What say you?'

Beelzebub only blinked, the glassy brilliance of his eye communicating no information. My imagination cast itself into that vitreous pit – if I could enter the nobly shaped skull, what would I find swirling there? Echoes of harsh words, a flurry of petticoats, perhaps the sting of the whip? Escape thwarted, fury mounting, the offending burden flung off – fiery dreams of stampede and mayhem? Though I could feel his rebellion, the vision of its cause was closed to me.

Looking longer into the huge eye, I saw my own image reflected convexly: the dark face and head dwarfing the tapering body and legs below, and reducing to tiny patches the field and sky beyond. This was what Beelzebub saw when he saw the world, and it was what I had taken pains he should see: me, and me only, his friend and comforter, eclipsing all else, embracing and controlling his wildness. So much was accomplished. Now it was my business to enlarge that circle of control till it encompassed more and more, till it included within its scope his mortal enemy: woman.

I must bring a woman within Beelzebub's purview – gradually and surely, as I had done all else. Should I beg Leah's help? No, the task would take many hours, many weeks, and she and all the other maidservants were occupied with their own duties.

I could not have a real woman assistant, but – it struck me – might I not have a feigned one? From where I stood in the field I could just see the top of a stone column that marked the stile where the path to Hay crossed the wall. It was about the height and girth of a person, and had the further advantage of being mostly hidden by a slight swelling of the ground as viewed from most parts of the pasture. Perhaps I could make a kind of dummy-woman out of the column; a kind of reverse scare-crow, where the purpose was to banish fright, not create it. Female clothes draped on stone would be just as objectionable an object to Beelzebub as the same clothes hung on flesh; in accepting the simulacrum (as I meant to make him), he would be accepting the whole female race.

At first I thought I might borrow some old clothes from Mrs Fairfax or Leah, but doing so would necessarily involve detailing my plan to them. This, I found upon reflection, I would rather avoid. Since the privacy of the pasture had already been secured, with a little care I could keep all secret.

Accordingly, I went to the establishment of a seamstress who I knew dealt in second-hand clothing cast-offs of the quality and gentry, full good enough to festoon the farmers' wives and burghers' daughters thereabouts as they strutted down the aisle to their pews Sunday mornings. From her store I picked out a canary bodice, a blue-sprigged petticoat, a scarlet cape, and a buff-feathered round hat (the latter I chose because you used to have one like it). Looking rather askance at this gaudy assortment, the woman asked the name of my sweetheart, probably thinking that whoever she was, she had a gypsy taste in men to go with a rainbow taste in clothing. I said nothing, only paid and left with my bundle. Let them believe what they liked.

When I took the clothes up to the stile-column, I saw that it was carved with curious slashing marks. I heard later it was called the Runestone by the old people in the neighbourhood; the characters supposedly the boasting records of those ancient northmen who a millennium since came rummaging and pillaging down the coast of England, and even so far inland as this peaceful valley. Some regarded the Runestone with superstitious awe; it was said that any who meddled with it would bring death and destruction to the neighbourhood. But none of this was known to me as I covered the queer carvings with my ill-sorted finery, tugging and pinching and pinning it into the semblance of a human form.

My handiwork was in place; I stood back to view the effect. What a thick, lumpish, comic dame stood before me! Still, a dame and not a column she appeared, and that would be enough for Beelzebub.

I was eager to test my scheme. I ran back to the stables for Beelzebub. After having ridden him to the pasture, I eased him at a walk towards the centre, to where I could just see the plumes of the dummy-woman's hat. Bracing myself for his reaction, I carefully let him walk a few steps further.

I pulled up short. Not because the horse had spotted the figure; he had not. I *had*, and to my confoundment: the sight took my breath away. For, in the first moment the hat beneath the plumes was uncovered, I thought (against all reason) it was yours, that it was *you* crossing the stile.

Though I knew the illusion for what it was instantly, still my heart throbbed painfully against my ribs and I sobbed aloud. I wheeled Beelzebub in his tracks and rode him back to the barn, hard.

Though I sought to shake off the memory of this weak and foolish hallucination, its half-sweet, half-painful effect lingered through the afternoon and rekindled the keen grief of our parting. I went about my stable duties unconsciously; remembered scenes passed through my mind with the vividness of tableaux in a pageant – you and me hunting birds' nests, or racing the stagecoach to Gimmerton crossroads, or reading a forbidden book in the garret by rushlight. Other, acid scenes, replaced them – Heathcliff, sunk deep in a bog of self-hatred, pulls away from Cathy's kisses with a growl, or curses her for spending an hour with anyone but his loutish self. By day's end I had tortured myself into a frenzy of memory so intense that some anodyne, even one concocted of falsehood, were necessary to maintain my sanity.

In desperation I took my set of coloured inks (I was then receiving lessons in architectural drawing) and painted on a pillow-case a woman's face life-sized, trying as much as possible to make it resemble your own. Then I took it to the field, where the dummy-woman still fluttered on the column, and fixed it under the hat. Though I had committed many errors in detail, the likeness seen from a little distance was haunting. It may give you some sense of my sad state at the time to know that I covered that limp piece of dyed cloth with kisses then, and every evening when I brought the whole masquerade in from the field – for the autumn rains had begun and I dared not leave anything out of doors overnight.

It was the day after I had painted your likeness that the incident of the spilled ink occurred – a petty matter, yet one fraught with serious implications, the full nature of which I have understood only in the past few days.

After having taken a solitary breakfast (I avoided joining the servants' mass feedings; except for the suppers with Mr Are, I ate alone), I went to the morning room.

There Mr Are sat, as he usually did at this hour, reading a paper from London in his dressing gown.

'Sir – ' I began.

'Bravo!' he clapped, his Pygmalion apparently turned impresario this morning. 'That is distinctly better, Heathcliff. We are getting on. You walked into the room with your head erect, your face unclouded, your hands held gracefully, and you gave me my proper address. Two months since you would, like a young bull, have butted through the door, your hands pendant hams, and snorted out your orders – orders, not requests – without preamble.'

I bowed slightly. 'Perhaps I should revert to what I was; my present state gives you less matter with which to paint your metaphors.'

'By no means; a paler palette suits me well; subtler gradations permit finer wit. For you flatter yourself, sirrah, if you imagine you have cropped the brush of satire.'

'Your meaning?'

' – is this, Heathcliff: though you have learned to stand tolerably, and to address a person without offering positive insult, you have learned nothing else. It is bare, it is cold, it is graceless; you might as well be a junior clerk at a warehouse asking his senior for tallow-money. To learn this much and no more is an empty triumph.'

'One I feel sure you will show me how to fill.'

'Cool, sir, cool – but you are right. A true friend does not pass over his fellow's failings, but puts him in the way of correcting them. Now, to the point – you must learn to *enter* a room.'

'Sir?'

'Any dolt can propel himself across a threshold, but only a gentleman can make an entrance. Observe!' Putting down his coffee-cup and casting aside his newspaper, he snatched up a tricorn hat that lay on a side table, along with the poker from the fireplace. 'We will say that this is my stick, since the real one is not at hand, and we will say that I am a gentleman who has come to pay you his respects.'

'Would not any gentleman hereabouts ride over, and hold a riding crop rather than a stick?'

'Do not tease me with quibbles, Heathcliff; we are speaking hypothetically, and hypothetically we are in London. Now, your hypothetical butler announces my hypothetical gentleman, and he comes to the door.' Here Mr Are stepped out to the hall. 'His head carries his hat, his left hand carries his stick, crop, sword – it is all the same – his right hand carries nothing, but is held in a state of graceful readiness.'

'Readiness to be shaken?'

'Certainly not; observe; you will see. Now, our gentleman thrusts one well-turned leg across the threshold – so – he casts a pleasant eye, alert yet calm, over the company assembled in the room – so – and steps in. As he does this he points the leading foot towards the chief person in the room -- yourself, Heathcliff! – describes a pleasing arc with his right hand as it ascends to his hat, and grasps the brim of said hat between thumb and third finger. Then, lifting the hat off the head, he bends forward from the waist, inclining head and hat in unison – thus. But when head is raised, hat stays behind, under the left elbow – so. Then my gentleman fixes his host with a cordial eye and utters his greeting. What? Why do you laugh?'

'Excuse me, but I have never seen *you* perform this monkey's minuet, and it is impossible that *I* should dance to it.'

He held his pose for a moment longer, then flung poker and hat on to the hearth in mock fury. 'Damn it, man, I have danced many such measures in my time, and so must you, till you earn the right not to. First you must show you know what is proper to be done. You must prove your respect for society. You must sufficiently teach others the worth of your character and parts. Then you can do what you like, as I do.'

He would have said more, but at this moment John came in, carrying his rather stout figure with what dignity he could and pulling a very long face. At first I thought he had entered to investigate the clatter the poker had made when it fell, but the case proved otherwise. 'Sir, there is something amiss in the library.'

'Amiss? What could be amiss?'

'Someone has made a mess.'

'Well, clean it up, John. Why tell me?'

'There is something suspicious about it.'

'What could be suspicious?'

'It is hard to describe, sir, I think you had better look.' On Mr Are's rising and my standing still, John added, 'And Mr Heathcliff, too – you might want him to look too.' He cast me a strange, almost humorous glance. I followed them out.

Since our midnight skirmish John and I had not spoken to each other except in way of duty, and then only in monosyllables, but I knew by his dogged guarding of his master (who he had served since both were boys) that his distrust of me had not lessened, despite my peace-abiding conduct in the intervening months. That peace had been hard kept; my fists had tingled to return in kind the inch-long keepsake over my right eye with which John had gifted me at the end of our encounter; all he had for memento was Mr Are's request (the sole notice the latter had given of an altercation that must have been a local nine days' wonder) that John call me *Mister* Heathcliff in future. My consolation was this: the pain Mr Are caused by these few words must have been far greater than any my fiercest blows could have imparted.

John led us to the windowed alcove where I habitually sat to study. It was several moments before I could rightly interpret what I saw. At first it seemed my corner had been garlanded with gay ribbons, as for a jubilee. But no – the books I had left neatly stacked in one corner the previous day were now opened – torn and scattered over desk, chair, and carpet. Moreover, what I had first taken for ribbons on the desk and window hangings were actually, I now saw, ink stains – the varicoloured contents of all the bottles in my drawing set splashed where they would make the greatest show.

I looked at Mr Are, expecting to witness an outburst; instead I saw a grim smile. 'Right,' he nodded. Looking at John, he said, 'Tell me, to whom would you attribute this foolish act?'

John examined the buckles of his shoes.

'I'm afraid I could not say, sir.'

'And I'm afraid you could. Come, speak up.'

He looked slyly at me. 'It's Mr Heathcliff's ink.'

'Yes,' said Mr Are, 'so it is, but what follows? Go on.'

'Well, last night about nine o'clock I heard a noise in the hall, so I looked out and there was Mr Heathcliff closing the library door, very soft, and peering right to left. Not noticing me, as I stood in shadow, he passed out the front door.'

This was accurate, and I thought I saw John's game. I had in fact been returning the inks to their accustomed place in the library after having used them to paint your portrait for the dummy-woman. Naturally I wanted to keep this enterprise to myself. My secretive air had made John suspect wrong-doing. He had entered the library; then, finding nothing amiss, decided to supply the lack and blame it on me.

Now Mr Are turned my way. 'And what have you to say, Heathcliff?'

The matter was beneath my contempt. 'John is right. I did enter the library last night.' I folded my arms.

'On what errand?'

'That is no one's business but my own.'

He gave a half-laugh. 'Strange and stranger still – this looks like guilt – but what is the motive? The act is pointless to the extent of lunacy!' Suddenly his features recast themselves in the mould of resolution. 'I will get to the bottom of it, I will understand it. Stay here.' And he strode out of the room.

John and I were alone together with the evidence. I looked at him coolly and steadily, thinking to make him squirm, but he returned my stare with an impudent grin, which I deigned not to notice. The ticking of the small timepiece on the mantel kept pace with the click-clack of the pendulum clock in the hall, then got off the stride, then back in again. Finally John spoke:

'Tripped yourself up, haven't you, now? We'll see who's so high and mighty after Mister Edward's done this day!'

'Fool!' I said softly. 'With what a feeble device you seek to discredit me! I would have expected better, even from such a dunce as you!'

He laughed. 'We are alone, *Mister* Heathcliff – there's no need for pretending between us. And it's you is the fool, to foul such a soft nest as you've feathered.'

'Yes, keep up the disguise, act your part,' I said, bruising my own flesh with my fingertips to prevent them finding the death-grip they craved on the churl's fat throat, 'for you will be unmasked soon enough, and to your grief.'

A look of genuine puzzlement, it seemed, passed over his face, but just then Mr Are re-entered the room. We looked at him expectantly.

'Well?' he said gruffly. 'What are you staring at? Does the pattern of my dressing gown put you out of countenance? Or is it simply the habitual arrangement of my features that you disapprove?'

John was speechless, so I answered. 'There is the mystery of the ink to clear up.'

'It is the ink itself that wants clearing up, I should think. John, see it done, will you please?'

John bowed, but lingered, unwilling that the matter be dropped. I, too, found that I wanted further clarification.

'Mr Are,' I said, 'certain charges have been made, or implied, against my conduct. I should like them removed.'

'Your conduct? Oh, yes – certainly. Yes, yes, you are cleared of all blame.' He waved his hand impatiently.

I inclined my head. Gathering up such of my books as were not ruined, I prepared to leave. John, however, was not so easily satisfied. 'But sir! I saw him walk out of the room! With my own eye!'

Mr Are's brow darkened. 'I do not doubt that you saw him leave the room, but can you swear that no other left it, no other entered it? Is your eye so all-comprehending? John, *remember orders*!'

During the first part of this speech John looked confused, but on hearing the last phrase his expression changed. He bowed low, muttered, 'I will see to the cleaning,' and left.

At that time I thought that Mr Are's admonition referred to the orders he had given John concerning my title and status in the household. Later, however, I wondered. John's puzzlement had been real, I thought; then it had seemed to disappear at Mr Are's last two words: 'remember orders'. Did they in some arcane way reveal to him the perpetrator of the mischief? If so, there was some conspiracy between servant and master, the nature and purpose of which I could not begin to fathom.

This incident added to my anxieties about Mr Are and his relation to me, but I did not at this time have much leisure for examining them. A golden prize had been placed within my reach; I had but to grasp it to make it my own. Not being quite an idiot, I did grasp it; I applied myself diligently to the lessons Mr Are taught me, and to the tasks set me by the weekly masters who had been hired to tutor me in fencing, dancing, and music. I succeeded well enough: you would cry shame had I not, for (as John had said) my nest was softly feathered. A few times I did fail sadly; then I consoled myself with the knowledge that of the gentlemanly science of horsemanship I was already master, and could have given lessons in it, even to Mr Are.

The training of Beelzebub was indeed the best of my tasks. Part of my pleasure was in the horse himself, part in steady progress towards a difficult goal, but part, I confess, was in the thrill I received the first time every day I caught sight of your likeness in the field, Cathy – the dummy on the column becoming in my love-lensed eyes the very figure of YOU – reproducing the bob of your gay plumes, the lilt of your face, just as I had seen them of old when you would run to me across the furrows I ploughed. I teased myself with glimpses as we circuited the far side of the field (I was as yet keeping Beelzebub from all but distant views of the dummy-woman), and sustained the illusion by spinning out tales whilst I rode: Hindley having drunk himself to death at last, you somehow had traced my whereabouts and were come to fetch me back to the Heights. Or, by fabulous chance you were stopping at Hay on the way to London: you had walked out to view the country and were just crossing the stile. Any moment I chose I could crest the hill and ride to your side. You would look at my face. For a moment the evidence of your eyes would bewilder you. Then – joyful recognition and outstretched arms, and I would pull you up and we would ride – where? There the fantasy broke, as indeed it should have before, since at any near sight of you Beelzebub would have done his best to trample us both.

So I continued in relative content, floating on a wave of real and fancied activity. Something changed, however. One day during a training session John hallooed me from a corner of the field, and, forced by my desire to keep the dummy-woman secret from him, I had to leave her assembled as I followed his summons to the house.

It happened that the errand Mr Are wanted me for – aiding him with some legal business in Millcote – took all the rest of the day and part of the evening. Further, the weather turned very cold and windy, and we rode back through biting whiplashes of thin, icy snow. My mind kept foolishly reverting to the representation of your visage atop the column in the field stung by cold and wet. By the time we reached home I had goaded myself into almost a frenzy of inward torment over what was, after all, only a false and graven idol.

Knowing this, still I excused myself as soon as decency permitted and ran out towards the pasture.

The snow had stopped falling by now but the intense cold remained, accompanied by a most bitter wind. Shreds of black clouds scuttled wildly across a crystalline full moon, alternately phosphorescing the frozen scene below and blotting it out. As I ascended the slope of the pasture the smooth soles of my riding boots slipped and skidded under me. Just as I gained the crest a great cloud brushed away from the moon and the dummy-woman flashed into full view.

As usual, my first thought was that you stood before me, but no! not you – never could you look thus! What stood there was flesh and blood, a woman, but vile, foul – misshapen, bloated face; blackened eyes; grinning, gabbling purpled lips; a long tangle of hair that whipped in the wind. The blood rushed from my head and I half-swooned. I fell to my knees and covered my face with my hands. Then reason returned. I opened my eyes. Though I thought then and do still believe that ghosts sometimes walk the earth, this apparition, I knew, must be only the bundle of cloth and feather and ink I had arranged myself that afternoon, and no cause for fear. Its ghastly appearance was but a trick of the moon.

As I drew nearer I saw what had happened. The snow had wetted and blurred the fine lines of ink I had drawn on the pillowcase, and the wind ripped it, causing a gap corresponding to the great flapping mouth I had seemed to see. What had been a faithful shadow of your beautiful face was changed to its grotesque, debased parody.

Shuddering, I snatched the thing off the post and rent it into a hundred pieces. I scattered them to the wind. Having thus disposed of what was monstrous in the image, I found the composure to calmly and carefully remove the remaining trappings from the Runestone. Still, I was chilled by the sight of the runes where the face should have been. The fitful moonlight, or my imagination, re-created of the runic strokes that same bloated mask that had so revolted me a minute before.

Then, just as I turned to go, I saw a movement out of the corner of my eye. It seemed to me that a white shape fluttered over the wall at the lower end of the field and disappeared into the thorn thicket. Chattering with cold and emotion, I raced after it, but by the time I reached the edge of the dark, tangled wood, there was nothing to be seen. Nothing, except what looked like a few small slippered footprints where the snow had drifted on the lee side of the wall. Then the clouds reclaimed the moon. Further discovery seemed unlikely, so I went indoors.

I slept ill that night, and for many nights following.

My dreams were haunted by the image of the dummy-woman. In my nightmares she strode down Thornfield's upper hall, opening every door. She crashed from room to room with a horrific stride – a relentless, inhuman progress of lithic limb. Sometimes she had the distorted mask's face, sometimes yours, once she even had my own. At length one of the doors she opened disclosed not a bedroom, but the star-studded arch of the firmament. She stepped out into it, and dissolved. Thus would the dream end.

Once there was a variation on this pattern. Starting up in my bed, I heard a hard, heavy step traversing the stone floor of the stable below. My heartbeat filled my chest – I knew that tread! Then I must listen to the rhythmic leaden thump climbing the stairs, anticipate the clumsy lifting of the latch, watch it happen. Then *she* stood in the patch of moonlight at the end of my bed, and – climax of horror – her face was not a face but a mossy, dumb stone, even the runes sunken so far they were but mute swellings in the lichenose surface.

Yet the thing was a woman, and desired me. She fell on me like the lid of a granite sarcophagus slamming down on its corpse. She pressed my forehead with her heavy face –

I woke sweating, though ice rimmed my water pitcher. I remember I spent the rest of that night sitting below with the horses.

By day I fared better, though dread formed a secret, leaden thoroughbass beneath the public counterpoint of study, conversation, and work. Every day I felt a mild loathing when I took the clothes for the dummy out of their closet in the stable (where I had moved them from my room at the onset of my dreams), every day when I crested the hill in the pasture and saw the figure I felt not pleasure but a *frisson* of disgust and terror. Still I continued using the dummy for Beelzebub's training, for to give in to my fears and abort the plan would be to admit a kind of madness, and this I was not willing to do. I only changed in the assembling of the costume on the column: where formerly I had striven for the utmost verisimilitude, now I no longer worked to arrange it with any kind of nicety, rather the contrary – I carelessly cast on bodice, skirt, cape, and hat all askew. But with malign perversity, and against all logic, the thing seemed to order its own toilet while my back was turned, and gather more and more of vivid life to itself as the weeks progressed.

Mind, all the time these delusions persisted I knew them for delusions, and, abhorring them, resisted them with all my power. With what success you shall hear.

We trained through the winter; by April Beelzebub was almost habituated to the sight of the dummy-woman. I daily rode him round and round the field, taking him twenty times within ten feet of her. I am sure I felt much more at each passage than did the horse; he, at least, *seemed* to take no notice.

However, I hesitated to declare him cured. I sensed a hard knot of resistance in his muscles, one that might explode into frenzy at any time. I determined, therefore, to put him to the test; instead of riding past the dummy I would make Beelzebub walk straight towards her and halt directly in front of her. If he remained calm, I would reward the horse then and there with some apples, of which he was especially fond. If he did not, I could do no better than bind my wounds and comfort myself with the fruit.

That day was a thawing day, I remember; though pools of snow still glowed in shadowed wood and orchard, the tops of the hills were already green. The turf was soggy underfoot and mists rose from the folds of the becks. A pale sun shone; a blackbird trilled from the highest branch of each tall tree; the earth-smelling wind blew soft. Having prepared the usual masquerade, I rode Beelzebub to the encounter.

I did not notice anything amiss with the dummy, nor did Beelzebub – he was steady and calm as he walked towards it. Indeed the thing seemed if anything less animate than usual. It stood upright in the clear spring light, its garments wafted a little by the breeze – a stone column with some clothes hung on it – that, and that only.

But in a second, transformation. Before my eyes the figure took life: its hips swayed, its skirts flared, its arms lifted themselves to the sky. It began to walk towards me.

Under me the horse writhed and sprang. Screaming and frothing at the bit, he attempted to bring the fury of his hatchet-sharp hooves down on the woman, or whatever it was.

I pulled back with all my might. He resisted: he reared and wheeled, but a little in the direction of my tug. I sweated to keep my balance as I worked with rein, knee, and heel to control the raving beast beneath me, all the while aware of the continuing eerie motions of the figure we now both abhorred.

I was making some progress in moving away; then suddenly Beelzebub twisted under me, took a running leap, and cleared the stone fence in a tremendous bound, a few feet shy of the still-gesticulating figure.

In mid-air (the flight suspended itself between seconds) I could not help turning my head, in horrified fascination, towards the woman. I dreaded to see – I knew not what.

I looked, and met the frightened eyes of John. He was huddled up to the fence close behind the dummy-woman, still holding in his hands long sticks attached to skirt and sleeves – sticks that, if wielded cleverly, could make a few articles of clothing seem a moving, living creature.

I vaulted clear of saddle and flying horse and struck ground a few yards short of John. The momentum carried me through a somersault and right up against him. With a jolt we hit the wall. My hands were at the man's throat and squeezing hard before I knew it; only a kind of death rattle issuing from his contorted maw suddenly brought me to the awareness that I must desist or pay the price of murder. I shifted my grip to his shoulders and shook him till the spit flew off his teeth.

'Why?' I choked out when I could catch my breath.

'It was a joke,' he panted. 'Lay off, Master Heathcliff.'

'It was not a joke,' I said. 'You knew the danger. Why? Why do you hate me?'

'I told you, it was a joke. I found out your mummery, and thought we could have some game of it.'

'It will not do!' I shook him again. 'You have hated me since you first laid eyes on me. You said you feared I would harm your master, but I have not done so. I have done nothing against him. Instead I have striven hard to help him. Yet you hinder me. Why?'

His eyes rolled back in his head. I saw I had tried him beyond his bodily endurance. I released my hold. Gasping and choking, he raised shaking hands to his neck. I helped him loosen his cravat.

'Now,' I said when his breathing had subsided to a normal pace. 'Tell me.'

His teary eyes sought mine, then broke away. He actually made the sign of the cross. 'Oh, none of that!' I said, losing patience. 'Tell me the truth!'

He winced and blurted out: 'If you want the truth, look at your face in the mirror.'

'What! What mystery is this?' I grasped his shoulders again, but released them when I felt how much he shrank from my touch. 'I'll not hurt you, only tell me.'

I thought: it is my dark skin, my gypsy eye. My neighbour's hand will ever be raised against me.

'I can't speak clearer,' he whined. 'My oath has been taken, and I can't forswear it.'

'What oath?' I said wildly. 'Mysteries! Riddles! What has your oath to do with my face?'

Evidently fearing my re-kindled wrath, he began again to shake. 'All is not well and fair at hall as may seem,' he said, 'and you coming with that face on you is a black omen – a black omen for Master Edward and for us who depends on him.'

Here I remembered Mr Are's reference to my resemblance to his dead elder brother, but still I could hardly credit this as constituting an omen. As I puzzled, John got up and wiped his mouth with the back of his hand. 'If you're the devil you look, then naught will move you, but if you're innocent, take fair warning: leave this place, or you'll bring us and yourself down to death and ruination.'

I let him run off; he was not worth chasing. I sat on the stile, my mind aswirl with sinister servants, stone-striding women, rearing horses, splashes of ink and blood – all devolved to a dense cloud of pain and hostility, enveloping me.

After a space – I know not how long – I looked up, and saw Beelzebub beside me, calmly grazing on some new spring growth. He had apparently run out his fury; when it was gone his affections, or force of habit, had brought him back to me. I reached up my hand and stroked his nose. He nuzzled my head, then began crunching on something he found on the ground. It was one of the apples I had brought for him; they had spilled out of my pocket during the fight. A wayward breeze moved the dummy's skirt; Beelzebub started, then warily resumed his meal.

In my mind's eye I saw horse and man, both strapping specimens of their species, and both undone utterly by a little pile of ragged clothes. How could I allow this state of affairs to continue? I rose to my feet, turned round, and resolutely began stripping the garments from the column.

As each came off – petticoat, bodice, cape, hat – I showed it to Beelzebub and rubbed its fabric against his face. He snorted a little but suffered it, being still occupied with the apples.

After I had treated every item thus, I put them on over my own clothes. I ripped and rent my way into openings never intended for my large frame. As the seams were weakened by wear and weather, I had little real impediment, except what the shaking of my hands made for me.

Beelzebub watched gravely as I donned each garment. I had his attention now. I began singing the old ballad I had formerly used to calm him: 'An earthly maiden sits and sings, & etc', just to remind him that the being before him was me, his master whom he loved, who yet was taking the form of the enemy.

When my costume was complete I stopped singing. 'Well,' I addressed him, 'what will you do now? Will you mash my brains to a pulp under your hooves? Or, like a rational creature, will you let me mount and ride? You offer no answer, so we must try to see which it is.'

I put my foot in the stirrup and swung myself up, sticking half-way because of the skirts, but at last gaining the saddle, which had marvellously stayed in place throughout all Beelzebub's rantings.

I held my breath. I let it out; the horse stood still as a lamb.

I rode Beelzebub back to the stable, holding the hat but still wearing the ragged rest, bunched up around my knees. I was in that brand of temper which cares nothing of the world's opinion. It was as well, for I found Mr Are waiting in the yard; perhaps he had caught John in his battered condition and had gathered from him or from his own deductions the tale of that day's doings.

He smiled, but did not laugh, when he saw my strange garb. 'I would never have believed I would behold anything in skirts mounted upon Beelzebub's back!' he said. 'I had an idea you were up to something of this sort, but I had not known it had come so far. You are triumphant!'

'For the moment,' I said. 'There may be other battles to wage in future, but this particular campaign is at an end.' And, slipping from the horse, I tore off the now-crumpled and ripped garments and tossed them into the stable trash-heap.

Mr Are shook my hand warmly and offered congratulations. 'But what is this, Heathcliff?' he asked, pointing to my forehead and shoulder, which bore bloody evidence of the fray. 'A casualty of war?' He observed me closely, waiting, I thought, for an account of my encounter with John.

'It is nothing,' I answered. 'I took a tumble going over a wall.' I was not going to give John the chance to call me a tale-bearer; besides, some of my suspicions pointed to collusion between man and master against me, though from what cause or to what end I could not imagine. Yet it behooved me to be cautious where such mysteries remained unsolved. And what of the white shape I had seen disappear into the thorn wood that stormy night last winter? John's broad foot never made the slim footprint I had discovered in the snow.

Whatever the truth of that, so much is certain: the ghost of the dummy-woman was laid. Never again did she climb the Runestone stile, and never again did she stalk Thornfield Hall – not in my dreams, at least.

I am alive. It seems I will live after all, and I lie in bed with nothing to do but talk to you, who have ever been near when the other side of my heart called. You hear me, I am sure of it.

Do you remember when I used to pretend your legs were mine? You had grown suddenly taller than I, and stronger, and your legs much longer, yet I would not let you be my master. I'd leap on your back and pinch your ears, and you'd give a little shrug and say, Where to, then, Cathy? and off we would go, the same as if the legs that were running were my own.

And they were, really, you said, because you could feel my thoughts moving in your limbs, just as though the impulse had come from your brain; your feet, willy-nilly, would turn the way I wanted – to the wall, say, if that's what I fancied, or back to the house, or out the gate. You couldn't call your body your own, you laughed. And I could feel the grit in the bottom of your boots between my toes.

When did we stop that game? When was the last time? Why do you not answer?

7

By high summer and the anniversary of my arrival at Thornfield, Beelzebub was pronounced cured: he became Mr Are's favoured mount and I inherited Minerva, the bay mare.

But before I go further I must tell you the rather strange issue of that last skirmish with John. It happened that I had struck my head on the wall harder than I at first knew, and following the mishap fell into a fever, which for a while looked like being dangerous. Mr Are called in an apothecary, who bled me and confined me to bed. Impatient with the restraint and (because of the fever) insensible of the reasons for it, I attempted a few times to get up and go down to my work in the stables. The apothecary had declared that if I jarred my brain he would not answer for the consequences, so for a day and a night, till the fever broke, a kind of guard had to be set over me. Daniel watched first, then came John's turn.

You can well imagine my reaction when I awoke from a fevered dream to see John sitting in a chair by my bedside. I thought he had sought me out in my weakened condition in order to murder me – smother me with a pillow, perhaps, and call it natural causes. I sat up and cast about clumsily for a weapon with which to defend myself, but John said, 'Nay, Master Heathcliff, do not take on so. I wish you no ill any more.'

I lay back, unable almost to move (my broth had likely been seasoned with an opiate), thinking that surely the man was toying with me, savouring his hour of triumph before serving me a feathery *optima mors*. But every time I struggled out of the sea of dreams that insistently pulled me down, I saw him sitting in the same quiet attitude as before, the only change, the shortening of a candle that cast soft glowing shadows through the night room.

After a while I caught hold of the idea that perhaps John had come under notice of Mr Are's suspicions, and was held to good behaviour by the threat of dismissal. But, through my fever- or drug-induced haze, I perceived an attention to me, a *noticing* of me, that surely went beyond any imposed imperative. His gaze was constant and strange – as before, he seemed to see something in my face that intrigued him, but with this difference: before, what he had found had inspired him with fear and loathing; now his eyes, if I read them aright, held a species of slavish fascination.

Once, out of a doze, I woke to find my hand grasped. John was holding it in both his own; I pulled mine away with the revulsion of one who discovers he has been caressing a nest of snakes.

After I had recovered, I assumed that John's odd actions had been part of my sick dreams, and would vanish with them, but no! the inexplicable devotion continued. Gone were the manservant's contempt and hostility; in their place were deference, solicitude, and what I can only describe as an intense curiosity. I would catch him spying on me at unexpected moments, peering in at the library door as I received a lesson from one of my tutors, or perhaps looking on as Mr Are and I fenced in the gallery. This made me uneasy, and I soon heartily wished the old John back.

Meanwhile my studies progressed steadily. I had regained that facility in reading which had marked my childhood, and was able to get through a prodigious amount of learning in a short time. The physical arts – boxing, shooting, fencing – I also mastered with ease. In fencing, indeed, I had lately challenged Mr Are's supremacy, once even flicking his foil out of his hand with a swift turn of the wrist. But my successful rivalry in this matter and others he resented not at all, rather welcomed with generous, though sometimes satiric, praise.

As the months passed I formed a more extensive idea of Mr Are's character. I say more *extensive*, instead of complete, advisedly – for to establish one sound fact about this man was to uncover two mysteries. Still, my total impression at this time tended more and more towards the favourable.

One strong point in Mr Are's favour was the sincere devotion displayed towards him by his servants, despite his despotic behaviour. At first I had thought the shifts and changes of his mercurial fancies to be self-indulgent exercises of power, more likely to incite terror and hatred than love and respect in those unfortunate enough to be subject to them. Yet love and respect were his almost universally, as far as I could make out. Daniel, Mrs Fairfax, Leah, and the other servants sang his praises continually, as I overheard in the halls. (Me they did not make their gossip – my ambiguous position in the household at the time, added to the forbidding aspects of my character with which you are well acquainted, ensured my immunity from that role!) But what was the secret of their attraction to this bombastic, capricious master?

Gradually, I began to see the answer. Although Mr Are's words were harsh, though he often bellowed his orders at the servants and frequently threatened them with dismissal or bodily harm, no one at Thornfield was ever actually punished.

One incident will serve for example. John was over-fond of his bed, and had the habit of yawning through his attendance of Mr Are in the breakfast room. This practice irresistibly drew Mr Are's irritable notice: 'John, I shall flog you personally the next time you gape in that shocking manner!' Then, one morning, leaping from his chair and overturning the coffee: 'There! You have done it again! It is the last straw; you must be corrected! Leave me now, but return to this room at five p.m. precisely; at that time, in the presence of everyone at Thornfield, I shall administer twenty lashes!' To my amazement John left the room notably unconcerned, barely stifling yet another yawn as he shut the door. And that afternoon at five, I and the rest of the household witnessed this:

instead of twenty welts, John received from his master's hand twenty shillings, with the admonition to buy with it a sleeping draught!

Though friendly satire, it *was* satire. Mr Are's daily discourse was laced with ridicule of human frailty. This, when directed towards a particular person, as it usually was, I would have imagined to be really offensive – I know I often had to grind my teeth in the effort to contain my rage at his broadsides – but then I noticed that when he railed or gibed at anyone *but* me (I was, you see, a privileged case) his barbs were never aimed at a vital point; they were meant to tickle, not to wound, to flatter by their attention to a trivial and perhaps attractive weakness – Leah's readiness to giggle, say, or Mrs Fairfax's extreme respectability – and so tended towards a general expansion of spirits rather than the reverse. The sum of it was that Mr Are's wit and unpredictability kept the servants in a state of bubbling good humour, spiced by laughter and leavened by their master's undeniable liberality in the matter of wages.

Knowing this much you would assume Mr Are to be a type of the superior rural squire, high-living, exuberant, a gentleman for whom all life was a holiday, all the world a carnival. But this was not the case. In fact as I knew Mr Are better I came to hear his frequent peals of laughter as cries of desperation, hysterical attempts to defy – what? Some gigantic enemy visible only to himself? I did not know, I only saw he danced to it on the edge of a chasm.

So he would joke and laugh one minute, and the next fall silent, his whole being almost palpably enveloped in gloom as he lost himself to whatever demon was devilling him. On these occasions he might, after a period of dark abstraction, abruptly abandon whatever it was he had been doing and leave – either on the back of Beelzebub, harrowing all the byways of the neighbourhood, or else in his carriage, without a word of warning quitting the neighbourhood altogether: twice to London during that year and several times to his other country residence. Leah told me that this was nothing for him; he had lately been a regular homebody compared to the decade previous, during which period he had scarcely been at Thornfield as much time altogether as he had in the few months since my arrival.

Did my heart swell with pride as I heard these words? Was I gratified to have apparently created such an interest in another human breast? I cannot say, for I then thought and acted within a cloud of unconsciousness from which my mind has only lately emerged (of this I will speak more later); but what I can honestly recall feeling (apart from the pain, fundamental and constant, of my separation from you) is a sensation of rightness, that the world had at last fallen into its proper arrangement after having been set cosmically askew.

Mr Are continued his eccentric practice of taking supper with me in the stable throughout the year, except in the middle of winter, when cold rendered the scheme impracticable, and we ate in my room. But we resumed our equine banquets as soon as the frost broke, and regaled the horses with ever finer displays of manners.

On one such occasion, in high summer, we sat drinking wine after having nibbled asparagus, gulped oysters, and eviscerated pomegranates. (It was one of Mr Are's fads to order dishes he thought might baffle me to manage; high was his delight if they did, higher still if they did not!) It being a hot close night, we had doffed waistcoats and quit the stable, wineglasses in hand, for the orchard behind, seeking a fresh breeze on the round hilltop. We sat in the cool grass, our faces and shirts reflecting a faint pearly glow from the brilliant band of the firmament arched above. The moist air submerged us in a dark palpable pool. The din of crickets throbbed up and down the valley.

A flare and ensuing orange glow in the murk signalled that Mr Are had lit and was smoking a cigar, a circumstance that touched me with a mild disgust, as all pollutions of body and mind have increasingly done.

'Your position is falsified by its basis on a contradiction.' Mr Are, speaking above the crickets, resumed the conversation we had broken off ten minutes before. 'You would enjoy the fruits of a societal order made possible by laws, yet you would flout those laws yourself.'

'What have I, a man outside family and property, to do with laws others have made? and made, if you examine them with any care, only to protect the families and properties of themselves and others of their class.'

'Yet you might acquire property, and then expect those same laws to protect it.'

'In such an eventuality I would not require anything of the law,' was my retort. 'If I gathered property to me, it would be by means of my own unique magnetism, my own essential genius, and the acquisition would be inevitable. I would retain the property by the same principle. If I lost my holdings, it would be because I had ceased to be myself. In the knot of identity are one's being and belongings tied; when it is undone, all is undone.'

'That I do not allow,' he answered, 'but let us put the general assertion aside for a moment and take up just one point, where your error is laid bare. Your present identity is entirely dependent on the laws of property, because those laws keep the populace hereabouts from rising up and claiming for each his fair share of a single acre, that taken by the hundred in my estate, provide the means by which you are tutored and clothed.'

'This has to do with *your* identity, not mine – it is your magnetism which preserves the integrity of your estate, and mine which makes you my benefactor.'

'A cool and sophisticated reply, quite worthy of you, Heathcliff. But your ideas are beyond serious consideration – your theory of the primacy of personal identity, if taken as a general principle, would lead to enthusiasm – mysticism – anarchy!'

'Not at all. My system, if realized properly, would lead to an unprecedented universal harmony. I will demonstrate it to you. Under your system, your precious laws are determined – how?'

Mr Are's glowing cigar end beat time with his answer: 'By the best of what custom and reason have built up over the years, codified in civil and moral laws. Properly followed, these laws allow for peaceful co-existence of individuals, untroubled intercourse between interests. Granted, the laws allot sacrifice and suffering to some, but in general they provide the greatest happiness for the greatest number.'

'And I spit on your "greatest happiness" – the tepid result of a compromise which produces only one positively good thing: a vigorous exchange of the coin of the realm, but at the cost of all true, deep, strong existence.'

'Your "true, deep, strong existence", if unchained, would be likely to crush all commoner forms of life in order to feel its being in the exercise of cruel power. Your creed would benefit only the strong.'

'But it is in strength that life is truly manifested,' I said.

'If you believe in life, in a life-force which goes beyond mere mechanical motion of the atoms we are taught make up the universe – then is not its most intense manifestation, the sentience of an individual focused into *will*, is not that supreme life worth a thousand little will-less lives?'

The floating orange ember made a long arc in the black air; Mr Are had tossed his cigar down the hill into the apple branches. 'You say that only because you imagine yourself to be such a supreme being, and you do not give a fig about what others might imagine themselves to be.'

'No, I say it because it seems to me irrefutably true. You are right; I do not give a fig for the welfare of society at large, yet I believe that if all followed my creed, the world would enter an exaltation of existence previously unimagined. If each psyche allowed itself to become attuned to its destiny, if each soul placed itself open to inspiration, then would individuality blossom in an array of beautiful colours inconceivable to our present starved organs of sight, in a profusion of ravishing forms yet unknown and unknowable.'

'Then would anarchy, madness, and mayhem destroy the earth. Your system, Heathcliff, would provide *carte blanche* to any madman who wanted to impose his diseased philosophy on others. The more extreme the madness, the more seductive its influence and the greater its power to harm. No, it will not do.'

'You are an atheist, then?' I said.

'Why do you say that?'

'You posit a world in which inspiration originates only from disease, from pathology. My world contains a god, and a devil, and spirits to guide us. It is they who determine our destiny. It is for us to make ourselves sensitive to their meanings, to rightly interpret their callings.'

'Your system is medieval, grotesque,' he answered. 'God gave us reason; *that* is our bright way to the good, not the murky road downward and inward, which can only lead to madness, melancholy, delusion.'

'You lack faith,' I said. 'And no wonder – your distant God does little to inspire it. Mine does permit extremes of pleasure and pain to exist side by side, but in that way ensures a climax of *being* – only in knowing these extremes can we be truly alive.'

Mr Are's face flashed briefly out of the night like a spectral mask; the flare he used to ignite another cigar showed it set in a sarcastic smile. When he had finished his task he said, ' "Pleasure and pain" – to you these make up the essence of being. Yes, I have no doubt that you have felt both, and felt them exquisitely. But there are extremes of experience you have not reached; perhaps you do not even begin to apprehend their existence; how could you, at half my age – you have not lived intimately with un-hope, daily communicated with horror – God forbid that your path lead you there. But if it should, then as you walked it you would whistle a different philosophical tune.'

This is how our discussions usually ended – with his dismissal of my arguments as effusions of youthful ardour, too slight to be refuted. I shrugged in the dark. What difference could his contempt make to me? I *knew* where he only conjectured.

As it happened, the hill on which we sat was about on a level with the battlements of the house, though some distance from them. The thorn thicket rose up far enough to obscure from our sight most of the building, but past the silhouette of Mr Are's head and shoulders I could see three narrow yellow rectangles; a lamp was burning in an attic room. I knew that one of the woman servants had as her domain a sewing room on the top floor; she must have had extra work on hand, I thought, to be labouring so far into the night. As I watched I distinguished a rhythmic pulsing of light and dark within the room; I took it to be caused by the periodic passing of a hand over the source of light, as might happen in thrusting a needle in and out of a piece of cloth held near a lamp. But then the windows flickered and disappeared, and the bulk of Thornfield Hall became indistinguishable from the outline of its owner's form.

'By the bye,' said Mr Are after a pause, 'do you know what tonight is?'

'No,' I said (though I did know).

'It is the anniversary of your advent on my horizon. Let us drink to what has been an instructive year for us both.'

We drank; he drained his glass and poured another from the bottle he had brought. I abstained.

He continued: 'I know you do not care to hear my praise, yet I will say this much: you have progressed far in the year you have been here. When I picture the dirty, hulking troll I stumbled over in Liverpool, and put him next to what I see before me now (with my mind's eye, for the darkness renders you to my bodily one but a misty outline against the stars) – well, rhetoric will hardly swell to contain the comparison. No, do not bother to answer; you would have to lie, or praise yourself, and by either choice break the rule I have taught you. We will seek another topic. You remember Colonel Dent, who called here today?'

'Yes, I happened to enter the library while you were engaged with him.'

'You bowed and excused yourself as soon as you saw that I was not alone, as prettily as any paragon in Lord

Chesterfield's book. Well, after you left he asked me the identity of that well-set-up young man. I told him you were a young relative of mine from the north, whose parents had sent to me to broaden his education. He suggested that, as his nephew also was coming for a visit, and since you appeared to be of an age with him, we bring the two together. My first impulse, born of established policy, was to demur, but I checked it – why should I keep you hidden any longer? You have the bearing, the discourse, all the parts of a gentleman. Why should you not be tested?'

'Tested? How, exactly? By conversation with the nephew?'

'Yes, that is the plan, but with these addenda: I will invite a party of the local gentry to stay at Thornfield for a week. I will entertain them with diversions of the usual sort – riding, picnics, excursions, games during the day; music, dancing, festivities by night. In all, you will participate in your character of my "young relative from the north" – a youth slightly rusticated by geographic misfortune, perhaps, but none the less a gentleman born and bred. You will dine, dance, converse – all on equal footing with the rest. If you slip, if you forget the lessons I have worked so hard to teach you over the past year, you expose yourself as a fraud and me as an untrustworthy trifler. If you succeed, you prove me a genius and yourself a gentleman. You will *be* a gentleman. Do you agree to this test?'

'Yes,' I answered.

'Good. But I expected hesitation, resistance – you are confident.'

'Indeed. You have mentioned nothing that is outside my power to accomplish.'

'Perhaps you are too confident. You do not properly anticipate the thousand accidents that might befall you, the ease with which one careless word could give you away. We will raise the stakes. We will make you exert yourself to the utmost. Hear this, then, and see if it shocks your confidence out of that cool monotone in which, I wot, it has inwardly sung an endless paean to Heathcliff's ability.'

'Go on, then. What Herculean labour would you contrive for me?'

'You have already played Hercules in the stables; I will not ask you to reassume the role. No; rather you must take the part of Tantalus. I will place a prize before you, which you will have to strain hard to attain. Here it is: if you succeed during this one week in convincing everyone you are a gentleman, if you raise no one's eyebrows, cause no whispered doubt about you to circulate, but conduct yourself in all respects in a manner befitting a nephew of mine, then I shall take you with me when I leave Thornfield next month.'

'Where do you go?'

'To the Continent – an extended tour of Italy, France, Spain, the lowlands, perhaps Russia and Germany. If you succeed you shall have the grand tour that finishes every fine young gentleman's education.'

'And if I fail?'

'Well, I need an overseer at Ferndean; I suppose you could stay behind and fill that post. It is an honourable one, beyond your deserts perhaps, but still far below the glittering prospect I offer you, if you have the luck and nerve to succeed. What say you to the wager?'

'Of course I accept, with the fullest expectation of winning.'

'Ah – beware! Overconfidence is a traitorous helpmeet – you would do better to mate with Prudence, or Caution. But I am glad you agree, since I have already set the date for the party – Tuesday se'ennight – and invited the guests.'

This surprised me not at all. I enquired their names.

'I asked the colonel on the spot, so we have him and Mrs Dent, and their nephew, a Mr Linton.'

Linton! That name! Linton – he *had* said *Linton* – the nephew of Colonel Harold Dent. My mind leapt the gap of logic to make of this unknown nephew, *Edgar* Linton, my boyhood enemy. But surely Colonel Dent's relative was not the same Linton whose tender breast I had knifed a hundred times in fantasy (despite the civilizing effect of my recent education), whose handsome face I still longed to batter until it was a welt of blood, whose violent dispatch had been accomplished a hundred times in a hundred most satisfying ways in my dreams? *Could* it be the same? It could, but surely *was* not. Linton was not an uncommon name; there must be a dozen families of Lintons in the country – the colonel's nephew could be from any of these. Why should it be *my* particular Linton? For he and I could not be in the same place at once without time stopping, the world shattering.

The sound of Mr Are's sentences, which had roared past my ears like a river for two minutes past, now ceased; he had prated on about the other guests and the supposed beauties of the young ladies amongst them. But only one subject could interest me now. 'This nephew,' I asked, 'what do you know of him?' My voice sounded strained in spite of my best efforts to make it offhand. It was well the darkness hid my face.

'Why do you ask?' Mr Are's response was quick – he would seize on any anomaly in my behaviour as fiercely as a hawk to a sparrow.

'Colonel Dent saw me, and mentally paired me with him; I am curious.'

'Yes.' Apparently satisfied with my answer, my companion took a swallow of wine and continued: 'You do well to fix on him; being most your counterpart in age amongst the company, he will be your severest judge. Let me see what I can remember, for he made a visit to his uncle several years ago and I happened to meet him. He was not much like you, not then at least – a slight, fair, bookish lad, who wanted heartening – but the colonel says he has improved of late, he even contemplates making this sprig in the family tree his heir. Still, you will have no trouble besting him out-of-doors. Better keep him there as much as you can, for the drawing room may be another matter. I remember him as rather a prodigy of refinement.'

'What did you say his name was?'

'Linton, his name is Linton – like you he is from the north. His first name is something like mine, but *not* mine – Edmund – no – Edgar! Edgar Linton.'

Edgar Linton! It was he! As if by magic, my most hated object was bodied up out of the shadows before me, my two worlds brought together – not in the way I had dreamt, by your miraculous appearance, but by the imposition of my rival, who matched my detestation of him with contempt and loathing for me. What would prevent him instantly unmasking me? The scene, as I imagined it, crackled with hidden fire. He would enter the drawing room with a group of elegantly appointed gentlefolk. His blue eyes would meet my black ones. His eyebrows would raise slightly. He would point a languid finger and say, 'That man is an impudent imposter, a runaway, a dung-slave. Remove him at once to the servants' quarters.'

This was my first panicked reaction, sitting there on the dark hill beside Mr Are, but after the first shock I saw its absurdity. I was thinking like a criminal, though I had committed no crime. Not having been indentured I had done nothing wrong in leaving Wuthering Heights and coming here, where my position, if unusual, was fair and legal. I was using my real name, or at least the only name I knew; any imposture was on Mr Are's part in saying I was his nephew.

But how could I prevent Linton's disclosure of my history? After a little thought I saw that it would be less difficult than I had at first imagined. Unless he involuntarily blurted something out when he caught sight of me, Edgar would be temporarily silenced by Mr Are's introduction; the heir of Thrushcross Grange would not be able to contradict his host's identification of me as his nephew without a serious breach of good manners, one my young gentleman's breeding would render him incapable of committing, and I would undoubtedly be able to forestall later, more politic disclosures. My only care, then, must be at our first encounter – the rest would follow almost automatically. I remembered how when we were boys the super-fine Master Linton had bawled when I spilt a dribble of hot apple sauce on him; we were men now, but he would still be delectably easy to silence.

But I had to put aside these thoughts for the moment. Mr Are was rising, was speaking, I must attend to what he was saying.

He requested I walk with him to the house, now darkened except for candles to light him in the door.

Once we reached it, he turned to me and shook hands with unwonted formality. 'Tonight was our final banquet in the stable,' he said. 'We must part from the old ways, for you have risen above them. From tomorrow forward you will take your meals with me in the main house.'

Thus, in the space of a year, I had advanced one link in the great chain of being, from the animal to the human. Whether or not my new status would suit me was yet to be proved.

I thanked Mr Are and, making my blind way through a wild whirl of imagined scenes, walked back to my quarters. At some point I became aware that I was not alone on the path. John had fallen into step with me.

'I have somewhat to ask you,' he began.

'Ask away,' I said, not being in the mood to spend my words in dispute of his right to question me, or to remark on the unusual incidence of his appearance at this time and place.

'Master Edward spoke to all of us at tea-time. He said you were really his nephew, who had been restored to him after having been lost.'

'Well? What of it?'

'Did he speak true?'

I stopped and turned towards him then, though I could not see him for the darkness. 'John, why do you ask me that? What has your master to do with truth or falsehood?

'At Thornfield, his word is the alpha and the omega, the beginning and the end of all matters. So it is, so it must be, and so will you and I be satisfied.'

'It is a deep game master is playing.'

'And if it is? I have my own game, and you do too, if it comes to that.'

'Games within games, as may be, but Master Edward's gameboard is biggest. So beware, Mister Heathcliff, of losing yourself on it.'

Here he put his hand on my shoulder, but I shrugged it off and left him behind me on the path. I was weary of his croakings; whatever he might know or suspect, it could be of little import compared to what I knew would happen in seven days.

I had a week, then, before the house party to fill with delightful anticipation – of humiliation, of exposure as an upstart, of revelation of my patron as a betrayer of his caste. Or perhaps I could look forward to swinging from the gallows in a month's time, having in an unguarded moment struck out at my enemy. Then again I might triumph over myself and over the others, might best Linton and all his class, and be the proudest gentleman of all.

But strangely, as the days went by my thoughts turned from these fantasies. Now, compelled by an inner dictate, I abandoned the momentous encounter with Linton to the future, and bethought myself instead of the past. There I found something much more alarming.

Cathy, I have said I left you and the Heights because I overheard you say that you preferred Linton's company to mine, and that it would degrade you to marry me. Those galvanic words had shocked me to action; it was those words I remembered – but what had you said just before you uttered them?

I had been dozing on the bench behind the settle where you and Nelly were talking. I awoke gradually to the sense of your voice, started to full wakefulness when you spoke my name, then heard the sentence that propelled my doom.

But what *had* come before? Now, waiting for Linton, my mind forced to consciousness what it had previously held back as too terrible to know; if I had known it a year ago my being must have dissolved instantly, my heart burst. But now, compelled by some new unwelcome strength, reluctantly and unhappily, I knew.

You were engaged to marry Edgar Linton.

You had told Nelly that Linton had asked you to be his wife. You had told her that you had accepted.

Could it be true? Had I really heard it, or was treacherous memory playing out my fears? Your flirtation with Linton was no news to me, for you had been tormenting me with him for years already, but had matters between you gone so far beyond flirtation?

Could it be? Or had I dreamed it? Again and again I went over the scene – the defeat of the dead fatigue I had felt lying on the hard bench, my only escape stupidness and sleep – the murmur of voices – the comfort of your voice being one of them – Nelly saying I wasn't there – That did happen, didn't it? Then –

Did you engage yourself to Edgar that day? Of that I still have no certain intelligence, though as you will soon read I have had other accounts of the matter. It cannot make a difference now. As you know in part and will soon know in whole, I took certain steps to ensure that such a marriage could never take place. Besides, tomorrow you and I will be joined forever. What does it matter if you have in the meantime amused yourself with teasing Linton? He is an insignificance, a cipher, a vacuum – it is impossible to take him seriously. You would marry *that*? The notion must be a product of my self-tormenting fantasy, not my memory.

Yet the fantasy, or memory, brings with it some degree of comfort too. In the nightmare in which you say you *will* marry Linton, you also say that you cannot. Your soul rebels against it. And I have faith in your soul, since it is my own.

It might be that this incident came from that dream world, which was and is almost as large a part of my experience as outward events. But it might have been a true memory. If it were, if you were indeed engaged to Edgar, what a blind fool I had been to bolt, to so utterly leave him the field. Yet, could I have prevented anything had I stayed? I had no alternate life to offer you, a beggar's wife I would have made you. I was right to leave, to raise myself. But to leave without a word!

It had been a year since I left. I was trusting to the ineffable, unutterable permanency of our connection – that you would KNOW that I was striving for you, and that I would return – but was the tie really so strong? Had you lost faith in me? Had you forgotten me? I must get word to you. This I resolved to do, as soon as Edgar Linton had supplied me with the clue that would tell me what my message must be.

Finally, a day or so before the house party, along with all these tormenting thoughts came a contradictory wave of pleasurable feeling. In meeting Edgar I would be face-to-face with one who had, mere hours before, seen you and talked with you. He might have touched (oh, pain!) your hand. Some of the air you had breathed might linger round him, your light would shine from his eyes. It was well; from this defiled connection I could yet draw a sacred essence. Through this false priest of your love I could know holiness, could renew my consecration.

Incredibly, this strange happiness grew stronger, in time blurring, then hiding altogether the hatred that surely should be my chief sentiment towards one who stood between me and my love. But when I examined my heart I found not hatred, but desire; not dread, but throbbing anticipation! More strangely still – and this in itself became a torment to me – when I attempted to call up your face in my memory it resembled his – I could not keep the two apart.

So, by the day of his arrival I longed to see Edgar Linton cross the threshold of Thornfield Hall, impatiently, intensely, as one might yearn, breath hitched in his throat, for the first glimpse of his lover. Deny the feeling though I would, I longed to annihilate Edgar Linton, not by a blow of my bodily fist, but with the turbulent wrench of my soul's embrace.

8

Edgar Linton came to Thornfield at last. We approached each other in the entrance hall, our eyes met. Contrary to my expectations, the sun did not darken, the stars did not fall from their courses; in fact the universe wheeled on pretty much as before. Yet I recognized, in the moment our glances locked, the beginning of a new phase of my existence.

Before his arrival I had watched all day at the library window. Finally there came a sound of wheels on gravel; a fine coach pulled up before the house. Edgar emerged first: he was dressed in dark clothes against which his fair hair blazed. His back to me, he supported his gouty uncle in a cautious descent, then handed down the richly dressed blonde woman who must be his aunt. He turned and smiled at something Colonel Dent said; I saw Edgar's face in the sunlight. Bittersweet memory bodied itself before me; Edgar Linton was handsome as ever, golden-haired and even-featured as he had been the last time I glimpsed him, when he called on you that afternoon of the night I left. No wonder you had admired him – even my eye perversely rejoiced in the exquisite line of this young man's profile, the perfect incline of his head as he escorted his aunt towards the house. But as in my imaginings of the week before (had some necromancer caught me in his spell?), his form, as I watched it, kept slipping into the image of *your* form, coinciding with memories of *your* features, *your* movements. Had Edgar spent so much time in your presence as to pick up your traits, your mannerisms? Or had some more mysterious alchemical transmutation taken place, so that part of your soul adhered to this, your masculine counterpart in natural gifts? I could not judge – if spell it was, it was well cast, and held me in it.

Now we stood across from each other in the entrance hall. Mr Are was engaged in greeting his friends. Edgar stood waiting, cautiously surveying the features of the environs, in the manner common to new guests. I regarded him alertly and steadily. How many visions of you, in how many dear aspects, multiplied from every flicker of his eyelid, every shift of his hand! It was as though he and I stood, not amongst French-spewing, satin-hung gentry in a mirror-lined anteroom, but in the smoky, copper-lumined kitchen at the Heights, Nelly and Joseph nattering by the fire and a wonderful, terrible presence – you – troubling the air between us.

His glance at first passed over me. Two heartbeats, then it jerked back. His brows lifted, he stood speechless. I held his gaze fiercely, mentally begging him not to speak.

During that intense second I saw myself through his eyes – a black-haired, Moorish-looking wildman, standing straight and menacing, inexplicably got up in a splendid wine-coloured velvet suit with gold-embroidered waistcoat – this superimposed on his mental retina over the shadowy image of a slouching, mean-looking gypsy boy in mud-spattered leather breeches, whose function it was to hold Miss Earnshaw's pony while its rider flirted with Edgar. This stableboy had vanished a year ago, doubtless to Linton's thorough satisfaction: it had been a troublesome blot in the background of Edgar Linton's courtship of Catherine Earnshaw and was better erased. Then the same ugly face turns up, washed and framed in fine lace, in a gentleman's country house.

He did not believe it at first, I think; his eyes bent from mine; he was trying to persuade himself that this was some fantastic coincidence of resemblance.

But he could not; his eyes returned in alarmed fascination. My features were, after all, exceedingly familiar to him; he had seen me more times altogether than he had any other person in the room. He could not escape the conclusion that I was myself, Heathcliff. Besides, I was staring at him with abundant intelligence of *his* identity written on my face. His expression changed – he began to speak – but Mr Are had taken my arm, was introducing me to the Dents:

' – and allow me to present my nephew, Heathcliff – Edward Heathcliff. He is my namesake, you see; we call him by his surname in our family to prevent any little confusion.'

A slight, smiling yellow-haired lady stood before me with her hand outstretched: I must needs go through the polite motions that had been drilled into me. I took the hand and bent over it. Mr Are presented Colonel Dent, a barrel-chested man with a large freckled pink face and small white rolled wig.

'Aye, we've seen your lad galloping over the fields on that devilish fine stallion of yours,' said the colonel, pumping my arm heartily. 'Or taking walls that nobody's dared since Hern's Hunt. I was saying to Sir George Lynn the other day that next he'll be jumping Hay steeple.'

'Yes, Heathcliff is quite the horseman,' said Mr Are. 'Remind me to tell you sometime the full history of his escapades with Beelzebub; there is matter there to surprise you. Yes, I'll warrant he's a match even for you in the saddle.'

'Good – good,' said Colonel Dent. 'I am delighted to hear it, for I am eager for a nice companionable gallop, if only this demned gout will spare me for a day. And maybe he will get my sprig of a nevvy' (here he thumped the embarrassed Linton on the back) 'out of the library and on to the back of a horse. He has half-ruined his health by poring over his book, and I am determined that this week at least he shall entirely abandon it, and pursue sport with the men by day, and the beautiful Misses Ingram by night, eh?' Here he leered and poked his uncomfortable nephew in the ribs. I must have looked my fellow-feeling for the embarrassment his uncle's vulgarity was causing Edgar, for he shot me a surprised, sheepish half-smile.

Mrs Dent came forward and squeezed her husband's arm. 'Harold, you are teasing Edgar. His health is tolerable enough, and you would be a better man yourself for opening a book from year to year.' Then, to me: 'But my nephew does need diversion; you will companion him this week, will you not, Mr Heathcliff?'

'With the greatest pleasure,' I said, 'especially since you request it.' Her eyes were blue and shaped like Linton's; I smiled into them. She dimpled at me.

Now it was Linton's privilege to make my acquaintance. When I regained his eye I saw it was excited, his face was flushed, but his mouth was firm: the danger of his blurting something out was over for the moment. 'Mr Linton,' I said, and inclined my head. He returned with 'Mr Heathcliff', the emphasis slightly on the first word.

Mr Are drew the elder pair apart in conversation; it seemed I must do the honours of the younger generation.

Edgar Linton and I stood regarding each other. Now that he was actually before me, my breast heaved. I could not move or speak. Linton was for me at this moment surrounded by a sublime and numinous light; his face shone with your beauty. I wanted to reach out and touch his cheek, so strong was the latent impression of you. My throat thickened as I searched his great blue eyes.

Edgar appeared to wax nervous under this scrutiny. He gave his head a little shake, then said lowly, wonder in his voice, 'Heathcliff – is it really you? How can this be?'

My paralysis lifted; I clasped his hand. 'Edgar! I am glad to see you! So glad – '

He withdrew his hand quickly (though not so quickly as to point an insult) and said, 'But it is bewildering! You are so altered, and to find you here in this company – How did it come about?'

'I will tell you – ' I started to touch his shoulder, but held back, fearful I might embrace him in an excess of emotion. Instead I indicated with a gesture that we walk to an alcove that would afford us some protection from Mr Are's quick eye and ear. 'I will explain,' I said in a low voice, 'but there is no time now. I will only say in haste that my friends here do not know of my history at the Heights. Will you help me? Will you keep my secret?' I forgot myself and pressed his hand again.

This time Linton responded with a slight pressure of his own. 'Yes, of course, Heathcliff; I am glad to see you rising in the world, if there is nothing wrong about it.'

'There is nothing wrong.' A vision of a golden future unscrolled itself before me. Edgar and I would be brothers – we would ride through this week side-by-side talking of you. He would tell me all that you had done in my absence, I would tell him of my hopes for the future. At the end of the week he would carry my love back to you, and two or three years hence, when I had secured a fortune and could claim you in person, he would be our treasured friend – the perfect third in our shining communion.

'But Heathcliff – how came you to leave without a word? No one knew what had become of you!'

'I was in a hurry; I could not stop.' The image of the happy triumvirate wavered in my mind as I remembered the murderous jealousy that had fired my departure. What of your relation to this man? I had not yet laid to rest the terrible spectre of your engagement. I must determine the truth, yet I was loath to abandon the shimmering bubble of feeling in which I floated with Linton at that moment.

'You should have left word,' he said. 'Catherine was very ill.'

Catherine ill! I shuddered – you ill, who had always been so hardy, and those dreams I had – ! I forget just what I said to Linton, I suppose I sputtered some enquiry about your present health, for Edgar continued coolly:

'Catherine is better, but, I fear, susceptible to any unpleasantness still. Doctor Kenneth has cautioned her friends not to speak of you.'

'Of me?' I repeated stupidly. 'Not to speak of me?'

'She displays a dangerous agitation at mention of your name. It seems she thinks you abandoned the vicinity in anger, or have been murdered, or some other absurdity.

You really should have informed the family of your resolve to leave.'

The insanity of my action tumbled in upon me. How could I not have seen it before? It was criminal to have left so. But my remedy stood before me. I appealed to Linton. 'You will make all right, you will explain, you will tell her – '

'Yes,' Linton smiled, 'I will tell her everything when I return to Thrushcross Grange next week.'

At that moment I felt that anything was possible – any act of forgiveness, any prodigy of redemption, any reprieve from catastrophe. 'Thank you,' I said, 'thank you.'

At this moment the drone of Mr Are's voice swelled: 'Heathcliff! Bring Mr Linton here; we are making plans for the morrow and you are wanted.'

We joined the other group. 'Mrs Dent tells me, Heathcliff, that Linton has just such a taste in landscape as yours.'

'I am pleased to hear it,' I said, 'but I must confess myself puzzled; I had not known I had acquired a reputation for a particular taste.'

'Oh, do not be disingenuous. All around here know of your thirst for the sublime,' – here Mr Are's eyes twinkled – 'your affinity for desolate, isolated nooks to which you can retire to think your lofty thoughts and read your Ossian – '

'Ah, Ossian,' murmured Edgar. ' "Who comes so dark from the ocean's roar, like autumn's shadowy cloud?" '

Edgar was looking at me quizzically, so I responded, ' "Death is trembling in his hand! His eyes are flames of fire," ' to prove I knew the tag.

Mr Are continued: ' – and though we have no wave-swept shores hereabouts, or secret fairy caves, we do have some authentic antiquities. Tomorrow you must eschew the habitual solitude of your rides, Heathcliff, and escort Mr Linton to one of your haunts.'

'And not only Edgar!' said Mrs Dent.

'I suppose we could go to the abbey,' I said.

'The abbey!' she exclaimed.

'Yes,' said Mr Are. 'It was sacked in the days of Henry, and is not an hour's easy drive from here. It is wild enough to satisfy the most exacting of gothic enthusiasts!'

'How agreeable! Just the thing!' Mrs Dent clapped her hands.

'Yes, it is quite intact,' I put in, 'though given over to owls and bats these days. You can still see implements of torture in the dungeon, perhaps used by Henry's men to persuade popish monks to English orthodoxy, perhaps by the monks themselves to mortify the flesh and thus lighten their souls for heaven – a spiked wheel, an iron rack – '

'Oh!' said Mrs Dent. 'It is too wonderful! You and Edgar shall not keep these pleasures to yourselves! We shall accompany you, especially to the dungeon. It will be the perfect object of an excursion.'

'The very thing,' I said, 'Linton and I will ride vanguard.'

Mr Are nodded approval. 'I shall give Linton Beelzebub to mount, and the two of you will be our squires, scouting any spectral monks Henry might have left behind.'

'When we reach the castle we will dispatch them,' I said. 'Smite them with bell, book, and candle!' laughed Linton.

'That's the spirit,' said Colonel Dent.

'If the weather holds we'll go tomorrow,' said Mr Are. 'I will ask Mrs Fairfax to organize refreshments. But now, come with me. I have a shorter excursion to propose. The gardener has bred a new strain of rosebush in the arbour; I would like your opinion.'

We had not been in the arbour above five minutes when John came to inform us of the Ingrams' arrival. Mr Are and I hurried ahead; the others, awaiting a gardener sent for clippers, lingered over the roses. Directly we turned the corner down the alley of trees to the house, Mr Are jigged a delighted caper and clapped my back.

'Well, Heathcliff,' he said, 'you have succeeded so far.

Our guests like you well. Mrs Dent compliments your *beaux yeux noirs* by the spark in her blue ones when she looks at you. The colonel thinks you are a manly spirit, quite the thing for firming up young Linton.'

'I am very glad to have been approved.'

'And young Linton himself is behaving in really an extraordinary manner – flushing red and white, laughing, displaying positive animation – quite another person from the reserved young man I remember. You and he are already thick as thieves. Have you cast a spell on him?'

'I simply greeted him as you taught me.'

'Hmmm . . . There is more to it; your eye has that singularly opaque cast that signals hold! to those who would trespass its secrets. But we will speak of it later; here are the Ingrams.'

We entered the hall, and my light-dazzled vision had at first some difficulty in making out the details of the scene. Then the glare evened and I saw Mr Are greeting a tall, haughty-looking raven-haired woman, who by her age must be the dowager Lady Ingram. There was a young man lying half-prone on a bench fanning himself with his hat; young Lord Ingram, thought to have been hot on the trail of London pleasures, had after all arrived home in time to chase whatever rustic game he might start here.

That left the two daughters to distinguish one from the other. From both I received the impression of beauty, certainly – but in one, the taller and more striking of the two, that beauty partook of hauteur, force, control – a surface perfection that – it struck me as her dark eyes flicked over my form – distilled a deadly venom within, unseen but ready.

This notion was perversely inappropriate as applied to a fresh young woman whose only offence was a superfluity of white ribbons fluttering on her girlish straw hat, so I squelched it well enough, and went through the ceremony of homage to the honourable Miss Blanche Ingram, the charming object of my prejudice, with no positive *faux pas* – but I own I was glad when I heard a crunch on the path outside and our other guests came in, laden with roses. The Dents had long known the Ingrams, but Edgar had not, and must needs be introduced:

Linton, Apollo-like, holding a sheaf of white roses, stands in a strong beam of sunshine issuing from the fanlight over the door. Then, as if in a pantomime (I had entered into that trancelike state that sometimes overtakes me in a crowd, where sounds blur and sights stretch in time), Miss Ingram steps into the golden shaft and extends her proud hand. Linton takes it and bows (a curl of his haloed hair, displaced by the motion, falls forward to brush her arm), then presents her with the roses.

A tableau sure to charm any viewer, you would say, but it had for me the reverse effect: the moment I saw Edgar Linton and Blanche Ingram together, united in their beauty, wealth, and assurance – all charm was suddenly and decisively drained from them, from the gay chatter of the group, from the brilliant sunlight reflected and re-reflected in the mirrors. I was left with a residue of dread – which gathered itself most thickly around Linton.

If he had been covered so far in my sight by a magic lantern slide of you, a palimpsest that read friendship into his image, and imbued this world with a promise of happiness – if he had been so illumined, I say – now someone had snuffed the lantern out. Your face extinguished, the residuum was cold and hostile. Linton was godlike still in his fair perfection, but this god was of the vengeful variety. If he condescended to extend his hand to me it would be to smite, not to bless.

I now saw my dreams of brotherhood for what they were – stupid, vain longings born of loneliness. The fact that only one of us could marry Catherine Earnshaw divided Edgar Linton and me, but something further did too: the great gulf between our births, our temperaments, our essences. His cordiality was condescension, perhaps only a polite cover to active malice. I must be on my guard.

During this episode John had come in with a letter for his master; having read it Mr Are called me aside to request that I be his emissary to the lawyer in Millcote – a matter of business suddenly come up and necessary to settle this day. I accepted the commission with such alacrity that he seemed almost displeased; only promises of the speediest possible execution of my errand reassured him. But in fact I took my time; this latest violent shift in my apprehension of the world had depressed and discomposed me; the few hours the ride gave me to regain my equanimity were a distinct gift. I did not return until after tea, at the hour when the company would cluster in the drawing room for their mutual entertainment.

As I walked past the thorn thicket, which had gathered a deeper spectrum of dusk to itself than the rest of the tender summer evening, I heard snatches of scales and arpeggios played on the pianoforte quite brilliantly, beyond Mr Are's forceful but flawed execution. Approaching the house I saw a hazy golden glow dissolving into the shrubs outside the drawing room windows – the twenty-four tapers on the crystal chandelier must have been lit for the evening. The nearest casement was opened outward; the filmy curtains, pulled rhythmically in and out of the room by the breeze, seemed to beckon me thither. The music stopped; there was a burst of laughter; I caught a whiff of hot tallow; instead of entering the house I swerved from the path, edged among the bushes, and looked in the window.

The curtain caught against my face, then, brushing past it, unveiled the scene inside.

The floor was a little elevated above the ground where I stood; perhaps it was that, or the brilliant illumination of the chandelier, that lent the figures I saw the aura of painted gods moving on a stage. There were two groupings in the room (neither included Edgar Linton), one at a card table in the back, the other, nearer me, around the piano. Miss Blanche Ingram sat at the instrument.

She was laughing up at Mr Are in a pose that displayed to best advantage the flash of her teeth and the milkiness of her uncovered shoulders. Mr Are stood with his head tilted to one side, the lines of his face drawn together in humorous quizzicality – a pose he often held for a few seconds after having delivered himself of a witticism. The shrug that always completed the gesture now drew another ripple of laughter from his companions.

'But he is *your* nephew, so we expect some manifestation of despotism,' said Miss Ingram. 'Only *he* confines his rule to the equine race, while you wreak your will on your own. One's only suspense with you is in conjecturing the direction and nature of the next imperial order.'

'There are many I crave to impose on so lovely a subject,' said Mr Are, 'but for the present I will limit myself to only one.'

'And what would that be, sire?' Miss Ingram slightly inclined her jet-massed head. The single rose that crowned it looked like sculpted marble.

'That you will play this new music I've had sent from Vienna – there is an aria I would try, and I lack an accompanist.'

'Ah – it is Mozart – this edict, at least, is a benign one. I shall obey it with pleasure.' And she leafed through the pages, testing out difficult passages.

Here Colonel Dent leaned forward and said something to Mr Are, but I was prevented from hearing his first words by a sudden gust that ripped through the leaves of the bushes, sucked the curtains into the room, and caused the candelabra on the piano to flare violently. Then it died down: ' – beyond anything,' the colonel was saying. 'Perhaps your young blade would come over one day and take a look at Cromwell. The demned thing shies if you so much as sneeze at him.'

'Yes, then Mr Heathcliff could effect a miraculous cure by riding the beast past a series of dummy handkerchiefs,' said Miss Ingram, not turning her head from the music.

'What! Do you scoff at my nephew's superequine powers?' exclaimed Mr Are in mock astonishment.

'I do not – there is nothing wrong with your nephew or his powers, but that horse is a brute and should be put down. I speak from experience – he threw me when I was here a winter ago. Nothing and no one could have changed him that much.'

'I wouldn't have believed it myself, but I've seen the horse,' put in Colonel Dent. 'Gentle as a baby now. The boy's a wizard. It beats everything – using a dummy to cure woman-shyness – perhaps I should set one on my nephew!'

Here the colonel alarmed me a little by looking, it seemed, through the window directly at me. I started and drew back, but a voice immediately within the room (Edgar must have been sitting on a chair against the wall) spoke:

'Uncle, you have no cause to say such things!'

'Yes, yes, I heard about your liking for that pretty neighbourhood lass from your poor mother; she had taken quite a fancy to the gel herself. But that's as may be – you're here now, and there's no reason for you to go moping around in company. Why, you would never have found me at your age sitting alone by the window when there were pretty young ladies in the room. Fie, Edgar, fie!'

Perhaps to turn the conversation from himself, Edgar addressed Mr Are: 'Sir, Mr Heathcliff's skill with animals is remarkable. He must have been brought up on an estate where horsemanship was prized. Is your brother-in-law a horse-fancier?'

'Yes, Heathcliff was raised in the country, but I must tell you that I call him "nephew" from custom and affection only. He is the son of a cousin.'

Edgar rose (the back of his head materializing within inches of my eyes) and walked to the piano. He looked graver, more self-possessed than he had in the afternoon. 'What side of the family would that be, sir?' he asked in a bland tone.

'That would be the northern side, by the distaff side,

out of the side of no consequence,' answered Mr Are smartly.

'Are you ready, Miss Ingram?'

For reply she began cascading through the introduction. The card players lowered their cards and raised their heads, the colonel subsided into a chair with a look of resignation on his face, Edgar drew near enough to see the music, and Mr Are, taking breath, sang.

He had a fine baritone voice; both he and Miss Ingram were spirited performers; the sprightly aria suited their talents. After a minute even the colonel listened with pleasure, nodding his little wig in measure with the music. And judging by the increased animation of Linton's face, his spirits gradually lifted, so much so that when the score called for a tenor counterpoint, he unhesitatingly rendered it, and rendered it beautifully. His throat throbbed like a bird's; his sweet note floated easily over the rich flow of the baritone line and the turnings of the accompaniment.

As I watched from my hiding place in the bushes, my brain buzzed with new despondency. The figures within – the musicians, their audience – cauterized my eye with their glitter. They existed in a separate realm from earthbound spirits like myself. I could, with concentration, copy their gestures, the balanced set of their shoulders, even the forms of their conversation; but their easy grace? their effortless brilliance? I had been taught how to make the transition from drawing room to dining room, how to hand a lady out of a coach. I had memorized a hundred compliments with which to sweeten conversation. But no matter how much I drilled, how many lines I conned, I would always be imprisoned by my role; I could never, as one bred in it, live through it. How could I have dreamt that Edgar Linton would accept me as an equal, embrace me as a brother? I carried a nimbus on my back: the hulking outline of the real Heathcliff, shoulders bent to the plough, head lowered against blows.

'Why are you outside looking in when you should be inside amongst 'em?'

It was John's voice, whispered low behind me. I had been so intent I had not heard him creep up. Angry that he had caught me spying, I raised my fist, but his face when I saw it stayed me. He waited for an answer.

'Perhaps I have found my proper place.'

'Nay, here is the place for bats and moles and the likes of me, in shadow. Your place is in the light with the gentry. You're finer than any with your brave gold lace. Yon twig of a Linton looks a wisp of a boy beside you.'

Something in me must have thawed. At any rate, perhaps from the need to hear John contradict it, I said, 'You mistake the suit for the man. My gaudies may show finer than Linton's grey silk, but his manners are real gold, mine but fairy gilt, likely to crack and scatter at the first shock. Sure as I enter that room I will make some blunder and lose the wager.'

'Never think it!' John spat contemptuously.

I laughed bitterly. 'Would that you were right. But you know not how to judge.'

'I know more than you think. I promised you from the first that I would keep my eye on you, and so I have done. I've seen the paces master has put you through, and I've heard his threats. Now Master Edward has his own way of doing things, and I don't fault him, but sometimes he goes too far, if I do say.' John shook his head. 'I've been thinking on it this week past. He's in such a sweat to pump you up to the mark, he makes you overshoot it. Even your first week here you spoke as well as many a great squire hereabouts, and had as much book-learning too, I'll warrant. And as for manners – well – you should have seen the colonel laying into his squab tonight with both elbows square on the table and grease dripping down from chin to waistcoat. We did laugh in kitchen, and said how you had them beat.'

I looked at him in astonishment. The servants taking my part? He continued:

'And if it's missing Master's grand trip that's worrying you, put it out of your mind. He would no more leave you here than he would stay home himself. The trip was planned for you all along – he's been writing about it to his foreign friends for months. But he must needs play out his game.'

'Why do you tell me this?'

'I see how you take it all too hard. It's a shame to let a body suffer when everyone else can see plain there's naught amiss.'

During the latter part of our conversation we had forgotten the close proximity of the singers. During a pause in the music Linton must have heard the sound of our voices, for suddenly he walked to the window. I quickly pulled John into the shadow of the bushes. I held my breath. Linton, his handsome countenance flushed, leaned out and peered one way, then the other, but could see nothing (it was quite dark now). On impulse I stepped forward into the light. He jumped back. My eyes caught his. His features convulsed in a curious amalgam of amusement and contempt; he withdrew, not to rejoin the singers, but, smiling faintly, to sit beside his uncle.

'There's no love lost between the two of you,' whispered John beside me.

'We are fated to be enemies,' I replied. I fear I trembled. My last layer of self-deception was removed. Linton might smile in company, but the mask was false. In fact he despised me – merely despised, for of such an intense emotion as hatred I was not worthy. Why should he hate what could not affect him? He was secure in what he had – wealth, position, beauty, and, as he thought, your favour. Perhaps he imagined that I had not the power to wrest away any of his prizes. I must make him see his mistake.

'Put him out of your mind,' said John. 'He's a poor snail, not worth crushing; he'll stay in his shell.'

'He had better,' I said between gritted teeth. And I paused no longer, but entered the house.

The musicians finished their performance with a flourish just as I walked through the doors; I joined in the applause. But Miss Ingram, seeing me, rose and turned the clapping in my direction. On my bowing a question to her, she said:

'You have occupied the centre of our stage in your absence, Mr Heathcliff, and must now pay the penalty of celebrity.'

I crossed the room and took her hand. 'Any penalty paid to Miss Ingram swiftly becomes a reward, if she exacts it in person. I am your servant, in this and all else.'

'Very pretty,' said Miss Ingram. 'But you are no one's servant. As I have been telling Mr Are, you are like him in your ambition to become the despot of all, man and horse alike.'

'Ah, Uncle, you have brought out that old tale,' I said.

'You have done wonders with that animal, sir,' rumbled the colonel. 'Wonders.'

'I thank you, but not at all,' I protested. 'I merely applied firmness and consistency of behaviour to the poor brute. Such a system will work at any time, for anyone.'

'Well, I would take it as a great favour if you would ride over one day and educate my groom to your system,' said Colonel Dent. 'It is a thing he sadly lacks.'

'I should be delighted,' I answered. 'Have you had trouble in your stable?' The colonel started to reply, but Miss Ingram, probably fearing that the conversation might descend wholly to the level of the farrier, broke in:

'No, it will not do, Mr Heathcliff, I do not accept it. It was not your system that transformed the horse, but rather your force of character. You have the unmistakable air of one who delights in command.'

I smiled. 'Were command my ambition, horse-training would give me a rather limited range for realizing it.'

'Oh, but that is merely the surface, the cover for some more sweeping activity. You are very deep altogether. For instance, Mr Are would have us believe that you were absent to discharge a commission for him; I think you were bent on another errand entirely. I think you are really the notorious Dick Turpin, the highwayman, resurrected from hanging. You have held up two stages in the hours you have been gone, and have deposited the jewels and strong-boxes in the apartment your uncle says you insist on locating in the stables.'

Lady Ingram leaned forward. 'Blanche, my own, you go too far with your raillery,' she remonstrated. 'Mr Heathcliff does not know you and will misunderstand. He will resent your freedom.'

Miss Ingram dismissed her mother's remark with a wave of the fan she had taken up. 'No, Mother, Mr Heathcliff understands me very well.'

'How could I resent what is but the plain truth, my lady?' I said, smiling. 'Miss Ingram has all unknowingly hit the nail on the head.' I glanced at Linton. 'I *am* a highwayman by profession, I have taken three diamond necklaces at knife point this evening, and perhaps I shall take more before I sleep. You ladies had best lock your bedroom doors tonight.'

At this Mrs Dent and Miss Mary Ingram smiled and giggled, Edgar Linton looked askance, Lady Ingram raised her neck up to its marble fullness and sneered, but I could see she was not displeased.

'There!' she said to her daughter. 'You have been matched!'

'Yes,' I continued, 'I am a merciless and desperate fellow. If anyone, woman or man, has something I want, he had better give it to me straightaway with a smile. Otherwise, well – !' and I mockingly drew my forefinger across my throat. Out of the corner of my eye I saw Linton grimace. It seemed he was, as I had hoped, reading my speech in light of certain passages from our joint youth.

'I say,' drawled Lord Ingram, raising himself from the sofa upon which he had hitherto been reclining, 'Dick Turpin was the toast of society in his day. We are in better company than we knew.'

Here Linton, biting his lip, rose also, saying he was tired and would go to bed early. His uncle protested, swearing that what he needed was not sleep but merriment, and suggested a round of charades. Lady Ingram said it was too late for that. Someone said cards – 'Yes! – whist! A whist tournament!' and so it fell out. We sat to cards the rest of the evening.

Miss Ingram, her brother, Mrs Dent, and myself made up the winning table. I continued my impersonation of a highwayman, and Lord Ingram (who, it developed, was only a few years older than I) set himself up as Jonathan Wild, a rival member of the brotherhood of the open road, and we kept the ladies in high good humour all evening with mock attempts on their property and honour. The other table was just as lively: Mr Are flirted outrageously with the younger Miss Ingram (less brilliant but better-natured than her sister), and the colonel was merciless both in his teasing of Ingram mother and daughter and in his sarcasms towards his nephew, who kept company with his fatigue and a book in a corner.

Miss Ingram was not one likely to let such a slight as Linton's apparent indifference to her charms pass unpunished; she commissioned Dick Turpin to steal the book; it was apparently a great treasure, since Linton valued it above the whole of his acquaintance. On Turpin's regretfully refusing – he dealt only in specie, not in scrip – she pressed Jonathan Wild into service. He proved more amenable, finally coming up behind Linton's chair with a fruit knife and commanding him to stand and deliver. The joke backfired, however; Linton handed the volume to Ingram with a smile, saying he was happy to relinquish even what he prized very highly to one who had the superior claim of an urgent and obvious need for it. Upon inspecting the spine of his prize, Ingram blushed, then laughed, 'Touche!' It was my well-worn copy of Lord Chesterfield.

The evening ended with Mrs Dent reminding everyone to rise early next morning for our excursion to the ruined abbey, and Colonel Dent promising us a fine day for it.

And what of the reactions of polite society to my secret debut? Edgar Linton answered my good night with a silent bow, but Lord Ingram shook my hand and pronounced me a fine fellow, his elder sister passed me the rose from her hair under cover of her fan, and Mr Are thumped me heartily on the back as I left for the stables. On my own reflections as I lay in bed going over the night's doings I will not dwell – only say that they bore little resemblance to the thoughts any one of the company could have imagined me thinking, unless it were Edgar Linton.

As I read these last pages, the light on the eloquent black script had begun to flicker and fade, and I had had to hold the surface ever closer to my eyes, so close at last that it had become impossible to distinguish any one character – they became instead grey blurs, through which I thought I began to discern a powerful dark shape, a clouded face, a rough hand reaching out to lay strokes on the other side of the paper –

The startled realization that I was entering a kind of waking dream jolted me to the effort of wrenching my eyes from the manuscript. The lamp was dimming; I must trim the wick. I extricated myself from my bundle of blankets, and was instantly rendered fully alert by the extreme chill of the air, so intense as to stiffen the exposed skin of my face and hands in the few seconds it took to adjust the flame.

I quickly reassumed my cocoon, in all my movements careful not to touch anything that might jar Mr Lockwood, since he was still sunk deep in slumber. I positioned the manuscript on my lap. But though the yellow paper's glow attracted me as if it had the power to warm, I did not immediately draw near. I had already been burnt with unwelcome knowledge.

Now, against reason, I had reversed my former conclusion. I could no longer deny it: this Heathcliff and Emily's Heathcliff were, inexplicably, identical. I was in a position to judge: even if I had never actually laid eyes on Emily's friend, I felt I knew him intimately. Heathcliff had been the only person outside the immediate family circle whose company my sister enjoyed, so naturally he had been the object of our intense interest. But always at one remove – we were never allowed to meet or even see him. If Anne and I thought it odd that the daughter of the Curate of Haworth should walk on the moors with a stableboy, or eccentric that she should jealously maintain the exclusivity of her acquaintance with him, then we kept our mouths shut about it, for she would go her own way in this as in everything else.

But though we said nothing to her, we thought a great deal, and certainly discussed *en tête-à-tête* – of course, the whole subject was kept secret from Father and Aunt – all she told us about her strange companion. I had heard from Emily's lips, and then reviewed with Anne, accounts of incidents at Wuthering Heights, descriptions of persons, even certain phrases, that had now, *mirabile dictu*, turned up verbatim in reading matter passed me by a stranger. It was the same man.

Reader, you might suspect me to have been the victim of an elaborate hoax, and not on my sister's part. You might reasonably think I should have risen and waked its sleepy perpetrator with cries of denunciation. But I did not; nor did I for an instant suspect Mr Lockwood of being or knowing a jot other than precisely what he had represented. Nor would you, had you experienced first-hand the extreme respectability of that gentleman.

No, the answer to the mystery lay with Emily; but, oddly, it was not this that disturbed me now, and kept me from immediately returning to my reading. I had passed beyond that; my frame quivered with indignation from another cause.

What kind of monster was this Mrs Dean, to have withheld Heathcliff's letter from Cathy? Surely, if she had delivered it, the two lovers, parted so long, would have joyously married. Instead, another marriage, one based on deceit and trickery, had been accomplished. How could this woman have taken it upon herself to pervert fate, and then expect forgiveness for it! It was insufferable! Unbearable!

It *was* unbearable that such intensity of feeling as Heathcliff's should go unrewarded, should come to nothing. He had loved his Cathy so constantly, with such force, had striven so mightily! Surely a love of such desperate concentration would create a volition of its own, would mysteriously but inexorably bend fate into a channel that must bring the two longing hearts together at last. I could not believe otherwise, even against the contradiction of history.

A movement from the bench opposite made me lower my eyes to the manuscript.

'Well, Miss Brontë,' said Mr Lockwood after stretching and consulting his pocket watch, 'I have dozed away half the night while you have been reading. What think you of my friend Heathcliff thus far?'

'I am not finished yet, but on the evidence I have gathered, I believe he has been poorly treated. He has been wronged.'

My companion leaned forward to peer at the pile in my lap.

'Ah – you are about half-way through. I would not wish to prejudice your verdict one way or another by expressing my own opinion, but another hour of reading may change your mind.'

'We shall see,' I said, privately thinking that my opinion was not of the order that could be prejudiced by any expression of *his*. 'But my present sympathy for Heathcliff has made me curious as to his fate. You say Cathy really did marry Edgar Linton, then?'

'Yes, and they lived together very happily, by Nelly's account, till Heathcliff came back again.'

'When was that?'

'About half a year after he had left the letter, and after the wedding.'

'How did he act at the first meeting? Was he angry? Anguished?'

'Undoubtedly, but reliable testimony has it that he kept any such feelings to himself; he had had six months to rend his hair and gnash his teeth in private, after all.'

I disapproved of the jocularity of Mr Lockwood's tone, and let my next words show it: 'If that is so, he behaved with generous courtesy toward those who had wronged him.'

'So he did, for a while.'

'And then?'

'Then he began courting Miss Linton, Edgar's sister.'

'He had a right to love another, since his first love had married.'

'Except that he professedly did not love Miss Linton, but retained his passion for Cathy in all its original force. And, she returned it, at the last, even though both were married to others.'

This silenced me for a moment. Finally I said, ' "At the last." You mean just before Cathy died?'

'Yes, and – ' he cleared his throat ' – afterwards, as well. I have told you something of my experience there. They say she haunted him for twenty years after her death, till finally she persuaded him to join her in the grave.' He shivered and pulled the blankets closer around him. 'The house was boarded up soon after Heathcliff died; but they say it is not empty. They say it is inhabited, by them.'

This turn of the conversation was quickly making me uncomfortable, so I switched it to more mundane matters. 'I had thought that Mrs Dean still lived there, with her mistress, and that was where you were going.'

'No, the family lives at Thrushcross Grange, the old Linton estate. It came to Nelly's present mistress, the daughter of Catherine and Edgar, after the elder generation had died.'

'Oh – so Cathy's daughter is living.'

'Yes, I will see her tomorrow, or rather today, after so many years. It is odd – she must be altered, she is nearly as old as I am, yet I cannot help picturing her as I last saw her, with the evening glow on the moors lighting her golden hair. Ah! She was exquisite, with the most extraordinary dark eyes – '

Mr Lockwood trailed off and seemed to stare into the

far distance. So tender had been his voice during the last speech, and so wistful his gaze, that I could not help suspecting another motive for his trip, making it a happier pilgrimage than one to a death bed.

Gradually Mr Lockwood's eyes, made heavy by the vibrations of the train, flickered shut, and I was left to my own thoughts. I lifted a corner of the blind and peered outside. The snow continued, yet the train roared through the darkness on its predestined course.

Though the safety and comfort of train travel increase prodigiously with each year, and the noise, dirt, and danger of even a decade ago are gone forever, still I could not be insensible of the extraordinary *unnaturalness* of this folding of time and space – this fragile capsule coughing and rumbling headlong against its future through the darkness, plunging in and out of tunnels, through storm and cloud, heedless of all.

To let one's mind dwell on it was to summon terror. Though the glow Heathcliff's letter cast through the small chamber now seemed less warming than sepulchral, I sought refuge there.

9

I woke knowing that if I did nothing else on this day, I must at least determine if there were really any formal attachment between Edgar Linton and you. If such an attachment existed, I must give him reason to break it. How exactly I would do this I had not thought out, but this morning I was charged with a grim confidence that I would find some way or other to carry my objective. I walked to the house, therefore, resolved to bide my time quietly and take my chance when it came.

The weather was the chief, the only object of interest amongst those gathered in the drawing room. Despite Colonel Dent's optimism of the night before, the morning had dawned doubtful. The pleasant winds of yesterday had blown in today's low, chill clouds and made of the sun a questionable bright spot behind them, though Mrs Dent swore she could feel the heat of it, and that the clouds would burn off by noon.

'I am sure you are mistaken,' said Lady Ingram. 'These are the sort of lowering clouds that always bring wet weather, and carry fevers too. For my part I would never venture my health in it for mere *pleasure*, though others may dare.'

Then the colonel, for whom meteorology was something of a hobby-horse, said he would go out and settle the question by reading the signs. The ladies watched out the window in suspense as he limped back and forth twice under the trees. He licked his finger, held it skyward for a few seconds, and walked back to the house.

'It will rain,' he pronounced to the anxious faces turned towards him. 'You must give over your excursion.'

Lady Ingram smiled and nodded sagely, but the colonel's wife clasped her hands to her breast.

'Oh, Harold!' she wailed. 'Surely not! Pray reconsider!'

'My dear, the signs are as clear as I ever saw them; I cannot alter the laws of nature to please you!'

'But this weather is very like that on my birthday, when the signs said it would storm, and so we put off till the morrow my birthday excursion to the Norman dungeons. But it did not rain at all; in the afternoon it turned sunny; perfect haying weather, everyone said; however the next day I took a fever, and what with one thing and another I did not see the dungeons till autumn.'

'You see!' said Lady Ingram with the air of a debater whose point has been proved. 'There is so much sickness about! I am sure I would not risk my own health, or that of my girls, for any such excursion.'

'Speak for yourself, Mama!' said Miss Blanche Ingram, who had just flourished down the stairs in her riding habit and great plumed bonnet. 'I don't care whether it rains or no, I am going abroad today!'

'But my darling! If you should take a chill! Think of me, or if you will not, only think of what your poor father would say if he were alive.'

'Poor Father would say what he always said, which was precisely nothing!' and she stared challengingly at her mother.

'Surely it will turn fine soon,' murmured Mrs Dent, looking from one fierce countenance to the other.

'No, Aunt, I am afraid you will be disappointed,' said Edgar Linton, coming in the door from outside. He avoided looking at me. 'I have just been for a stroll, and I distinctly felt a shower of rain.' He held out the sleeve of his jacket for his aunt's inspection. Blanche Ingram came over and fingered it.

'Pooh!' said she, flipping it away. 'That is nothing. How could you notice a little sprinkle like that?'

'It was not a *little* sprinkle,' said Edgar indignantly. 'My sleeve is quite wet. I could wring it out.'

'Nonsense!' Blanche exclaimed with spirit as Edgar

flushed. 'I could *cry* a greater shower than that! You are a namby-pamby if you let such a trifle deter you.'

'Edgar does take cold easily,' said Mrs Dent. 'Perhaps you should stop at home, dear; do not overtax yourself.'

'Letitia, you will ruin that boy with your babying of him,' rumbled the colonel. 'If the weather turns fine, he must go with the rest. But – ' he folded his arms and glared, ' – it will NOT turn fine!'

After this there was nothing to do but look out the windows in silence till Lord Ingram and his younger sister came down the stairs, her chattering and him yawning. They stopped short when they saw the long faces assembled.

'Everyone is moping because Mama has taken a whim that we must all stop at home,' said Blanche.

'My love, blame no whim of mine. It rains!' pronounced Lady Ingram.

'Then let us raise thanks to a merciful providence for sparing us a day of endless tedium and pointless exertion!' exclaimed Lord Ingram, flinging himself into the sofa of which Linton had taken possession of one corner. 'I have a shocking headache.'

Miss Ingram's nostrils flared and her eyes flashed. 'You two are a pair – Mr Linton with his cold and Theodore with his headache! All that is left is for Mr Heathcliff to discover he has the vapours, and must stop at home with his toes elevated. How now, Mr Heathcliff, why do you continue to stand? Pray take your place with the invalids!'

'On one condition,' I said to her, the elders having resumed their court of inquiry by the window.

'And what is that?'

'That you have undertaken to play apothecary, and bestow an anodyne.'

'It is impossible; I can only diagnose, never cure.'

'Ah – perhaps you cannot cure *them*, but you can cure *me*!'

'You *are* ill then?'

'You must know; are you not a diagnostician? Besides, having caused the disease – '

To my relief, the bursting entrance of Mr Are put the plug to this palaver, of which I had learned enough from the dancing master to spout by the hour (he actually sold textbooks on the subject!). Instantly both parties appealed to their host:

'The excursion must be postponed; a storm is brewing – '

'Surely, Mr Are, we must not be put off our pleasure by a few clouds – '

He held up his hands. 'Would that I were Doctor Johnson's Philosopher and could manage the weather,' he smiled, 'but as I am not, we shall have to wait for it to manage itself. In the meantime the servants are making all ready, and we shall leave the moment a sunbeam dares to show its face!'

'There! There!' said Blanche Ingram suddenly. 'Mama, see!' Triumphantly she turned her mother to the window, and not waiting for any reaction, took her sister's hand and tugged her out of doors.

All looked at Lady Ingram.

'The sun *does* shine,' said she at last, in such tones as wondered at its audacity in doing so.

'It is settled then,' said Mrs Dent, and clapped her hands. Mr Are began shouting orders to everyone within calling distance. We were to fetch wraps, parasols, sketching pads, etc.; the servants would bring the carriages around in fifteen minutes. Lord Ingram groaned and pulled a plush pillow over his face.

An hour later carriages, horses, guests, and servants were assembled in the circle drive. There was a flurry of shawls and hampers. Then came a crack of thunder, which all politely ignored. But in a few seconds followed such a burst of rain that no one could ignore, not even the Honourable Blanche Ingram, whose sweeping filmy plumes looked like monkeys' tails by the time she reached the hall, shuddering with chill and vexation.

Chill and vexation became the order of the afternoon.

The rain streamed down the outsides of the windows and the insides of the chimneys; in defiance of John's best efforts the fires repeatedly sputtered and went out. The company's spirits were in like case; despite a sincere wish to please itself, it remained plunged in collective gloom. Mr Are, of course, proposed entertainments, but nothing seemed to suit. Charades were too much trouble – everyone had had enough of struggling out of wet clothes to care to bother with any more costumings. A game of forfeits was begun, but as a difference of opinion between Lady Ingram and her elder daughter over the legality of a penalty made imposing it impossible, and not imposing it out of the question, the project was abandoned. The company moved on to part-singing, but this proved the doleful occasion of Lady Ingram suspecting a hoarse throat in Mr Are. For a time the spirits of the group revived over the convivial task of prescribing remedies and predicting calamities, but even these pleasures palled.

I was hard put to stifle my amusement at the spectacle: eight prime specimens of the English gentry, each wearing upwards of fifty pounds on its back and each standing, figuratively speaking, on a pleasure-island of six thousand or so a year, but unable for all their advantages to produce a smile amongst them. How you would have laughed, Cathy!

After dinner (the picnic hampers were damply opened in the conservatory), the library fires had finally dried themselves out enough to produce some heat, and gradually the company found itself in a condition to begin to be happy. Someone proposed we reproduce the entertainment of the night before: a whist tournament. This alarmed no one, and when stakes of a penny a point were proposed, pleased most.

Mr Are, I knew, was an exception. He disapproved strongly of gambling; I had often heard him declaim on its evils – how the current mania for gaming had ruined more than one family in a single night, where ten thousand pounds could change hands in a sitting of faro.

Therefore I was pretty sure that the stakes would not be raised from their present modest level.

Nonetheless I inwardly determined a limit of money beyond which I would not venture. By this time I had put by a tidy nest egg – almost all my quarterly stipend from Mr Are, combined with Hindley's golden leavings, I had invested in Millcote, according to the advice of Mr Are's bankers, so that I had in the bank at that moment about four hundred and fifty pounds – though for me a fortune, and the basis of my hopes of reunion with you, mere pocket money to any of the other players. Keeping this in mind, I resolved to limit myself to five pounds' loss, after which I could emulate Edgar Linton and, as he did now, read a book by the fire.

But as the afternoon progressed I had no need to resort to that stratagem, having in a few hours accrued in winnings more than twice my limit in losses. You will remember, whenever we would play a round game in the kitchen at the Heights, or when in the old days Hindley and I would wager on coin tosses, how Nelly said I had lucky hands, that drew winning to them. Hindley swore I'd witched the coins, and more than once thrashed me for it (though he never could resist wagering the next time just the same). Even you teased me to admit I'd marked the cards. But I never did anything of the sort – I was as astonished as you were at my repeated triumphs – only that too turned sour on me as we witnessed Hindley's degradation through wild play, and I had refused to touch a deck these past several years. Now I was pleased to see my luck returning, and continued to win moderately throughout the afternoon.

After tea Lady Ingram, disappointed by Mr Are's persistent vigour, discovered a hoarse throat in Miss Mary Ingram, and sent her upstairs to bed; Edgar Linton was recruited from the sofa to make up a fourth with the remaining sister, Lord Ingram, and me.

In this account to you his advocate, I must scruple to record that Linton's earlier defection from play had been accomplished with modest grace; he had volunteered to be the one to sit out the rubber (our numbers leaving one over), murmuring he was unwilling to do anyone the disservice of partnership, since he had such a regrettably poor head for cards. Now that he was actually to play, however, his objections took on more bite:

'I am afraid cardplaying is not a pastime I enjoy overmuch,' he said. 'Its virtues as a laudable instrument of social intercourse are lessened by the demands of the game on one's attention, and often positively damaged by those little rivalries and resentments that competition invariably produces. Besides, the practice of play sometimes leads to vice.'

'Never mind, Mr Linton,' said Miss Ingram. 'No one could believe it possible in your case; yours is far too strong a character.' Linton's *amour-propre* admitting no possibility of the satire that was really intended by this speech, he smiled and sat in Mary's chair.

In doing so his leg brushed against mine, and we both jumped back as from the touch of a red-hot poker. For a second, I suppose, neither of us hid the revulsion he felt; Linton, at least, looked his vividly, but then quickly dropped a mask of civility over the truer expression and murmured, 'I beg your pardon.'

Lord Ingram's attention being engaged in calling his servant for a new deck of cards, he missed the incident, but Blanche Ingram caught it, and looked back and forth between us. I tried to appear bland as milk (which was Edgar Linton's habitual expression anyway); however it was, Miss Ingram found something in our faces to satisfy her and did not then pursue the matter.

The new cards arrived; we sat to play. At first Miss Ingram seemed bent on running the conversation on the lines of the previous night's, and declared that if Mr Heathcliff, with his mysterious savagery, was Dick Turpin, and her brother Tedo with his naughtiness was Jonathan Wild, then Mr Linton, who made such a perfect picture of gentlemanliness and morality *on the outside*, was surely Beau Nash. The Beau had been a model of propriety – THE model of propriety – at Bath, and had been so very strict about the limits of gambling & etc – yet everyone knew that he had founded his fortune by robbing stages in a mask, and had regularly fed his hungry pocket by the same means, even after his reputation as an arbiter of gentility had spread throughout England. So Mr Linton need not think he was fooling anyone with his refined manner; we all knew he could shout 'stand and deliver' with the best of them.

'If I had been the Beau,' said Linton, 'no matter how proper on the one hand and avaricious on the other, I surely would have known what to do when presented with this puzzling array of cards! For I must confess myself absolutely at a loss as to how to proceed.'

'Heigh-ho, Mr Nash, but that is the cream of your cleverness!' exclaimed Miss Ingram. 'Naturally the Beau would be a master of deception, able to feign knowledge where none existed, and equally able to produce a very creditable aspect of ignorance to cover wicked intelligence!'

Linton shook his head. 'Again you flatter me far beyond my deserts, Miss Ingram. I have little power of dissimulation; the outward man, whatever his merits or lack of them, must satisfy, for he is the mirror of the inward; I can only marvel at the prodigies of deceit some can accomplish.' And here he shot me a cold glance.

Lord Ingram, as Linton's partner, now bent over his shoulder and explained to him the rudiments of the game; my fair partner, finding her sport gone in that quarter, turned to me instead.

'Well, Mr Turpin, and what spoils of gold and silver did *you* take last night?'

'None of gold and silver, but something infinitely more precious; gold and silver I would spend, but this prize I will keep forever; it is beyond price.'

'And hyperbole makes your riddle beyond guessing. What is this treasure?'

'A rose.' (Truly without price – I had thrown it out the window two minutes after it was handed me.)

She smiled. 'A rose? How can a rose be priceless?'

'When it takes its value from the hand of the giver.'

'Is this, then, the hand of a Midas?' and Miss Ingram stretched her rather large member across the table.

I took it up and kissed the air above it. 'No, it has a stronger magic than King Midas's – it is more like the bow of Cupid in its fatal effect.'

Miss Ingram drew her hand away (but not before giving mine a faint squeeze) and tapped my arm with her fan. 'You are bold, sir; those who are pierced by Cupid's darts often bleed to death!'

'I will risk it; for one who is so beautiful must also be kind; you would not be cruel enough to allow such an accident!'

Lord Ingram, catching the end of this as he resumed his seat and redealt the first hand, said, 'Do not depend upon it. Blanche is cruel enough for anything. She skewers her suitors on long pins just like she used to spiders, so she could rip off their legs at her leisure.'

'Pooh-pooh!' exclaimed his sister. 'Shall we all bring in tales from the nursery then? Shall I tell how you used to tie Mary's wrists to the bedpost with your suspenders and beat her with your toy whip?'

'Since you have just told, I need hardly bother to give permission. However, as I recall the incident, though the suspenders may have been mine, the whip was yours, and it was you who actually wielded it.'

'Come,' said Blanche, 'stop your naughty lies. You are making Mr Linton blush. Mr Linton, would you treat your sister thus?'

Edgar hoped no true brother would treat his sister in the way described.

Miss Ingram threw a grimace at Lord Ingram and continued, 'What age is Miss Linton?'

'Isabella is sixteen, two years younger than myself.' Miss Ingram supposed she was very beautiful.

'She is generally much admired.'

'She has many suitors then.'

'No – she is still very young, and besides our neighbourhood is extremely isolated and we have always led a very retired life; and further, our parents died last year and we are barely out of mourning.'

I started a bit at hearing this, but now the consistent sombreness of Linton's garb was explained; as was perhaps his late lowness of spirits (though I hoped I had made my contribution there too).

We murmured our condolences and played a round in silence.

'Well,' said Blanche, taking a trick, 'considering the isolation in your neighbourhood, Mr Linton, I suppose there are no other young ladies worthy of admiration. I suppose they are all sad rustics, below your company.'

'In fact,' returned Linton warmly, 'there is one who could claim her place at the head of any company, who I admire – I mean, who everyone admires – ' He looked at me in confusion.

'Oho, Blanche, you have hit a tender spot!' cried Lord Ingram. Then, when Linton remained silent, he half-whispered to his sister: 'Can't you ever leave anything well enough alone?'

'Do shut up, Tedo, I'm simply being civil. Mr Linton knows I take a friendly interest in him, and that I meant nothing amiss with my question, don't you, Mr Linton?'

'Oh, yes, certainly – '

'Well, then, who is she? What is her name?' Here Lord Ingram threw up his hands in mock horror of his sister's audacity, but she pressed on: 'And when may we congratulate you?'

Linton attempted to take a detached and superior tone: 'Oh, I meant to imply no particular connection between the lady and myself. We are acquaintances merely.'

'Fie, Mr Linton, that is a shocking fib! We had it from your uncle last night that there *was* a particular connection, to a pretty neighbourhood girl – a liking, he said – and that your mother had approved.'

'Well,' said Linton petulantly, 'what if it is true? I suppose no one would contest my right to like whom I please!'

'Take it easy, old man!' said Theodore Ingram. 'Of

course no one would dream of it. Blanche *will* tease; no one has ever succeeded in stopping her, so you might as well decide to notice it as little as possible. Just ignore her; that's best all around.'

'Tedo, you are absurd,' said Blanche. 'I am sorry, Mr Linton. I was wrong to press my question. It was impertinent. I think I now understand your need for discretion.'

There was a pause before Linton spoke: 'Thank you, Miss Ingram, but I would not have you misapprehend the situation. The relation between the young lady and myself is honourable; there is no need for discretion; nothing is hidden.'

Miss Ingram looked at him in expectant silence. Then: 'Except her name . . .' she trailed off.

Edgar glanced at me, then raised his chin defiantly. 'It is Catherine Earnshaw.'

'She lives near you?'

'Yes, her family are substantial landowners, the oldest in the district.'

'And your attachment is of long standing?'

'She and my sister have been friendly for years now.'

'And you have made a third in the friendship.'

'Yes.'

'But there is no engagement.'

Linton again turned away from my eyes. 'No.'

Miss Ingram nodded wisely. 'But it is plain you wish that there were . . . ?'

At that interesting moment John came in and announced that supper would be ready in ten minutes.

'Just time for a cigar!' Mr Are exclaimed. We put down our cards; the ladies hurried off to make adjustments in their toilet; the elder gentlemen and Lord Ingram went to walk and smoke on the loggia; suddenly Edgar Linton and I found ourselves alone.

When he looked about him and saw what had happened he rose hastily from his armchair to leave the room and my presence, but I reached out and jabbed his shoulder hard enough to topple him back in his cushions.

'A word, sir, *if* you please,' I said.

Edgar tried to stand again but I shoved the table hard up against the arms of his chair, so as to make him a prisoner of it.

'I shall call out for help!' Edgar's voice climbed hysterically.

'No, you won't,' I replied.

'I am not speaking to you!'

'And I am not touching you – yet,' I said in a very low voice.

His face went white, but he stifled his protests. I went on:

'Now,' I said. 'Let us get some facts straight. Do you imagine yourself engaged to marry Cathy?'

He answered, with more spirit than I would have expected from him, 'What do YOU care? You abandoned her, and never sent word.'

'You said that yesterday, sir; Lord Chesterfield would tell you that repetition is doltish. But I will overlook the fault and answer you anyhow. There is no need of words between Cathy and me.'

'Yes, that is right; it is well you think it. She has forgotten you at last, and needs no further torment.'

'You know not of what you speak. She could no more forget me than she could forget herself.'

'She *has* forgotten you!' he exclaimed.

'Forgotten, when by your own account she was made ill from worrying about me?'

'But that is past. I promise you she never mentions your name, and has not for six months or more. You are erased, you are nothing to her.'

'Never. Not for an instant am I out of her innermost thoughts, as she is ever in mine.'

'Oh, yes, your devotion to her was strikingly apparent tonight.'

I reached out to his neckcloth and twisted it in my fist. 'Explain!'

He made some attempts to wrench my hand away, but failing, probably decided that cooperation was his best hope of early escape, and ceased his struggles. I loosened my hold enough for him to answer:

'Your pursuit of Miss Blanche Ingram makes nonsense of your fine professions of love for Catherine.'

'My pursuit, as you term it, is mere polite attention, and you know it.'

'Take your hand off my cravat or I really shall call out. The servants are moving in the corridor.'

I let go my hand but still fixed him with my eye. He went on, his voice shaking with pique and fright:

'You may think your flirtation with Miss Ingram is nothing – perhaps it is, it *is* nothing to you to break a lady's heart – but Catherine will not think it so. She will find in this evening's occurrences sure confirmation of your total disregard of her, and I shall tell her.'

I would have struck him, but was stayed by the sound of voices in the hall. The gentlemen had returned from their smoke; they might enter at any moment. I contented myself by putting the whole force of my soul into my next words:

'You will tell her nothing. From this moment forward you will have nothing at all to do with her.'

'What an extraordinary speech!' Linton's voice steadied as he spoke; he was stealing courage from the proximity of his friends. 'What business have you, a bastard half-breed, with ordering me about? Of course I shall do what I like about Catherine. You have not the least power to stop me. I shall certainly marry her as soon as ever I can.'

'You will marry in hell, damn you; not in this world, while I am alive!'

He was prevented from answering, and I from saying more, by the hurried interruption of Mr Are, who, blinded to discord by his own high spirits, stuck his head in the door to bid us to supper. I rose and bowed very deeply to Linton. 'You may depend upon my promise, sir,' I said, and walked out.

They say you can never see yourself truly, not over your shoulder or in a drawing or even in a mirror. I never saw you truly till Edgar and Isabella saw you. And then I felt ashamed, as though they stared at my naked body.

But when you and I were together, it was all right again. For a long space it was all right, and we chose not to measure it, almost as it was when we had no words.

It was better without words. Where there were no words an eye could not mark its own barrier, nor the point where another eye began.

Your eyes were dark as mine still, but I began to measure their difference from mine after Edgar saw you.

The measure taught me fear. Could you exist apart from me? And if you could, who was I?

When I was with the Lintons I felt light as a feather, glad to rise above the whirlpool that claimed me when you and I locked eyes. But there was no rest floating apart from you, only giddiness and fever.

And in the night, what was it that happened?

It did not happen

It was not that

But the next day when our eyes locked, did we know? Or was it part of not knowing?

And did it happen?

And if it did, how could I float away to the Lintons? How could I escape the maelstrom?

But it did not happen

10

Linton was not present during supper (a hurried affair – the company had caught the gambling fever, and cared not to stop over such inessentials as food and drink), so I was surprised to see him, newly attired in grey satin, waiting in the library, where one large table was set up for a round game. He appeared suddenly to have regained the animation he had showed upon his arrival, but had lost since – he did not address me, certainly, but exclaimed upon seeing Mary Ingram up and about (she had revived enough to eat) and led her to a chair on the far side of the table to quiz her about her present symptoms and regale her with reminiscences of his past ones. For my part, I was glad to avoid him in company, where nothing further could be said to the point; besides, I saw that with Linton events had progressed beyond speech – I would have to discover a more surely impressive mode of discourse.

I took a place, then, as distant from Linton as possible. Miss Blanche Ingram smilingly approached, but by a bit of smart manoeuvering I was able to interpose Mr Are between us and make it seem chance – to all except Mr Are himself. He knew me so well as to instantly recognize the stratagem. Smiling slightly, he nudged me in the ribs. I, in turn, knew him well enough to be sure of the direction of his misapprehension: he imagined I played hard-to-get with Miss Ingram. Well and good, his blunder suited my growing plan. I nudged back. We began to play.

The tide of luck, which in the afternoon had run moderately in my direction, now turned in force towards Lord Ingram. He won round after round, raking in the pool. Further, this pool was not the paltry affair of the afternoon, for – wonder of wonders! – Edgar Linton insisted on raising the stakes! The heightened manner he had briefly fixed on Mary Ingram now fastened itself to the game; his eyes glittered with unhealthy excitement as he threw more gold into the centre of the table, even though most of it made its way into Ingram's pockets.

Have you seen your pretty Edgar gaming, Cathy? Do you know how the fever takes him? Have you witnessed his noble forehead sweat, his lucid blue eyes glaze over till they have all the depth of two china saucers? God grant you have; even such a low order of affection as you have felt for him could not easily survive that sight.

Mr Are, of course, opposed the increase in play, though he could not absolutely forbid it without positive rudeness. But his moderating influence, combined with Linton's ignorance of the amounts society *commonly* wagered in an evening, kept the limits low, relatively speaking. By the time the ladies retired for the night, I had won just more than I had lost, taking the games in total.

John brought in a rack of fine old port, and Mr Are poured us a nightcap, toasting the reign of Morpheus.

'But it is not yet midnight,' said Edgar Linton. 'There is time for another game!'

'What!' said Colonel Dent. 'You haven't squandered enough yet?'

'Well, Uncle, you complained when I did not play – now that I do, you are complaining still.'

'And so I will continue, till you learn to read Lady Luck's moods aright. Do not put your hand on her knee when she's kissing another!'

Edgar blushed. 'If everyone took your advice no one would play at all, for there must always be someone who wins and someone who loses!'

The colonel drained his glass and set it down. 'Odds bodkins, boy, play or not, it is all the same to me. Just remember not to venture beyond your own estate, for not a penny will you pinch from mine, now or after I'm under ground.'

He raised his spectacles to view the effect of his threat

upon the heir hopeful, and indeed Linton, after a moment's hesitation, bowed towards his uncle in seeming acquiescence – he was not so far gone in an avaricious stupor as to completely lose sight of the main chance. Satisfied with his nephew's show of obedience, Colonel Dent hoisted himself up. 'I'm for bed.'

'I, too,' said Mr Are. 'You and I will leave these young blades to their folly, Dent; we old fellows must rest tonight or pay the consequences on the morrow.'

Before our host left he motioned me to the sideboard, ostensibly to discuss some detail of the cellar. His back to the company, he pointed to the label on a bottle of port, but mouthed, 'Watch Ingram', and raised his eyebrows.

It was enough. I too had suspected something more than Lady Luck's favour in the sudden flow of gold into Lord Ingram's pocket. In fact I was almost sure the pack in use, which Ingram had earlier bid his servant fetch from his valise, was marked.

Talking of vintage and corks, I peeled back a corner of the port label and crimped it slightly with my thumbnail. I looked at Mr Are. He nodded almost imperceptibly. We understood each other. He smiled and took his leave. The object of our suspicions walked out with him, saying he would bring back something such avid gamesters as Linton and myself must find diverting.

For the second time that evening Edgar Linton and I were left alone. Neither of us spoke. He held the curved bowl of his empty wineglass up to look at the fire through it, then twirled the stem between finger and thumb. A log in the hearth split and sparked. I silently uncorked the new bottle of port and poured Linton another round. He as silently drained his glass, looking at me the while, and thrust it out for more. I filled it to the brim, spilling not a drop.

Theodore Ingram now came back carrying what appeared to be a large hat-box. He caught up his glass with his free hand and proposed a toast: 'To fair weather, fair maidens, and fair play!' to which we all three drank,

Edgar immoderately, I sparingly; I wanted to keep my wits about me during the transactions to come. I noticed Lord Ingram did not indulge overmuch either; perhaps he too anticipated need for a clear head.

Ingram swung the hat-box up on the sideboard. 'What do you suppose I have in here?' he drawled.

'A severed head, by the look of it,' I said.

'What say you to six of 'em?' and he flung the cover open.

Linton gasped. Inside were six faces – masks or half-masks, some with hats or wigs. Set on a revolving hexagonal stand, staring blankly in six directions, were a white-teared Pierrot, a sinister Harlequin, a dashing red-hatted soldier, a scowling ochre Indian with long black hair, a bloody-mouthed tiger, and a creation that looked like a butterfly in one light, and a feathered face in another.

'What? – Are these for charades?' asked Edgar.

'No, for gambling,' answered Ingram. With a flick of his wrist he set the stand whirling. The grinning faces changed to an unpleasant blur, with only a dismembered eye here, an isolated lip there, leering crazily at the viewer. 'They're all the rage in London. You wear a mask, you see, and nobody can tell what's behind it. You can grin away when you draw the pam, cry when you get a deuce – it's all the same, all under the lid, don't you know.'

'I'll take the soldier,' said Linton, and reached out to stop the wheel.

'No, not so fast, there's a good fellow. That's not how it's done. These are gambling masks, so you must gamble to get one. See, put your hand on one of the stations at the base' (six outlines of skeleton hands were painted on the black metal) 'and the mask that stops above it is yours.

He did so; the wheel creaked to a halt; Pierrot was Linton's lot.

'Good. He can be a lucky fellow, especially when the moon is full – of course I haven't the slightest notion whether it is or not tonight; how *does* one tell such things when it rains? – Now Heathcliff!'

I drew the tiger; Ingram, the butterfly. I poured more wine; we drank, donned our masks, and sat to play.

Though Ingram may well have been the fool of fashion in affecting these masks, I thought after I had worn one a minute that he had shrewder reason too – his partners would have that much harder a time crying cheat! through the holes. Yet my tiger eyes sharpened themselves in readiness for the kill.

The game was three-card loo. I drew first play, and wagered low. I won that round, but I thought I saw Ingram press one of his cards with his thumbnail. Glancing at my cards as I put them down on the table, I saw similar tiny indentations scoring the patterned backs. He who knew the system could determine suit and number from the marks. Cathy, I remember you laughing over the mumbling pains Hindley took to get his scratches by heart; then he would sit down with his cronies to cheat but stay to drink, and soon lose the sense of his own fraud. Ingram was not quite such a bungler, but like Hindley he must pay the devil at last.

I watched through one more hand to be certain. To accuse a gentleman of cheating was a weighty act. It was Ingram's deal – I saw him glance at the faces of his own cards, then peer very hard at the backs of ours, before placing his bet, a large one. He looed us.

I delayed no longer. I reached for my wineglass and tipped it directly on to the spread.

I sprang to make my apologies – 'A thousand regrets! – It was your deck, I believe!' – and to ring the bell for John. I mopped up the cards in my handkerchief just before Ingram's hand could reach them, and well before Linton became sensible of the dribbles from the table that were staining his satin breeches.

'Here, John,' I said when he entered, 'I'm afraid I've been clumsy. Would you please clean these cards carefully and put them in my room to dry?' I handed him the sticky mess.

'No, no!' cried Ingram, 'I am sure they are not really ruined. Give them over, fellow – let me see!'

John, confused by the masks as well as the contradictory orders, hesitated; I sent him a flash of my eyes. I said to Ingram, 'But I insist. I have damaged your property, a fine hand-painted pack by the look of it, and must repair it as best I can.'

'Oh, very well,' said Ingram. 'But I am sure it does not signify. Perhaps your man would take the trouble to ask my man to bring down a fresh deck?' The lord waved his hand languidly in the direction of his bedroom.

'There's no need for that,' I answered. 'The hospitality of this house can surely run to a supply of playing cards. John, would you be so good as to find some?' John bowed and began to leave. 'Oh, John – ' I added, as if in afterthought. 'Make sure to bring one of the *plain* sets – the ones with the *unpatterned* gilt backs.' John clicked his heels and left.

Ingram took off his mask and twiddled it between his hands a minute before he spoke. 'Well, Mr Heathcliff, I fear I have underestimated you!'

'A common tendency, it seems,' (I looked at Linton). 'Yet you will find it an easy habit to break.'

'I promise you I am cured already! You have gamed a great deal?'

'Not at all, but I have had ample occasion to observe the practices of others.'

Here Edgar, who was rapidly becoming the worse for wine, sputtered out something that sounded like 'Hindley!' But I gave him such a look through my tiger-eye slits that he suddenly found great occupation in dabbling the wine-stains from his trousers.

Just as Ingram reassumed his mask, from the darkened doorway there came a peal of laughter, a woman's laughter. Its perpetrator stepped into the light, holding her hand to her mouth to contain her merriment. It was Blanche Ingram. I saw that her feet were bare and that she wore a white nightdress and mantua. Linton turned his head away and averted his eyes. I rose and bowed.

'I am sorry to laugh,' she said, 'but truly, you are ridiculous – especially you, Tedo! *C'est un beau papillon! Mais cela est digné de lui*, don't you agree, Mr Heathcliff?' She accompanied these words by leaning over her brother's chair and fluttering the delicate lace mantua out behind him like wings. He swatted her away irritably.

'I say, Blanche, you're going it some, aren't you? You'll catch your death in that nightgown.'

'I intend to do no such thing!' and she whipped Lord Ingram's frock-coat from the back of the chair where it had been deposited and, with a swagger, put it on. 'You can look, Mr Linton. I'm as decent as you are now.'

'Blanche,' said Ingram, in a more decided tone than before, 'do stop your nonsense and leave us alone.'

'Oh? You are drinking and gambling in painted masks – I can see that you want no nonsense.'

'You can't stay here.'

'Whyever not?'

'You're only a girl, and should be in bed.'

'You are wrong; there's no girl here.' She went over to the fireplace and blackened a finger by smearing it along the edge of the chimney. Then she drew upon her upper lip and cheek the curve of an upturned moustache. 'Lord Ingram says there is a girl in the room. Do you see one, Mr Heathcliff?'

'No,' I answered. 'You must inform the gentleman that he is mistaken. But there is present a personage whose name I do not know; a young man *avec l'air farouche.* I crave an introduction; I would invite him to join our revels.' I glanced at Linton; he was so slumped in his chair as to look unconscious; perhaps he was so in fact.

'Don't encourage her, Heathcliff,' said Ingram, but not bad-naturedly; my return of his sister's jest had broken the back of his opposition. 'She wants severe putting down to keep at even a bearable level.'

'Tedo!' wailed Blanche lugubriously, and pulled a long lip.

'Oh, all right,' said Ingram, 'since you're so undeniably here, you can play a round with us, I suppose.'

She kissed her brother (he exaggeratedly rubbed at his cheek with a handkerchief), then walked to the sideboard. 'I'll have this one!' She lifted up the soldier mask.

'No!' exclaimed Ingram. 'You must spin for it, as we did! It's bad luck not to!'

'But I've already touched it, and it would be bad luck to put it back.' He lunged towards her suddenly, but she dodged and feinted. 'There now – you can't get it – but to appease you, I'll wear just the hat.' She replaced the staring face, then took the high busby that went with it and thrust her heavy hair up into its cavity. With her locks hidden, and seen by candlelight with cork moustache, coat, and hat, she made a fair counterfeit of a young man; her beauty was of that strong classical cast that suits either sex.

Ingram shrugged. 'What's the use, anyway? Girls never understand fair play.'

Turning her back to her brother, she put one bare foot on my chair, leaned on her knee, and thrust out her jaw. 'What about a cigar?' she asked.

I reached one from the humidor, clipped it, and put it into her waiting mouth, then held a candlestick in front of her. She steadied my hand with hers as she stoked fire into the tip. This was not the first time she had smoked a cigar. She glanced over my shoulder. 'Here is your servant, Heathcliff,' she exhaled. John had returned with the fresh pack. He placed it on the table with only the slightest of winks.

I indicated Miss Ingram. 'John, will you serve this young gentleman a glass of wine? Then you may retire for the night.'

John served, bowed, and left. Miss Ingram drained her glass with a flourish. 'Now – ' she said, 'what are we playing.'

'Loo – but you won't be able to meet the stakes, Blanche,' said her brother. 'You lost all your money this afternoon.'

'You must stake me, Tedo. That's your pile of gold on the table, isn't it?'

'How will you pay me back?'

'Oh, I'll probably win enough to do that, and if I have bad luck, Mama will pay. You know she always does what I ask.'

'Yes, the more fool her,' he sighed. 'Well, sit down then – here you are.' And he counted her out a pile of the shiny dross. She sat in the chair across from me, tucking her feet under her for warmth.

Ingram looked at me inquiringly and nodded in Linton's direction. 'Is he – ?'

Linton certainly looked in no condition to play. His mask had slid down around his neck and his breath was like a snore. But when I touched my hand to his shoulder he shrank back; something like alertness animated him.

'Don't touch me; I have no need of your aid. I am quite ready to play.'

I shrugged and shuffled the cards. The game began.

Now that Lord Ingram had only the blank gilt backs of our cards facing him, his bets and play were alike conservative. I, too, was modest in my ventures. The audacity of Miss Ingram, however, knew no bounds; or rather would not have, had we not imposed a rule limiting our hazards to what could actually be placed on the table – else she would have lost her hunter, her emerald necklace, her copy of *Evelina*, and her sister's spaniel.

Lost, I say, because lose she did – virtually every hand, not that it daunted her. She played carelessly and quickly, throwing down her money without counting it, and taking every new loo as an occasion for fresh jollity.

Edgar Linton lost too, though not as extravagantly as Blanche Ingram; either his uncle's admonition had had some effect, or the wine he had drunk had drenched his spirit. He counted out his bets silently, with a kind of sodden contempt. Still he continued to drink, and each glass worsened his temper – the more so because now I was the one who was winning.

It was the first real manifestation of what was to

become a major fact in my life – my ability, when I concentrated, to sway the fall of cards as I wished. As I have said, I had long enjoyed general good luck at games of chance, but never before had I known that I could *consciously* influence the particular direction of play. Or perhaps the ability was born that night, of this particular conjunction of people and circumstance – the storm outside, the late hour, my old enemy near, the grotesque masks glaring in the firelight, myself behind a mask – perhaps this confluence of essences awoke in me a latent power, gave that unique part of my mind the range and boldness it needed to make the leap from its unknown and unknowable cell outward into the world.

Now I felt my mind quick and quiet beneath me; I saw everything with extraordinary clarity – all the scene: the table, the glasses, the masks, the cards, the hands that held them – all seemed illuminated within. The very shadows glowed with meaning. Suddenly I knew my power; knew with a certainty that if I pictured the jack of clubs falling into my deal, so it would fall. I sighed. I was not at all surprised; once the thing had come upon me I could see that it was likely, even inevitable; only now a way into the future was confirmed that I had before only glimpsed, and half-feared.

'Too bad, Linton,' said Ingram as he swept gold coins from the centre of the table over to my side. 'Lady Luck has turned towards Heathcliff. But she is a fickle wench. Who knows – she may smile in your direction ere the night is done.'

'No, she will not,' said Linton. 'Not while Heathcliff and I sit at the same table. She always liked him best, even when we were boys.'

'He's raving,' I said aside to Ingram, and it was easy to credit this. The candlelight caught the dry glitter of Linton's eyes even through the eyeholes of his mask, and sweat ran down his neck.

'The lady does like him best,' said Blanche Ingram, taking a drag on her cigar. 'What is the secret of your wooing, sir?'

'She loves him best, but she'll marry me,' mumbled Linton. 'She'll marry me in the spring, if he can be kept from her door. More wine!'

Ingram gave me a significant look and covered his glass with his palm.

'Sorry, Linton,' I said, 'I'm afraid we're out. See, the bottle's empty.' I upended the first bottle we had drunk.

'Miser! Niggard! Thief!' Linton staggered to his feet, tipping his chair backwards on to the floor. 'I saw you push the full bottle behind the screen with your leg. What right have you – ! You're no better than a beggar! Here – keep away from me!' This last was to Ingram, who was attempting to lay hold of him and quiet his drunken thrashings.

'Sir, you are drunk,' said Ingram to Linton, 'and you grow offensive. Let me help you to bed before you insult our host.'

'Our host? Our host? That's rich!' In struggling away from Ingram Linton kicked over a bottle (which I *had* pushed behind the screen) and it rolled noisily across the floor. He laughed wildly. 'What a joke! he's no more our host than the scullery maid is. He's a gypsy, a changeling, a cheat – '

'*C'est vraiment incroyable*!' murmured Blanche.

'Shut up, Linton, or you'll regret it later,' said Ingram. 'What have you got against Heathcliff? He's a good fellow; he hasn't harmed you.'

'A good fellow! You think he's good? Can't you see he's the devil?'

'You're distracted, man. Go to bed.'

'All right, what about this? He's a cheat, he's cheated all of us at cards tonight.'

Ingram stared, burst into laughter, then abruptly broke off. 'Linton, upon my honour, if Heathcliff had cheated, I would have known it.'

'But he has cheated. He's as good as picked our pockets.'

'Be quiet, Edgar,' I said.

'How did he cheat, then?' asked Miss Ingram.

'How should I know? I'm no gamester – perhaps he has extra cards in his pockets. Make him turn them out.'

Ingram had finally succeeded in getting his arm around Linton's shoulder. 'Linton, I don't think you understand the gravity of the accusation you're making. Heathcliff could call you out for this – indeed, if you carry it much further, he will be compelled to. And I will back him.'

'It you do care to call him out, my dear fellow,' said Blanche to me, 'I'll be your second. I may not have much practice at it, but I believe I am already more of a man than Tedo.'

I looked at Linton with contempt. 'Fight him? That limp newt? I'd sooner duel with you, Miss Ingram.'

At this Edgar Linton wrenched an arm free from Ingram's restraint, grabbed the empty bottle off the table, and flailed out at me, but the blow went wild, just nicking the ear of the tiger mask. Ingram pinned Linton's arms against his sides. Blanche had reached out to restrain me (at that second I really intended to exterminate the worm), but stopped in mid-gesture, her eyes transfixed by something over my shoulder.

'Mary?' she said.

I turned. In the gloom by the sideboard stood the figure of a dark-haired woman, robed in a white gown similar to Miss Ingram's. She took a step closer, and I saw that the long black hair was not her own, but attached to the red Indian mask, which she must have put on while we were occupied with Linton.

'Mary? Why do you wear a mask? Why do you not speak?' asked Blanche.

The figure took another step towards us.

'It is a servant girl playing a trick,' murmured Ingram, but none of us believed it. There was too much of serious purpose in that step.

'Mary, you begin to frighten me,' quavered Blanche. 'I *command* you to remove that mask!'

Still the figure advanced. It drew into the circle of light that surrounded the card table.

Blanche cried, 'It is not Mary! It is not Mary!'

Blanche, Theodore, and Edgar seemed to draw back, leaving only me and the mysterious woman in the luminous centre. The woman came up to me. Something kept me from moving back, or from checking her. Time slowed; sound drained away. She reached up to my face with both hands, lifted my mask, and stared into my eyes.

The edges of the room blurred and dissolved, blasted by the force of that stare. In its light the mask changed before my eyes – the Indian's chiselled cheeks and cruel mouth bunched and deformed themselves until I saw only the gloating countenance of – the dummy-woman!

Something sprang between me and the figure – it was Blanche Ingram. 'I will unmask her!' she cried, and attempted to suit her actions to her words. There was a struggle – flashes of white drapery – then something, a mask – the Indian mask – spun across the floor. The woman was fleeing – a swirl of her nightgown and a high, shrill laugh, and she was out the door, Miss Ingram hot behind her. But the woman managed to kick a footstool into her pursuer's path, and Blanche went tumbling headlong, bringing down a side table and its contents on top of her.

By the time we had helped Blanche Ingram out of the tangle she was in, and determined that she was unhurt, pursuit of our mysterious visitor seemed pointless. Besides, summoned by the noise, John and Leah had entered and were putting the furniture to rights. Then Mr Are appeared in his dressing gown, but before Ingram could finish his account of what had happened, the elder man wheeled abruptly and vanished into the dark of the hall, probably disgusted with our drunken revels, as he thought.

'Who was she?' I asked Blanche in a low voice, brushing candle wax off the coat she wore.

'Not Mary,' she said, and only shook her head when I pressed the question. She slipped out of the room, eager to escape the scandalized glances of Leah.

Edgar Linton had collapsed on a sofa and now sat with his head buried in his hands.

'Bed for him,' said Ingram, and we hooked his arms up around our shoulders and between us hoisted him upstairs to his chamber.

'I'll take care of it,' I said to Ingram when we reached Linton's door.

Ingram shook his head wonderingly. 'You're a good-natured fellow, Heathcliff, to forgive him his insults. I've seen men killed for less. Still, he *was* very drunk. Good night!'

For the third time that night Edgar and I were alone. He lay on his back on the bed staring at me glassily, his eyes twin mirrors of the candle I held. I sat down on the edge of the bed.

'Edgar – are you conscious? Can you understand me?'

'Yes.' He spoke as if in a trance.

'We are old friends, are we not?'

'We have never been friends.'

'But there is a tie between us – a deep one, and of venerable vintage.'

He tried to cover his eyes with his hands. 'Go away.'

I held the flame closer to his face. 'You are drunk, and cannot remember. It is understandable.'

'There is no tie. You are nothing to me.'

I took his limp hand in mine. 'I am everything to you.'

'No.'

'Yes.' I pinched his clammy palm to get his attention. 'And, because of what we have been to each other, tomorrow I will have the utmost tenderness for your safety.'

'My *safety*?'

'Indeed. You and I will be riding abroad together, alone some of the time, and accidents may befall those who ride far in this countryside. There are many out-of-the-way lanes and stray paths where a man might slip from his horse and crush his head against a rock, and no one the wiser.'

Edgar was a little more alert now. He stammered, 'Oh, but I prefer to ride in the carriage.'

'I do not think so, when your uncle has determined otherwise. You want to please him. You want his estate, do you not? Dent House would companion Thrushcross Grange handsomely, don't you think?'

'You have no right – '

'No right to anything. I know. No right to love Cathy. No right to act like a gentleman. No right to notice anything at all about you. Isn't that a fair representation of your opinion? Come, answer!' I pinched his stupid palm again.

'No! – Yes! – Leave me alone!'

'But that is precisely what I will *not* do. I will *not* leave you alone – especially not tomorrow.

'Tomorrow?'

'Do not distress yourself about tomorrow. Come what may, I will be near to watch over your every move, to make sure you do not meet with a *fatal* accident.'

'Fatal! – but – '

'Yes. Cathy would not want your accident to be fatal, and both you and I are slaves to her wishes, are we not?'

Linton's face had turned positively ashen, and a new sweat had broken out on his forehead. I touched his cheek and rose.

'Good night,' I said. 'May your dreams prove as sweet as the future I foresee for you,' and I left him.

11

'Do not touch that cord.' Mr Are's voice emanated from the shadow that clouded his bedchamber, gathering its thickest umbra about the velvet-hung bed in which he lay. I had been summoned thither early in the morning by John, who when I asked the reason only shook his head and uttered a phrase he had applied to Mr Are's affairs before: 'It's a deep game the master's playing.'

Now the master's face was a pale blur indistinguishable from the paleness of his pillow. The gloom in the chamber was intense; sunlight insinuated only one knife-thin sliver between the heavy window drapes I had intended to draw apart.

I lowered my hand.

'What is amiss? Are you ill?' I asked. Never before had I been summoned to Mr Are's bedroom.

'No,' he said. 'That is to say – ' he trailed off.

I reached out again and gave the curtain pull a yank. The hard-edged shaft of sun exploded; it slashed through the bed's soft cavern.

'Damn you!' cried its occupant, curtaining his eyes with his arm. 'Mutinous ingrate!'

'You are ill!' I exclaimed. The harsh light showed Mr Are's face drained, his hair dishevelled. I came a step or two nearer; there was blood on the sheet, which was caught in a tangle around his right arm. 'What have you done?'

I leaned across the bed for a better look, laying my hand on his shoulder.

Mr Are shook me off irritably. 'What have *I* done?' he said. 'Ask rather what *you* have done! – Drinking and gambling and carousing through the night – I have raised up a wastrel for my pains.'

'You are bleeding,' I said, ignoring his grumbles. 'From what cause? Where is the wound?'

For answer he disengaged his hand from the bedclothes. A handkerchief had been twisted round it tight; with a grimace he pulled it off. The action apparently split an ochre crust that had dried on the palm; it oozed crimson. I carefully took hold of the injured hand (the skin was dry and hot) and inspected it.

'The palm has been slashed by a sharp blade; the web of the thumb is cut quite through,' I said. 'Had the weapon been wielded with one degree more of force your thumb would have been off.' The thought of last night's mysterious woman entered my mind. 'Who has attacked you?'

'What makes you think I was attacked?'

'Some human agent held the knife that made that wound, and I do not think it was yourself. Besides, we had an intruder.'

Mr Are's eyes flared like bellowed coals. 'What did you see?'

'A woman in white.'

'A woman in white, you say. A woman in white, indeed. A spectre, no doubt, summoned up out of a dissipated funk of smoke and alcohol and bad heads.'

'This spectre had, corporeal substance, enough to knock over Miss Ingram.'

A smile momentarily relieved his strained expression. 'She did for Miss Ingram, eh? I had not heard that part.'

I suddenly lost patience. 'Evade it as you will, there was a human woman among us last night, one who hates you and seeks to do you harm, who *did* do you harm! She attacked you, and attacked to maim, or worse!'

'Hold your tongue!' shouted Mr Are, starting up from his pillows suddenly, and as suddenly falling back exhausted. 'I was attacked by no one,' he almost whispered.

'You were attacked, sir, and by someone, but do not think about it now. I must fetch the physician.'

'No, no!' He stayed me with his good arm. 'No, *you* must be my physician.'

Again I started to rise, thinking he was raving, but again he pulled me back. 'I am serious, Heathcliff. I have reasons – good and sufficient reasons – why no one must know of this. Even John – I would not let him in the room this morning, I shouted my orders. No, I would have only you – nor must you let what you see here pass these doors. Do you swear?'

'Let us waste no more time in talk. You must allow me to fetch Carter.'

'First you must swear.'

'Yes, all right, I swear. Now let me go.'

'Do not be tiresome. I have said you must be my surgeon. You have assisted Daniel in his operations on the horses, have you not?'

'Yes.'

'And you have acquired some skill in the procedures?'

'A little.'

'Hmph. Daniel says you surpass him. At any rate, you shall sew me up. Yes, you heard aright. You saw for yourself how my thumb has parted company from its fellows; you must bring all together in brotherly reunion. Come, lad, the needle will join severed manflesh as tight as severed horseflesh. Go; get the tools of your gory trade; it is scarce dawn; no one will see you – if they do they will think you are returning from an amorous errand – Miss Ingram's bedroom is next mine.' Mr Are was not too far gone for a leer.

I none-too-gently rebound his hand and left. When I returned ten minutes later with my case of instruments, he had fallen into a doze, but jerked awake at my footfall. 'Did you meet anyone?'

'No, all is still.' I selected the smallest needle and clamps from those in the case. 'This will be painful. Shall I fetch some brandy from the dining room?'

'There is something better nearer at hand. Open the middle drawer of the toilet-table – just there – and take out that little phial and glass.'

I drew out the articles. The phial contained a dark liquid that flashed ruby as I turned into the light.

'Good. Now half-fill the glass with water; then, to the mark with the elixir.'

'Is it an opiate?' I asked as I measured it out.

'No – or rather, I know not; it is as likely to contain opium as ear of mouse or wing of bat, of which I believe it to be chiefly concocted. I had it from a herbalist in Italy; I did not need it for the duel for which I had procured it, but have superstitiously kept it by me ever since. It is purported to simultaneously banish pain and strengthen the heart; there – I believe I feel its virtue already.' And he swung his legs over the edge of the bed and thrust his hand on to the table. 'Commence!'

I cleaned the wound with a sponge, then began my operations. The laceration was deep; I had to sew together layers of muscles before suturing the skin. Even to one fortified with a quasi-magic Italian potion the process must cause considerable discomfort, if only to the imagination, so I sought to distract my patient the best way I knew – by angering him.

'This is a vicious wound,' I said. 'The knife was twisted as it was thrust, and only deflected by the bone. Who is this masked woman, and why did she attack you?'

My barb found its mark. Mr Are's cheeks flushed and his brow lowered. 'I have said: *no one* attacked me! – '

'Nonsense!'

' – at least no one who has legal and moral status in this world. You must drive the thought from your mind; or, if it will not be driven, at least enchamber it there; let no one glimpse it, or I am undone. But stay; you said she wore a mask?'

I proceeded to explain the exact circumstances under which last night's encounter had taken place, drawing out the tale to match the length of the seam I sewed. I told about Ingram's cheating, Miss Ingram's appearance, and Linton's accusation – leaving out, of course, my access of power over the cards and the undertext of my dealings with Linton.

Mr Are's face brightened during the telling – something in it relieved, it seemed, an anxiety that had festered before. By the end he was chuckling heartily. He chattered on, stimulated by the drug beyond even his normal garrulousness, as I packed my case.

'By gad, Heathcliff, you have bested them all! Your forbearance toward Ingram was at once kind and shrewd; poor puppet that he is beneath his cloak of modishness, by his folly he has given over to your hand his controlling strings – you may jerk them as you will in future. And you have behaved with like circumspection and generosity towards Linton, who I must say has astonished me with his deportment, by turns sullen and uncontrolled, with little rhyme or reason attached. As for Miss Ingram – tut-tut, Heathcliff, you have made a conquest! But have a care; your booty is no haremish slave; she is enough of a Turk herself to turn and make *you* the prize!'

I shrugged. 'She can mean nothing to me.'

'Very proper; you are faithful to your nameless one. But Miss Ingram has one advantage: she is present in the delicious flesh whilst her rival is but the shadow of a shadow.'

This line of discourse did not please me. 'I hear movements below,' I said. 'If you want my visit to remain secret, I must leave.' And I moved towards the door.

'No – hist – a moment – there are footsteps outside.'

'There is another exit.' I indicated the window.

'Good fellow. You noticed the loggia roof beneath. It was a route much frequented twenty years ago, when I and my brother were your age, but now fallen into severe disuse; however I am sure it will still serve. I will bundle up this bloody linen – there – thrust it into your case; you will burn it later. Oh, yes, Heathcliff – you must take upon yourself all the duties of the host, at least for now. Tell them I am indisposed – the morbid throat they suspected yesterday has materialized – that tale will have the double advantage of following from precedent, and fulfilling a dire prediction; Lady Ingram will be much gratified. But perhaps I will spoil her fun by joining you later.'

I bowed, then dangled my farrier's case above the vine-covered roof below and let it drop. I hooked one leg out the window, but Mr Are detained me again.

'By the bye, Heathcliff, had you heard?' he called airily. 'There was a prowler surprised within the premises last night.'

I perceived that my guardian had decided on an official version of the incident and was in this arch manner teaching it to me.

'What manner of prowler would that have been?'

'A woman robed in white – a masquer, a fakir, a gypsy, by all accounts. After making a little appearance at your revels, she passed to the kitchen, whence, after a brief encounter with the cook, she managed to escape.'

'There was nothing stolen?'

'She attempted to take a toy belonging to Lord Ingram, a mask; but in her flight, dropped it.'

'It is well no more serious event occurred – from your account (and from my own observations – we are alone, sir; there is no need to pretend) she was a desperate character, in the extremity almost of rage or pain – I know not which – but with a rancour of eye that would blink no more at a throat cut than a thumb severed.'

Mr Are stared at me for a second, then abruptly dropped his light-hearted manner: 'Get you gone! Get you gone! You perch on my sill like a great black raven; a monster bird of ill omen. I like not your splenetic croakings; change them for something more sanguine, or – !' and in a surprising rush of strength he suddenly sprang from the bed as if to push me from my vantage, but I vaulted down to the loggia roof and was away soon enough.

As I approached the breakfast room two hours later I could hear in the excited buzz of the voices inside some intelligence of what had happened the previous night. I opened the door. Ingram looked at me over the heads of his mother, his sister Mary, and Mrs Dent, clustered around him.

'I say, Heathcliff, exciting news! Our fair visitor of last night was a gypsy – one of a marauding band, it seems, encamped on Hay Common till this morning, when it was discovered they had taken French leave.'

Lady Ingram raised both her hands. 'We might all have been murdered in our beds by this unnatural female!'

Colonel Dent interrupted his nursing of a dish of coffee to wag an instructive finger at us over his propped-up gouty knee: 'You were in no danger, Lady Ingram, not from her. I know the tricks these people are up to. The wretch was only a spy deployed by confederates waiting outside. She was to stealthily determine the nature and location of the valuables, and the disposition of their owners; having done so, report to her principals in the bushes, who would then have taken the house by storm.'

'Her stealth was of a singular nature,' remarked Blanche Ingram, who stood apart from the others drinking her coffee by an open window, 'since she insinuated herself into our midst with all the secrecy of a shrieking banshee. And her chief object of interest was not any bauble or bangle, but Mr Heathcliff.'

Lady Ingram raised her lorgnette. 'My love, you cannot mean you were *there*? At a gentlemen's card party, in the middle of the night?'

'Why not, Mama? Tedo was present; who could be a fitter chaperone? And even our cadet host, that model of propriety, found it circumspect to extend me an invitation.' She bowed to me mischievously.

Of necessity I confirmed the card party's entire respectability (ignoring Theodore Ingram's wink), then changed the subject to Mr Are's indisposition, which indeed provoked great interest where it had been predicted. Then I proposed a plan of action for the excursion, ending with seating arrangements for the carriages. This deflected Lady Ingram's alarm to a new area; the Honourable Miss Blanche was keen to ride, but the dowager wanted her dangerous daughter close under her eye. They finally found a compromise in a small open gig put at their disposal; Blanche herself would drive Mama to the abbey.

'But Mr Heathcliff, that leaves you and Mr Linton out,' Mary Ingram said.

'Linton and I are to ride,' I said. 'Mr Are has given him the use of Beelzebub.'

'By God,' said Colonel Dent with some feeling, 'if it weren't for this blasted knee I'd join you!'

'Oh, no,' said Mrs Dent to me, 'I'm afraid it cannot be. Edgar is indisposed this morning; he says he will stop at home.'

'Indisposed?' growled the colonel, face instantly crimson. 'Indisposed? The young pup! I dare say; he is *indisposed* to our company, and *disposed* towards the contents of five or six books!' He grunted as he struggled to free himself from his chair. I lent him my arm; he heaved himself upright and reached for his stick. 'I'll *dispose* him!'

'Please, Harold, do not be so very precipitate!' fretted his wife. 'Edgar was much upset by the events of last night! The gypsy woman – '

'Is that it? Snivelling and hiding from a woman, is he? And *this* is what you want me to make heir of the Dents? We'll see about that!' As Mrs Dent wrung her hands the colonel left the room. We could hear his cane thumping heavily down the hall towards the stairs to the bedrooms.

So it fell out that, just as I had foreseen two days previous, Edgar Linton and I rode vanguard to our little procession. But not speaking loving words of you – nay, speaking not at all, for Edgar was silent and distant. His plea of indisposition had probably been no lie; he had downed enough wine the night before to fell an ox; besides, there was our final conversation to consider. I do not know how much of it he remembered, but that he remembered something was apparent in his avoidance of riding too near me, or out of sight of the carriages.

Still, I had ample occasion of observing Linton's horsemanship. He was a conscious, stiff rider: his knees tense yet rattling against the saddle, his boots jammed in the stirrups, his knuckles white with squeezing the reins. Beelzebub tossed his mane and rolled his eyes towards me – What is this spiritless thing on my back? they seemed to ask. His rider allowing him no more than a moderate walk, the whole procession crept towards the abbey at Linton's snail's pace.

As for me, I did not care; since last night I had felt my destiny bearing me along as steadily as the tried and true bay mare beneath me; no cause for undue speed when my sure passage was inevitable.

Miss Ingram, however, had no such motive for patience; enduring the drive under the conviction that fate owed her a debt of excitement for the gallop she had given up, she was determined to exact payment despite Linton's caution and her mother's resistance. So, smartly whipping her horse to as much exertion as it could muster, and ignoring Lady Ingram's appeals, tugs, and tears, she several times forced the gig past the two riders for a run down the open road ahead, probably thinking I would be tempted to a race.

Finally a lack of response from me and threatened hysterics from her mother made her give over this game; she must needs amuse herself in quieter ways. First she tried flicking Linton's hat off with her whip; success in this endeavour was too easy to hold lasting charm. So, driving up next me, she initiated a game of catch with some fruit (she had got herself up as a shepherdess for this pastoral occasion, and every proper shepherdess must have a pretty basket of apples and pears on one arm to balance the crook on the other). For a while I consented to pitch fruit back and forth over Lady Ingram's forbidding lap, then tired of it and urged Minerva to a gallop, leaving the others behind on the pretext of scouting the road ahead. In fact, it was no pretext, for this road was unfamiliar to me. On my solitary rides I had always taken an opposite approach to the abbey, on a path too narrow to admit any but a single rider.

It was just the sort of day you used to love, Cathy, with a fresh prankish wind exposing the tender undersides of leaves in glittering bursts. Such sharp pleasant gusts – you could so follow the progress of each as it flattened grasses and twisted branches that it might have been a wood sprite or elemental spirit, beckoning all to its revels. Higher up, the wind spun small white clouds across the golden sky, obscuring the sun's rays only long enough to add piquancy to their renewal. It was on such days that you and I would delight most in pure motion – when we were children lie down at the top of as steep a grassy slope as we could find and roll to the bottom (how Nelly would scold at the green stains on your pinafore!); or, when we grew older, gallop down the same hill on moor ponies.

I remembered all this as I raced on ahead of the others, and especially when I reached the top of a steep declivity, at the base of which lay the bridge that led to the abbey, just visible over the treetops on a hill at the other side. The festal procession being not yet in sight behind me, I determined to ride down to inspect the bridge, to make sure of safe passage for the carriages.

Once I had passed the first turn on the road down I felt myself in a distinctly different element, a different climate, almost, from the one I had just inhabited. The trees grew densely, their trunks, because of the steepness of the slope, nearly parallel to the bank in which they were rooted – so densely that as soon as I entered under their umbrella I was in near darkness. The pervasive murk made difficult not only sight, but breath – it seemed to weight the air with vapours inimical to living lungs. The hairs on the back of my neck prickled. I pulled up Minerva sharply.

There was no wind; the playful rustle of leaves that had filled my ears all day was absent. It must have been this unexpected blank that had disturbed me; and its cause was after a moment's reflection obvious: the steepness of the ravine and density of the foliage must bar any movement of air short of a gale. In fact the silence in this dead air was profound – no wind, no bird calls – only an undersound of the far-off murmur of water: the stream at the bottom of the chasm.

I eased the bay into a walk; we proceeded downhill. I noticed a moist, feral smell in the air; it increased as we neared the bottom.

Turning the last bend and seeing the tops of the heavy stone arches of the bridge that spanned the still-hidden stream to the abbey, I remembered an old story I had heard about this place. It was haunted – not by the standard mad monk, but by an eccentric presence called 'The Red Lord of the Hill', though he was more black than red, being covered all over except for his rufous face with short sleek black fur like a cat. And, oh yes, instead of feet he had two sharp cloven hooves, red as red can be.

The Red Lord had been here long out of memory, before the time when Christian men had erected the abbey, and other Christian men had cast it down. The stone edifice grew and shrivelled on the roof of his house, for he lived inside the hill.

The hill was hollow, the hollowness immense – and lined, ceiling and wall, with enormous crystal mirrors doubling and doubling again the silent silk and satin and gilt furnishings, and multiplying the nameless succulent fruits piled high on mounds of gleaming shaved ice. It was as grand as any palace you could imagine, but empty of movement except for the clumsy reflected caperings of the lord, whose loneliness and bile made him in fits playful or vicious.

As legend had it, the Red Lord liked to lure mortals into his beautiful abode, tempting them with promises of life everlasting, a life of uninterrupted revelry in all the luxuries of the senses, on the condition only that they never contradict anything he might say. This would seem a simple enough requirement; most would get through the first half-hour of riddles and tricks, sucking delicious nectar from fruit the while. But as soon as the unfortunate mortal uttered 'yes', or only nodded assent to one particular assertion (what this was the story named ambiguously – either that the world we think we inhabit is but the dream of a sleeping giant, or, oddly, that the world around us is real but *we* are illusion); as soon as the guest in the palace, I say, agreed to one or the other of these statements, the lovely fruits withered, the mirrors dimmed, and the poor dupe found himself starving in eternal darkness, with only an occasional triumphant cackle from the Lord of the Hill's throat, or a spark from a kick of his hoof, for company.

It was said also that, contrary to what might have been expected, the abbey had been built where it was *because* of the Red Lord; in those days a religious might reasonably have ambitions of sainthood, and here in resistance to the red one's clever temptation and (some thought) torment, was a short cut to beatitude. But many, succumbing to the demon's seductive arguments, had found it a short cut to a very different state.

Was he here still? If I called out his name would he burst from the rocks and drag me below?

A low whinny from Minerva made me notice that we had reached the bottom of the hill and I was sitting motionless, as if in a trance. Shaking off my morbid thoughts, I dismounted and walked the bridge, gauging the prospects for crossing.

These were poor. The ancient stone arches, supposed to have been built by the Romans, were probably sound as they had been the day a couple of millennia ago when their keystones were heaved into place, but the relatively modern oak beams that covered them were in a bad way. The south edge, especially, was rotted; in one place near the centre of the span was a great hole, big enough to swallow a carriage entire.

I walked to it and looked through. It was a dizzying drop to the stones and rushing water – fifty feet, perhaps more. I still had one of Miss Ingram's pears in my hand; on impulse I cast it down into the pit. After bouncing off the edge of one of the arches it fell sheer away, very slowly, it seemed, till it silently obliterated itself against a boulder in a green smudge.

It was clear that a carriage could not pass. But I tapped and tested the north side of the bridge, and this seemed perfectly sound all the way across. Edgar and I could easily transport the hampers on horseback; the others would be obliged to walk, in safety if not in contentment.

I shivered as I mounted Minerva. The air was positively cold here, and the smell grew heavier. I raced back up the hill rather faster, perhaps, than could be justified by the urgency of my errand.

Having left the carriages at one end of the bridge and made our way across it, we at length emerged from the noisome shades of the ravine into the brightness at the crest. When the ruins came into full view the company gasped with collective pleasure. A landscape architect could not have sacked the abbey to better aesthetic effect than had Cromwell's troops. Most of the roof had been reduced to picturesque mounds of rubble (with only an occasional arch left standing to sketch a ghost of what had been) – but Thomas's torch had only half succeeded. Providence, perhaps in the form of a rain storm closely following on the moment of conflagration, had preserved most of the standing walls. Some had crumbled down to eye level or lower, it is true, but this more enhanced the effect of the whole than otherwise, lending its outline a charming irregularity, and offering mortals roving its labyrinthine corridors surprising encounters of eye and ear.

The roof's having been so long demolished, nature had entered – wild roses grew where once robed figures knelt; birds' whistles rose and fell where once orisons droned. Earth covered stone floors; halls and rooms were carpeted with soft grass, cropped close by a local flock of sheep, for whom this was a holiday pasture. Only here and there did a gap in the green cover reveal, in polished mosaic, a haloed head, a shining cross, to remind the walker on what manner of ground he trod.

Nor had the great chapel been granted immunity – its

roof too had fallen to the flames; only the high walls at east and west had been spared, and in the west wall a great stained-glass rose window stood intact. It was to the chapel area that Miss Ingram, who had run ahead, called us.

'Tedo! Mr Heathcliff! Bring the baskets here; I have found our spot. You see, there is a legation to greet us!'

'Fallen down on their jobs a bit, haven't they?' murmured Ingram. 'But then, they've been waiting a long time.'

The fitful sun lit a fantastic scene. A number of human figures lay peacefully on the grass, dozing, as it were – their eyes closed, their hands folded upon their chests. But these sleepers dreamed no ordinary dreams – nor would those closed eyelids flicker and raise at our coming, or even at the blare of the last trumpet; neither living nor dead, this band of slumberers could never change its state, no, not till the angel unleashed the seventh seal and stone itself crumbled.

For it was of stone they were made. They were the marble effigies of ancient knights and ladies, sleeping on their mossy coffins. The coffins themselves, however, which would have raised the statues to the monks' eye level, had been overcovered by rubble and earth – hence this white company's appearance of napping casually on the greensward.

'I have found our banquet table!' exclaimed Blanche, tapping with her shepherdess's crook a large round shield which covered the heroic stone chest of a particularly doughty knight. ' "Sir Wilfred de Parmelee!" ' – she read from the legend, then curtsied – 'we shall be delighted to dine with you!' With that she hooked her fruit basket over the uplifted pointed toe of Sir Wilfred's mailed foot.

I was playing servant (Miss Ingram having ordered John and the others to remain with the carriages – she *would* be free of their ill-bred stares for one afternoon at least), laying the cloth and spreading the comestibles, when Mrs Dent, who had wandered off by herself, ran up flushed and panting.

'I have found the dungeon! It is all there, just as you said! The rack, the iron maiden – and only imagine! There is a skeleton, chained to the wall!'

Her news revived the fatigued group. Even Lady Ingram rose, from the rather attenuated bishop she had made her couch, and followed Mrs Dent to the path behind the west wall, which I knew led to the torture room. The monks had located it, perhaps in spiritual jest, beneath the apse.

The stack of bones they exclaimed over held no novelty for me, so I let them go off, keeping to the task I had begun. Blanche Ingram too stayed behind.

Cathy, I approach a part of my narrative which will surprise you, which may cause you to fling from you in rage the pages upon which it is written – to tear them into bits and grind them beneath your heel – but I caution you, I beg you – act not in haste – remember as you read that I did all by design, and the design had you at the centre of it, the end of it, you always.

I have said there were wildflowers dotting the sward on the hilltop. Here, among the stone effigies, they grew in especial profusion – the sweet grasses of midsummer: wild roses, pinks, daisies, cinquefoil – where grazing sheep had spared them at the bases of the half-tumbled walls, in the crooks of the knights' elbows, and in the crannies between their ankles. Blanche Ingram now plucked the most showy of these blooms to strew in the centre of our makeshift table, while I laid plate and silver around its periphery. Acorns from a solitary oak nearby crunched pleasantly underfoot as we moved about.

I smiled to myself. The wheel of the day was turning; destiny was taking shape beneath my hand.

'You smile,' said Blanche, settling herself next the table with an apronful of flowers. 'Has Sir Wilfred whispered a joke in your ear?' (I was at that moment caching some wine in a shaded nook beneath the good knight's head.)

'Not a joke, but he did murmur an observation with which I am pleased to agree; that after long waiting I am at last alone with the most beautiful woman in the county.'

I bent on one knee beside her.

'Well, sir! And what then? Does this bold knight tell you what action is prompted by such a circumstance?' She gave me a roguish glance before returning her eyes to her task.

'No. He is silent, but my heart is not.' I snatched her hand from the flowers and pressed it to my lips.

She snatched it back. 'Fie, sir – ! You are punished for your presumption – you have snagged a thorn; you bleed.'

'I told you I was in danger from your darts. How will you heal me?' I held out my hand to her.

She took it in both hers and contemplated it for a moment. Then with a flourish she drew it to her mouth and lightly kissed the streaming cut. 'There! I have annealed the wound. You have no further cause for complaint.'

A drop of blood trembled on her lower lip; I rubbed it off with my thumb before it could fall to stain the white bodice that fast rose and fell beneath it; then I leaned closer.

Our breaths mingled, but she turned her head just before our lips could touch. 'Mr Heathcliff! What would Mama say?'

'That question is easily answered. I think she would swiftly demand to know the size and disposition of my fortune.'

'And what would your reply be?' Miss Ingram's tone was exceedingly casual.

'That question too is easy. I would say that my fortune is immeasurable.'

'Oh?'

'Yes. It cannot be measured, since it is composed at this time entirely of conjecture and expectation.'

She drew a flower from her apron, 'I do not think Mama would be pleased with that answer.'

'And I do not think you give a fig for your mother's pleasure.'

Another flower moved from apron to table. 'Whether or not that bit of impertinency may be true, one has one's own pleasure to consider.'

'Exactly.' I took a flower from her apron and began to pluck the petals from it.

'But what is one to do,' she went on, 'when one's pleasure apparently conflicts with one's best interest?'

'One weighs the one against the other; a pleasure of sufficient intensity might in itself constitute a considerable interest.' I tossed away the stripped stem of the flower, and, hooking my finger through the laces on Miss Ingram's shepherdess stays, drew her towards me.

'But how is one to know?'

'One cannot, except by experimentation.' I brushed my lips across her cheek.

'An experiment – ?'

'Come to my room tonight, after the others are asleep.'

She pulled away slightly. 'Your room in the stables? What would I do there, pray? Take a midnight ride on Beelzebub?'

'If you like.' I kissed her.

'I cannot,' she breathed. 'I am watched.'

'By whom? Your mother?'

'Yes. She thinks that you and I – ' I quieted her by kissing her again.

'Then you must mislead her,' I said.

'How?'

'She thinks I have designs on you; my fortune is an unknown quantity; naturally she is on her guard. But Edgar Linton is unquestionably rich, and likely to be even richer when his uncle Dent dies. Divert her attention to Linton; she cannot disapprove, nor is his ardour as a suitor such as to cause a parent alarm; her anxiety will be dispelled; her vigilancy in all directions relaxed.'

Blanche laughed; the scheme was much to her liking, as I had known it would be. 'I see. I am to *conter fleuret-*

tes in Mr Linton's ear just loud enough for Mama to hear; then I can do what I like.'

'And I can do what *I* like. But wait, I must forsake you; if I am not mistaken I hear your unknowing *cavalière servente* approaching now.' In a few seconds Linton rounded the corner of the abbey leading Beelzebub, who bore Colonel Dent on his back.

Miss Ingram sprang up, and with a wink showered me with the petals that remained in her apron. Then she greeted Edgar and his uncle, hands outstretched, and soon was sitting between them on the bishop, arm and arm with each, much to the colonel's gratification and his nephew's puzzlement.

As if on cue Lady Ingram and the others came from the other direction, loudly expatiating on the grisly charms of the skeleton. Catching sight of her daughter with Linton, the dowager mother raised her lorgnette; what she saw apparently satisfied her. The plan was in motion.

Now nothing prevented us from eating, so we set to. As I passed slices of joint and glasses of wine over Sir Wilfred's shield, I inwardly chuckled to think how surprised those I served would be to know the full extent of my experience in picnics.

As I handed around the pudding, Blanche and Mary Ingram gathered more flowers, and by the time we had swallowed the last bite, each of us, Olympian-like, wore a fragrant garland round his head. The Honourable Miss Blanche playfully hooked Linton's arm with her crook and drew him near her, in order to adjust Edgar's wreath at just the proper angle to best frame his handsome face. She appealed to Mary and her mother to admire the effect: 'The blue of the cornflower against the gold – *c'est ravissant*!' Edgar smiled and blushed; he was beginning to dance to Blanche Ingram's tune. Little did he know who really played the pipes.

Even Sir Wilfred received a flowery crown, but before the bishop could be served the weavers' industry waned, the warmth of the sun without and the wine within having weighted their hands. Conversation gradually flagged; wreathed heads nodded; a bee buzzed unmolested above the remains of the pudding; for fifteen minutes the company dozed.

As for me, I walked over to the lone oak and hoisted myself into its branches. Mr Are had been right about my frequenting this place, but I did not come here to read Ossian.

At the top of this, the only tree on the highest hill in the neighbourhood, I could see on the far northern horizon a peculiarly shaped tower. This tower, I was convinced, was the same one you and I used to descry on the edge of the southern horizon when we looked from Pennistone Crag. Do you remember, it was shaped like the letter 'h'; we used to call it the giant's chair; we imagined he sat in it to look towards the western sea. In exile I could derive some comfort from thinking that you might be gazing at that very tower the same moment as I – our eyes touching the same point in space simultaneously.

Now, as I gained my habitual seat near the top of the tree and caught my glimpse of the tiny dim tower through the swaying branches, an inner voice sounded, as from vanishing memory, and seemed to speak. 'Be sure,' it sighed. 'Be sure.'

'Cathy?' I whispered, so vivid was the illusion of speech. 'Cathy?'

But my heart, and the air around me, was mute – no other message was vouchsafed me, though I long studied the flickering image on the horizon, seeming almost a mirage today, for any remnant of meaning. At length it faded out altogether, perhaps obscured by gathering haze. The living sleepers below stirred; I silently lowered myself through the leaves and passed among them on the way to the dungeon before they opened their eyes. I had an appointment to keep; with Brother Bones and with one other personage.

I sat in the hewn stone room regarding the skeleton and waiting for Edgar Linton. I knew he would come – logic dictated it; he had not seen the torture room yet, the others would make sure he viewed it, I could detain him afterwards – but beyond logic, I knew it anyway. I had had a message from you, or from the part of you I kept in my heart, telling me to make sure, make sure of Linton, and I knew that destiny would find me the chance.

The room was dark, of course, but lit in unexpected areas from gaps in the masonry opening to grass-screened light from the surface of the slope outside, for the dungeon was really within the dome of the hill. It might be that this circumstance had given rise to the legend of the Red Lord; perhaps the screams of tormented heretics had been romanced into his demonic cries, or the cries of his victims. Or perhaps, as the legend itself had it, the interrogation room had been located near the lord's abode to take advantage of the special horror inhering to his environs. This I thought I could feel, but the old machines of torture hulking in shadow, and the skeleton sagging from its chained wrists and spotlighted by a greenish glow, would in themselves explain any depression of spirit in an onlooker.

The wind wafted down sounds from time to time. I heard a guitar strumming (Mary Ingram had brought her instrument); first, strains of 'Cherry Ripe', then a song of Ben Jonson's, I believe, celebrating love and longing. Nothing for a while, then footsteps. It was a man alone – Linton – he hesitated in the doorway, his wreathed hair a golden halo around his head.

'A word, sir,' I said. Before he could move I laid a firm grip on his arm. 'The ladies will not come to your aid; they are too far to hear. You have only me to deal with, unless you count *him*.' I indicated the grinning witness behind me.

He tried to shake me off. 'Heathcliff, there is no need to hold me; I was looking for *you* just now. Stop these absurd games and drop your hands from my person.'

I held him fast. 'You think they are games, do you?'

'It is impossible to take you seriously. That is what I wanted to tell you. You threaten, but your threats are hollow. You are powerless to substantiate them. For the instant you harm me, you lose – not only what you so absurdly seek to wrest from me, but what you already have; which, it strikes me, is considerable, for a stable-boy, anyway.'

'It would seem that I am caught in a *dilemma*!' I said, on the final word spinning him around and thrusting him back on to the slab next to the skeleton. I stood over him. 'But as I am only a stableboy, perhaps I do not understand aright. You, as a gentleman and scholar, will be able to correct me if I have got it wrong. First, you mean to marry Cathy.'

'Yes, I shall marry her. And she has willingly agreed.'

'We will put aside the question of her will for a moment, though we both know it to be strong enough to blow the two of us before it like dry leaves in a gale. However, we will stipulate for the sake of this conversation that you and she are engaged to marry.'

'Right.' To his credit Linton had regained his composure sufficiently to cross his legs and lean back next to the skeleton as though quite at home.

'I wish to prevent it. How shall I do it? Can you teach me, schoolmaster?'

Linton sniffed in disdain. 'The only sane and rational course would be to return to Wuthering Heights and consult directly with the young lady in question. But naturally it is impossible *you* should follow the sane and rational course.'

'Exactly – and the reasons I cannot, are no concern of yours. It is enough that you understand that whatever is done, must be done between the two of us – between you and me only.'

'That brings us neatly back to your dilemma, does it not?' said Linton.

'Yes. And to resolve it, I require that you break off relations with Cathy. If you will not do so willingly, I will force you to it.'

I noticed Linton glancing at the shadow of the rack beside us, but he continued quite bravely: 'That you cannot do. You have nothing with which to bribe me;

there is nothing you have that I want. You have nothing to threaten; any violence you perpetrate on my person will doubly rebound on you, and where are your hopes then?'

Upon my saying nothing, he continued in a kind and reasonable tone, 'I am a magistrate now, and could in fact have you jailed for the threats you have made, but for old time's sake I will refrain. So let us call quits. I will not expose you to your new friends, and you will discontinue these ridiculous assaults. Agreed?'

Instead of answering directly, I seized the skeleton's neck and with a lunge swept the dried-up thing off the bench. Linton flinched and shuddered, but did not flee, as he watched it disarticulate itself across the floor. Its bony fingers still dangled, amputated, from its chains; I snapped them backwards and flung them aside, then sat in the cleared place.

I gently cupped Linton's knee with my hand. 'Edgar, I want you to think very carefully about what I am going to say. Do not answer out of preconceived policy or prejudice; try very hard to understand that I am a force to be reckoned with; that I exist; that I *will* carry out what I determine to do. Can you listen in this spirit?'

'Yes – very well.' His eyes ever strayed to my hand, despite his efforts to focus them elsewhere.

'Good. Now, unless I receive from you this hour a solemn undertaking to drop your courtship of Catherine Earnshaw, I will force you to do so in a way that will be must uncomfortable, most inconvenient, one could say most *terminal*, for you.'

'Do you mean to kill me then?' Linton blanched under his nonchalance.

'Cathy, through some unfathomable whim, is fond of you, so killing you would be a last resort. But if you refuse to promise, we have entered the realm of last resorts, have we not?' I squeezed the knee. 'Well, what is your answer?'

Linton suddenly shrank from my touch. 'Take your threats, and be damned,' he cried (Your lapdog can snap on occasion, Cathy!). 'I will simply tell my uncle what you have just said, and then your game is broken.'

'I think not. I think your good uncle, so rich, so wilful, in such uncertain health, is not in a humour to hear any whining reports from you of improbable threats, that would certainly be laughed off by me.'

'Then tonight I shall write a letter to my uncle to be held in case of accident, detailing the history of our recent intercourse, and everything else I know about you.'

This was clever, and coolly delivered; however it only confirmed the necessarily speedy execution of the plan I had in place. 'Is that your answer, then?'

'It is.'

I patted his knee and rose. 'So be it. You have replied as I expected. But I was compelled to make sure.' Kicking aside the heretic's shattered skull, I left Edgar Linton to his musings.

It is not you who comes to me with his arms filled with blossoms, who whistles bird notes and reads me poems of his own devising. I am peaceful with him, he never makes me shake by merely walking into a room or my belly lurch when our eyes lock

But oh how it was then you and I nuzzled like colts in the winter with all outside the circle of our backs ice, and we knew, we knew the centre, the safe place

something changed.

The wind blew and the clouds hid the moon and you turned to the door and I was afraid. We were older and I made a drawing of a lady wearing a high wig and diamond buckles and a satin sash. The man with her had golden hair and a golden carriage. You reached over my shoulder to put your muddy palm on the paper and I hated you.

When he touches me it is sweet as stroking a cat. You had been safe and then you were not safe.

You were never safe. I never wanted you to be. I wanted you to swallow the world.

12

No matter what happened under the hill, on top the day wagged on as before, and within a half-hour Edgar Linton and I, whatever our true feelings, were making such polite remarks to each other as chance and propriety dictated. At length it was time for tea, but the Misses Ingram and Mrs Dent clamoured for one more game first. We had played at blindman's buff till everyone was caught, at field-tennis till the wind grew too strong, at anagrams till Lord Ingram fell asleep from boredom. What was left? Bowls! But the balls and pins had been left below in the carriage.

'Never mind,' I said, rising. 'I can ride for them in five minutes. Stay! the cases are awkward; we had better have two horses. Linton, will you come?'

Linton thought that after all it might be best to have tea first, but the sentiment of the group rose up against him; after tea people would be too stupid with food to play, or the light might give out. When Blanche Ingram offered to ride and Lady Ingram's indignant protest directed itself less at her than at the derelict Linton, he bowed to fate.

'Don't imagine that I am blind to your plan,' said Edgar as we paced our mounts to the edge of the ravine. 'I see what you're about, and I am on my guard. You must descend first – I will follow at a secure distance. And if you make any move back towards me, that instant I ride to the others and tell everything; never mind the consequences.'

'As you like,' I said affably. I tapped Minerva's flank and we tore down the slope like a whirlwind, catapulting chunks of turf and leaf-mould into the air with every gallop. A dip at the bottom, then we burst out of the dense growth on to the bridge, and crossed it at the same rough pace. As we flew by the hole in the bridge floor, the extent of the void disclosed made my stomach tighten slightly. I pulled up and waited for Edgar on the far bank.

Through gaps in the leafy curtain that shaded the opposite hillside, I could see Linton making his way down very slowly, picking and choosing his path around the rocks. Beelzebub held his head at a peculiarly retracted angle; the nervous Edgar was apparently maintaining a constant pull on the bit. The horse would be ready to bolt at the slightest additional irritation.

I had time to toy with a new idea. Should it be here? Anyone who happened to fall into that chasm under the bridge would be unlikely to bother me further. I called up from memory what I had seen when I cast the pear into the void: a sheer drop to the rocks, except far to one side, where two of the Roman arches intersected. The chain of painful experience I had contrived for Linton, scheduled to begin (but not to end!) with a minor injury incurred unloading bowling balls, would be rendered unnecessary if he took a plunge into that hole. His seat on Beelzebub was precarious. If the horse were to, say, break into a run at the proper moment, Edgar would certainly fall, and might well fall fatally. Beelzebub would have me in sight as they traversed the bridge. I had but to raise my arm, and it was done!

I figured the odds. The carriages were placed so that if the servants happened to be looking in the direction of the bridge, they would witness the accident. What would they see? A horse running, a man falling – a heavy copse of trees blocked me from their view.

Perhaps to have witnesses of so much and no more would be well; then there could be no question of foul play. But why should such a question arise in any case? The surface of my relation to Edgar was unblemished; any bad behaviour last night had been all on Edgar's side.

Still, what of you, Cathy? There could be no secrets

between us; sometime I would have to render up my true account. How sharp would they be, your grief and anger?

But wait! At the verge of the bridge horse and rider had halted – rider, clumsily grasping the pommel, was sliding off horse! I had counted on Edgar's caution, but it exceeded even my expectations. Your lambkin was actually afraid to cross, Cathy, though his mount was surefooted as a goat; the distance to ground from saddle probably gave him the vapours! I had to laugh; for once his finicking timidity was justified.

Edgar, witnessing my mirth, tipped an ironic wave of the hand in my direction as he began leading the horse. He approached the centre of the bridge. I reckoned the paces. Four more and he would be next the hole. If Beelzebub bolted, Edgar might stumble through anyway.

Then events moved very quickly, much more quickly than I can record them. There was a commotion on the opposite hillside; something was descending the ravine from the abbey. A horse and rider – a ripple of skirts behind the foliage – Blanche Ingram, riding one of the horses from our stables! I knew in a flash that Mr Are must have recovered sufficiently to join us, had taken the more direct bridle path to the hill above, and Blanche, who had been chafing all day for a ride, had overmastered her mother's protests and wheedled Are's mount to surprise us.

Edgar turned to see what was coming. Beelzebub, gripped by the short and inept lead, must needs turn his head too.

I had thought I rode fate, but fate was riding me. Blanche Ingram disappeared into the wooded dip at the approach to the bridge, then burst out at a gallop. Her horse's hooves made their first clatterings on the wooden floor. Of a sudden finding her way barred, she forcefully pulled back on the reins. Her horse shied but did not stop. She cursed and brought her whip down on the beast's rump. Skidding just short of Edgar's boots (Edgar jumped back, very near the hole), the horse screamed and reared, topped by an explosion of petticoats.

Beelzebub, seeing those petticoats, hearing those curses, witnessing that whip raised, saw his old enemy emerge from ancient memory. He snapped the reins out of Edgar's hands and galloped past me as though the Red Lord himself were on his back. Edgar, unbalanced by the sudden removal of what he had been pulling, staggered for a long second, then, with a cry, toppled through the hole in the bridge.

I was off my horse and to the edge of the hole in a trice. Ignoring Blanche Ingram's continuing struggles with her mount, I looked down.

Now, Cathy, note well and remember if you feel inclined to blame me as you read the pages to come: at this point all I had to do was stand still, or even move a fraction less quickly than in fact I did, and I would have been rid of Edgar Linton without taking a whit of trouble or incurring a trace of blame. But instinct, or perhaps fate again, seeing more perfectly than I could into the future, made me act.

Edgar, by an extraordinary effort, or, more likely, a piece of fantastic luck, had caught hold of a bridge support about ten feet down, in the angle where two of the great rounded arches met. His arm had hooked at the base of the stone 'V' perhaps after he had slid down the roof of one of the arches. The rest of him dangled above a sheer drop of at least forty feet on to the sharp rocks below.

Edgar's face looking up at me was white; he was silent out of breathlessness or terror.

I took off my coat and, lying on my belly, hung it down by the sleeve, but of course it would not reach, and even if it had, Linton lacked the strength to grasp it. I would have to go to him.

I tried to assess the problems of descent; how could I reach him, and avoid falling myself? If I hung off the far edge of the hole Edgar and the angle of the arch would be directly beneath me. From there the tiny platform from which he hung would be only about a four foot drop under my feet, but Edgar's arm covered most of that. To avoid knocking him off when I landed I would have to swing forward and stick to the arch wall like a fly.

But there was no more time to weigh odds; I could see the muscles of Edgar's wrist begin to quiver with the strain of bearing his weight.

I found a grip on the edge and swung down through the hole.

My heels lurched sickeningly into the void; my hands slipped slightly; I struggled; caught hold. In the few seconds I hung there gasping, my mind catalogued my perceptions with extraordinary speed and clarity. With cold precision I noted the mossy surface of the long timber underside of the bridge floor, which seemed to turn the light and air and the stone of the arches a pale sickly green. The sound of rushing water was very loud; the timbers must have acted as a sounding board, reflecting and amplifying what came up from under my feet. I thought about what was under my feet. I felt the sweat start out on my forehead.

The wood under one of my hands began to crumble. I must act.

I took a swing backwards, then let go, reaching through the air to the surface of the nearest arch. I let myself impact with the flat of my body the whole stone curve, simultaneously clamping down hard on its sides with legs and arms. Grunting with the punch of the stone in my belly, I slithered down a bit, but not so far as to interfere with Linton.

'I cannot hold,' gasped Linton.

'Yes, you can,' I said. I wedged myself like a chimney-sweep between the two arches, and reached down. I gripped Linton's arm, or rather the fabric of his sleeve, with both my hands, and began to pull. The angle was awkward, so it took an agonizing time to inch him up, with nothing to look at but his blanched face, or worse, the rocks down below, that resembled pebbles at this distance, but were really great boulders, as we would see (I imagined) the instant before they broke us like eggs.

I knew that part of Edgar's fear was the mortal terror that I would drop him on purpose; to prevent me he kept snatching at my clothing, which put me off balance. At any second he might make the panicked movement that would send us to perdition together. But finally I managed to drag him far enough so he could get a leg up; at length he weakly straddled the ledge. I lowered myself into like position to steady him, noticing his breeches were torn and there was blood on his thigh – he must have snagged a nail going over.

'Now you're all right,' I said. We were safe for the moment, but fixed in a ludicrous embrace, balanced chest to chest in the narrow cleft of stone. Edgar seemed dazed to the point of paralysis.

'Edgar,' I said, trying to fix his attention. 'Take your hands from my neck and put them on to the bridge.'

He gripped my neck the tighter, almost in a strangle hold. 'I will not! If I let go, you will push me over! Now, if I fall, you fall!'

'The reverse is true as well, and if you do not stop struggling with me I will not answer for the consequences, for either of us!' This impressed him, and he was able to become calmer, and to substitute for his grip on my flesh, a grip on the stone.

I heard a voice from above and looked up. Blanche Ingram, face white and strained, was looking down through the hole, and beside her appeared John.

'I have a rope, Master Heathcliff!'

I ordered him to fasten the end of it to one of the bridge parapets and to lower the other end to me. Linton was soon harnessed securely; John, aided by several servants who had followed him from the carriages, carefully hoisted him up, to the relieved cheers of those assembled – the maidservants, Mr Are (puzzled at the time our errand was taking us, he had strolled down from the hill), and of course Miss Ingram.

I wondered how that proud lady would bear the humiliation of her role in this matter, but I need not have worried; while I was waiting for John to lower the rope for me I heard her excited recitation of the precipitative events of the mishap two or three times; by the last telling she was its heroine rather than its perpetrator.

At last, cheered, congratulated, and thanked (though not by the one who might have been thought to have most cause), I stood safe on solid ground.

I drew Mr Are apart from the crowd that fussed over Edgar. 'Let us not alarm the rest of the party over this,' I said. 'I can drive Linton back to Thornfield in the gig, and you can break the news to them gradually. Otherwise we will have Mrs Dent in hysterics over her nephew.

'He may be hurt; his leg bleeds.'

'All the more reason to get him away quickly. If we tried to move the whole party at once the delay would be endless.'

Mr Are wavered. 'Well, that much is true. And between the attentions of his aunt and the Ingrams he would be worried half to death by the time he reached Thornfield. But what of his wound?'

'I can patch that easily enough.'

'Yes, you are an able surgeon.' He lifted his bandaged hand and winked. 'But what if his injuries prove more extensive?'

'I will ride for a physician.'

'Perhaps I should accompany you then, to stay with him should you have to ride.'

'Yes, perhaps so – but you are wanted here to manage the others. If need be I could leave Linton with Mrs Fairfax, or in such a case it might be quicker to convey him to Carter.'

After a few more difficulties were raised and laid to rest it was settled that I would take Edgar to Thornfield alone, and Mr Are would stay to calm the company, and convey it back to the house. In briefing my guardian on what had been done, and what left undone, I did not forget to warn him of a defect I had noticed earlier in the latch of the bowls case.

During this colloquy Mr Are and I were witnesses to an eloquent dumb show. After the rescue Blanche Ingram, having imperiously waved the servants away, had led Linton to the end of the bridge, where she helped him sit beside her on the causeway wall. She, talking the while, alternately dabbed at his bloody thigh with her handkerchief and fanned him with her hat. He, by motions of head and hand, denied the need for these attentions, yet by white face and trembling smile solicited them.

Then the nature of their preoccupation seemed to change – their smiles vanished, their hands stilled, their attention towards each other became more concentrated. Each leaned forward, intent on the other's words. Upon Blanche's starting back slightly, Edgar caught up her hand as though to insist on a point. He glanced quickly at me as he did so. Blanche withdrew her hand from his and made some very decided speech (her head nodding angrily at certain points of emphasis). She rose from her seat, looked over in my direction, made some parting remark to Edgar (from which he recoiled as from a blow), and began to walk towards us. Edgar lowered his head as though faint; a servant moved to aid him.

'It looks as though Linton has just taken another fall,' chuckled Mr Are, 'perhaps a worse one than the first. It's as well you're carrying the poor fellow back to Thornfield; the number of his comforts here is fast dwindling.'

Miss Ingram approached us, chin in the air. 'You had better see to Mr Linton, sir,' she said coldly to Mr Are. 'I fear his wits have been scattered in this unhappy spill.' Then, to me, as Mr Are, grinning, left us: 'It seems Mr Linton gives you small thanks for saving his life.'

'What did he say to you just now?'

She shrugged. 'Mad things.'

I endeavoured to look concerned. 'Perhaps he has knocked his head. I must take him away to a physician.'

She smiled. 'I think it is his *amour-propre* that is knocked. But yes, take him, take him away by all means. He fatigues me.' She levered my elbow to turn us away from the bank where Mr Are was leading Edgar towards the carriages. 'You, however, do not.'

I leaned near her ear. 'Tonight?'

'Tonight.' And with a secret pressure to my arm, she turned to mount her horse. I gave her my palms for a stirrup and jumped her up. Then I joined Linton and Mr Are.

Through all the hubbub, Linton was probably not cognisant of our exact arrangements for conveying him to the house till the gig actually moved, and Mr Are vaulted off the back and waved us away. Linton put his hand on the handle of the door, as though to follow.

'Don't be absurd, Edgar,' I said, encouraging the horse's pace. 'If you leap out now, not only do you make yourself ridiculous, you risk a broken leg.'

'Take me back immediately, you blackguard,' demanded Linton.

'What! Is this how you address your saviour, he who has within the hour hazarded his own neck to salvage yours? I had heard that gratitude was dead in the world, but I had not seen proof of it till now.' We were nearing the crest of the hill.

Edgar drew up into his dignity.. 'In light of your previous threats, I cannot understand your present behaviour as other than criminally mischievous. I insist, I require that you stop the carriage and put me down at the side of the road instantly, if you will not take me back.'

He was looking so wild that I thought it best to quiet him, so I slowed the carriage and said in a reasonable tone, 'Only listen to yourself, Linton! Yes, I admit that I have said some harsh things to you – we are rivals in love, after all; you would hardly expect me to make no protest – but if I seriously meant you physical harm, surely I would have let you fall to your death back there at the bridge instead of exposing myself to the considerable danger of bringing you up. And I assure you the danger was considerable!'

Seeing that my words were making an impression, I brought the gig to a stop. 'Now, granted, there is no love lost between us, nor will there ever be, but to oblige Mr

Are I am willing to take the trouble of your transport to Thornfield. I am just as willing to turn the horse in the other direction and deposit you back at the abbey. Which shall it be?'

Indecision swept Linton's face as he weighed his persistent distrust of me against the common sense I had spoken. Probably the awkward prospect of explaining a return to the abbey, more than any diminution of his doubts, determined the outcome. 'Drive on, then,' he said. 'But let it be in silence. I have nothing more to say to you, and certainly wish to hear no more of your speeches.'

So we drove on into the darkening east. The wind had continued to rise and was bringing in storm clouds from the North Sea. The sunset behind us, where the sky was still relatively clear, cast a lurid sanguine glow to the gathering dark bank ahead. By the time we skirted the thorn thicket, the first drops of rain were falling.

When we reached the fork of the drive, I turned the horse towards the stables rather than to the house. I glanced at Linton. It took him a second or two to comprehend what was happening. The instant his face convulsed in alarm I clamped my left hand on his collar. 'Not so fast,' I said. 'I find I cannot dispense with your company just yet.'

'No – let me go! Heathcliff, what do you mean by this?' He kept up this sort of panicked patter the rest of the way to the stables. I said nothing – he had requested silence; I would give it him.

My luck held. The west stable door was wide open, as I had left it; any who would close it were in attendance with the carriages; Thornfield was deserted except for Mrs Fairfax and some maidservants in the house. I drove the gig into the dark maw with a struggling Linton still in hand. Once inside, I let the horse lurch on into the shadow by itself while I let go Linton's collar, jumped down, and barred and padlocked the door behind us.

Linton did not lose this chance to attempt an escape – I could hear his frantic stumblings down the centre aisle of the stable away from me as I secured the lock. 'It's no good, Edgar,' I called into the semidarkness. 'There's no other way out. I've seen to that.' I followed the noise of his steps at a leisurely pace.

I heard his gasp of discovery as his hand hit on the latch to the storeroom. He went through and slammed the door.

I had pressed it open again before he could find the bolt to draw against me. Falling backwards away from the swing of the door, he clattered against some bottles in the dark. I located lantern and glass phosphor match in their accustomed place. (The room having only one small high window, the air was almost completely black.) The flaring light as I twisted up the wick revealed Linton shrinking in the corner against a cupboard. I opened a drawer, drew out padlock and key, and locked the door to this room too.

'There,' I said. 'Now we are secure against superfluous guests. For I want you all to myself, Edgar.'

He looked about wildly, assessing opportunities of escape or defence.

'As you see we are very cosy here – no drafts or unwholesome vapours – you needn't fear for your health; there is only the one door and that lone window. Yes, placed rather too high to afford a view. It is the only blemish to an otherwise agreeable situation. This I know, for I spend a lot of time here, it is my headquarters, my workroom. Were you forgetting that, Edgar? But of course not; you are so fond of reminding me that I am a stableboy. A stableboy's place is in the barn, with the animals. Well, here I am in my rightful place.'

During this speech Edgar was, unhindered by me, opening first one of the cupboard doors, then another; hoping against hope that the next might lead outside.

'Ah – you condescend to take an interest in my trade. How good of you. There are the medicines – those bottles contain pills and doses for fevers, unguents for wounds. Careful! That was clumsy of you – mind the glass now! But feel free to look further. Yes, in that cupboard are bandages for binding wounds, cat gut for closing incisions, irons for cauterizing, all complete; we are well stocked here, ready for any emergency. Go on, do, I undertake you will find what is behind the next door most intriguing of all.'

He flung it open, gasped, slammed it shut. I strode over and swung it open again. 'Don't be so hasty; this is the best part! Here are the tools of my trade – specifically, for I am a surgeon, did you not know? In fact I have done a neat job this morning, with these very clamps and needles and knives – see how their edges glitter! I keep them well honed.

'Here is the lancet for piercing boils (for horses are heir to all the ills of humankind), saws for grinding through bone, forceps to aid in difficult foalings – all much larger than those used on humans, of course – but look, here is an exception – this particular set of tools is of a scale suitable for either horse or man.' I picked up a box of sharp-clawed instruments. 'Are you acquainted with the purpose of these?'

Linton shook his head, backing away from me till he brought himself up against the wooden pegs and iron hooks upon which hung the leathern tackle. I moved towards him. 'No? You have not seen these before?' I held the box close for his inspection, indicating to his attention a set of sharp circular pincers. 'Well, can you guess from the shape of this tool what it is fashioned to excise? The parts in question are not that much smaller in a man than in a horse, though in your case the disparity may be greater than is usual.'

It was at this moment that Linton began to scream. 'Bawl away,' I said. 'Any passerby would think it only the shrieking of wind in the eaves' – for the storm without had struck; wind and rain lashed against the glass of the small window, and the timbers above and around us groaned in ghostly harmony. I knew I had to complete my task soon; the wind would quickly cross field and hill to the abbey, and hasten the return of Thornfield's inhabitants.

He did not suffer, Cathy – not then, at any rate. To his credit he rallied sufficiently to attack me with a series of quite painful buffets, but I put a stop to that with a blow to the chin, which, as I had intended, stunned him out of consciousness for a space. For good measure I pressed over his nostrils the species of *spongia somnorifera* we used to calm the horses – he moaned softly, but his half-open blue eyes saw nothing.

I worked quickly. I trussed him securely, wrist and ankle, to the hooks on the wall with lashings of harness, to get him in good working position and in case he should wake up betimes. Then, baring his body, I used the gelding tools to perform a very deft operation, one I had done many times with Daniel but never in circumstances that required such precision of workmanship, such care in excision, such meticulous regrafting of tube, muscle, and skin.

It was done in minutes. There was very little bleeding. The incision, which I rubbed with a healing unguent, was as clean as any the finest opera surgeon could have made, the stitches as small and even. I bandaged him, buttoned up his breeches, undid his bonds, and put smelling salts under his nose.

I abruptly slapped the manuscript face down, then, cheeks burning, peered through my lashes in the direction of Mr Lockwood, fearing that the sudden movement might have awakened him; I wanted no witness to my shock and embarrassment. But the mound of blankets that encased that gentleman remained safely motionless.

Heathcliff! Brute! Fiend! Madman! The scales had dropped from my eyes; I saw him for what he was. Surely he richly deserved the misfortune that dogged him; yes, even to the thwarting of his mighty desire!

I was angry. I wanted to shout Heathcliff into sensibility of his egregious errors of self-justification. I wanted to make him admit that as a moral being he was grotesque, misshapen. But of course he was out of reach of my preaching. I could not talk to him, though he could talk to me.

All I could do was refuse to listen. Surely I was under no obligation to read more; I *should* not read more; I needed no more evidence to form my verdict: in foiling the schemes of this monster Nelly Dean had acted wisely. There was no more to be said.

And yet – and yet –

I seemed to hear the voice of my sister Emily, as I had so often heard it in the reaches of the night carrying across our darkened bedroom, spinning out the web of a story in the starlit air. 'Coward!' it sounded in my inner ear. 'You would turn away from what *is*? You would admit only a soft imitation of life, deny the stony fundament that supports it? If you are too puny to live yourself, at least acknowledge life in others. Existence is for the strong; know that fact; bow before it!'

My hands reversed the bundle on my lap. My eyes lowered to it. I resumed reading.

Linton retched into the straw while coming around, and I saw he was too numbed and sickened from the anaesthetic to understand what had happened to him, or what I was about to say. Then I bethought myself of the scarlet elixir which had worked such wonders for Mr Are that morning. Having had at that time some anticipation of a need for it later, I had packed it in with my instruments. So now I forced a few drops on to my patient's tongue. In two minutes his convulsions had ended and he sat quite calmly before me, though still dumb with bewilderment and shock.

I trimmed the lantern wick and sat across from him.

'Do you know what I have done to you while you were unconscious?'

He shook his head.

I said, 'Be brave, then, and I will show you.' I held before him a tray upon which lay the bloodied but still recognizable evidence.

After a second of incomprehension he screamed and hit it out of my hand. Tray and contents rolled into the straw. He doubled over and sobbed.

'Stop blubbering and listen,' I said. 'You saw only one, did you not? I took off only one. I have left you half a man.'

I forced him to take a few more drops of the liquid. At length his mewling was stilled. He stared at me.

'Now,' I said, 'do you feel pain?'

He shook his head in the negative.

'Nor will you, not for some hours at any rate, and not much then. I have done a first-class job on you. You will suffer hardly at all – a little lameness on that side for a few weeks, but nothing more.'

Edgar began to be able to comprehend his rage. 'How could you – ! Unspeakable – You will be hanged! Hanged! You are destroyed by this deed! This night you will spend in prison!'

'I think not.'

'You think not? You think that any judge in England will spare you for this?'

'No,' I said. 'But it will not come before a judge.'

Linton was speechless in his indignation, so I continued: 'You have been injured in a fall, which was witnessed. Also witnessed was my daring rescue. Afterwards at least half-a-dozen people remarked the blood on your trousers. Then Mr Are, the leading gentleman in the county, commissioned me to take you here and inspect your injuries. If you let the nature of this operation be known, I will say that I performed it as an emergency measure – that the part had been crushed, was haemorrhaging, and had to be removed immediately. There was no time to fetch the surgeon, and Mr Are himself would attest my complete competence for the task.'

Linton was shivering now: 'You will not get away with it. It will be my word against yours; and even if mine should not immediately prevail, believe me, I will persist in my charges against you. Eventually my superior station and character will tell; the authorities will see the truth.'

'It is possible that you are correct,' I said, 'though I think it unlikely. But we will never know whose theory is sounder, for you will never utter one syllable of your story.'

Linton held his head between his hands. 'Why not? What fantasy will you spin now?'

'Because there is the matter of the other testicle.'

Linton stared in horror and puzzlement.

'I have left one *in situ* for a reason. The minute I discover you have been bearing tales, is the minute I begin my plans to complete the job I started here tonight.'

Linton shrank a little away from me.

'Oh, yes,' I said. 'The more you struggle against the noose, the tighter it draws around you. For the more success you might have in convincing others of my criminality, the less I would have to lose by confirming it.'

He was silent. I continued, 'Consider your situation. As matters stand now you are still capable of fathering a family, of continuing your race. You may find some luscious girl – Miss Ingram, perhaps – and bed her and wed her (though even at full power you've had little enough juice for that sort of enterprise). But if you accuse me, the whole line of Lintons comes to an end. Finish. Exit Edgar, exeunt all.'

He sat still, staring at the floor.

'I have your attention now, do I not?' I said. 'Well, good, for here we come to the crux of the matter.' I waited till he looked up before continuing. 'As I told you earlier, you will drop your suit of Catherine Earnshaw.'

I paused for effect. A shudder ran through Linton's body.

'Ah, you see what it's all about, don't you? Yes, you're right, your choices are unpleasant enough. You must either give up Cathy's company, favour, conversation, caresses, and et cetera (and even to your puny passions this must be a mighty blow); or, should you persist, become a full gelding in time for your wedding night.

'No, do not turn from me; face your destiny, listen to your fate. Should you marry Catherine Earnshaw here is what I would do. I would hunt you down and eunuch you, with pleasure (there is nothing you could do to prevent me – there is no hiding from me – you know that in your heart of hearts). I would repeat tonight's operation, only on that occasion not denying you the opportunity of experiencing to the most exquisite extent all its various sensations.

'Then I would systematically dismantle your house, your wealth, your family. I would suborn or destroy all those you hold dear (with one exception), and laugh in your face at the end of it. Is that clear?'

He looked at me a long space, then slowly nodded.

'But none of this need come to pass, if you keep your mouth shut and stay away from Cathy. Then I will molest you no more; on the contrary, I will dance at your wedding – to anyone but her – drink a heartfelt toast to the bride, and lay down a handsome gift into the bargain.'

We went backwards and forwards over this ground a few times more, but the upshot of it was that finally he agreed – with however profound a depth of resentment and hatred – Edgar Linton agreed to my terms.

Events then in actuality moved quickly, though in the measure of experience they dragged with maddening slowness; every minute I expected to hear the rush of carriages in the drive. I removed the evidence of that hour's doings while Linton sagged into a passive stupor in the corner. Then, after shaking him awake so that he could copy a certain document, I locked the storeroom door while I went to the house to get his trunk. Here was the weakest part of my scheme – I ran the risk of encountering Mrs Fairfax and her questions, which could have been awkward, but this by luck I avoided.

When I got back to the stables with my burden Beelzebub was waiting outside, steaming where the raindrops pelted him. Rather than take time to rub him down, and as I could see he had not yet got his run out, I hitched him and another horse to a small covered carriage. I put

Linton and his trunk into it and set out through the waning storm for Millcote. He was by this time so weak and dizzy that I had to drive one-armed – the other was occupied with supporting him against my shoulder. Oh, I was tender with your pretty Edgar, Cathy.

We were in good time for the night stage to Leeds. I settled Linton within it, then had a word with the driver. Tipping him liberally, and laying my finger aside my nose, I told him that the silent pale young gentleman I had just tucked up in blankets had had a grave disappointment in love and was sick with sorrow, and drunk besides. The driver nodded me a wink and undertook the watch-care of the young gent; he'd see him safe into the Gimmerton connection that next morning in Leeds Innyard.

I let the horses set their own pace back to Thornfield. The storm had blown itself away to the western sea; incredibly, after the aeons that *seemed* to have passed, there was still some light in the sky – it was tinted a pure glowing azure blue; a lone star shone bright on the eastern horizon. A clean smell rose from the washed grass. I folded back the hood of the carriage so the air would clear my head; occasional leaf-fuls of rainwater baptized me with fresh spills as I passed under a tree. There were two more tasks I must accomplish before I slept that night. I tried to ready my wits for them.

As I had anticipated, Thornfield was in tumult when I arrived. Torchbearers criss-crossed the lawn. Lights flared in rooms upstairs and down. Mr Are, followed closely by Mrs Dent, had run out the front door to meet me before my carriage could roll to a halt. The colonel thumped and lurched not far behind them. I jumped down; a waiting servant took the horses.

'Well!' said Mr Are. 'And what have you done with young Linton? Taken him up to the physicians in Millcote, I suppose?'

'Oh, tell me that he lives!' cried Mrs Dent, plucking at my shoulder. 'I shall never forgive myself if he has come to harm!'

I bowed to them. 'Have no fear; he is well,' I said quickly. 'Here, Madame, he gave me a letter for you.' (The literal truth, though I had given it to him first!) I handed it to Mrs Dent, but the colonel, having advanced within arm's length, swiped it from her, then, grumbling, handed it back when he recalled that his spectacles were in his dressing case and not on his nose. Mr Are snapped his fingers at one of the torchbearers, who held a flare so that light fell upon the missive.

'Why – how extraordinary!' exclaimed Mrs Dent, after a moment of breathless reading. 'He has gone home!'

'Home! To Dent House?' asked her husband incredulously.

'No! Home, to Gimmerton, to Thrushcross!'

'You've read it amiss!' shouted the colonel. 'Robert, fetch my spectacles!'

'No, I've *not*, Harold,' said Mrs Dent, pushing the paper two inches under his nose. 'To Thrushcross Grange, and he gives no explanation, only that "pressing circumstances compel him to take his leave, and that he regrets the necessity for his precipitous departure". And he signs with his best love.'

'Well, here is the limit. Here is what passes understanding,' fumed the colonel. 'Letitia, I had persuaded myself to think that your nephew was not entirely a dunce, but now I see my fond error. Indeed in the wake of this latest slight to us I hope he *is* a dunce! A total vacancy of wit would at least leave room for a moiety of honour!'

At this Mrs Dent, putting her hands to her face, fled into the house. I could see the Ingrams clustering around her inside, offering comfort and getting news.

'Heathcliff,' said Mr Are. 'What light can you shed on this matter? You have taken Linton to the stage. What did he tell you?'

I motioned the gentlemen out on to the front walk, well away from the ladies' possible overhearing, and, cautioning them to use discretion in repeating what I should tell them, recited the story I had prepared. I did well and honourably by Linton, Cathy; by the time I had spun out my tale Colonel Dent was not only satisfied with his nephew's behaviour, he was disposed to think more highly of him than ever he had done before.

Mr Are too accepted what I said; it dovetailed with what he himself had witnessed. But when Colonel Dent re-entered the house, chuckling, 'These young fellows must sow their wild oats,' my other companion lingered.

When he had come home, Mr Are said, to find Linton vanished, he had gone out to the stables to look for me. The gig was back; the closed carriage was absent; this suggested that I had driven Linton through the storm, probably to a physician – but what had made him certain of the latter was what he had found in the the stable storeroom – the bottle of Italian elixir. This discovery had greatly alarmed him – why would I have used it unless Linton was in a very bad way, indeed? But now I was telling him that Linton was *not* injured. Was I holding something back, perhaps out of consideration for the Dents? Was he indeed hurt? Had I administered the remedy to him?

I thought quickly. 'Yes, I did give him a dose, but for his spirit rather than his body. He seemed in great distress, yet insisted on travelling. I thought it would sustain him.

Mr Are looked grave. 'I fear you did wrong. The stuff is not without its dangerous aspect; sometimes there is a reaction. It should be used only to alleviate intense physical suffering. How did he seem when you left him in the stage?'

I told him of Edgar's departure, and of the driver's promise to look after him.

'Ah, well, he sounds right enough. You were lucky this time.' Without further comment Mr Are took my arm and we walked inside, but it struck me uneasily that the look he gave me at parting was a singularly troubled one.

I had a word with John before leaving the house, then went to my quarters in the stables. Now I had only Miss Ingram's visit to anticipate.

I lay on my bed in waistcoat and shirtsleeves. The

London paper I held was black with words, but though my eye crossed and recrossed the lines and columns, somehow the meaning seemed to be drained out of them. It was after midnight, and, the weather having changed its face again, a light rain was falling. I had instructed Miss Ingram to approach the stables by way of the orchard. At last there was a tap on my window. I unlatched the door.

She entered, bringing with her a fine mist in the swirls of her voluminous grey cloak. I caught her by the shoulder with one hand and turned her towards me, so her face was illuminated by the light of the fire on the hearth. A subtle nimbus of glistening damp made her cheeks glow. I unbuttoned the frog fastening at her throat, then lifted the cape from her shoulders. She was wearing just such a filmy white nightgown as she had worn the night before, but this time no mantua covered it. Lowering the cape halfway down her back, I used it to pull her to me.

At first she returned my kiss, then after a minute laughed, put both hands on my chest, and pushed me from her. 'You take away my breath, Mr Heathcliff! Don't you know it is customary to hang up a lady's cloak when she visits you, and offer her a chair?'

For answer I whipped the wet cloak from her back and flung it towards the hearth, where drops from it sizzled on the hot stone. She looked at me quizzically. Before she could speak I swept her up in my arms, then dropped her on to the bed, not over-gently. I stood looking down at her. 'Will that do?'

She lay still and smiled up at me. 'Perhaps Mr Linton told the truth.'

'What did Linton say, then?' I sat down on the edge of the bed.

'That, despite the evidence of today's events, you wanted not to preserve him but to kill him!'

'Extraordinary! Did he assign a motive to this peculiar wish, or did he put it down to indiscriminate bloodthirstiness ?' I laid my hand on her white ankle where it peeped out the damp lace edge of her nightgown.

'He did not explain, but I could read his thought.'

'Oh beautiful oracle! What did Linton think?' I removed her velvet slippers, sodden from the rain, and warmed her feet between my hands.

'I cannot of course say for certain, but perhaps he imagined you resented his apparent success in – a certain area,' she said, wriggling her toes.

I lowered myself next to her. 'Ah! – and what area would that be?'

'Mr Heathcliff! You have better cause to know than anyone!'

'Did he mean this area? Or perhaps *this* area?' She laughed and struggled for a minute, then sighed into my caresses.

There came a loud knock on the door, followed almost immediately by a lifting of the latch. We both started upright, but there was no time to do anything else. John stood in the doorway, staring at the two of us on the bed.

'Will you be wanting anything, Master Heathcliff?'

'No, thank you, John. Come see me first thing in the morning – for further orders.' John bowed and left as abruptly as he had come.

Miss Ingram was gasping hysterically. '*Further* orders? What did you mean by that? Why did he come?'

'I told him to.'

'What! Are you mad? Have you set out to ruin me?'

'Calm yourself. You need not be ruined. He is a loyal man, and will do what I say. He will be quiet – unless I tell him not to be.'

'Unless you tell him – ! *Unless* you tell him? Why under heaven would you tell him to talk?'

'I would do so only if you refused to cooperate with me.'

'Oh, you despicable – ' She stared at me, her face slowly changing. 'You are not only a wretch, you are stupid with it!'

'Indeed?'

'Yes, stupid! There was no need, none! for these elaborate machinations! I loved you, or thought I did.' Now the tears started to pour.

'Oh – you think I want *that*. You are mistaken. I require something quite different.'

This struck her silent for a long space. Then with an effort she straightened her spine and met my eyes with a semblance, at least, of pride and composure.

I must confess I felt a pang – not exactly of remorse, but of regret at my degree of necessity in this action. Miss Ingram had courage and nerve. But I hardened my heart; I had set myself on a course from which there was no looking back.

'What is it you want me to do?' she asked.

'I want you to behave in every way as you would have done had a certain sequence of events taken place. I want you to substitute this sequence for other events in your memory. If you are questioned, it is to these new events you will revert as fact.'

'That is mysterious, but doubtless you mean it to be so. The events are – ?'

'You and Linton have been carrying on an intense flirtation from the first day you came here. Your attentions to me were so much smoke, a screen for your preference for Linton. I agreed to go along with it out of good will towards both parties.'

'Good will – infamous! But go on.'

'He had made you an offer of marriage which you had half-accepted, but this afternoon, his passion fired by his near brush with death, he urged you, as you talked together by the bridge, to agree to engage with him in illicit congress, and suggested an assignation for this very night. This of course outraged your very tender sensibilities. Unwisely, he pressed his request until he became impossibly offensive. You not only refused the assignation – you broke off all further relations with him. He took it very hard – I suppose that is why he has left so suddenly; there can be no other explanation.'

She looked at me speculatively. 'I wonder what you have done with Linton. Perhaps you really have killed him. I wonder.'

'Any inquiries will find him alive and well at his home in the north.'

'You're confident of that. I suppose it must be so. Yet why except to cover his disappearance would you do this – out of sheer malice, sheer wickedness?'

I shrugged. 'Perhaps I am malicious and wicked. Perhaps I am mad. Or perhaps I am only bored.'

'Do you have any idea of how much I loathe you?'

'Do you have any idea of how indifferent I am to any feelings of yours?'

She grasped my shoulder. 'You are lying. You are not indifferent to me; far from it. I am never mistaken about these things, and I was never more sure of anyone than I was of you.'

'They say even goddesses are fallible, when their blood is roused.'

'Blood answers to blood, and ours is like. Deny it if you can!'

I detached her hand. 'It matters little now. I have done this thing. You must agree to my story. It will hurt no one, and in fact will more improve your reputation than otherwise.'

'Not hurt – ! Well – !' She raised herself from the bed, where we had both been sitting, and stood erect. 'Yes, I will go along with your story. You give me little choice. But first I will tell you exactly what I think of you.'

I stood to face her. 'What do you think of me?'

'I think you have had the whole world in your grasp this day, and you have flung it into the fire.' Her face was a mask of scorn.

I must have smiled, for she reached out and began shaking me, as hard as she could. I did not hinder her, but she soon tired of the exercise, probably seeing that she might as well be shaking a marble statue, for all the satisfaction it would yield her. So, giving me a thwack on the chest in lieu of a farewell kiss, she caught up slippers and cloak and opened the door to leave – then, pausing, without turning around: 'Oh – one more thing, Mr Heathcliff – I *did* see that woman's face.'

'What woman?'

'She was no gypsy,' she said, and slammed the door.

I was alone. I took off my clothes and went to bed.

That night and every night, I was alone. The darkness within the circle of my embrace was empty. Cry as I might, dream as I might, when I reached out my hand in the dark, you were never there – never there.

13

Heathcliff must indeed have been mad! In this latest outrage, a betrayal not only of Miss Ingram, but of his sworn fidelity to Cathy, the doubts he had expressed earlier about his own sanity were all too clearly justified. Wondering what new maniac grotesquery I might encounter, I turned the page. To my relief, I saw that the next sheet was scripted in the hand I had come to recognize as Nelly Dean's:

Sir –

Here are missing some pages of Heathcliff's story, destroyed by my self. After Mr and Mrs Linton had returned from their honeymoon I deemed it dangerous to retain the evidence of my meddling, the mistress having such curious ways about her, ever making free with other folks' affairs, and their things too – so I determined to get rid of the letter.

Accordingly I got up my courage and took my workbox down to the kitchen, meaning to burn what was at the bottom of it in the fire kept lit there even in such hot weather as we had that spring. I actually did thrust a good handful of pages under the grate, and had another ready to follow, but just at that moment my mistress entered the room.

I nipped my apron over my arm, then thought unhappily that the action would call attention to what it hid rather than the reverse, but Mrs Linton was too exercised by the troubles in her own mind to bother about any guilty secrets in mine.

She said, 'Nelly, I have had a shock.'

'Yes, Miss?' I stuttered (I kept the privilege of calling her by her old title sometimes).

She laughed tremblingly and put her hand to her throat. ' – A visitation, I think, and a singular one. I scarcely know how to describe it – have you ever felt like an icy hand reached into your breast and squeezed your very heart?'

I had rallied enough by then to put a face on it and laugh, 'No, indeed, Miss, nor do I think it likely that any sensible person would, who had just been to London and back with more kind and handsome a husband than ever she deserved,' for I thought I saw the direction madam's fancy was taking.

'Well, I did feel so, just now. I was unpacking a box from the Heights – it contains my old treasures – Isabella would think them paltry enough, if she saw them, and smile, but they are precious to me – and my hand closed on this.' She opened her palm, and on it sprang up a hank of thick black hair tied with a scarlet thread.

'It is the only bodily thing I have that remotely connects him to me; I found it in our hiding hole in the barn after he left. Nelly, I wondered sometimes if he put it there as a sign to me, that he would return. Do you think so, Nelly?'

'I should think it unlikely, Miss,' I said. 'A handful of hairs can signal no clear message, especially when followed by no other.'

'Well,' sighed Mrs Linton, 'at any rate as soon as I touched it a chill ran through me till I shivered, though it is so hot, and I felt bad enough to die. I think Heathcliff must be dead, and today he reached up from the grave, or from wherever he is, to try to grasp my happiness from me.'

'Now ma'am,' I said, my alarm having taken a new twist, 'you must not go that road, or we'll have a return to the fever and fretting of three summers ago. You should put your old playfellow from your mind; that one never did any good in his life, and, if he really is dead, now at least may be hindered from spreading his ill-luck to others.'

Instead of defending her old comrade to me as she was

wont to do at this phase of her existence, she shook her head. 'Cold! Cold! To take himself from me without a word, and then to take my peace!'

She left the room distracted, without teasing to see what I held beneath my apron, and I could have completed what I had begun, but now I thought that if I burned any more of what had come from Heathcliff I should bring his curse down upon the Grange, and destroy us all. So back the letter went into the workbox, and so it comes to you.

It has been half a century and more since I laid eyes on the missing pages, but as I read them many times over before they were burnt, and have a pretty good memory still, I think I can supply their sense.

However, before I revert to Heathcliff's doings, I must voice my wrath at his treatment of my dear master. I refer not only to the horrid mutilation he visited on him, but to his lying account of Edgar Linton's behaviour towards his Aunt and Uncle Dent. I knew Mr Linton well, Mr Lockwood, and served him for twenty years, and am mortally certain that never would he behave in the way described, slighting his friends to pursue selfish pleasures. No one could deny that he was fond of study, and increasingly with the years kept to his library, but a kinder man than my master never drew breath, nor a more considerate one.

Well, to continue – You may be sure Heathcliff kept a sharp watch during the next few weeks for signs that his wicked attack on Mr Linton had come to light, but none appeared. The latter did arrive at Thrushcross Grange safely, and went into a period of seclusion that puzzled us greatly then. He shut himself away with his books and would see no one, not even Miss Cathy, and certainly not Dr Kenneth, though that worthy man told me he was summoned more than once by Miss Isabella, only to be snubbed outside the study door for his pains. I thought it at the time a delayed nervous reaction to the death of his parents the year before, and so it may have been, in part.

The worst of it was that once Mr Linton had been home a few weeks he never could tell Catherine what Heathcliff had done to him, for to do so would be to disclose his own concealment of her foster brother's whereabouts. Sad to say, Catherine would have forgiven a hundred mutilations over one such omission in regards to Heathcliff. She was as wicked as he was.

So Heathcliff was left a free hand to weave his web, though for all his labour it was to come undone. He made much in his narrative of some letters he wrote after Linton left Thornfield, to his darling, and to me, too, in case of Miss Cathy's going astray or being intercepted, promising to come in a year or so like a fairy prince in a golden coach to heap all manner of riches on Miss's lap.

For my part I never got such a letter, and can answer for it that my mistress didn't either; there would have been no secrecy in that quarter about such news – we would have had jubilee ringing in our ears for a fortnight out of it.

No, those letters never arrived, and I can make a pretty shrewd guess as to why. Heathcliff had another enemy besides Linton in our parts – being so intent on squashing the suitor he forgot the brother, who had less love for him even than my master, and so his careful schemes went for nothing.

It had been for years the custom for Curate Shielders to bring the post to the Heights when he came, twice or thrice weekly, to tutor Cathy, but time had wrought an alteration in this as in so much else; Cathy's long illness after Heathcliff's disappearance had interrupted the lessons; they had never been resumed; the post must be got in some other way. Hindley rode into Gimmerton almost daily, ostensibly on business but really to drink and roister at the tavern; he picked up the post on these trips, and, if he were sober enough to read, would thumb through it at his leisure while jog-trotting back to the Heights. Any letter with Heathcliff's mark on it would have quickly found its way to the bottom of Blackhorse

Marsh, if it had not fallen unheeded out of his drunken pockets before.

I remember Heathcliff had a deal more to say about his fine new friends and their affairs – the upshot of every episode, of course, being the glorious triumph of His Majesty, never mind how many crimes he had committed to achieve it. I must say that I have seldom met with a more self-congratulatory apologia than that you hold in your hand, Mr Lockwood, not even in the speeches of politicians, and the part that is missing was no exception.

At length, they all went home, and Heathcliff was left alone with his master to prepare for their tour. The latter was as mightily pleased with Heathcliff's acquittal of himself at the house party as even the principal actor could wish, and so they had a pleasant enough time of it together before setting out on their travels.

Over these travels Heathcliff's pen passed with unaccustomed speed, perhaps because the events recorded had necessarily more to do with matters of general interest, and less with his favourite topic – himself. They went to France first. That country was still dirty with light-minded courtiers and antique aristocrats – there was a court to be presented at, and so Mr Heathcliff must needs be presented. Of this event we had a full account, you may be sure.

They stayed hob-nobbing with the great of the land some months, long enough for Mr Are to have visited on him the result of a past folly: a little Parisian by-blow, a girl of some five or six, abandoned by her actress mother. The newly-made father, who, I'll grant, possessed something like a conscience, acknowledged the slip and with the aid of his other ward brought it back to Thornfield, leaving it, and the order to find it a governess, with the housekeeper.

Back this bold pair went to the Continent, to Italy this time. There they became entangled in an intrigue, the details of which I forget, except that it ended in Heathcliff's disguising himself as a bishop and skewering a masked prince of the Church with a rapier concealed in his crosier.

They visited some other countries – I remember they frequented the opera in Vienna, and came across their old friend Lord Ingram in Switzerland, where he was taking a cure for the pox – but the place that made the greatest impression on Heathcliff was Germany.

Ever a fool for the mystic, Heathcliff had in his earlier studies sniffed out the works of a certain obscure German philosopher and now was wild to meet him. So off they went to the town where this philosopher taught at a university. There Heathcliff enrolled as a student, and soon became so mired in metaphysics as never to know top from bottom again.

Mr Are, in the meanwhile, was caught in a different sort of mire, with a certain Grafin Clara. It was as well that urgent business called him back to England. That would have been in January of 1783.

His master greatly wished Heathcliff to go along, but the latter refused, though strongly urged, owing to his stubborn infatuation with the incomprehensibilities the philosopher opened out to him; this was a grave mistake, for the refusal caused some little coolness between him and Mr Are, that brought a bitter frost later.

Heathcliff could not, or would not, tear himself away from his studies till the summer of that year, and by that time affairs at Thornfield had shifted from what they were before, when Heathcliff was the idol of Mr Are's eye. Now a new graven image squatted on the altar, the sun and moon rose and set by *her* comings and goings; she was beyond the sun and moon indeed, to Mr Are's besotted eye: it was the little governess, hired to teach Mr Are's ward Addle but retained to beguile the warder.

Heathcliff's pen had her a whey-faced chit, a snivelling brach, a sharp-toothed ferret, as he said – oh, he waxed positively eloquent in his anathema of her. None may now know whether his inspiration were truth or jealousy, but something it certainly partook of the latter, for while Mr Are may have *felt* love for Heathcliff as much as before, he certainly *showed* it less – all his show was now for his new mistress, who, holding back the only trump card one of her station might play, led him a merry game, refusing him what he wanted so he would want it the more.

This was Heathcliff's view of the situation (you and I, Mr Lockwood, knew him well enough to realize that where his own interests lay, he was capable of considerable torturing of the facts); however, he was sure that the governess schemed after Mr Are's fortune (which Heathcliff probably already considered his own). Miss Eyre (that, fantastically, being her name) was therefore a hypocrite and adventuress and must be exposed – for Mr Are's own good.

Heathcliff also caught the notion that the governess disliked *him* – as any sane person in her position would, subjected daily to such poisoned glances as Heathcliff could shoot down a corridor or level across a tea table. He would have it that she was turning the master's mind against him – slyly filling his ear with doubts about Heathcliff's origins, sanity, and love of Mr Are.

These suspicions smouldered on underground for awhile, till fuelled to full flame by a recurrence of the kind of vandalish prank Heathcliff had recorded as taking place at Thornfield before – but this time instead of tricks with dummies or ink, there was damage done to Mr Are's clothing: several waistcoats were ripped down the middle.

Heathcliff ups and accuses the governess of this foolish deed. Her motive, as he said? To do down Heathcliff; since, as happened when the inks were spilled, the face of the deed makes Heathcliff its author.

Then there is a grim scene between Heathcliff and his mentor-that-was – Heathcliff incriminating the governess, exposing her base motives as he thought, Mr Are sitting stern and silent, refusing to entertain suspicion of Miss Eyre, yet as steadfastly refusing to offer a counter-theory to explain the enigma of the ruined coats. Instead (as I recall what I read) he leaps to the heart of the matter:

'Am I not allowed to fall in love, Heathcliff? Is that it?'

'Of course you are, sir,' says Heathcliff. 'But your friends must hope that you will settle your affections on one who deserves them!'

'And who will deserve them if not she!' flares Mr Are. 'So modest, so pure – you think you can see through her as through a crystal – but then – one twist, and she flashes with wit, and bite, and pluck! Where could I find another, to whom my heart would bend as it does to her?'

Heathcliff, to give him credit when it is due, refrained from making aloud the sarcastic response to this question he *thought*.

'You are silent; you think ill of her,' Mr Are continued. 'You think you have reason; you think you protect me; I must be patient. Heathcliff, believe me when I tell you that she is blameless, as blameless as yourself. I know who did this thing. But there is reason – oh, such strong reason! – why I *cannot* tell you more. You must trust me, believe me – '

'As I believed you when you told me that there were strong reasons, *inalterable* reasons, that you could never marry?'

At this Mr Are slammed down his hand so hard it cracked the glass on the writing table (they conducted this conversation in the library). 'You know not of what you speak, Heathcliff, or even you would not be so cruel as to cast my words back in my teeth thus. Reasons *have* altered; she has altered them by her existence, and I *shall* marry her! Neither hell nor heaven will stop me – and if my creator cannot, then you, my creature, can scarcely hope to succeed!'

This line of discourse did not sit well with Heathcliff, and thereafter relations between the two men cooled even more. The winter of their friendship was reached two or three weeks later, when Mr Are almost perished in a mysterious fire in his bedroom, very obviously set on purpose to kill him.

This time, to Heathcliff's astonishment, it comes out that the governess accuses *Heathcliff* of the deed, that all along, while he has been pointing the finger hard at her on one side, she has been pointing back just as vigorously on the other! And with what unspeakable grief and indignation Heathcliff learns that Mr Are refuses to deny the charges the governess makes against his former favourite! That he equally refuses to affirm them does not signify – Heathcliff is wounded to his heart. He himself requests that he be posted to Ferndean Manor as overseer, a position you will recall he had scorned previously, though to most of his station to secure it would have seemed like dying and going to heaven.

Heathcliff moves into Ferndean through a black funk of his own creating, for the duties are pleasant enough, not at all taxing, and the financial rewards are considerable. His new abode being near Ingram Hall, he is thrown much in the company of the compliant Lord Ingram, back from his prolonged cure in Switzerland and ripe to be tempted to new folly. As Heathcliff's mania is for gold rather than flesh, they fall to gaming every night, and draw to them local rakes of sufficient means to make their losing profitable to Heathcliff.

This unsavoury turn of events has one salutary outcome: the lumination of Heathcliff's growing pile of gold allows him to begin to see his way clear to feel his attachment to Mr Are, and although he did not say this outright, we can hope that he experienced some part of the gratitude to his benefactor he should have felt. But this is reading between the lines – what Heathcliff actually expressed was a resentful longing for the elder man's company, a kind of mutant breed of his pining for my mistress.

But my pen has run on, just as my tongue used to during our long gossips, and I have overshot the place where Heathcliff's interrupted narrative resumes. I only want to say one thing before I give over – it has been my experience that a body often becomes a portion of what he is thought to be, though it runs against his natural bent, bad or good, and Mr Are in the main thought Heathcliff good.

I have now told you the gist of the burnt part. Read on, sir, and see if I did right to suppress the whole.

14

Ingram and Boy Ferrick laid their money down on the table and rose. The latter, with a surly, hangdog look, left the room without speaking, but Ingram lingered; he put his arm around my shoulder as we walked to the door together.

'Forgive him, Heathcliff; Ferrick's a bit of a lout when he loses, though he can afford it well enough, but in the main he's good company. May I bring him again?'

'As you like.' I little cared what species of boar raised itself on its hind legs to come to my table, as long as its purse was fat.

We passed from the smoky dark interior to the fresh morning outside. Ingram's servant was waiting with the carriage, into which Ferrick's pink coattails were just disappearing. But from the mouth of the drive emerged another carriage. I recognized it as Mr Are's.

'Company, Heathcliff!' said Ingram. 'You won't mind if I leave before the fireworks commence!' And as the second carriage arced around the drive and stopped behind the first, Ingram walked to it, spoke through the window to its occupants, bowed himself backwards to Ferrick's carriage, and left. I took a stance on the front doorstep and awaited developments.

Mr Are got out, stood a minute talking to someone within (I could see the little white patch of her face in the shaded interior); then, with the air of a man who has steeled himself, walked towards me. As he approached, I was struck by how well he looked: glossy and high-coloured, like an animal put in prime condition for a fair. So love suited him.

'Well, Heathcliff,' said Mr Are, smiling, 'will you invite us in?'

'*You* may walk in, and welcome,' I said. 'But as for

your companion, I do not receive any person who has accused me of being a vandal, and a bungling one at that!'

Gone were Mr Are's smiles. 'Then we must stand outside.'

'Very well.'

'What of your accusations towards her? It seems to me that this matter cuts both ways – and you see she is here, ready to forgive and forget.'

'It is easy to forgive and forget when you have won the field.'

'Won the field? In what sense? You left of your own accord.'

'When I made my suspicions known to you – in decent privacy, by the way, not as a public circus – you assured me not only that you were certain of Miss Eyre's innocence, but that you knew who the real culprit was. This carried weight with me; I was quiet, if not entirely satisfied. But when she made *her* accusation, you made no similar assurance to her – only sat mute and grim, leaving her – and me – and such servants as were present – to understand that you believed her!'

'Then it is I with whom you should be angry, not she!'

'To be sure I am very angry with you, yet in your case, one ungenerous deed must be put in the balance with hundreds of generous ones; and besides, understood if not excused as the product of a kind of madness induced by love. I can apply neither the first, nor the second justification to Miss Eyre's action.'

'So you think my Jane does not love me, at least not to the point of madness?'

'I have told you my opinion on that score.'

'Yes, damn you, so you have, in terms that left no room for mistake. Ah, Heathcliff – if only I could compel you to see – I *had* to let her think you did it.'

'That makes no sense. I cannot even imagine an explanation for such a compunction, so unjust to one party, so false to the other.'

'If you knew with what I must contend,' Mr Are

mused. 'If you knew with what difficulties I am beset, what dangers threaten me – !'

' "If you knew, if you knew – "! Why do you not *tell* me?'

Mr Are rubbed his chin. 'Should I? Should I? He tempts me – how he tempts me! What a relief it would be to unburden myself! But if it went wrong – I would lose her, I would lose him, lose all – '

'Do you not trust me?'

'Yes, but can I trust you to see things the right way, as I do?'

'I am your creature. I am as you have made me,' I answered with some sarcasm.

'Do not flatter me or yourself! You have a hard, cold core that I have never touched. It is cruel, it is pitiless, I fear it, I dare not – '

I grew impatient with this waffling. 'Oh, have done with your whining! Let the chit imagine that I have committed these mad deeds, and am like as not to cut to shreds the wardrobes of my friends, and burn them in their sleep too. One day, perhaps, I shall oblige her with such attentions, and live up to expectation!'

'But she really does not believe it of you any more. She is sorry to have misjudged you.'

'Oh? And what motivated this remarkable change of heart?'

Mr Are shuffled a bit. 'Well, in fact there has been a recurrence – '

'A recurrence? What has been shredded, painted, or burnt this time?'

'The incident was in the nature of a personal attack. A visitor to the house, a Mr Mason, was stabbed.'

I thought of last year, when Mr Are's thumb had been nearly severed by a mysterious assailant. 'Did you see his attacker? Was it that same woman in white?'

'It was a woman, but Mason did not mention the colour of her dress, and she was gone before I could reach him.'

'Who else was in the house at the time?'

'Miss Eyre – it was she who helped me bandage Mason – and others you know, the Dents and the Ingrams.'

'How strange that Ingram did not mention it to me, then. It must have made a terrific sensation.'

'Not so strange, when he did not know. I thought it best to keep the incident a secret.'

'Thought it best! Just as you did when the woman attacked you! Secret piled upon secret, deception on deception!'

'Have you done with anathematizing me, sirrah? How much examination will your own life bear? Will your every action prove without blemish when exposed to the harsh light of conventional sanctity?'

My thoughts turned inward for a moment. Even if he suspected something about Linton, he could have no proof. 'What foul deed do you now imagine I have committed?'

'I *imagine* nothing. I need not, when I meet at your very door the most scandalous wastrel in the county, accompanied by one so bad he puts the first in a parsonic light. And I'll wager they were *not* concluding a genteel levé. No, they have been here all night, gaming. Do you deny it?'

'No, I do not.'

'How could you lower yourself thus?'

'Lower myself, by receiving a peer of the realm?'

'Come, Heathcliff, we both know a higher measure of man than that!'

'Yes, you taught me one, but then you taught me to call Ingram friend as well.'

'That accusation is petulant and childish. We have together watched him go from the merely weak to the actively bad. Do not turn your back to me; we must have this out. Report had told me that you had fallen into bad company and low ways; I had hoped it false, but I see it was not.'

'Oh, and has report confided anything to you about my management of the farm?'

'No, but I daresay your other preoccupations have left little enough time for it.'

'You daresay? When I came here two months ago, I found – not a farm, but a wilderness, not a house, but a kind of rough camp site set up in two rooms of a neglected building. The other dozen were empty, the drains were clogged, the stables a shambles. Writing to you for instructions but receiving none, I supposed *your* other preoccupations had left you little time, no time,' (I glanced towards the carriage. Its occupant was fanning the door from inside; the sun was already hot) ' – so I had to fashion my own plan.

'I considered how to make this place a paying proposition. The situation is low and damp, woods choke the house into the valley; all the open fields are far from the barn. But, distant as they are, they would be ideal for horses. And I know horses.

'Yet it is a tricky thing to turn a profit in horseflesh. I wrote to you again. Again getting no answer (you were, I am sure, *very* preoccupied!) I took it upon myself to make improvements on the stables and pastures, and to order breeding stock. In addition, I have had the drains dredged, that jungle of growth near the house cleared, and the house itself aired, cleaned, and partially furnished.

'In short, I have applied a rational system of stewardship to your property; you may approve or veto it any time your busy schedule permits. If you approve, you will realize a very tidy profit in two years' time. If you veto, the devil take you!'

Anger, surprise, and some other emotion warred on Mr Are's face as he listened to what I said, but I was never to hear his reply, since we were, at the moment of my final rather unpolitic ejaculation, interrupted by the governess, walking up to us across the grass.

Mr Are's eye, as it turned from me to her, softened; his chest seemed to swell; he reached out to her; she met his grasp, then, quickly, as if on the wave of impulse, extended her other arm to capture my unsuspecting hand.

Her flesh was surprisingly warm for one in whom the life force seemed ever at a low ebb – but of course she had just been steam-heated in the carriage.

She was such a low, sallow thing, with her dry rusty hair pulled back from her pinched face, and Mr Are was in those days a striking, a vivid, man – but I now noticed that next to him she was *not* eclipsed by his brilliance, but reflected from it a faint glow. It was the only time I ever saw Miss Eyre look almost pretty.

Now she pressed my palm into Mr Are's. My immediate inclination was to back off, but the sudden pressure of his grip forced me to look in his eye, which seemed to say, 'We are not finished, you and I, but for the moment let us shake hands anyway.' Accordingly I let my hand be pawed for a few seconds before it was dropped. I said nothing, but the happy pair appeared satisfied.

'Perhaps Edward has told you that I discovered my mistake about you,' said the governess, pushing her spectacles up her nose (a habitual gesture which never lost its power to irritate me). 'I am more sorry than I can say, especially since I have lately seen something else to which I had previously been blind: that you are very dear to Edward. I hope you will generously let bygones be bygones, and allow me to be your friend too.'

What could I do but smile and bow? I still had many reservations about Miss Eyre's motives, but if her change of heart was policy, it was *convincing* policy, and so deftly administered, that it left its object no room for outward resistance.

'There!' said Mr Are, beaming. 'We are friends again! And Jane, Heathcliff has informed me of such changes begun at Ferndean that will make it the showplace of the county!'

'From what I have heard of his abilities, that cannot surprise me. But Edward, have you told Mr Heathcliff the other object of our visit?'

Mr Are drew the governess close against his side. 'Heathcliff, Jane and I are to be married. You are the first to know, and are likewise unique in being the only friend invited to the event. Will you come to our wedding?'

Again, I could do no other than congratulate them, however strong my misgivings. I was, happily, excused from accepting the invitation because of a horse fair in the next county, on the very date named, that it was really necessary I attend to get the breeding stock I needed.

Since Friend was my role I thought I had better act it thoroughly, so I urged them to enter the house and stay for dinner; my housekeeper, Mary, was an excellent country cook and would relish an occasion to display her art. Mr Are and the governess, however (to my relief and probably theirs), had pressing business back at Thornfield.

I watched their carriage into the stifling tunnel of trees that was the drive, then sat down heavily on the front doorstep. Tired though my body was, my brain worked at top speed. Oddly, it did not run over the scene that had just taken place, did not surge with remembered resentment of my unjust treatment, or wonder at its sudden reversal and the still unexplained events behind it, or despair at the coming union, which, even if the governess were sincere (which I doubted), must be damaging to my interests – no, it did not. All of these things fell away as though they had never been, or were part of a story told long ago by Nelly.

A door had been closed in my mind, swallowing Mr Are and Miss Eyre. Hand in hand they receded from me. Receding with them was the fairy dream of Heathcliff, heir of Thornfield, overwhelming his childhood friends and enemies with his new-grown splendour.

What was left was the image, bright and strong, of Catherine Earnshaw, *not* fixed in the memory of our shared past, but transported – here, to Ferndean; imperfect, present Ferndean – you could be here, with me, Cathy, truly here.

Why *not* bring you here?

Smarting under the sting of the final humiliation you had dealt me, bowed under the hundred-fold pain built up over the years previous, I had vowed not to return to Wuthering Heights till I could do so in utter triumph, could burst through the old gate in a coach as big as Edgar Linton's, descend from it in clothes twice as fine, urge my love to you in phrases ten times as eloquent as any he could muster, and toss enough money in front of Hindley to buy up Wuthering Heights many times over.

But now that vision, the necessity of realizing that vision, melted like a fairy ring when the dew dries.

I had not that dream in my hand to offer you. I had something less – yet something more, in its mundane substantiality. By this time I had amassed, by investing my earnings (and lately by winning at cards), upwards of five thousand pounds. I had a dependable yearly income, likely to steadily increase, from my managerial duties. I had the use of a house that, while not distinguished in its architecture or setting, yet had its solid good points, upon which much could be built.

Why should I worry further about besting Linton? That I had done pretty decisively already; besides, was not the real point, the only important point, to gain you? Had I not always insisted that we were *one*, had a single heart beating in two breasts? Yet here I was, intent on amassing wealth, not so much to offer you in love (if I let myself whisper in my own ear the truest truth), as to fling at you in bitter reproof of your having underestimated me.

What joins us was, and is, purer and simpler than that. We could come together without the elaborate mechanism I had planned. To doubt it were treason to us both.

I had a life to share with you – a position, friends – could you and I not be happy in a normal way? Could I not travel to Gimmerton by stagecoach, court you as any swain his mistress? Even Hindley – could I not bring myself to pretend, for a week or two, that he was a human being, and parlay with him for your hand? I thought so.

To have you here! To witness your delight in planning improvements for the interior of the house, your enthusiasm in landscaping the grounds, your interest in the horses! How Mr Are would amuse you, how his midget bride would give you matter on which to sharpen your tongue! How Ingram and his cronies would overnight find themselves thrall to your charms –

But no, that last part must not be. I must put a stop to my gambling. I must not resemble Hindley in any way.

To touch you in reality, not in phantasm – to press with these fingers the round warmth of your flesh, to inhale the scent at the nape of your neck –

Yes, I would do it. From this moment onward I would think differently. I would lay aside my pride, or try to change its nature.

Upon my return from Europe some months before, I had employed a spy to make sure Edgar Linton had remembered his limitations. The report I had received was satisfactory. Edgar was fast gaining a reputation as a recluse, not often venturing beyond the walls of Thrushcross Park. You still kept up a connection with the Grange, but local gossip had it that your object was your friend Miss Isabella Linton, that Edgar had "gone off women", and stayed in the library during your visits. I was sure that you, having received the explanatory note I dispatched before leaving for Europe, were waiting for me – but with what increasing exasperation over my delay I could (then and now) too well imagine.

Over the next few days I began to lay practical plans. The date for the horse fair (and the wedding) was a little less than one month distant; I determined to start my journey to Gimmerton the day after I returned. But how would Ferndean fare while I was gone? While I could not think of hampering my activities in Yorkshire by putting a limit on my stay, neither did I wish to jeopardize the success of my growing enterprise here, so necessary to our future happiness.

I soon hit on a solution; Mr Are had mentioned that John would be at loose ends during his master's honeymoon trip. I rode over to Thornfield; it was settled in an afternoon. John would oversee Ferndean while I was gone, and in the meantime keep his mouth shut about my plans.

All was settled, but I had several weeks to live through before I could leave. My first impulse was to transform the house to receive you, to make it into as close a copy of an earthly paradise as my wits and the shops of Millcote would allow. This I checked, knowing how well you would like to please your own fancy, yet I did indulge myself to this extent: to take the sunniest room in the house and prepare it as a kind of bower, like one of those high-feathered birds in tropic lands who attempts to please its mate by dragging orange petals and green beetle wings into its nest, then struts and crows in admiration of the effect.

Millcote's gaudies, I found, were not fine enough for my bower: in the end I had to travel to Liverpool to get them. Remembering my past experiences there, I marked well the difference in perspective the possession of a few thousand pounds can make. The thieves and beggars who once towered over me like ogres, seemed more like rats as they postured for pennies, or scuttled out of the way of my horse. The grand merchants who used to curse me from their stores, now bowed and scraped for my custom. And, on a mount worth a hundred pounds, I could laugh as I rode past the madhouse that had been my bitterest bane but two years before. It pleased me to seek out the very watchman who had threatened me with his pike. He probably still wonders why the rider in the plumed tricorn flipped him a gold guinea.

Such sweet things I bought for you, Cathy! – a porcelain music box with gypsy dancers spinning on top, a gilded French bed painted with gods and goddesses, a dozen kinds of scent in gold-topped crystals, a spinet and music to play on it; from the Orient a crate of scarves and bangles, from Italy tins of sweetmeats, from Africa ivory and ebony chessmen, and other toys as light as air, as light as my heart as I gathered them.

The time I spent in and out of that chamber, readying it for you, marked one of the happiest periods in my life, certainly happier than any I have known since, even till the present night I spend writing this letter. For I lived in the certainty (as I then thought) of seeing you in three, in two, in one week's time. The culmination of all my longing approached; I fancied I saw its wings fluttering in the filmy bed curtains, as the sun through the latticed window caught in their iridescence and shimmered rainbows.

What Mary, the housekeeper, thought of these goings on I never knew; for her natural phlegm revealed nothing of reaction: neither surprise, nor blame, nor approbation. The only sign she made that she took any notice of an alteration to the household fittings was to ask how often I would be wanting the new chamber aired and dusted.

She was marginally more voluble on another subject. After one of John's visits (he came once or twice during those weeks to familiarize himself with the workings of the farm, and stayed to gossip with Mary) she made this pronouncement:

'They do say that Master has sommat he don't want the governess to know.'

I put down my newspaper (I remember I had been reading about the Paris treaty ending the American war) and looked up to where she leaned against the door jamb, familiarly fondling a plucked fowl destined for the kitchen pot. 'What would that be, Mary? They are to be man and wife within the week; it is an ill time to be keeping secrets.'

'Ill it be, sir; happen you hit on John's very word: "It's an ill wind," he said, "and like to blow ill to all at Thornfield, and further than that, too." '

But either John had said no more, or Mary chose to style it so, for that was the end of communication on the subject, only she hoped John was wrong; she hoped nothing would come of it.

The next week I went to the horse fair as planned. It was Mr Are's wedding day, but I gave scant thought to that. I succeeded in buying some very good breeding mares – sleekly long and elegant of limb, not as powerful as Beelzebub but built along his lines. What a race of horses would be started at Ferndean!

As I rode over turnpike and country lane, every few minutes I was overcome anew with the joy of near anticipation. I was to leave early on the morrow for Gimmerton; my trunks were packed and corded; all was ready. Two or three times my heart pounded to the point of nearly sending me faint off the back of my horse. But I arrived at Ferndean without mishap, to what reception you shall now hear.

I had expected to find John waiting for me, but not in the drive holding the reins of his own saddled horse, with anxious face and the air of someone who can scarce pause to draw breath.

'Master Heathcliff,' said John. 'You must come to Thornfield at once! There's no time to waste!'

Before I could voice my puzzlement at this extraordinary statement, Mary emerged from the house, her hands wound up in her apron (the autumn was drawing in; there would be a degree of frost that night) and vigorously accosted John:

'There! You mun' let him draw breath before you carry him off to your master's nonsense. Such goings on! Mr Heathcliff, you get off your horse – here's Tom come to put her away – and sit to supper. You too, man, you can say your piece while he eats. I'll not have him ride off again starving!'

So, while swallowing tea and devouring chunks of bread and butter, I heard the story of Mr Are's strange wedding. And strange it was: though Mr Are certainly entered the church a bridegroom, when he left it he was not a husband – at least not a husband to the governess!

For – wonder of wonders, and my cup of tea suspends itself midway to my mouth as I hear it – it seems Mr Are is already married, and this fact was disclosed during the ceremony, at the very altar!

'By the true wife herself?'

'No, but by her representatives,' John replied. 'One of them, a Mr Mason, had been a guest at the house before;

the other was a lawyer. We saw them when they came to Thornfield after.'

'After the aborted ceremony?'

'Aye, that was the way of it. Master had gone out that morning blooming and shining, looking the picture of himself at eighteen; when he came back his face was like a stone statue, and his hand around Miss Eyre's arm was like a stone hand – Leah thought Miss would faint with the pain of it. They said not a word, but passed through the hall, past the luggage piled up for the honeymoon, with that Mr Mason and the lawyer and the long-faced parson trailing behind. They all locked themselves in an upstairs room and talked for hours. Then the three outside men came down again, looking like three hanging judges. The lawyer said to Miss Eyre that she was cleared of all blame, not having known of the marriage, and left the house. The clergyman canted on awhile to Mr Are about the sins of bigamy, then he left too.

'Miss Eyre broke away from Mr Are, and ran up the stairs and slammed the door to her room. The master followed and pulled a chair up outside her door. When he saw us peering around the corner of the staircase (we could not think what to do, or even what to think!) he charged at us as though he were a wild animal, telling us to begone unless we wanted our brains dashed out on the landing. You may be sure after that we took ourselves to the kitchen, and did not soon venture from it.'

'But John – the supposed wife – who is she? Why has Mr Are repudiated her?'

'Well, Master Heathcliff, all agree she was beneath him. Some say she was a servant at the house, now paid off and sent away; others say she was gentry, a rich heiress, whose loose morals and shocking behaviour caused the break many years ago.'

'*Some* say these things. John, what do *you* say?' I watched him narrowly.

He fingered the hat he held in his lap. 'You'll remember I warned you that all was not right at Hall, Master Heathcliff?'

'You knew about the previous marriage, then?'

John shook off the question as a dog would shake off water after an unexpected soaking. 'What does it matter what I knew, or thought I knew, Master Heathcliff? The worst has happened, and Mr Are is in that pitiful a state, as would make you weep to see him. You must come with me now, you must help him.'

'I would think it is Miss Eyre's help he wants, not mine.'

'That's just it, sir! She's gone!'

'Gone? What do you mean?'

'Gone – vanished – disappeared into thin air, or so Master rants. From what I can make out he sat outside her door till she did finally open it, deep in the night, and they talked in the library – this I know myself from hearing the murmur of their voices; I did not sleep, but prowled the halls so to be on the spot if needed. I heard the lady's sobs, and Mr Are's voice raised, in pleading or in anger, perhaps both. After a long time Miss Eyre went up to her room again, and Mr Are stayed in the library. After a space I crept in and saw him dozing on the sofa. I covered him with a rug and was finally able to go to bed myself, for a few hours.

'The next thing I know Leah is at my door crying and saying Master is taken in a fit, and out I go to find him wandering from room to room, distracted, tearing his hair and saying over and over: "She is not here, she is not here!" '

'Miss Eyre had left in the night.'

'Yes. She had gone off, with only the clothes she brought with her to Thornfield and very little money, Master thinks only a few pounds and shillings. She left everything else. Master is beside himself; he keeps moaning that she will starve or freeze. Then he calls for you: "Where is Heathcliff? Why is he not here?" Oh, it is pitiful to hear!'

'Have the grounds been searched?'

'Aye. We found nothing, only a little bit of lady's

fabric caught on a thorn, but it may have been there for months.'

'I do not see what I can do. I cannot conjure her back out of thin air. I have my own plans; you know their importance to me; I must be on my way.'

'Nay, Master Heathcliff, you would not speak thus if you had seen him! Only stop one day. Come back with me; have your trunk sent to Thornfield. You can leave from there to the north tomorrow. You are not expected at the other end, and will lose only a day, or a half day, by doing it.'

At length I was persuaded, with what an inner struggle you know, knowing my nature. Having set my course towards Gimmerton, it was a terrible wrench to alter it even by such a slight degree; but after all, John spoke true. The detour could not delay me much.

So I agreed to go, but with an inordinate sense of foreboding. I could not prevent the feeling that I was, in so agreeing, committing an error whose consequences would be punishing to me far out of proportion to my transgression.

I paid one last visit to the room I had prepared for you. I left a bud from a late-blooming rosebush in a glass on the ivory table by your bed as a covenant that you would be there to see it when it had opened out into its blossom. I locked the door behind me and put the key in my pocket. Alas, as I write, the crumbling petals of that rose must lie as they fell, fell day by day like the dry tears of one who is beyond hope, for I have not been back.

We reached Thornfield just at dusk. It was a chill, wet evening, with intermittent gusts of cold rain. We were struck at once with the unwelcome idea that something further had gone amiss, we dreaded to imagine what, for several carriages stood in the drive and servants were loading things into them.

We soon were made to understand that the Master had dismissed the entire household, saying everyone must leave immediately, even Mrs Fairfax and Adèle. At the great ensuing lamentation, he had paid off all handsomely, literally throwing money at them, only saying that they must be gone that very night; he would not be tortured one hour more.

This was clear madness. Ordering John to detain the flitters for as long as he could, I went in search of my all-knowing mentor, my noble protector.

I found him sitting quite quietly in a straight chair, in what had been the governess's room. He was studying something very intently; he looked up.

'See, Heathcliff,' he said. 'She took nothing – not even these pearls I gave her, she left them on the mantel – nothing to sustain her in the wide, wide world. I have driven her away, I would never have forced her, she will die, I am a murderer!'

'Endeavour to calm yourself, sir! Did she not leave of her own choice? You wished her to stay, did you not?'

'Yes, yes – but you do not understand. It was my sins, my sins that drove her away.'

'Your previous marriage?'

'You have heard then!' He suddenly coiled into action; he sprang up and grasped me by the shoulders. 'What did they tell you?'

Calmly as I could, I told him what I had heard. I ended with a question: 'Is this the secret, then, that you have been hiding from me so long, and feared to tell?'

'Yes – no – it is part of it, but not all. Heathcliff, do not torment me with what is past. Help me.'

'Yes, I will help you, but I cannot do everything all alone. Why have you dismissed the servants?'

'They worried me; I could not bear to see their looks: pity or scorn, I do not know which is worse.'

'It does not matter. You must hire them back.'

'I cannot. I can do nothing but think of her. She may be perishing for want of succour, while we sit here – ! Oh, Heathcliff!'

'You will not help her by carrying on in this way.'

'But my head spins; I cannot concentrate my mind. We must find her. How can we find her?'

Putting aside the considerable curiosity and irritation I felt, I addressed the problem at hand, ascertaining what had been done and what had not been done. First it was needful to settle the problem of the servants; we must have at least some of them to help with the search, if for nothing else. Mr Are agreed to keep on John and a few of the men to search for Miss Eyre, and Leah and the cook to keep the household functioning, so the runaway would have something to return to.

That night we sent riders to every house within a ten-mile compass, asking for news and leaving a request that we be notified of any sign of the fugitive bride. I knew this step to be as sure a way of spreading scandal as any we could have devised if we had studied a fortnight, but Mr Are was not to be dissuaded – anything that could be done to speed the return of his darling, *should* be done.

By the next morning all the riders had come back empty of news. It was now twenty-four hours since the governess had vanished, and the very hour I had set for starting the journey to Gimmerton. But to do so now seemed out of the question. Mr Are was in a dangerous way; his eyes glittered; he had neither eaten nor slept since the disappearance, only galloped wildly over the countryside searching for his Jane, or dashed in panic home fearing he had missed her return.

At last I succeeded in quietening him, by the proposal of a plan. The governess, with no money or possessions, must have gone to friends; there were two places where we knew she had them: Lowood Institution, where she had received her education, and at her aunt's house. The aunt was now dead, but a cousin survived, a Miss Georgiana Reed, presently staying with other relatives in London. John would ride to the school with all possible speed; I ditto to the cousin in London, where I could also arrange for advertisements in the newspapers.

After Mr Are had been made to see the sense of these actions, he was satisfied; enough, at least, to pass from a state of near mania to one of collapse. We got him to bed; I left for London.

When I returned a week later, though with no clue as to the governess's whereabouts, I possessed at least the consoling belief that I had exhausted the possibilities of what could be done. I had set advertisements afloat all over Britain, had alerted hospital and civil authorities, had posted rewards, and had supplied a heap of grist for the mean mills of a pack of lawyers, headed by the very lawyer who had stopped Mr Are's wedding: they would write to their brothers all over the land; if anything could sift Miss Eyre out it would be their screen of words.

All was set in motion and would continue in motion without me. I was now free to leave for Gimmerton.

Fate had decreed otherwise. Dr Carter's gig was in the drive when I arrived. Mr Are wasted with a dangerous fever; he called for me continually; only my presence would quiet him.

That was last autumn. Mr Are was very ill and continued so for a weary time. With what mixture of concern, impatience, and resentment I sat by his bedside, thinking of you while I ministered to him, you may judge by your memory of my character.

Cathy, just now the candle I wrote by guttered out. Waiting for more candles, more ink, more paper – waiting long (the boy who answered my loud summons was sleepy and slow), I leaned out the open window and inhaled the fresh night air. I suddenly felt your presence most urgently. You are less than two miles away; your body – shifting in sleep? breathing my name? – displaces the very atmosphere that now cools my skin. I sighed in ecstasy. The boy returned; compelled by a lover's rapture, that must speak the adored name to all who will listen, I asked him if he had seen Miss Earnshaw in town.

He proved, now that he was fully awake, a most observant and voluble boy, capable of serving up to me not only what his own eyes had gathered, but also the full harvest of general gossip. Yes, he had seen Miss Earnshaw, in church with the Lintons: she sits with them in their pew, since nobody else at the Heights goes to church any more (Hindley being too thoroughly occupied in going to the devil!); all say that Mr Linton is again set on marrying Miss Earnshaw, after having jilted her two years since – that was a strange affair, folks said he was bewitched or mad for a while, but he had lately recovered, and loved Miss Earnshaw as much as ever. Or even more: he had formed the habit of sitting on the servants' bench with his back to the altar so he could better worship his own divinity; Miss Earnshaw looked brave in church Sunday fortnight, with three outlandish white plumes, the biggest ever seen in Gimmerton, in her green hat; Mr Linton never took his eyes off that hat and its fair owner, even when others bowed their heads in prayer; and during the sermon Miss Earnshaw was observed to repeatedly tease Mr Linton's silver shoe buckle with the toe of her velvet slipper.

So the poor one-horned snail has after all crawled out of its shell! He will regret it, though what he does or thinks will after tomorrow be nothing, less than nothing to us – but Cathy! You! I will not believe that you really intend to join your life to this fop's! I will not believe, even, that you might be toying with the notion of taking this puny lapdog to mate. You are merely tormenting him out of boredom, and punishing me for my tardiness in returning.

I wonder, could the letter I wrote to you after the business with Linton have gone astray? But I wrote one to Nelly too, to guard against that eventuality, and I had notice that postage for both had been paid, so I was sure they were delivered.

Well, all will be explained within the day. I must finish my tale, for the eastern sky begins to show light; I would be at Pennistone Crags before the sun reaches its zenith.

Every day it is the same. He asks to marry me and I say yes, by and by, I will live in a fine house adorned inside with white satin and outside with peacocks on an emerald lawn. Their cries the only things that speak of you.

When the sun shines I will take his arm and say yes and no and I will hold myself erect as I walk from room to room. My legs will not touch the lining of my stiff skirt.

And why should I not be happy? I will be, happy, happy! For you will never return. If you were alive, you would have sent me word. You must be dead.

No, not only dead, but damned, for heaven would have let you speak a branch bent groundward on a still day, a single leaf spiralling from a blank sky, an egg rolled out from nowhere across the floor – I would have heard.

No, not damned, but annihilated. Hell itself would not hold you from me. There is neither hell nor heaven in the place where you are.

On the day I am married I will walk from room to room in the spotless house, but that night I will slip from his bed and move barefoot over the silent clean carpets down, down through the kitchen to the cellar where they hide the earth smell (they cannot scrub it away)

moving through the thick dark my feet will find the patch of damp earth in the corner. If I stand perfectly quiet in the dark, if I listen very hard, I will hear

the dry rustle of dead vines climbing the cellar wall
see
pale flowers flash
behind the lids of my eyes
nothing to do but stand still

15

I hasten over the events of the next months, Cathy, for two reasons: first, because little happened till the end; second, because the news I have just had makes me anxious to condense my tale, the sooner to deliver it to the Heights and make sure of you.

Many heavy weeks passed before Mr Are was pronounced out of acute danger, and after that he lingered in a state of wasting invalidism. Day by day he clung to me as fast as a shoat to its teat; day by day, I resolved to shake him off and come to you, yet, day by day, did not.

Every morning was the same: I would ride to Millcote for news of the governess, and, getting none, ride home. Five times during the trip I would wish Miss Eyre, however distant she might be, further – all the way to Tophet, in fact. Each of the five times, however, I wished her back, if only to raise Mr Are – and me – from the slough of despondency into which her departure had sunk us.

The injured party would receive me in depressed silence, within the recesses of his dimmed bedchamber – he would not suffer the drapes to be opened; in fact he had caused extra panels, heavy and quilted, to be hung over his windows and doors. He had become hypersensitive to the least light or noise; any such stimulus, he said, sent pains shooting through his head. The servants who remained tiptoed and whispered past his room; indeed they shunned the upper reaches of the house for the most part; I had moved from the stables to the chamber adjoining Mr Are's, and could see to his wants.

The prospect of getting the report from Millcote would each morning inject the master of Thornfield with enough spirit to falter out of bed, fumble on a dressing gown and the smoked-glass spectacles he wore against the danger of glare (very great in that bedroom!), and endure the rigours of a chaise longue till my return. I suppose it was his matinal fantasy that I might bring his precious Jane back. This kept him alive, though to dignify that vegetable existence with the title of *life* is to mock the meaning of the word.

And daily I would be forced to offer him the same unnourishing budget of news – that there was none, only that the lawyers were busy as possible with the motions of advertisements and rewards, and with adding figures to the bottom of the column on their quarterly bill.

Then I would try to tempt him from his wearisome state with gossip, London papers, new books, and music – all things that before had been his delight, but from all the pleasure they created now, might as well have been dust stuffed in his mouth. I usually left his room in a temper; my feeling for you was twenty times, a hundred times stronger than his paltry attachment to the governess, yet there he cowered, the older and supposedly wiser man, a blinkered worm propped up on a plush pillow; *my* distress was at least vertebrate.

Of course I consulted with Carter, and then with other physicians too. Each prescribed a different combination of bleeding, purging, dosing, dieting, bathing, etc. to secure Mr Are's complete happiness – but after several bouts of wrangling, all concurred on one point: physically, their patient was restored to sound, if lowered, health; it was his mind only that wanted strengthening now.

When I was satisfied that this was indeed so, I decided to tell the invalid that I was going to Ferndean. Of course my real object was not Ferndean, but Gimmerton, where I would speed the minute I had put my affairs in order, but this was no business of Mr Are's, and besides could not possibly interest him – all he cared about was his priceless governess and his headache.

He was dragging on his goggles when I entered, and winced a little at the light from the hall, like a mole spaded up in a garden.

'You are early,' he said, lowering himself into his couch. 'Never mind; tell me the news. No, pray sit down, you make me nervous hulking over me like that.'

'I have no news. John has ridden to Millcote this morning. I have come to talk of something else.'

He sighed and lifted his hand an inch. Taking this for assent, I briefly told him my plan. 'The doctors say you are recovered,' I concluded, 'and Ferndean is but a few hours' ride.'

His answering voice sounded dry and bitter (I could not see his face because of the thick murk he found so comfortable): 'So you too would leave me, Heathcliff.'

'Sir, as I have just told you, and as you must allow, I am of little use to you, and of none to myself, as things stand.'

A pause. Then:

'To be of use – that is a strange motive, coming from you.'

'Can you supply me with a better one?'

'I can, and her name begins with "C".'

Upon my remaining silent, he continued, in a feeble echo of the teasing tones he used to use, 'Come, "H", confide in me. Who is "C"? You must love her still, else there would be no reason for your continued avoidance of the sex. You are no natural monk, yet I have seen you time and again repel the blandishments of the most beautiful girls in Europe, and, what is more, slip out of their mamas' snares. "C" – Caroline, Celestine, Charlotte – why do you never speak her name? "C" – Celia, Cora, Catherine – how can you bear the distance between you? If she be alive, if her whereabouts be known, how can you stay away? Tell me, H.'

This was cruel. 'You mistake my case for yours. I merely stifle from inactivity here, as you would too if you were in my place, or in your own right mind.'

'You lie – or conceal. Still you withhold your confidence.' He seemed to draw into himself, to brood. 'But if I upbraid him for this, he will merely refer me to my own example. God knows he has reason. What to do, what to do – ? Heathcliff, stay but one night more!'

'Why? To sit in the library and make conversation with the spines of the books?'

'No – I will come down. If you will stay but one night more, I will come down to sit with you. I will keep you company.'

Though I was twice as loath to incur any delay now than I had been, I hesitated. Mr Are had not been downstairs for months. And it was only for one night.

So I again was persuaded to stay at Thornfield – to my confoundment.

As I waited for Mr Are in the library that evening, my impatience to be done and gone, or perhaps an influence cast off from Thornfield's prevailing state, made me feverish. First I was chilled; nothing would warm me, I must needs pile logs on the hearth. Then I felt smothered, and had to open the window, though it was November.

At length the master of the house appeared, supported by John, who positioned him near the fire. His face had changed; what had been these last months sodden with grief, now glittered with burning intensity.

'John! The card table! Heathcliff, sit near! I would have a game!'

'Sir?'

He patted the seat next him. 'Let us play cards. You are a famous gamester; come, play with me.'

'I have given up cards.'

'Yet you will play this once, with me, for old times' sake.'

After a degree more of persuasion, I assented: 'Very well; one time more can make no difference.'

That I won was no surprise, but my usual method of winning was rendered redundant by Mr Are's utter incompetence at play, though he had insisted on setting the stakes high. Instead of paying attention to which cards he put down, he looked at me. He gazed on my face with an inexorable scrutiny, that, however unceasing, yielded him no satisfaction; if anything it made him wilder-eyed and more feverish. I waxed exceedingly uncomfortable; his eyes, so hot, chilled me; I piled more logs on the fire. Still Mr Are stared silently.

Finally I asked him what he found in my face to interest him so. He said, 'The parable of how a man may be a devil, yet walk out of hell with a word.'

Whatever game the master was playing now, I wanted no part of it. I set my mind and called to myself the lowest cards. They came to me. I put them out, confident that Mr Are could do nothing but take them, and break the morbid pattern his fancy had spun.

The second after I had cast down these paltry cards, Mr Are flicked his glance up over my shoulder, as though someone had come into the room. My eyes followed his involuntarily. When I looked back to the spread, one card had been altered – Mr Are had cheated! But not on his own account: in place of *my* deuce of diamonds, was the jack of clubs!

'Very cleverly done,' I said in a light tone, 'better than anything our old friend Ingram ever pulled off. But you have miscalculated – that was *my* deuce you replaced, so it is my loo and my ten pounds!'

'What deuce?' said Mr Are, meeting my eye squarely. 'You played no deuce – nor have you all night, your luck is so infernally good.'

I inspected his face to find what satire was intended, but discovering none, shrugged and swept in the ten pounds. If indulging him in his fancy would fill my pocket, so be it.

But as the night wore on, indulgence became weary work. I was literally unable to lose. If I left the fall of cards to luck, I would draw high and win. If concentration brought low cards to my hand, Mr Are would substitute better ones, and I would win again. Further, nothing would induce him to acknowledge his deception, even catching him at his trick; once I seized his sleeve just as he was performing a substitution. Still he kept a shameless surface, and only said, 'Mind, Heathcliff, how you go – you have ripped that lace. Now it will trail in the game!'

I was baffled, and finally gave over any attempt of control, and let the cards fall as they would.

When we ceased play at last, Mr Are bowed low and said, 'Tomorrow night, at the same hour?'

I left the room without answering, the weight of my winnings bumping against my leg. When I poured the gold out on my bed, I counted over four hundred pounds! Mr Are was handing me money; nay, cramming it down my throat! Had I stayed at Ferndean, how many deals in horseflesh would it have taken to clear such a profit?

Mr Are's whole manner had been disturbingly aberrant: its unhealthy heightening fixed on me, and its profligate outcome the deliberate wasting of his resources (though, as I had found out since his illness put me in charge of his affairs, these resources could not soon be depleted – he had holdings in the West Indies to make Thornfield look like a poor relation's potato patch). I tried to calculate a motive for his strange behaviour, but could not; I would stay one day more, to consult the physicians.

I will admit to you, Cathy, another reason for my delay: the pile of gold I had heaped on the counterpane had warmed my ambition to wealth. Might I not, in only a few days' or weeks' time, add substantially to that nest-egg which represented our joint future? Though I had enough now to form a basis for our happiness, would it not be pleasant to have *more* than enough?

But I did not quite let this line of thought surface to articulation, not that night. Instead I compacted with myself to abide by the decision of the physicians.

As I had anticipated, they advised me to humour my benefactor; let him air whatever sick fancy mouldered in his brain; at least it was a turning towards life; his former course could have only the opposite destination.

So I stayed on, Cathy, that night, the next night, and the next, and on and on, gaming with Mr Are and piling up gold. I could not stop winning, I could not stop, and

I could do little else, nothing else seemed worth the effort. I was infected – infected with a moral miasma that infiltrated the furthest corner of Thornfield Hall. I was dizzy with gold. After I had counted ten thousand, I stopped counting – only watched the pile grow.

I became almost as much a recluse as Mr Are. John now rode to Millcote for the news; I ventured out only deep at night, after the gaming and the counting were over. I remembered my old fears – was I indeed mad? But the question no longer interested me. I roamed amongst the trees, restless, fevered, baring my hot throat to the elements – finding in autumn's winds and rains, in the snow of winter (*this* winter – remember how it stormed?), fit counterpart to my inner state.

And what of my noble protector, my high-minded mentor? He increased in vigour and energy, yet it was energy of a mutant breed, expressing itself only over the card table. He continued to remain in his bedroom during the day, doing I know not what; I too kept to my room, and slept, but even in sleep I was infected – a plague crept under the door from his chamber to mine, like a sulphurous cloud, and swept my mind with unwholesome dreams.

Of some the meaning was clear enough: I saw a heavy shower of gold coins poured steadily from Thornfield's battlements on to the helpless bodies of Edgar Linton and Hindley Earnshaw, in the courtyard below. Relentlessly it fell, till their bodies were crushed, and blood ran from beneath the glittering pile.

More obscure scenes habitually replaced these. Untranslatable sighs and whispers invaded my sleep – and visions of cats, birds, flowers, twisted together and writhing, becoming huge, billowing over my head, urging some message, but in no known language.

Anxiety – hot cheeks, clogged throat – might cause me to wake. I might stagger to the window to find relief – fling it open – only to see the same dread forest awaiting me outside: the dream had tricked me.

One night – or evening, my sleep had taken me through

the afternoon – my awakening was to the flapping of enormous wings. One of the birds in the jungle had metamorphosed into a great angel, the angel of death, covered with glittering sharp black feathers; they filled my chamber with their rasping.

I woke with a start – or had I awakened? – for so sluggish was my state that I could not be sure. But dream or reality, there was a fluttering in the room; it disturbed the atmosphere; I felt my cheek brushed by feathers.

I leapt from the bed – the soles of my feet hit the cold floor; this was no dream! – there was something substantial making great swoops through the room, though I could see it but dimly by the line of light that showed under the hall door. I flung it open, and as I did so, sensed a rushing of air, heavier than wind but akin to it – one instant, and the thing had passed my ear and escaped to the corridor.

I followed it. Light radiated from a candle, stuck in its own wax to the floor. A motion in the other direction caught my eye. Something moved near the entrance to the attic.

It *was* a bird, fanning its bright wings as it settled on the top of the half-open door. It did not fly off as I approached, only nodded its head up and down. It was a parrot, such as sailors bring back from the Indies, said to outlive man and equal him in dexterity of tongues. This one was silent. Its body and wings were scarlet, but splashed with the most brilliant epaulettes of blue and yellow. It regarded me, its head cocked to one side. I offered my wrist to it.

But at that moment there was a low laugh from the other side of the door. The parrot twisted itself to peek in that direction, then dropped down to whatever it saw. I pulled on the latch. But my unseen counterpart was too quick for me – I had time only to glimpse a flash of white, before the door was slammed and bolted, and the bird and its companion, if companion it had, were beyond my ken.

I waited for Mr Are in the library as usual that night,

though not to the usual purpose; the game I had in mind would surprise him. However, I was to be surprised first.

My honoured guardian made his entrance dressed with unprecedented care, in a formal dark suit sporting fresh Flanders lace at wrist and throat. He was clean-shaved, another innovation (since his illness he had affected a rough beard), and had tied his hair back with a ribbon. In fact he was at all points accoutred in the style habitual to *me* – a piece of insolence which puzzled rather than offended, in light of his recent mental state, yet it put me off balance; I had entered the room resolved to begin my agenda as soon as he appeared; now I hesitated.

We waited while John fetched a new pack of cards: I reading the newspaper by the light of the fire in the hearth, he drumming his fingers on the card table and perusing my face.

This I pretended not to notice.

Apparently moved by a sudden impulse, Mr Are kicked back his chair and strode to the centre of the room. 'Heathcliff, come here.' He held out his hand. Ignoring a twinge of superstitious dread, I complied. I stood next to him in the spot he indicated.

He was staring at a large mirror that extended floor to ceiling on one of the library walls. In it we could see doubled the ranks of books, the leaping fire, my newspaper draped carelessly over the card table, our chairs just pushed out from it, and ourselves standing side by side.

'There you see us, Heathcliff. Do we not make a pretty pair? An edifying, uplifting spectacle? Matching pinnacles of happiness and virtue, eh?'

No answer seemed possible, so I made none. But he pressed my shoulder – of late I had had to school myself to endure his touch without shrinking, I felt such a violent antipathy to it.

'Come, Heathcliff, tell me. What do you see there?'

'I see two gentlemen dressed with suspicious similarity. They might almost be twins.'

'Yes, yes, as to dress – but what of their physical being? What is the contrast between them?'

'Though they share a darkness of skin, eyes, and hair, and have athletic builds, the younger is at all points superior to the elder. He is taller by half a head, and holds himself calm and erect. The elder slouches and twitches. Perhaps he is the victim of some nervous affliction, or perhaps some guilty secret goads him.'

'Perhaps.' Mr Are's eyes flashed as they met mine in the mirror. 'Time will tell. And their expressions – what of their expressions – ?'

'Fierce, wild, and unbending are the aspects, in both.' Indeed, as I looked long, the mirror cast its spell and our faces blended, it seemed, to one interchangeable mask.

'Heathcliff, are you a good man?'

I said nothing.

'Well? I asked you a question.'

'Why should I respond, when I know you have the answer ready and would be disappointed if I pre-empted it?'

'Hard – hard! Ever the unfeeling retort! Is there any pith of mercy in you, any morsel of forbearance and loving kindness? Sometimes I have thought so, other times I see only pride and cruelty.'

'In the mirror before us is duplicated faithfully my whole being. Look upon it. In what your eyes see, there must truth lie.'

'My eyes see courage, fortitude, intelligence, even duty, in plenty. But pity, benevolence, truthfulness – ?'

'I would scorn to tell a lie.'

'Perhaps. But you conceal much. You have let fall only snippets about your past – I know nothing of your former friends – the mysterious "C" – she who must not be named, she upon whom your whole being depends, of her you have told me nothing.'

'*You* have no secrets?'

'We both know I have secrets; I know *you* know their boundaries. But what of yours? You have more than one. For instance, what of Dent's nephew, Linton? There was something strange that summer – What was he to you? There was something there I did not understand – '

I turned to the man, away from the reflection. 'You have mentioned the boundaries of your secrets. Do they encompass a red bird?'

He stared.

'A red parrot,' I continued. 'It paid a visit to my room this evening, and was polite enough to invite me to its abode in the attic, but then it forgot its manners and slammed the door in my face. What manner of bird is this?'

The sweat started out on his brow. 'A parrot – ? Perhaps one of the servants – '

'There are only a few servants left, and none has such a bird, as you well know. Its like has not been seen at Thornfield. Yet it knew the way to the attic, well enough to lock the door after itself. Tell me, what manner of bird can do as much?'

Mr Are grasped my shoulders with both his hands and gazed long, and longer still, into my eyes. This time he did not speak it aloud, but I heard, as well as if he had shouted, the interrogation he had often undertaken of himself: Should he tell me? *Could* he tell me? The hesitation in his eyes betrayed the inevitable outcome, unless I began to ride fate again.

I raised my hands to his and removed them from my shoulders. 'Well, while we both want information, neither is willing to impart it. Would you say this is a fair definition of our impasse?'

Mr Are nodded.

'Very well; I have a way out. We must game. Not for money, never for money again. Knowledge will be our prize; the cards will determine its recipient. The loser must pay the winner by answering his question, any question, fully and with absolute truth.'

'Fully and with absolute truth,' repeated Mr Are.

'Yes,' I said. 'And we must solemnly vow to adhere to this rule, else there would be no point to this game, or any other.'

After an intense pause, Mr Are answered: 'I agree. But we must have a prearranged schedule of play, lest either winner or loser think better of continuing and call halt to the proceedings.'

'Good. Say five questions in total, then?'

Mr Are nodded. 'And five answers, true and complete answers.'

'Done.' I sat down and picked up the deck.

'Oh, one thing more,' said Mr, Are, nipping the cards from my hands. 'Let us put these by. You are too damnably lucky with them. Dice are what we want, to level the odds. Agreed?'

I shrugged. 'Agreed, though I might justifiably point out that of late *you* have been my lucky genius!' Inwardly, I warmed myself with the knowledge that my powers were not limited to cards.

Yet, during the minute or two it took John to fetch dice and cup, I had time for self-doubt. I did not *know* that I could control the dice. Perhaps not; or perhaps it would take two or three tries before I got the knack of it – even that might spell disaster for me – Mr Are was suspicious about Edgar Linton. What if I were forced by his questions to incriminate myself? Of course I might choose to lie, but I had just bound myself to truth; that was a bond I would somehow tremble to break.

John put the things on the table, bowed, and left. Mr Are and I shook hands.

He rattled the dice in the cup; the leaping flame behind me was reflected in his eyes. 'Let it be as God wills it,' he said, and let fall the bony cubes. He had rolled a seven.

I tried to gather up my will, but his eyes hindered me. A puny trey was my roll. My chest clogged with panic as I awaited his question.

'Who is "C" – I mean what is she, to you?'

I laughed in surprise at the question, and at the sudden knowledge that I was going to answer it. Though I had steadfastly refused to talk about you for three years, hugging even your name jealously to my secret self, now my instinct to hide my heart's treasure, rigid though it had been, melted.

'"C" stands for Catherine – Catherine Earnshaw. I was adopted by her father, and raised with her.'

'She was your sister?'

'My sister, yes, and more-than-sister.'

'You loved her, of course.'

'Of course.'

'She returned your love?'

'Yes.'

'How were you certain of that? I suppose you pledged eternal faithfulness to each other?'

'It was more that we were, and are, eternally one. I am part of her, she is part of me.'

'Hmph. Very fine, I am sure. But then, how could you leave her?'

'She said it would degrade her to marry me – and so it should have done, at that time. For after Earnshaw's death the heir, Hindley, had banished me to the stables, and I became as you found me, base and ignoble.'

'You are base and ignoble no longer. Do you still wish to marry this Catherine?'

'Marriage is too feeble a word to describe the union I wish with her, but yes, I would marry her.'

'Then marry her you must and will, man! We will seek her tomorrow!'

I blinked with astonishment. A tangled knot had been cut loose; what had seemed difficult was rendered simple; the labyrinth was mapped.

Meanwhile, Mr Are had reached a mighty pitch of excitement. His breath came fast, he paced between table and fire, the eyes rolled in his head. But his frenzy was now recognizably one of elation, not despair.

My powers failed again on the next roll. Mr Are had the question. I tried to steel myself for his words; now, at the very moment of my release, it was possible I would hear my doom pronounced.

'What were you doing outside the madhouse at Liverpool?' he asked.

'What?' This was an unexpected turn.

He repeated the question.

'I had travelled there in an attempt to learn the secret of my origin,' I said.

'Fully, fully!' he remonstrated. 'Your answer is not complete. Why Liverpool? Why the madhouse?'

'I had been told that Mr Earnshaw had found me in Liverpool, and my memory – partial, dim memory – guided me to the madhouse. I thought I remembered having lived there. A low whitewashed wall, kicks and curses, a tunnel to the outside – '

Mr Are's eyes glittered. 'It was thus, it was thus, so they said, so I saw! Go on!'

Struggling to reckon the dizzying implications of his comments, I continued: 'I escaped and lived for a while by my wits in the street, stealing from thieves, begging from beggars. Then Mr Earnshaw carried me back to Wuthering Heights and named me Heathcliff, after a son who had died.'

'Well and bravely answered! Roll!'

This time *I* was the winner. Mr Are set his jaw as if readying it for a blow. 'Ask!'

'Why were *you* outside the madhouse in Liverpool?'

Studying his face, I could perceive that thrice an answer was born on his lips, and twice a paralysis settled there to stifle it. The third time he managed to utter, 'I was seeking my son.'

My lips, too, stiffened. 'Why seek him there?'

'Because I had put him there fifteen years before that time. His mother was mad, and as he resembled her greatly in body and seeming disposition, I feared him equally afflicted, and could not abide to watch the malady develop in one who bore my blood. I left him there, supplying a false address for myself, but I caused money to be sent every year for his keep.'

'What did you find in the madhouse, then?'

'Nay, that is a separate question. You must roll for the right to ask it!'

I knew I would win the roll, and I did. 'What did you find at the madhouse?'

He licked his lips. 'I found that nine years previous my son had escaped, and had never been seen again. Still receiving my money every year, they had kept his little whitewashed room as it was, and had preserved the tunnel under the wall as he had dug it, only plugging up the outer end. He must have been a strong, brave lad to have escaped so.'

The dice had fallen to the floor between us. My eyes were held by his eyes.

'What is my name?' I asked.

'Heathwood – Heathwood Are,' he said. 'Earnshaw must have come upon you by chance and been struck by the similarity of your name to that of his dead son.'

My heart swelled. I could not speak.

'Can you forgive me?' Mr Are asked.

Words would not come to me. I did not know what words were in my mind.

He continued: 'When I saw your face that night I knew you were my son, for it is your mother's very face in masculine mould. I followed you; your initial on the locket, your name when you told it me – confirmation of your identity. But given that, I feared, I feared. The astonishing resemblance, your savage aspect, your strange behaviour, all seemed to draw to one conclusion – that you too were mad, tainted by your mother's fatal blood. Yet there was that in your being that denied madness. I would test you. Using all the stratagems at my command, I tested you. John was already suspicious because he had seen your mother and recognized the likeness; he feared you for me; I took him partly into my confidence; his fear changed to respect. I watched you, noting with despair your bursts of rage and cruelty, with elation your quickness of application. I gave you more responsibility. You rose to every challenge. I educated you, and you rapidly attained that level upon which a son of mine must exist – nay, you surpassed every expectation. I grew to love you – you flinch, but it is so –

yes, to love you, in spite of your hard exterior. Or mayhap because of it; what is that flinty carapace but a response to my neglect, and evidence of your superior spirit, that would survive in spite of all? There was much warmth between us – I felt it – '

'There was a change,' I said.

'Yes – a change – ' He strode to the fireplace and stirred the fire. 'The woman I loved feared you, perhaps apprehending your origin and what it implied. Secure in loving you, sure that all would be put right soon, I allowed her to believe that you wished me ill, since that belief served other urgent purposes. I felt your resentment and gloried in it, for it meant you were not indifferent to me. I meant to reconcile the two of you – my two most beloved – in time, and to restore you to your rightful place in the world.'

A log broke; sparks hissed through the room. Mr Are turned from the fire with an air of decision. 'And so it shall be, at least in part. She is gone and may never return, but you are here. You are my son, and shall be known so to the world from this day forward. My sweetheart is lost, but yours, please God, may yet be gathered to you. You shall bring her to this house as your bride.'

Still I stood motionless. How strange it was.

Father.

He studied my face as though seeing it for the first time. 'How dear he is become to me! How I would strain him to my heart, claim him as my ewe lamb! But he is no lamb, he is a wolf, he will eat me through to my vitals with his cruelty.'

Still I was silent a while longer.

He stood before me, eyes burning. 'Heathcliff?'

I must have made some sign, for he embraced me. Unfamiliar sensations flooded my body. I wanted to crush his head against the hearthstones with the poker, but I wanted to bury myself in his breast.

I found I was weeping. Weeping, I loosed myself from

his embrace. Weeping, I scooped the dice from the floor. Weeping, I placed them on the table.

'There is one question left,' I said. 'Roll for it.'

I won the toss. The look in his eyes said he knew what I would ask.

'Where is my mother?'

Of a sudden, his body seemed to shrink up into itself. The light in his eyes dimmed. Cold and silent, he turned, took up a candle, and beckoned me out of the room.

We ascended, as I knew we should ascend, to the upper corridor, to the door within which the bird had disappeared. He took down a ring of heavy keys, which I had never noticed before, from where it hung on a hook above the jamb. He unlocked that door; we walked up the stairs behind it to the attic hall. At the end was another locked door.

Mr Are paused outside it. 'Are you resolved to go through with this, Heathcliff? She is mortally dangerous; you have seen her handiwork on me, and heard what she did to Mason, who is her brother.'

'I am resolved.'

He knocked. Upon receiving no answer he inserted a key within the lock and turned it. He called out: 'Bertha! Bertha Are!'

'What name is that?' called out a clear voice from within. 'It is not mine; it never was. Why do you persist in applying it to me?'

'It is part of her delusion to deny her name,' said Mr Are, speaking low, as he pushed open the door, 'as she would deny everything else that is true. For God's sake be on your guard, Heathcliff. She is cunning.'

We saw two women sitting at a large round table in the middle of the room. The red parrot sat on the taller one's shoulder. A globular lamp at the table's centre, while illuminating the rolled manuscripts, bottles of ink, and stained quills that lay spread everywhere around it, cast the woman's face, now turned towards me, into deep shadow.

The other woman, very slight, with a gentle eye, said,

'She is quiet today. She never complains. Her fortitude under suffering is remarkable.'

'It is her sister,' explained Mr Are *sotto voce*. 'She is lately come from the West Indies to replace the servant woman who left.'

'Why will you talk of the West Indies?' asked the shadowed woman. 'That was never my home. Why do you insist that it was so? And why do you keep me imprisoned here? I want to return to my own house. Do you hear? Monster! Jailer! Answer me!'

Mr Are flinched and put his hands over his ears. 'Terrible! Terrible! To hear such intelligence as once was there perverted! To see such beauty decayed!'

The woman suddenly sprang forward, seizing Mr Are savagely by the neck. They struggled wildly for a moment amidst a great tumult of air from the parrot's beating wings. Then her sister came up to the woman from behind and touched her on the shoulder. She subsided instantly into her chair; the parrot settled in its former spot.

'Behold Bertha Mason Are, the Creole, the wanton,' panted Mr Are. 'I was tricked into marrying her when I was younger than you, and only discovered my mistake when it was too late. All her line is fatally infected with a pernicious madness, a madness that seems reason, but would have the world other than what it is, and strives to seduce others to a like delusion. Heathcliff, behold your mother!'

And Mr Are moved the lamp so that it at last cast its rays on – a mirror, a deep pool, that reflected him who looked into it, and drowned him.

'Mother? I am no mother,' said the woman in a wondering tone. 'And this is no son of mine. And yet – ' She reached out a hand to my cheek. 'Yet – '

'Do not let her touch you!' warned Mr Are, interposing his arm between her and me. 'She will turn on you in an instant, as she did me.'

'In all I do, I try only to free myself,' she said, drawing herself up proudly. 'It is the first, the only honourable task of the prisoner – to outwit his jailers and regain the world. I give you warning – both of you – to do this I will commit any savagery, any outrage. Powerful though you may think yourselves, ultimately you have no power to hold me!'

'Defiant and intractable wretch! Yet how pitiable. She had the appearance of sanity, of purity, once. Now she disgraces the name of woman. But she will never escape. It is my duty to hold her here. Chained, she torments only me. Loosed, she would harrow the world!'

'Vain and foolish man!' she addressed him. 'There are other channels of escape besides doors and windows. Bar those as you will; I am free in spite of you!'

'Rave on, rave on, dear wife. Be happy in the knowledge that you have ruined me.' Then, in my direction: 'Well, Heathcliff? Has the warm sentiment inspired by the sight of your mother melted your organ of speech? Is it the loving gleam of her eye that moves you so? Or perhaps the maternal care evident in her address? Are you not blessed to have such a mother? Are you not glad you asked to be shown her?'

I sat in a chair next the table.

'Leave us,' I said to Are.

He laughed bitterly. 'You cannot mean it.'

'I do. Leave the two of us together. I would speak with her privately.'

'I will not do it. You know not what you ask. She would destroy you.'

'That is nonsense. She is calm. She lashes out only at you.'

'It is her cunning. She would attempt to overpower you as soon as I left the room.'

'Faugh! Overpower me? I could snap her like a reed. Besides, you have said I am her son. As such, I can at least match her in ferocity and cunning.'

Though he held out long, and was loath to submit, Mr Are finally gave in to my request. After many cautions and conditions, he and the other woman went out into the hall. 'But remember, I am listening. One cry, and I return.'

Once the others had left the room the lamplight seemed to leap out and gather the two of us in towards it. I could see my mother's face much more clearly now. Where at first I had been struck only by its resemblance to my own, now I saw how wasted, gaunt, spectral it was. Did she wane before my eyes?

'Why do you say you are not my mother?' I asked.

'For a long time, almost as long as I can remember, I have been imprisoned in these rooms. There is nothing to do here – only plot for my escape, and write on the paper my captor provides me. So I do write. I write night and day. I write very small so that the paper will last longer.'

'What do you write?'

'Sometimes I write about prisons like this and savage men like Are. Sometimes I write about beautiful faraway kingdoms, floating in another ocean. Then I am free, for in the worlds I create I am free, and free to be other women, other men.'

'Where were you before you came here?'

'Are will tell you I come from a tropic land, but he lies. I come from the north, where the wind blows colder and fresher than here. I remember the moors – sunlight on the heather, open air in every direction. I remember horses in the barn, dogs barking, bread rising in the kitchen – '

'It sounds like my old home.'

'That is strange. And you look strangely familiar. Perhaps you are my son after all.'

Again she reached out to my cheek. This time I suffered her to touch it. I had found her. I closed my eyes.

A great blinding light exploded in my skull. My eyes filled with blood. Dimly, I perceived as from a distance my mother holding over me one of the rolled-up manuscripts, with something that looked like an iron bar protruding from the end. She had hit me with it, and only refrained from striking me again when she had satisfied herself that I was stunned, and unable to move against her.

I sprawled in the chair, seeing all that happened, but powerless to prevent it.

Next she wadded up a great gout of paper and crammed it down my gullet, I suppose to stop me shouting out, if ever I found my voice.

Mr Are had forgotten the ring of keys on a chair by the door; she tried them till she found the one that would loosen the heavy leaded windows. She flung them wide, then plucked the parrot from her shoulder and threw it out into the night; I heard it squawk and take wing. She seemed to glory in the strong wind that now entered the room – she danced before it, swinging her skirts wide and laughing.

I felt my consciousness slipping from me, but by a great effort of will sustained it. Time blurred and slowed in my eyes.

From the murky depths of a large inkwell my mother draws a tiny dagger – home-hewn by the look of it, but deadly sharp – and places it in her pocket.

Next she begins twisting up pages from the table. I see what she is about! Beware, Thornfield! But I cannot move, cannot shout, cannot even grunt a warning; my throat has turned to stone with all else. I watch as she ignites the twist with the lamp-flame. Gaily she torches the far curtain – then the hanging above the bed – then the tablecloth –

The door bursts open. She is ready, has drawn to one side, thinking to slip out unnoticed while Are rushes to put out the fire. But he sights her as she glides out, lunges towards her, knocks her to the floor. They rise, fall, struggle, rise again, locked together in a terrible dance that moves them ever nearer the blazing windows. I hear shouts from outside the house.

My heart pulses in a burst of pain; sensation is returning! I force strength down from my chest through my limbs. I choke out the paper wad, stagger towards the writhing pair, embraced in intimate combat. They teeter at the low sill of the open window. 'Father!' I cry.

He looks over his shoulder at me; the woman ducks under his arm to free herself. But not to escape; to draw the dagger. With both hands she raises it above my father's back as he turns, too slowly. I propel myself towards her.

It is done in an instant. She is out in the night, falling, flying. Her incandescent skirts billow in the wind – she is flying, floating, blooming like a great white flower in the black air.

A mighty cry ascends from the courtyard. I have toppled my mother out the window. She is crushed on the flagstones below.

Blaze; a crash. A flaming beam has fallen on my father's shoulders; he has crumpled beneath it. I am choking. With a terrible effort, I heave the fiery weight aside, raise the charred and bloody body beneath it in my arms, stagger – I know not where, but I am down the infernal staircase and John is relieving me of my senseless burden. I look at what lies on the flagstones. Mother. Though the brains lie dashed beneath it, my face stares unaltered back at me.

That was a week ago. They say Mr Are will live, but as a blind and maimed man – the doctors amputated one hand. I escaped with only the wound on my head and a few burns. Thornfield was completely destroyed.

Yesterday, the day Mr Are recovered his senses, he sent for his lawyer and settled upon me outright thirty thousand pounds. I sat by his bedside for a while, but finally pressed the groping fingers of his remaining hand and left. Let him find what it is to be abandoned and imprisoned.

Cathy, I have booked passage on a ship sailing from Liverpool to the new world. Come with me to America, far away from those who have oppressed us. There we can be happy and free – free as the aboriginal inhabitants of that vast and beautiful continent, free as the wild wind that blows alike over our native moor and the plains of our future home.

Send word for me to come, or come yourself – I have engaged the inn boy, he will lead you to my carriage. My love, fly to me! If I have lived till now, let me die in your embraces! I scorn a lesser existence.

Your

H–

Under Heathcliff's signature was appended a postscript from Mrs Dean. It said, 'Having hurried through these last pages while the boy whirred the top I had given him in the next room, I felt thankful for the wisdom that had led me to take matters into my own hands. To his list of sins Heathcliff had added matricide and the abandonment of his father. No matter how rich and polished he might have become (and, not having set eyes on him yet, I seriously doubted both points), he was still the devil we knew from before, and could only bring sorrow down on my mistress and those who loved her.

'Therefore I thrust the document into my workbox and returned to the boy. I told him that Miss Earnshaw had been married to Edgar Linton yesterday, and that the couple had just left on their wedding trip; I had gone out the back door in an effort to intercept their carriage where the road loops by Blackhorse Marsh, but had just missed them – that was why I had taken so long.

'For answer the stupid boy only stared at me doubtfully. In a terror to get quit of him before Miss Cathy returned from the Grange, I pointing to the wedding dress. 'See,' I said, 'there is the dress she was married in yesterday; I have the care and storing of it now, so get you gone; I must be about my business.' At that he turned tail and ran off with his message. I would not have been in his shoes for all the gold in the new world.

'Mr Lockwood, the rest you know. Heathcliff went

away again for half a year – you have heard of his return and what followed upon it.

'Sometimes it lies heavy upon me that I could have prevented those tragedies by delivering the letter to Catherine. I doubt not that her deep attachment to Heathcliff would have prevented her from marrying Mr Linton, and perhaps would have drawn her to the waiting carriage. But what worse tragedies might have ensued? A veil lies between us and the answers to such conjectures – I cannot rend it.

'Do not fail to let me know your conclusion.

'N.D.'

Tomorrow I will be a bride and he will come to me with his breast abloom.

But how can I flower without you? He is a stranger who comes for me, a gilded man in a picture, whose kisses are paper not fire like yours, my hawk, my eagle.

Not mine. You left me.

I dash you from the sky. You are nothing to me – never leaping the wall in the morning with the sun at your back, never reaching out from the barn shadows, never whispering a secret word in my pillow.

Never riding over the hill again.

I opened my eyes to the glare of a brilliant white winter sun, unoccluded by snow or cloud, spreading slantwise through the train compartment. The blind had sprung open, apparently by its own agency again, for Mr Lockwood, like me, was blinking in affronted amaze at the bright vigour of this new morning.

I gasped. Not only had I actually fallen asleep on a train, an unprecedented event; I had relaxed my grip on the manuscript and let go its pages, which were now slid helter-skelter down the crazy slopes of the blankets. I immediately sprang forward to gather them – making that which was bad, worse: what papers had been left on my lap now joined their fellows on the floor.

Exasperated, I leaned down to scoop them up. At the same instant Mr Lockwood too bent to similar purpose. Simultaneously we remembered the crack of heads that had initiated our acquaintance; simultaneously we jerked back to avoid a repetition, our exophthalmic stares locked in alarm.

At this interesting moment the compartment door was opened. 'Five minutes to Leeds station,' a train employee said, and shut it again.

Mr Lockwood smiled and raised his hand. 'Permit *me*,' he said, as he began to gather the pages; then: 'Were you able to finish?'

'Yes.' I paused; memory rushed forward with many questions. Was Heathcliff ever reconciled to Mr Are? Was that sad man reunited with the fugitive governess? What brought Heathcliff and Cathy to forgive each other before she died? Did he execute the terrible vengeance on Edgar Linton he had threatened? How exactly did Heathcliff leave this world – *if* he did? And what were the details of the haunting Mr Lockwood himself had experienced, and that was still rumoured at the abandoned farmhouse?

But even the first of these questions was interrupted by the re-entrance of the train employee, to collect the blankets. Then there was no more time; I must fasten my coat, wrestle with my gutta-perchas, collect my shawls and my wits. The train stopped. We were bustled out of the compartment and on to the platform before we knew it.

My companion, who had courteously preceded me to act as a breakwater against the surging crowd (since I am small of stature, the service was welcome), now stopped and faced me. People swirled around us like quick currents about an island. With one hand he held his stick and the sheaf of papers, sadly jumbled, against his chest. With his other he pressed my arm, his face communicating a singular attentiveness. 'Miss Brontë, your verdict – what should I tell her?'

I hesitated. What could I say? What could he say, to an old, old woman with only death ahead of her?

Behind Mr Lockwood I saw a small group of people making their way towards us, against the flow of the crowd, scanning the area and pointing. Chief among them was a tall, striking lady with large dark eyes and beautiful white hair. Somehow I had no doubt that here was the daughter of Cathy and Edgar, and that it was my interlocutor she sought. I must speak now or lose the chance forever.

'Tell Mrs Dean it was the only thing she could have done,' I said. 'Tell her she really had no choice. She had to follow the laws – '

But my last words were swallowed in the chug of a train approaching on a parallel track. A voice called out a name; hearing it Mr Lockwood turned; a final pressure of the hand and he was gone.

I found my own way to the Keighley connection, and was home by noon.

16

It was the early afternoon of a warm day in March. I sat by the bedside of an old lady whose face above the counterpane was withered and shrunken as a winter apple, but whose hand gripped mine with summer vigour. The room, spacious, bright, and well-appointed, had in it only the two of us and one other person, my sister Emily, who sat apart in a shadowed corner. Through the half-opened door muted voices could be heard in conversation.

The old woman was Nelly Dean; the room was in Thrushcross Grange; the half-heard voices, those of its mistress Mrs Catherine Earnshaw, recently widowed daughter of that Cathy whose story I knew so well, and Mr Charles Lockwood, my late travelling companion. And on the bedside table in front of my nose lay a familiar stack of yellowing pages.

Reader, you may wonder what stirring events, what startling disclosures, what high-flown speeches, had filled the three months between that snowy day in January when I bid Mr Lockwood good-bye at the station, and the quiet scene to which I now direct your attention.

The answer is, all too literally, none! – no occurrence with shape enough to be termed an event had varied the humdrum of parsonage routine; no one besides Father's boorish curate and Tabby, our housekeeper, had spoken more than two consecutive sentences to me during that period. And worst of all, *M* Heger had been silent, making no response to my letters – though, I feared, his silence in itself made a most speaking response.

Silence too had reigned between me and Emily. Though I knew it to be unwise, I had not been able to resist questioning her about Heathcliff; the result was a withdrawal of unprecedented distance and duration. She and

I scarcely spoke at all except about our father's illness, and necessary household matters. Even in the latter we were divided; Emily kept to the kitchen with Tabby, while I did the solitary dusting and bed-making.

And until now Mr Lockwood too had been silent. Though in the rush of our departure no arrangement had been made for a future meeting, I had more than half expected, given the short distance between Haworth and Thrushcross Grange, to hear something from him in the weeks that had followed our forced, but genuine, intimacy.

Nothing had come till yesterday, when a messenger knocked with a letter for me. For a half-second my heart pounded violently – *M* Heger, my beloved *maître*, had written! – only to contract when I put on my spectacles and made out a Gimmerton postmark; still, the reception of any letter was a feast to break the famine of those barren hours. I opened the envelope.

The contents were a surprise. With all the authority a waxy seal and creamy embossed paper could give her, the mistress of Thrushcross Grange begged a visit from 'Miss Brontë and her sister' (Emily, it must be, since Anne was from home). The invitation was the urgent request of Mrs Ellen Dean, of whom Miss Brontë had heard, for an interview with them – she specified both sisters. She, Mrs Earnshaw, and Mr Lockwood, who had made the acquaintance of Miss Brontë on the train, would deem it a great kindness in the Misses Brontë if they would pay this visit; a carriage would call at eleven.

So it had been arranged. I of course was eager to go; for someone to beg to speak to *me* was a novelty, and then Mrs Dean might answer some of the questions Heathcliff's manuscript had raised, and left hanging. To my surprise Emily readily agreed to accompany me. The coach came as promised.

Though I had languished in a kind of static limbo these past months, the rest of the world had not. This I felt with a pang when Mr Lockwood greeted us in Thrushcross's entrance hall, for he had so evidently prospered in the company of the stately woman to whom he introduced us. The brooding tension I had noticed in the train seemed now to have vanished, to have been replaced by a sparkling content that communicated itself to me in the glad pressure of his palm when he shook my hand, and in the pleasure with which he seemed to observe me, Mrs Earnshaw, indeed all that passed before his eyes. And for the most part he was content to observe only, and let Mrs Earnshaw do the talking.

That gracious lady, speaking in a hurried low voice in the entrance hall, begged pardon for taking us up to see Mrs Dean now, even before offering us refreshment, but the old lady was so very anxious for the visit, it would be cruel to defer it.

'She has been failing fast these past days,' whispered Mrs Earnshaw as we mounted the stair. 'But she still has her periods of lucidity, and then, she asks for you. There is a certain manuscript, or letter,' she pressed my arm, 'you know of what I speak – and lately the poor soul has been obsessed with the idea of delivering it, and seems to connect *you* with the task.' We traversed a broad corridor towards an open door. 'We have put her in my mother's old room; she is happiest there. She has asked to speak to you alone; Charles and I will wait apart.' And, after ushering us in and introducing us to the little figure on the bed, they left, and we were alone with Mrs Dean.

At first sight it seemed scarcely possible that conscious life inhabited this shrunken frame, but my mistake was speedily corrected; as soon as the old housekeeper saw me her eyes danced and snapped, betraying a lively mind behind them. She captured my hand in greeting, and, in her homely countrywoman's way, without further preamble set out to drain me of all intelligence I might possess concerning my family, its history, and its place in this part of the world, searching for some link connecting it with herself or her friends. Emily she ignored.

At length this interrogatory barrage found a mark; it developed that our servant Tabitha had once been a great gossip of Mrs Dean's, though they had not seen each other for many years. I resigned myself to a recitation of Tabby's affairs, and was mentally marshalling my knowledge of them to that purpose, when my contrary inquisitor said suddenly, 'Well, Miss! I have found out a good deal from you, and you have answered the questions of an old woman pretty patiently. It is only fair that I return the favour. What would you like to ask me?'

I was so startled at this sudden reversal that I opened my mouth but said nothing for a second, long enough for Mrs Dean to continue:

'Come, you do have questions. I can almost see them there balancing on the tip of your tongue. And you have been eyeing Heathcliff's letter this past quarter hour, as though you would eat it up if you could!'

At this I had to laugh. 'You are right, of course, Mrs Dean. I am very curious. I want to hear the real end of the story.'

With a little start she let go my hand. 'Of Heathcliff's story? The end? The real end?' For one so solicitous of questions, she seemed oddly baffled by this one. Her eyes dimmed; her fingers began idly pleating the edge of the counterpane. 'There was no end – only circles – like tendrils of bindweed – around and around – '

I attempted to fix her attention on tangible matters. I patted the stack on the table. 'But the letter, Mrs Dean, the letter – what happened after you got it?'

'Mr Lockwood knows; didn't he tell you? I kept it; Miss Cathy never set eyes on it. She married Mr Linton.'

'Yes, I know, but Mr Heathcliff returned, after you had intercepted the letter and after the marriage . . . ?'

The twisted fingers continued to pleat the counterpane, but the voice grew stronger as it picked up the trail of its story: 'Yes, he returned; that one would always turn up where he was least wanted. 'Nelly,' he said out of the night, 'it's me. Don't you know me?' and there he stood like a great sleek wolf in the moonlight, half devil, half man. And I daren't keep him out, for he would have got in eventually and the mistress would have taken a fit over the delay; so I went in to where she and the master and Miss Isabella were taking tea so peacefully, and announced him.'

'What happened then?'

'Oh, Miss Cathy was half mad to see him, you may be sure, but out of consideration for Mr Edgar, who stood by cold and silent, she kept her joy almost within decent bounds, grasping her foster-brother's hands and exclaiming over him, but not smothering him with kisses, at least not in front of her husband. And Heathcliff held himself stiff and taut as a strung bow, and danced out as many manners in that hour as your fine London gentleman could in a day! But I could see with him it was all policy; he was waiting for his chance.'

'His chance for what?'

'His chance to have her alone, so he could persuade her to undo what she had done and go off with him at last. But I knew his game, and I took care to be present at their meetings, though I had my ears boxed for it more than once. Besides, I feared that if they talked together too freely my suppression of the letter might come to light.'

'It did not?'

'No – they were so alike, you see – mirror pictures; each looked in the other's eyes and saw itself reflected there, and so loved, and so hated. Oh, they were selfish! – and they were proud, and wilful, and resentful of the injury each thought the other had done. So they talked around and around each other, never meeting head on till the day of her death, and so never came to the truth of the letter.'

'But what about Mr Linton? Did he never tell his wife about his meeting with Heathcliff?'

'Oh, no, Miss – he never would allude to it, least of all to Mrs Linton. She was that unjust and capricious, you know, to likely dismiss Heathcliff's treatment of my poor master with a laugh, then turn around and rage a fortnight over Mr Edgar's silence on the whereabouts of her lost playfellow. And the master knew it, too. Oh, he knew it!'

'He must have greatly loved her, to have overlooked such serious flaws in her character. Also, if I may say so, he was brave to have married her in defiance of Heathcliff's threatened revenge.'

'I have thought that myself, Miss, and wondered over it too. What gave him the courage after two years to try his luck? Of course he must have had news from his Aunt and Uncle Dent of the strange goings-on at Thornfield. Maybe when he heard of Heathcliff's retiring from the world with his guardian after the scandal, he felt it was safe to act. Yes, in the balance, I think that must have been the way of it.'

'Still, his love was great. Did hers match it?'

'Not by any means. As I say, Miss Catherine was her own true love, along with what she saw of herself in Heathcliff.'

'Then why did she marry Linton?'

'After self-love, ambition was her besetting sin. She wanted to be a fine lady, and have a handsome, rich husband. And so she was untrue, and so she paid. She died, in this very room it was.'

The bedchamber, which had seemed so gay and cheerful up to now, suddenly went a degree colder. Involuntarily, I swept its perimeter with a glance, as though expecting to see a corpse materialize on the window-seat.

'Yes, it was in this very room she died, on this very bed, after having given birth to my mistress, whose voice we hear now in the next room. And I had kept watch every night for weeks on the daybed in the corner; yes, that very one, where your sister sits now. It was a day like this one, a warm sunny day in March, with the winds blowing up the earth smell from the moors through the windows – yes, swung outward just as you see them; she said the moor air made her feel stronger. The master had gone to church, and I let him in.'

'Him?'

'Heathcliff. It was the last time, you see, so I let him.

I knew she must die. She was sick with the child, and had torn herself in half between the two men, and now they had both abandoned her for her pains: Heathcliff had married Miss Isabella out of spite, and Mr Edgar had shut himself away with his books. The look of death was upon her.'

'So you let him come up here.'

'Only the one time. They embraced, on that daybed. And I can bear witness to the fact that they were able to settle their differences, to understand each other at last. They even forgave each other – in *their* fashion – for what was loving to them would appear to normal folks like killing – afterwards she had bruises big as hen's eggs on her arm from where his thumb had pressed it so fondly! But she would have killed *him* if she could, to take him with her; she said so before she died that night.'

'She died. Then what happened?'

'Then? What more could happen? She had the baby. She was dead before the dawn.'

At this Emily leaned forward and started to say something, then only half-smiled and shook her head.

'Oh, you are thinking of Mr Edgar. Yes, he mourned, most grievously. He sat with the corpse night and day till it was buried in the churchyard. Not in the vault – she had said she wanted to feel the moor winds blowing through the grass above her.'

'And what of Heathcliff?' I asked.

'Well, he suffered mightily for twenty years, and made others suffer too – he wreaked what vengeance he could on the two houses, and finally by hook or crook became master of all. He very nearly prevented my mistress from marrying Hareton, Hindley's son – spiteful as Heathcliff was, he couldn't bear to see anyone connected with his old enemies happy – but he died before he could complete the plan. He was haunted by Miss Cathy's ghost (as Mr Lockwood witnessed), and she fretted and worried the life out of him at last, and he lies with her now in the same grave. Yet some say neither of them lies there, but they walk the moors still.' Mrs Dean shook her head and touched the corner of her eye, as though to blot a tear.

'Is that all?'

'That is all – except for the end of the ending, for now Mr Lockwood has returned in his old age, and he is to marry my dear mistress, who will not live the rest of her days alone, praise be to God, since it seems *I* must die.'

Suddenly her face changed and she rolled her head closer to me, this time with real tears wetting her cheek.

'Mr Lockwood has forgiven me. Do you forgive me?'

I had expected something of this nature (though not quite in the form it took) and so was ready with my speech: 'It is not for me to forgive. I have not been injured. But I can offer an opinion, especially since you have now given me the whole story.' I patted her hand. 'I am sure you have done the right thing.'

At this, with some effort she raised herself up from the pillow, and squinted in Emily's direction.

'And you, Miss? You so dark and silent in the corner? What do you think?'

Emily said without smiling: 'Excuse me, but I do not think you would really care to hear *my* opinion.'

Mrs Dean held a beckoning finger out to Emily.

'Come into the light, where I can see you.'

Without hesitation Emily rose, and moved to a seat on the other side of the bed from me, where the sun from the window fell full on her face.

Mrs Dean examined it for several seconds without speaking.

'Ah! Ah!' she exclaimed at last, and clucked her tongue emphatically. 'Perhaps you are right! Perhaps I would not care to hear from you. Sometimes silence is best.' Shaking her head, she closed her eyes.

She kept them closed, and uttered no further word. After a minute or two I felt some alarm, and looked at Emily.

She shrugged indifferently. Just then Mrs Earnshaw entered and gave Mrs Dean's shoulder a gentle pat. The old woman opened her lids, but remained mute.

'You are tired, are you not, Nelly?' Aside, to us: 'She is fatigued; it is best we leave her to herself now; if she does speak it will likely be to wander. Will you come downstairs and take tea?' We began to rise.

Then, sharply, from the bed: 'How now, Missy! I'm wandering, is it? When I have as many wits about me this moment as you on the best day you ever lived!'

Mrs Earnshaw smiled at us. 'Well, then, what is it, Ellen?'

'Only that I still have some business with these two. I still have a letter to deliver.'

'They are here; they are waiting.'

Mrs Dean reached over and laid her hand on Heathcliff's manuscript. With a trembling but purposeful gesture, she held it out. 'Here,' she said. 'It is right that you should take it.'

Emily glanced at me, smiling slightly at my amazed expression, then bowed and took what was offered her. 'Yes,' she said, 'I will take it. Thank you.' She rolled it up and buttoned it in her pocket.

Without looking more at Emily, Mrs Dean sank back in her pillow and closed her eyes. This time she kept her silence.

After tea, during which we received confirmation of the coming marriage and were able to congratulate the principals, the happy pair pressed us first to stay longer, then to accept a ride home in the carriage, but we declined both offers, saying that as the weather was so unseasonably fine we would like to walk; we would have scarcely a three-mile trip, cutting across fields.

As soon as we had smiled our way out of our new friends' sight, and were far enough down the drive to pass the danger of being overheard, I allowed myself to give vent to my feelings. My relations with my sister could not be rendered worse than they already were, and I would, for two minutes at least, have the pleasure of expression, if not of impression, for I conceded that however sharp and true my thrusts, my sister's mental hide would remain unbroken.

'Emily, I cannot understand or excuse your behaviour. How could you keep those papers? Perhaps courtesy to Mrs Dean could justify a feigned acceptance, but when we got downstairs! Then there was no excuse! You could at least have *offered* to give them back to Mrs Earnshaw; I saw she expected it!'

'Give them *back*? I was not aware that she had ever had them. What has Heathcliff's letter to do with her?'

'Ask rather what has it to do with you! It is a family document, and should be kept in the family.'

'Oh? Has Heathcliff suddenly been taken to the bosom of the Earnshaws? I should have thought the point, even considered posthumously, was precisely the opposite. Besides, the letter was given me by one who possessed it for sixty years; she alone among the living has the power of conferral.'

But I doggedly refused to be silenced: 'And your behaviour to that dear old woman! It was nothing short of cruel! How could you have withheld from her the comfort she craved, when it would have been so easy to give!'

Emily snorted derisively. 'That "dear old woman" was lying.'

'What!'

'Through her teeth. Lying. You know: saying what is not true.'

'In what respect, pray? She owned up to her lie; it is a lie no longer.'

'Oh, you mean the concealment of the letter. I did not mean that. I meant something else.'

'To what could you possibly be referring?'

'To her account of the events *following* the concealment of the letter.'

'But how could that be false? Mrs Dean hid the letter by herself; the other matters were public. Heathcliff loved and lost. Cathy died. Her daughter Catherine was born. Heathcliff damaged his enemies. Where in that is there room for a lie?'

'That is not the only story.'

'What do you mean?'

'There is another story, one that cannot be told.'

I stopped short and stamped my foot. 'When you are not insulting your friends, you are driving them mad by speaking in riddles!'

'All right, Miss High-and-Mighty Brontë, I will speak plain. Cathy did *not* die the night the child was born.'

'That is a silly assertion. Births and deaths are a matter of legal record!'

'Records can be falsified. Edgar Linton was a magistrate, remember?'

I was silent for a minute while I digested that. 'Well, if she did not die, but the records are falsified, how could *you* know?'

'I was told by one who had direct access to the facts.'

'By whom? Emily, tell me!'

'Why should I tell you anything? To give you the pleasure of calling me silly?'

'Do as you like, then.' We resumed walking. I, half-blinded with suppressed tears, steered my course by the bright flower pattern on the back of my sister's skirt, which I had to struggle to keep in close view.

I was, of course, inwardly frantic for Emily's explanation, but I knew a show of absolute indifference to be my only chance of getting it. In her present mood, if my sister thought you wanted the salt, she would hand you the pepper. So I hummed a little tune; I fashioned a pleasant expression for my face; I even studied to control my walk, to purge it of any little bounce of exasperation that might reveal my true temper. Emily, back stiff and straight, strode ahead, her long legs carrying her effortlessly over puddles I must needs skirt with exertion.

My attention was momentarily diverted by the sight of a heavy cart, drawn by oxen, approaching. The cart was so wide, and the road so narrow, that we had to stand a little way up a bank on the side to wait for it to pass.

As I watched it approach, my fancy took the sudden notion that we had abruptly been shunted to another, more primitive time. The cart was so clumsy and slow, and the two people in it, a man and a woman, so shapeless beneath their styleless garments, they seemed peasant incarnate: bowed under the weight of their labour, blank faces turned inwards, lost in the memory of the race.

When the cart drew abreast, I nodded and said good day, but they did not answer, though they passed within six feet of me. They would not even raise their eyes to mine. They were like people met in a dream.

They were gone; I looked about me. I shook my head to clear it; gone was the friendly sun of the morning; now the sky was low and dark. The landscape too was different than it should have been; the hills were steeper, the vegetation sparser, the road narrower and more lonely.

'This is not the road to Haworth,' I exclaimed.

'No.'

'Where have you led me? Where are we going?'

For answer, Emily pointed across a steep valley to the top of the long rough hill opposite. Squinting through my glasses, I made out a far silhouette of gables and chimneys against the grey sky.

'It is Wuthering Heights!' I exclaimed after a second. 'You are taking me to Wuthering Heights!'

Emily nodded.

'Why, Emily? You would never allow me to accompany you before.'

'Always before you have turned from the truth. Now I am going to find out if that is a permanent condition, or if it may be remedied.'

Here was a chance for reconciliation, and I took it. 'You are right. I have turned from the truth, but I shall no longer; I will face it head-on, if you will but show it me.'

Emily inspected my expression. 'You mean that.'

'Yes.'

'Very well, then. Not only will I take you to Wuthering Heights, I will tell you the true tale, what really happened the night the woman we just met was born. But I will tell you on condition.'

'Anything – only tell!'

'I will tell if you vow never to question me as to my sources.'

'Yes – I vow.' There was glad sincerity in my voice; I was more than willing to bridle my tongue in exchange for a partly satisfied curiosity and a share of sisterly affection.

'Right, then.' And, walking along the narrowing path, dodging the freshets from the melting bank that curled around our feet, she told, I heard, the tale that follows.

Emily said,

Imagine how it must have been, how it was.

Imagine this: three candles fixed by their own wax to the mantelpiece. (Someone was in a hurry.) Their flaring light illuminates a lady's bedroom (the bedroom we just saw), but elegantly appointed in the style of the last century. It has lately been turned birthing room, by the evidence a difficult birth. Everywhere there is blood – more human blood than is comfortable to see – blood-soaked rags, bowls of bloody water, the bloody swaddlings of a fitful infant lying in a cradle at the end of the bed, a bed covered with blood-crusted sheets, on top of which the woman lies.

The woman. Someone has put a fresh nightgown, a fine lace one, on her, as though to array a corpse. She is more than half a corpse already – her skin grey-white and pulled tight across her face – her eyes closed – not even a flutter of breath audible. But a pulse beats faintly at the base of the exposed throat, and more strongly deep in the wrist of the woman, held by –

The husband. He sits in a chair at the bedside, waiting for death. One of his blond curls has a gout of blood on it. He sobs lightly each time he breathes.

The nurse. Slumps in a chair in the corner. The child, pale-haired like its father, squalls. No one moves. The mantel with the three candles on it also holds two clocks. They tick in unison.

It is now the hour after midnight. The window is open, night air sucks the curtain in and out, in and out.

What is that? A rustle in the ivy outside? The curtain blows out and in. A hand gains hold on the sill. Yes. A shadowed face; eyes blaze from shadow. Ripple of powerful, dark-clad shoulder, white flash of lace, thrust of shining black boot into candlelight.

'Heathcliff!'

The cramped word comes from the husband's throat, but at its utterance the body on the bed stirs as if in unconscious response.

The husband sobs still, but finds the strength to move a vague hand towards the bell-pull.

'Stay!' says Heathcliff in an awful voice. 'As you love her life – or, if that weighs short, your own!' With one hand he displays a pistol, with the other he pulls from his pocket a small bottle filled with a scarlet liquid, through which the flickering candles flash a ruby brilliance. 'Remember this? With it I will save her, if you can muster intelligence enough to hold your interference!'

He moves around the bed, kneels by it opposite the other man, balances the pistol on the pillow by the woman's head. 'It is loaded and primed!' he snarls at the husband when the latter begins again to speak. 'And in my present mood I would liefer blow you to perdition than not.' Then the only sound the baby's whimpers.

Heathcliff smooths the matted hair from the deathly face, in the silent ear whispers endearments.

As the husband and the nurse look on (for she has roused herself; oh, yes, that one misses nothing), Heathcliff uncorks the bottle, forces a few driblets of the liquid through the woman's clenched teeth. He strokes her throat.

Husband, nurse, and lover lean forward. A convulsion animates the woman's body. 'You have killed her,' croaks the nurse, but the husband raises his hand. The body is still; then a blush rises from its breast up its thin throat to its cheeks. The eyes open. They are live, lucent, liquid, without bottom.

'Cathy,' says Heathcliff, and his voice sounds as over a great distance.

'You have come back,' says Cathy, very clearly, looking at Heathcliff. Heathcliff is too overcome to find more words, only presses her hands and kisses them. Her husband gasps, but otherwise holds his tongue.

'You have come back,' she repeats, 'this time. But you will part from me again.'

'Never, Cathy,' quavers Heathcliff. 'Never again.' His hands pass over her form, caressing it from foot to head, as though forming it anew from memory.

She reaches a hand to his face. 'Have I died, then? And taken you with me as I wished? Are we angels together in that glorious world we used to glimpse?'

'No, Cathy, we have not died. I am here, with you, in your bedroom.'

'But where are the oak panels? Where are our books? This is not our bedroom! And here are Nelly – and Edgar – What does it mean?'

'Remember, Cathy! We are not boy and girl, nor is this Wuthering Heights! You married not me, but Edgar Linton, this man who sits so quietly by your bed. You have had a child with him. You are mistress of Thrushcross Grange. But I am here to take you from them – from husband, from child, from all. Will you come? – Cathy?'

Cathy takes her time, looks around the room, seems to gather memory and being to herself as the seconds tick by on the mantel. When she speaks again it is not to Heathcliff, but to her husband.

'Edgar Linton, you will never see my face again in this life. Will you curse it or bless it?'

At first Linton chokes on his speech, then he manages: 'Catherine! What are you saying? You would leave me? Leave your child? Abandon your duties to live with this outlaw?'

'I do not care anymore what he is in your eyes or any

one's; in mine he is child, and mother and brother and husband. I have need of no other.'

'No need of me?'

'No longer. I have been happy with you, but no longer. He has returned, and I must go.'

'But what will I do if you go? What will I do?' The man presses his head with both his hands.

'You will do much as you have done; your books have ever been your best companions.'

At this the man's temper breaks; he reddens. 'Then be very sure, Catherine; if you pass out of this room you will never see me or your daughter again, plead as you will in the future, when this rogue tires of you.'

Here Nelly speaks out: 'Mr Linton! She does not comprehend the meaning of what she says; she speaks from the delirium that precedes death!'

'No, she is well enough; I know her.'

'Then only think of what *you* say! That she be out of her senses we can expect, but must you take leave of yours as well? You would let this man, who has already debauched your sister, walk out with your wife, too? Do you study to be the laughing stock of the county?' Then to Heathcliff: 'It is murder! She will die if she is moved!' For Heathcliff is tenderly lifting Cathy out of the bloody bed, is straining her to his breast. 'You are killing her at this moment.'

'Stand clear, woman. This moment I am saving her life. Yes, she will die – if she stays here, with you and this fine stud and the whelp he has sired – leeches to drain the life from her.'

Edgar, with whom Nelly's words have weighed, tries another tack: 'Catherine and I have been joined by the laws of church and state. We are man and wife. You cannot undo what has been done.'

Heathcliff smiles; his teeth look sharp in the candle-light.

'You expect such puling sophistries to deter *me*? I obey one law only, the law that joins my heart to hers, that beats so close to mine now.' And he presses the slight form he holds closer to his chest, brushing its hair with his cheek and tucking the folds of his greatcoat around it. Only Cathy's hand is visible now, twisting itself through Heathcliff's wiry locks where they are caught up in a ribbon at the back of his neck.

Still Linton persists in his idea. He lunges for the pistol, which has been forgotten on the pillow. Heathcliff watches him coolly. 'Be careful with that,' he says. 'It is quite likely to go off.'

'Release my wife, or I shall shoot you!'

Heathcliff laughs. 'If you kill me, you kill her.'

'Do not count on that stopping me!'

'Go ahead; fire away – I little care which world I inhabit, as long as she shares it. Otherwise, stand aside. I am leaving this place with Cathy. Her life with you was an error. Now it will be as though it never was. We will soon be on the far side of the world. You will never see us again. You will have nothing more to fear or hope. Forget us. Erase us.'

All this time Heathcliff, holding his treasure, has been circling the bed towards the door. Edgar follows them with the pistol.

'In my capacity as magistrate I arrest you for abduction!' Edgar cries.

Heathcliff smiles and bows. The action makes the coat Cathy is wrapped in fall open, and for an instant her face is visible. She is laughing.

Heathcliff backs across the threshold into the dark hall. Quick steps on the stairs, then the slam of the outside door. Nelly runs down, opens it, looks out.

In the drive a coach waits, its blazing torches blur the stars behind it.

'John!' calls Heathcliff.

A portly man leaps down from the driver's seat. 'All be ready, Master Heathcliff,' he says. He opens the door of the coach. A woman's shadowy face can be discerned in its recesses.

'Everything is arranged,' says Heathcliff to Nelly. 'She will be cared for.' And, aided by the waiting woman's white hands, he lifts his burden into the coach and follows himself. The door closes, the coach begins to move.

Emily's voice ceased, but my mind raced on. What *had* been her source? How could she know these things? Had she somehow, perhaps in her perusal of parish histories, gained possession of another manuscript, written either by Heathcliff or some other principal, that gave this version of the events? Or maybe Ellen had told it to her friend Tabitha years ago, and Tabby had passed it on to Emily, her favourite, over their shared work in the kitchen. Or it could be that Heathcliff himself had confided this tale to Emily? – but who could Heathcliff be to Emily but a ghost?

Be that as it might, I had promised not to ask. Emily had stopped walking; we stood looking down a slope to a ruined churchyard where the gravestones climbed crazily on each other's shoulders, just escaping the swollen beck that rippled through their midst.

'That is the graveyard where they are buried,' Emily said.

'Cathy and Heathcliff?'

'Yes, and Linton too – by his request he lies next to Cathy.'

'Considering what you have just told me, that seems strange.'

She shrugged. 'The ways of love are strange.'

'Still, in this case . . .'

'You can see for yourself, if you don't believe me.'

'No, no; of course I believe you! Only tell me what happened next!'

'Very well; but walk quickly; the light is waning, the clouds may bring rain.' We turned back to the path and continued walking, uphill, now.

'What happened next? – That we must deduce from the evidence, for no reliable witnesses remain,' said Emily, 'but it is simple enough.

'Imagine: after the coach has run out of sight, the

nurse's heavy climb back to the bedroom. She is tired to the bone, to the heart. She notes that no servant has come forth to investigate the noise; they too are exhausted from that night's work, and if they heard a carriage, must have thought it only the doctor, or the parson. All is still as she reaches the top of the stairs, walks down the hall to the room with a light in it.

'Imagine the two of them: the young husband, beside himself with rage and grief; the servant woman, perhaps secretly seeing in the events of that hour the results of her own manipulative folly. They look at each other in silence in the space over the child; it struggles fitfully in the tangle of absent bedclothes. The sound of carriage wheels diminishes in the distance.

'Left with that, what did they do? No one can now know for sure, but there must have been a barring of the door – a frenzied consultation – a hasty laying of plans.

'The idea to conceal what had really happened must have been Nelly's. Concealment, subterfuge and the like were meat and drink to her, and besides must have seemed light enough a sin put in the balance with the honour of two families. As for Linton, he was as ready to bury Cathy in his mind as he had been Isabella. Now that history had repeated itself, why not dispose of his wife in the same way? And this time, go one step further: since she was dead to him, why not make her dead to the world, their little world?

'Who would contradict him if he did? Not the fugitive pair, certainly. There was every reason to believe Heathcliff spoke the truth when he said the lovers would never be back, since the instant Linton knew Cathy's whereabouts, he could compel her to return by force of law; surely it followed that Heathcliff would keep his heart's prize beyond both Linton's knowledge and the law's compass; and if he heard of something that played into his interest so directly as a story of Cathy's demise, would confirm rather than deny it.

'So why not with that single lie preserve at once the family name, and some unspoiled corner of happy memory? (For remember, Edgar loved Cathy too, in his fashion.)

' "Why not?" Nelly put it to him.

'It was simple, really. The next morning an expected announcement of an expected death, and a conspicuous disposal of gory bedclothes. If the grief of the young squire kept him locked alone in the room with the beloved corpse, the servants, especially if schooled by Nelly's hints, would have understood ("Aye, Master'll keep the cuckoo out now, God love him!"). And they could be counted on to comprehend the practical need for a quick burial in a closed coffin ("Missus were that far gone before she went!"); likewise they would readily supply the reason for Heathcliff's disappearance ("Like as not the devil's followed his dam down to hell!"). Yes, they understood all that had happened at Thrushcross Grange, and quickly spread their understanding through the county!

'Edgar Linton buried a coffin filled with stones. Not in the family vault – he would not risk that – but in the concealing earth, and put up over it a headstone graven with his wife's name. The tears he shed were real. Over the years, Nelly told the bogus version of her mistress's death so many times that in the end she probably came to believe it; part of the distress we just witnessed was perhaps due to the nagging pricks of truth.

'So the stony mother was buried, the father lived on in increased seclusion (fearing a world that belied the reality he had chosen), and, as for the child, it lived and thrived, to this day.'

'But what of Heathcliff and Cathy?' I asked. 'Heathcliff lived out a solitary, misanthropic lifetime at Wuthering Heights, and Cathy, if there at all, was there as a ghost – we have Mr Lockwood's as well as Nelly's testimony to both those circumstances.'

'Yes – all that they told – of Heathcliff's revenge, of Cathy's haunting of him, of his death – all took place – but began five years later than Nelly had said; of course

Lockwood did not come on the scene till the end, and could not have known the beginning.'

'Five years – Cathy and Heathcliff had five years together.'

'Yes. With Mr Are's aid they acquired a plantation in the New World, near New Orleans in what was then one of the French colonies; they wanted to avoid the cold winters and colder morals of the lands further north. Cathy soon regained her health, but perished five years later, bearing their child, a son. Acting on his darling's final wish, Heathcliff brought her body back here for burial, which he accomplished himself, at night – laying her he loved in place of the stones Linton had put in the coffin. These he carried home to his bedchamber, where they were found after his death.'

Though I wanted to ask, 'And *your* Heathcliff?' I dared not – to do so would have been to stem the flow of words on the whole subject forever. But my fancy suffered no such check. Emily had just now mentioned a son. Could he have survived? Perhaps he – or no, the ages were wrong – perhaps *his* son, had been Emily's playmate, and had confided to her the secret history of the family. If not, I concluded, Emily's Heathcliff had been moonshine – a confabulation born of moor mists, my sister's loneliness, and Tabby's twice-twisted tales.

But I kept these thoughts to myself, and instead inquired, 'What was their life like in the New World, on the plantation?'

Emily slowed her walk. We were far up the slope; I thought we must be very near the farmhouse that was our destination, but the road curled around the shoulder of the hill just ahead, so the prospect was hidden. She looked up at the sky. It was the typical low grey dome of a Yorkshire March, but from the movements of her eyes across it I thought she saw loftier heavens, brighter clouds.

Emily said, 'Imagine this: In the middle of the plantation was a deep round lake. Encircling that lake were thickets of bearded oak, stands of tall pine, orchards of lushly clustered fruit. In the morning, through the shade of those scented trees, they might ride together on fine black horses (Heathcliff bred a famous strain for the Louisiana planters) till the air grew too hot. Then they might row out on to the lake in a red-canopied boat. When they got to the centre, perhaps Heathcliff trailed his hand in the lapping water while Cathy strummed a mandolin and sang to him. Or perhaps, if she dozed, he slipped over the side and slid like a seal to the dark lake bottom, then up to the light again. The tropic copper sun reflecting on the dimpled surface drew from it a haze so golden that you could hardly tell where the water ended and the sky began. But to the two of them, the glow was the glory of their coupling: that they were together at the last as they had been at the first.

'In the shade of the evening they walked and talked amongst the trees, black-barked and glistening from the constant mists of the lake. The wet spice of crushed leaves came up from the ground where they stepped. Dewy vines gently slapped their skins. Perhaps Cathy reached a globed fruit from a vine and rolled it over Heathcliff's forehead and cheek, telling him to savour the coolness. Perhaps Heathcliff took the fruit from her hand and broke it, then teased her tongue with morsels exchanged for kisses.

'Later, awakening in the deepest hour, they heard, not the wuthering of wind in fir they had heard of old, but the hidden life of the night forest – bird and insect and serpent – exploded in ecstatic cry. Their bed was not as it had been in childhood, oak-encased, a little room-within-a-room, but set on an open veranda, canopied by billows of gauzy net, that gleamed in the starlight like a great glowworm's cocoon, the two of them at its heart. And when she reached out her hand in the night, he was there; and when he reached out his, there was she likewise.'

We had been walking slowly; now we rounded the shoulder of the hill. Before us, very near, startlingly near, stood the house that was called Wuthering Heights:

ancient stone structure bulky against the troubled grey of the sky, skeletal branches fringing its corners, its windows narrow and blank.

The shock of it made me stop short. Emily turned. 'What is wrong?'

Still I paused. Something in me was dissatisfied.

'Well, are you coming?'

Instead of moving, I answered, 'You have vowed that what you have told me is *true*. I believe you, with all my heart. But did it *happen*?'

'What, precisely, are you asking me?'

'The scene you have just described – did it exist, in a literal and factual sense? You have told me that Heathcliff and Cathy emigrated to the southern coast of the North American continent, lived there in felicity for five years. They delivered fine love speeches to each other daily, and embraced in ideal passion. Excellent. In addition, given their characters, they must have frequently quarrelled, raved, ranted, wept, reconciled. Presumably they also ate, drank, worked, spent money, were bored – went through all the necessary forms of mortal life. These things *happened*?'

Emily with effort maintained a patient demeanour. 'Yes.'

'What you have given me is a true *historical* account, not "true" fable or allegory?'

Emily's patient look shaded into one of scorn. 'You have not listened well.'

'I have listened to every word; I have heard and valued all that you have told me. I am only struggling to ascertain how best to understand it!'

Emily shook her head. 'I see now that you will never understand.'

'That is grossly unfair! If you would only explain!'

'Some things cannot be directly explained. It is as I have said. Some stories can never be told. The heart of some stories can never be known. They can only be felt. And with you, the organ for such feeling is dead, or never existed.'

During the preceding speeches my glance had ever and again strayed from Emily's angry face to the house that loomed above it, and now something caught my eye.

'Emily! Is that a candle in the window?'

Emily turned, and, shading her brow, levelled a glance in that direction. 'No, it is only the reflection of the setting sun.'

'It was not, and you know it; the sun has been thickly covered for an hour, since the weather turned.'

'Nevertheless, just now one beam escaped for a second.'

'You are wrong! There – in the upstairs window! It flares again – it moves! There is someone inside!'

'It is a trick of the light.'

'No, Emily, I see it!'

'Impossible. The windows are boarded.'

'Oh! – It has been snuffed out – but come, let us look!'

She turned away from the house. 'No. After all, I will not show you. It would be of no use. If you went within you would see bare walls – unpeopled rooms – vacant and uninformative spaces. That is all.'

In truth, as I continued to examine it the house did look vacant. Seemingly, the windows opaqued themselves before my eyes; I perceived that they *were* shuttered and nailed. But I could not resist asking Emily, 'What would *you* see?'

She half-smiled. 'An allegory, or perhaps a fable,' she said, and began walking away from the house.

'No! Emily! You have brought me all this way! It is not fair! Let us go in! I want to know more!'

'For you, Charlotte, there is no more. For you the story was completed a long time ago, when Heathcliff and Cathy died. They are dead, the world they inhabited is dead, and there is the end of it.'

And that is all she would say on the subject, that day, or any other day.

But as we walked past Gimmerton kirkyard on the way back to Haworth, the rushing of the spring-swollen beck was loud in our ears, and that sound of the mingling of many waters seemed the very murmur of life, strong and insistent, continuous beneath the hardened surface of everyday existence.